Brian Kelly: Route 1

Brian Kelly: Route 1

Thomas E. Coughlin

Fitzgerald & LaChapelle

Manufactured in the United States of America

Library of Congress Control Number: 2001-131699

ISBN: 0-9666202-1-6

Cover design: Pearl and Associates

Cover photography: R. F. Hoffman, Nashua, New Hampshire

Book design and production: Tabby House

Fitzgerald & LaChapelle Publishing
852 Elm Street
Manchester, N.H. 03101
(603) 669-6112; fax (603) 641-4929

Dedication

For Elaine . . .
who keeps my feet planted firmly in the clouds

Acknowledgments

Lowell City Library, Manchester City Library, Kennebunk Town Library, Chester Town Library, *York County Coast Star*, the *Lowell Sun*, Manchester West High School, Lowell High School, Bobby Stephen, Flo's Hot Dogs, Congdon's Doughnuts, Billy's Chowder House, the Maine Diner, Alisson's Restaurant, The Beachcomber, Wells Historical Society, William McQuade, Joseph Sullivan, Marc Cote, Elaine Coughlin, Dennis A. Tito, Kate Kelly, John Garfield, Sharon Baldyga, WCAP-AM, WFEA-AM, Manchester Education Association, the Tallwood Motel, Wendy Fitch, Julia's Gifts, Duke Broder, Kennebunk Book Port, Richard and Ellen Chasse, Donna Lareau, Edward and Dorothy Coughlin . . . and finally, to all the businesses in Lowell, Massachusetts, Manchester and Bedford, New Hampshire, and everywhere in York County, Maine, that are no longer in business but managed to come alive within the pages of this book.

I

BRIAN KELLY SLID HIS HAND along the banister as his sixteen-year-old legs bounded up the stairs to the second floor of the tenement building. The lanky teenager took the stairs two, sometimes three at a time, as he returned home just before six o'clock on a Thursday afternoon. Opening the door, he caught sight of his mother seated in the living room, a cup of tea balanced in her lap. There was a thoughtful expression etched on her face that led him to believe she had something she needed to share, or perhaps discuss.

Elizabeth Kelly was a serious-looking woman with a plain face that one might label handsome but certainly not pretty. She was tall, just under five feet, ten inches. Her 165 pounds were proportionately distributed over a large skeletal frame. The woman extended her only child a gentle smile as he entered the living room, then took a sip from her cup of tea. Brian shuffled across the room and gave his mother a soft peck on the cheek. Beckoning him to take a chair, she was obviously arranging her thoughts before sharing them. Brian knew something was up. There was no other reason his mother would have seated herself in the only room in the house reserved for anything but everyday matters. Over the last eight years the Kelly living room had been limited to formal gatherings and was kept clutter free.

Brian pulled over a hassock, seating himself directly in front of his mother. Although there were only the two of them, Elizabeth Kelly had emphasized and reemphasized over the years that they were no less a family than the Flynns down the street with their eleven children, and he knew from all outward appearances he was being called into a family meeting.

"Brian, your uncle Jimmy is taking me up to Manchester in New Hampshire tomorrow. I have an interview for a job at a sweater mill up there. With any luck I'll be starting work in October. Of course, this means we would have to move." Elizabeth paused and waited on her son's reaction to this revelation.

"Geez, Ma, this is sort of coming at me from out of the blue," he responded, reeling from the bombshell she had dropped. Only weeks earlier, Brian had started his sophomore year at Lowell High School following nine years at Varnum School in the Centralville section of Lowell, Massachusetts.

"You know, baby boy, there's been less and less work for me in the mill yard the last couple of years and it's not like textiles are about to make a comeback around here real soon. I think you know how tight things have been and it's not like we can stay on St. Vincent de Paul forever." A proud woman, Elizabeth was haunted by the reality that the St. Vincent de Paul Society from nearby St. Michael's Parish had provided twenty-five dollars a week in food allowances for her and Brian during the past eighteen months.

"There's a sweater manufacturer in Manchester that's going great guns and hiring. It's something I just have to follow up on. Tell me you understand," she added almost apologetically.

The tall teenager nodded his head in silence before stepping over to his mother and applying an affectionate hug. "I won't know anyone," he stated pathetically.

"You'll know me, and besides, you'll make friends in no time. I wouldn't do this unless I had to, hon. Put it in God's hands; it'll be okay," said Elizabeth, expressing the faith that was the trademark of her everyday life.

Brian did not respond. Instead, he beckoned his mother and led her toward the kitchen. For the remainder of the evening, the subject of the job interview and possible move to New Hampshire was carefully avoided.

The next day Elizabeth Kelly was driven to Manchester by Jimmy Clarke, the nearest thing she had to a relative. Elizabeth had lost her father at age three, then her mother four years later. When no relative stepped forward to claim the orphaned girl, Helen Clarke, the next-door neighbor and closest friend to the deceased woman, opened her door to the orphaned Elizabeth. She was raised with Jimmy and George Clarke as an equal member of the family. Through the years she came to look upon the two boys as brothers, particularly Jimmy. George was nine years older than Elizabeth and moved out on his own right after high school, eventually settling down in Oregon. During the next twenty years only minimal contact had been kept up between the elder brother and his family. Jimmy, on the other hand, was a mere eight months younger than his adopted sister and the two remained bonded right into adulthood. When the need for transportation north to New Hampshire arose, Elizabeth did not hesitate to ask her kid brother.

On a Friday in early October, Elizabeth Kelly was driven north to Manchester where, after two hours in the personnel department of Pandora Industries, she was offered a full-time job in the sweater division of the company. She accepted the position on the spot and was subsequently treated to a celebratory lunch by her brother before returning home to Lowell.

The following day, Brian accompanied his mother and uncle back to Manchester where they combed the state's largest city in search of a suitable apartment. In mid-afternoon they were ushered through a third-story, six-room flat on the city's west side. Elizabeth was overjoyed to find an apartment larger than her present flat. She was further delighted by the weekly rent, eight dollars less than her Read Street apartment back in Lowell. Lastly, the landlord, a Mr. Giroux, seemed like a kindly old gent who appeared anxious to have the Kellys as tenants. For his part, Brian remained restrained throughout the whole apartment-hunting process. Not wanting to put undue pressure on his mother, he suppressed his feelings of desperation as he faced the prospect of being torn from the familiar faces, neighborhoods, and routines of his beloved Lowell. By late afternoon Jimmy Clarke was retracing his route from Montgomery Street on Manchester's west side to an access way onto Route 3 and the southward route home to Massachusetts. Brian sat mute in the back seat, listening to his mother's enthusiastic banter about the new life she was about to construct for her and her son in the Granite State.

"Take a look out your window, handsome—that's no doubt going to be your new school," crowed an enthusiastic Elizabeth. He shifted his head just enough to see the lettering cemented to the side of the colorless building that occupied all of a city block. SOUTHSIDE HIGH SCHOOL read the foot-high letters.

"Let me get this straight. We're on the west side of the city, but the school's called Southside. That doesn't make sense."

His uncle spoke up, trying to draw his nephew into the family discussion. "You heard what Mr. Giroux was telling us. Manchester's supposed to be the only city in the country that's main street is a dead end at both ends."

"Well, Toto, I don't think we're still in Kansas," muttered Brian almost under his breath. "Hey look, Ma, it gets even better. There's a naked man and woman carved into the building above the door. Nice place you're sending me to."

"You're not going to be an old grouch for the next month, are you?" asked Elizabeth, looking disappointed.

"Ma, I'll make it work. For you, I'll make it work." The teenager dropped his head back far enough to see upward through the back window. As his mother resumed her conversation with his uncle, Brian closed his eyes and attempted to block out the ordeal that confronted him.

Preparations for the relocation moved forward immediately following the decision to take the Montgomery Street apartment. Elizabeth spent the better part of every waking hour carefully packing and boxing the family's belongings for the move to Manchester. Assisted by her son, she managed to have everything prepared for shipment in a van borrowed from a friend of Jimmy's from work. They estimated it would take two, perhaps three, trips up Route 3 to transport all of the Kellys' worldly possessions.

When Brian was not hauling heavier items about the apartment, he was extending final farewells to the friends and acquaintances he had collected during the past sixteen years. The most difficult good-bye proved to be the one he had to make to his longtime mentor, a street-smart character who answered to the name Perez. A neighborhood fixture for the past seven or eight years, Perez had taken a liking to the young, lanky Brian Kelly years before.

Perez had appeared on the streets of Lowell sometime in the mid-sixties. No one seemed to know his first name. He had arrived on the scene with no apparent friends or relatives. Being of modest build, less than average height, and a member of a minority group, it had not taken long before his presence had been challenged by a local tough named Jake Shaw. A circle of onlookers formed around Perez and his muscular adversary behind the grandstand of Mayflower Park. There had been a visible absence of any support for the seemingly overmatched Puerto

Rican as he had asked for a volunteer to mind his leather jacket during the fight. That was until a pencil-thin, freckled kid stepped forward and offered to hold the garment for him. Perez handed over the jacket without even an acknowledgment.

The fight ended in ten seconds, fifteen if one considered the short time the men had circled each other in silence. With singular purpose, total focus and blinding hand speed, Perez dropped Shaw onto his back after one flurry of blows. Once on the ground, Shaw was quick to concede to his smaller opponent after Perez peppered his face while sitting astride his body. In just seconds, the wiry Puerto Rican had bloodied the stocky Shaw's nose and opened an ugly cut over his left eye. Perez dismounted his beaten adversary in silence and walked back to the grandstand to retrieve his jacket. The young boy helped him on with the jacket the same way a cornerman assists his charge in a prize fight, then tagged behind the warrior as he strode back to the roadway. On reaching the street, the victorious Perez turned back to his youthful ally.

"How 'bout I buy ya a Coke for ya work back there?" he asked with a smile. A wide grin broke out across the youngster's freckled face as he ran along beside his newfound friend. From that day forward, Perez and young Brian Kelly bonded in a friendship that transcended differences in age, culture, and social philosophy. Absent a father, Brian listened and learned from this tough character. From street-fighting to street-corner psychology, Brian Kelly absorbed the lessons and directions of his urban mentor.

And in Brian Kelly, Perez had found a friend in whom he could place his trust and confidence. He was known to state loudly, and in no uncertain terms, that Brian was the only person in the United States that he trusted completely. These statements of fact were known to be made primarily on those occasions when the Puerto Rican had drunk more than his fair share of alcohol and were generally accompanied by a measure of shameless weeping.

Their parting on an autumn afternoon, therefore, proved to be emotionally painful, tempered only by the mutual vow to remain in touch, no matter how difficult this might prove to be.

II

THE KELLYS MOVED THEIR MODEST FURNISHINGS over the weekend in mid-October of 1972. Elizabeth would not rest until the major part of all of their household effects had been removed from boxes and put in their proper place. Jimmy Clarke and Brian made two runs between Lowell and Manchester on Saturday, returning the borrowed van by late afternoon. Elizabeth used the time alone on this day to arrange the furniture and accessories in the spacious flat the way she wanted it. The exception was her son's bedroom where his personal belongings—table, chairs and bed—were deposited in the middle of the room, pending his layout preferences.

It was Saturday evening when an exhausted mother and son collapsed side by side onto the couch in their new home. Brian's uncle had offered to take the two out for dinner but, at his sister's urging, left for home and the company of his own family. The woman wore a satisfied look on her face as she glanced around the apartment. It was much roomier than their flat back on Read Street in Lowell. It also appeared to be in a better neighborhood. Montgomery Street, which ran north-south along the city's west side for just under a mile, was flanked by single family homes along its northern end and three-family tenement houses at its less affluent southern extreme. The Kellys would now occupy the third floor of one of these tenements. Not having the energy to cook, his mother asked Brian if he minded having pizza for supper.

"No, Ma, sounds great," he replied with enthusiasm tempered by exhaustion. "How's the TV reception?" he asked, staring at the aging console sitting across the room.

"I was afraid you'd get around to asking that. Let's see, how can I put this in a positive light? You weren't too attached to the Boston stations, were you?"

Brian rolled his head sideways towards his mother. "Tell me you're kidding. Ma, please tell me you're only kidding."

"No, I'm afraid all we're getting up here is channel 9. Oh, and I think we get PBS, channel 11."

"That's great, Ma. Channel 9 and the bug channel. Channel 11's the bug channel. Bugs killing bugs; bugs eating other bugs; bugs mating with bugs. And when they're not showing us bugs, we're treated to a parade of boring eggheads trying to impress us with their oh-so-superior knowledge."

"So, we'll keep it on 9 all the time and in a few months we'll buy a new TV. Is that a plan or is that a plan?" asked Elizabeth playfully.

"You're not going to let me watch my bug shows?" asked Brian, trying to sound pathetic.

His mother burst out in laughter and pulled her son up against her. "You're the best kid, just the best. You know that?"

That evening Elizabeth sent Brian out to purchase their first real meal in the new house. They had noticed a small pizza shop a couple of blocks away in the course of running trips between Lowell and the new apartment. They had not gotten the phone installed as of yet, forcing Brian to order and stand around in the pizzaria's crowded waiting area. After thirty minutes he returned to the third-story apartment to find the table set and his mother washing down the kitchen pantry walls. Elizabeth threw down her wash rag the moment Brian pushed open the hallway door. She removed a half gallon of cold milk from the refrigerator and placed it on the kitchen table.

"Everyone just serve themselves," she proclaimed as she removed the first slice from the pie.

While Brian sat quietly, staring at the unfamiliar walls and chomping down his dinner, Elizabeth beamed outwardly at the prospect of the new start this move to New Hampshire would afford her and her son. The job at Pandora represented a clear step upward for her and she viewed the move to Manchester as an improvement in her son's environment. When she noticed a prolonged silence at the table she made an attempt to get Brian to open up.

"You a little uptight about going to the new school? Is that on your mind, hon?" she asked.

"A little—no big deal, Ma."

Elizabeth reached over and warmly hugged her only child. "Wait till the girls up here get a look at my tall, handsome boy. I've got a funny feeling you'll be bringing home one of those French-Canadian gals we see all over the place," she said slyly. Brian responded by rolling his eyes.

Elizabeth reminded Brian that they were family and that he should not hesitate in sharing any problems and concerns brought about by the move and the new school. "It's just you and me, kid. We're going to be fine."

The Kellys retired to bed early, knowing on Sunday they would have to continue the unpacking process. Elizabeth rose the next morning well before her son. In her brief time in the neighborhood she had already located St. Patrick's Church down the street. She made her way to early morning mass, purchasing a box of doughnuts on the way home. Brian was not even fully awake when his mother pushed her way into his still unorganized bedroom, presenting him with a cup of coffee and a small circle of plain and powdered doughnuts. Breakfast was followed by a day of serious cleaning by Elizabeth, while Brian used the day to fully assemble his bed and arrange his bedroom to his liking.

On Monday, mother and son walked to Southside High, where Brian was officially enrolled in the school. Administration set about arranging a class schedule after a morning of filling out forms and meeting with guidance counselors. The tall sophomore was instructed to report for class the next day. He was told that a period-by-period class schedule would be waiting for him in his homeroom on Tuesday morning. Mother and son spent a full three hours at the school before finishing all of the necessary registrations and arrangements.

Brian found himself quite uncomfortable wandering the corridors of his new school, largely in the company of his mother, but under the watchful eyes of many of his peers. It was not so much that he was ashamed of being seen in his mother's company. His discomfort came more from the idea of being viewed as less than self-sufficient. He was relieved when they left the building and returned to the Montgomery Street apartment just after noon. Elizabeth talked enthusiastically about the prospect of starting her new job the next day, which brought a small measure of consolation to her son.

The next morning, over his mother's objections, Brian donned a pair of clean but well-worn jeans for his first day at Southside High School. His favorite shirt, an olive-drab military knockoff, was wrinkled from the move up from Lowell but he wore it nonetheless. Elizabeth had to leave for work in advance of Brian. However, she made a point of wishing him a good first day, applying an affectionate peck on his cheek on the way out the door. Her shift began at seven-thirty and she estimated the walking time from Montgomery Street, across the Notre Dame Bridge and down into the mill yard, to be in excess of twenty minutes. Following his mother's departure, Brian emptied the remaining coffee from the percolator into his cup and lounged around the kitchen for a half hour. Finally, he locked the apartment behind him and set out for his first day at a new school, in a new city, in a new state.

It was only a ten-minute walk from the front door on Montgomery Street to Southside High. Approaching the school, Brian scanned a sea of unfamiliar faces as he passed groups of conversing teenagers. His first duty was to report to the administration office, where he picked up his books. He muddled his way through the narrow corridors cradling two armfuls of books and searching for his homeroom, where he had been told his period-to-period schedule would be waiting for him. Finally, following two sets of contradicting directions, he happened upon it and strolled through the open doorway. Still laboring with his textbooks, he dropped one armful down on the teacher's desk and announced that he had been assigned to this homeroom. The news did not seem to come as a surprise to the teacher, a bespectacled, dark-haired man by the name of Mr. Sullivan.

"Where are you transferring in from?" asked the teacher.

"Lowell, Mass," Brian answered.

"Home of Jack Kerouac. You've got big shoes to fill," replied Mr. Sullivan.

"Home of Bette Davis, too," added Brian.

"Well, Mr. Brian Kelly, we'll be expecting big things from you, it appears," stated the teacher. "There's an empty desk in the last row—near the back," he instructed, pointing to the far corner of the room.

Brian nodded his head and, after removing the stack of books from the corner of the desk, turned toward the classroom filled with curious students, and began what felt like an endless walk to the rear of the room.

As Brian made his way down the far aisle, ignoring the stares, he caught sight of a girl removing items from atop his assigned desk. The girl made no attempt to camouflage her annoyance as she hurriedly removed books and other assorted objects from the desk. The young lady, a pretty thing with shoulder length light brown hair, glanced at him as she removed the last of her articles. On eye contact, he extended the girl a sympathetic smile but his gesture merely elicited a glare from his new classmate. She followed the glare with an audible sigh, clearly meant as a statement of her displeasure at his arrival.

Brian spent the next few minutes sizing up some of the people with whom he would share a homeroom. There appeared to be a number of attractive females, not the least of which was the less-than-amiable young lady seated directly to his left. Mercifully, the bell sounded for first period, which in his case meant English. There, the whole "new-boy-in-school" routine was relived as he reported to his first real class and ultimately found an empty desk in the middle of the room. He was sizing up this new group of Southside students surrounding him when his eyes caught sight of the girl from homeroom entering class. He was now able to take in, in more detail, physical characteristics of this extraordinary creature. She was tall, certainly above average, with a long, swan-like neck that made her seem graceful in her every movement. Long-legged, she was a female in the act of leaving girlhood behind, as each part of her body showed the promise of the beautiful woman that would soon be in full blossom. Brian stared across the room at her, engrossed in committing to memory every detail that his mind could save for recollection. The trance brought about by the appearance of this girl was abruptly broken by the arrival of Miss Royal, a middle-aged teacher with a scratchy, monotone voice. With the class called to order and the lessons for the day begun, Brian repeatedly caught himself shifting his eyes in the direction of the girl from homeroom. He was particularly interested in finding out her name. He was in luck— when Miss Royal tossed a question to the class on an element of the personal history of Herman Melville. The long-legged girl raised her hand, and Miss Royal pointed in her direction.

"Miss Keogh," she enunciated carefully, nodding at the object of Brian's absolute attention. He scratched the name into a notebook, then let the syllables of her name echo through his consciousness.

"*Miss Keogh—Miss Keogh—she is Miss Keogh,*" he thought as he began committing the name to memory. The girl provided the correct answer with a confident, almost brash, demeanor. He looked on, transfixed by this completely self-assured young woman. Never before had he found himself so profoundly impacted by the mere presence of another human being. At some point in the course of the period, he had to make a determined and conscious effort to focus on the academic material being presented by the uninspiring Miss Royal, pulling his attention back to English literature.

During the remainder of the school day the transfer student was introduced into what would be his scholastic routine over the next three months. Brian and the memorable Miss Keogh did not cross paths again until the short, interim period that separates the final class of the day and dismissal. Back in homeroom, he could only catch snapshot glances at the object of his now runaway imagination, who in fact seemed to make a conscious effort to avoid looking at him. This was accomplished by keeping up a stream of meaningless banter with the girl sitting on her left. A minute or so before the final bell, Miss Keogh stretched her perfectly contoured legs, extending them under the desk in front of her. His eyes were instinctively drawn downward, resting on these two perfect works of nature. Seconds later there came a flutter of giggling from the two girls. His eyes ascended to note that he was being observed by the girl engaged in conversation with Miss Keogh. As efficient as a second set of eyes, she had apparently conveyed to her friend the nature of his activities. Brian responded by burying his head in his desk, pretending to search for a nonexistent object.

Brian welcomed the sound of the final bell. From homeroom he set out to find his locker. He followed the reasonably sequenced locker numbers only to find his on a pitched section of hallway, causing it to lean at an approximately fifteen-degree angle. The door to the locker opened on first try and he crammed half his textbooks inside. As he did so, he realized that he had made no friends or acquaintances on his first day at Southside. If he were back at Lowell High or Varnum, he would surely have some fun with this strangely placed locker. He decided, on the spot, to give his new locker a name. He would call it—no, he would call *her*—Eileen. He smiled to himself then locked up his first symbol of belonging at Southside High School.

Turning to leave, he caught sight of Miss Keogh standing and talking to a boy. The boy, perfectly groomed and seemingly at ease in a sport coat and tie, was a handsome chap who came eye-to-eye with the flirtatious sophomore. Brian stood motionless as the two passed through the narrow passageway, totally caught up in each other and oblivious to his existence. He left for home after a leisurely walk around the building, making mental notes of where places of importance—library, auditorium, and the like, were located.

Arriving home in mid-afternoon, Brian poured himself a glass of milk and settled into what would become a familiar routine. This meant attacking homework only minutes after completing his final class of the day. There was something uncomfortable and foreign associated with sitting at the kitchen table at this early hour, pouring over assignments due two or three days in the future. Involuntarily, his mind wandered back to Lowell and what might be happening at the corner of Bridge and Third streets. He visualized Perez walking, a rolled-up *Lowell Sun* in hand, toward the Wonder Bar and the company of other males. Men leaving behind the confinement of the first shift for the companionship of others mutually trapped in the ongoing routine that would, in due time, rob them of each and every boyhood dream. Quiet desperation made tolerable by "the King of Beers." He rose from the table and walked to a window. A gust of autumn wind blew a collection of dead leaves spiraling upward, dancing before him before falling back to earth. Unwittingly, his thoughts returned to Southside High and the intriguing Miss Keogh.

The previous tenant had left the Greater Manchester phone book in the apartment, allowing Brian to begin some fundamental detective work. Opening the book and flipping to the K's, he noted that there were two spellings listed. These were K-e-o-g-h and K-e-o-u-g-h. The latter spelling was more common, with four listings. The former spelling of this fairly uncommon name had a single listing. Howard Keogh, Ministerial Road, Bedford. Even in his abbreviated time in New Hampshire, he had picked up on an implied class distinction between residents of Bedford and Manchester, both of whom attended Southside High School in West Manchester. Bedford was home to many of the area's professionals, entrepreneurs and academics, laced with a smattering of old money with proud Yankee names. Manchester, too, had its share from these groups but, unfortunately for them, they were joined by everyone else. When Brian brought to mind the image of the perfectly groomed, impeccably dressed girl from homeroom and English class, he was strongly inclined toward a single probability. The cool, confident manner reflected through a distinguishable air of superiority—Miss Keogh was a Bedford girl! He underlined the listing for Howard Keogh before returning the book to the telephone table.

By his third day, Brian was beginning to identify specific groups within the school, social, academic, and economic. He recognized what would be a major problem for him in the weeks ahead. Back in Lowell, his enrollment in a college preparatory program isolated him, by and large, from his friends from junior high. However, between periods and certainly before and after school, he would simply rejoin the friends with whom he shared common attitudes and mode of dress. At Southside, he had no group of social peers to return to from his classroom routine. His classrooms were populated by feeble bookworms and popular kids, which included jocks and the accomplished, both socially and physically. The same mix existed at Lowell High. However, back in Lowell, he had the ability to return to his less-polished buddies from the neighborhood or Varnum at any and all times except during actual classroom hours. Now, in his new surroundings, he was forced to conclude that he was entirely a breed apart from those around him and probably not likely to make meaningful friendships among his academic peers.

As his first week at Southside High wound down, Brian began to draw impressions from his individual classes. By far, his first period English class stood out from the remainder of his educational itinerary. Most importantly, this was the period he could observe Miss Keogh from a distance. It was clear she was one of the brightest students in the class, proffering articulate arguments with regularity. Over the first few days he avoided offering his personal insights in English class, but did answer correctly the only question tossed at him by Miss Royal. On the other hand, the confident Miss Keogh showed no apprehension to challenging her fellow students' answers or theories. What's more, she would confidently express her views not as opinions, but as clear statements of fact.

In addition to the presence of Miss Keogh, there was another, very real, undercurrent present in the person of Ben Turner, a well-scrubbed, good-looking kid who strode around school with absolute self-confidence, no doubt a product of his prowess on the football field. Ben, already a varsity standout as a sophomore, had been propped up by the adulation of his coaches and admirers since the age of eleven. One of the few nonwhites in the school, he commanded the respect of those around him through accomplishment and intimidation. For Ben, Southside High School was a stage, and he saw his role as a major one. Turner spoke louder than most anyone else, often using forceful hand gestures and extended eye contact. One of his favorite targets was an extremely thin, studious type named Jerome Jefferson, another black student. It was almost a daily routine for Ben Turner to torment the much smaller boy before class, to the amusement of onlookers.

On the Friday morning of his first week at Southside High, Brian noticed Miss Keogh was absent from her desk in homeroom. First period English lagged without the attendance of the young woman who was now invading his daydreams regularly, not to mention the thoughts that teenage boys torture themselves with lying in bed at night before the arrival of sleep. When Miss Royal assigned study material for a quiz announced for the following Monday, Brian wondered if he dared call the phone number in Bedford that he had theorized was Miss Keogh's. Throughout the school day, he wrestled with the proposition of calling this beguiling creature with word of the English quiz and details of the material to be covered.

However, the whole issue of calling the Keogh girl was rendered irrelevant when he cleared the homeroom doorway only to see her seated at her desk. Brian stepped quickly back to his desk, opened his English text, and hurriedly jotted down the homework assignment. Then, without uttering a word, he placed it face down in front of the young woman. The pretty girl's eyes grew wide for a moment, then a scowl replaced the surprised expression on her face.

"What do you think you're doing? Get that thing off of my desk," she snapped coldly.

"Miss, there is information of real value to you on that paper," answered Brian.

"Get that piece of paper off my desk," ordered the girl in a no-nonsense tone.

"As you wish," he conceded in a voice void of any hostility. "Just don't start whining around me when you blow the English quiz on Monday and I friggin' ace it!" Brian turned half sideways and stared right at the impeccably groomed teenager, who finally turned and locked eyes with him. His stomach knotted as Miss Keogh's steel blue eyes riveted onto his. She did not speak, opting only to stare directly at him, until it was he who became uncomfortable and broke eye contact.

"You're in my English class?" she asked as if in disbelief.

"That's right—Miss Royal's first period class. I noticed you were out this morning and I thought you'd like to know we were having a quiz on Monday. She gave us the weekend to study and the material we're responsible for is on the paper." Brian, his heart racing, kept a friendly tone in his voice.

Without uttering another word, Miss Keogh extended her hand and motioned him to provide her the paper. Handing her the note, Brian took the opportunity to study her face at close range. Her flawless complexion required only the slightest hint of makeup while her lips were set off in subdued pink. She scanned the piece of paper before lifting her eyes back to him.

"You write like a girl," she said sarcastically.

"It's even worse than that—I throw a baseball like a girl, too."

"Your parents must be very proud," she answered in deadpan fashion. Turning completely toward her, he extended his hand.

"Hi, my name is Brian Kelly."

The confident Miss Keogh did not respond to his gesture, choosing to let him remain frozen in front of her, hand extended. Brian became aware that a number of classmates were watching the proceedings.

"I'll leave my hand out here all afternoon if I have to," he snapped.

"That's up to you," said the girl. She turned away from him, folding her hands on the desktop.

A few seconds passed before the final bell sounded. Brian withdrew his hand and began collecting his things. He turned his back to the young woman, his repressed anger indicated by the stiffness in his shoulders. Conscious of some snickering from eavesdropping classmates, he grabbed a stack of books and made for the door. He had only taken a few steps down the hall in the direction of his locker when he felt a tug on his sweater. Swinging around, he confronted his tormentor.

"Sorry for being a brat back there. My mother says I'm a bad seed. Anyway, Mr. Brian Kelly, I'm Maggie May Keogh, and I think I owe you a thank you for the English homework and everything. I would have been screwed without it," she said, displaying a smile that showcased a row of white teeth. She spoke in a flirtatious whisper, and Brian searched for a reply. When she extended her hand, he considered showing this girl the same discourtesy extended to him only moments earlier, but could not follow through. Reaching out, he lightly squeezed the soft, white hand of the female that was sending waves of nervous energy through his body. The self-assured Miss Keogh resumed walking, and after a moment of hesitation, Brian joined her.

"Are you any relation to the clown in the circus?" she asked offhandedly.

"Yeah, as a matter of fact I am. Emmett Kelly's my dad. You wouldn't know it by the way I look but I'm worth millions. I just bum around like this to keep the phonies and fair weather friends off my back."

"Well, it appears to be working," replied Maggie May, without so much as a moment's hesitation.

Brian made a sudden stop and turned to the only person in school who had, to date, engaged him in conversation.

"I'm afraid this is as far as I go," he announced, pointing toward a locker angled against the corridor wall. "Maggie May, this is Eileen," he wisecracked.

The girl stared at the locker in deadpan fashion before speaking. "You've given your locker a girl's name. I don't get it. Why a name—and why Eileen?"

Brian bent down, laying his books by the locker door. Then, he stepped behind the angular sophomore and placed his hands on her shoulders. Exerting only the slightest amount of pressure, he caused her to incline in the same direction as his locker.

"I—lean. Get it? Eileen!"

Maggie May Keogh let her head drop in mock disgust. "On that strange note I think I'll go find my ride," she exclaimed, stepping away from him.

"Did I tell you—Grace Kelly's my aunt," called out Brian to Maggie's retreating back.

"No big deal—Gene Kelly's my lover," she tossed back, not to be outdone.

Brian stood in the middle of the hallway, his attention focused on the back of the incredible Miss Keogh, his eyes trained on her magnificently turned calves. He simply could not turn away until she reached the stairwell and disappeared.

Brian left the building amid a stream of chattering students and began the uphill walk back to Montgomery Street and home. His mind swirled with thoughts of his conversation with the sharp-tongued Maggie May Keogh. Arriving home, he decided to put off homework until later in the weekend. He did not anticipate his mother's return much before five o'clock. So, with less than a dollar in his pocket, Brian decided to check out Manchester's downtown area.

He set out just after three in the afternoon and, after crossing the Merrimack River, arrived on Elm Street, downtown. Proceeding south, he spent a good portion of his time taking in the new sights, businesses with odd-sounding names: The Rag Barrier, State Pharmacy, Ben Richards, Mass Camera Center, Pariseau's, Easler's, the Junior Deb Shop, the Slak Shack, Holland's Drug. He thought there was a noticeable lack of Irish names, something he had become accustomed to from his sixteen years in Lowell. Brian made note of details that might prove valuable at a later time. Movie theaters, restaurants, and department stores were of particular importance. There was something called Cine I and Cine II that reminded him of the Strand back home. Reaching an intersection that separated city hall from what appeared to be a bank, he trotted between a row of stationary and parked cars and began making his way eastward. Before him, another movie house could be seen up the street.

In an alleyway directly to his left, Brian's attention was suddenly captured by the sound of pitched voices. A grown woman was engaged in a shouting match with three youths, none of whom appeared to be even of high school age. Two of the boys taunted the woman with catcalls and profanity while the third was positioned behind her and appeared to be trying to place something inside her jacket and down her back.

"Hey, Judy, is this the best you can do?" they called out, distracting the outflanked woman. Brian was somehow reminded of nature programs where packs of hyenas would encircle a large beast and eventually bring it down through blindside and rear attacks. After two aborted attempts, the youth seemed about to deliver his payload when a pair of hands locked onto his wrist and coat collar simultaneously. The startled youth's eyes widened and he let out an astonished cry.

"Okay, jerk off, let's see how this puke shit looks on *you*," exclaimed Brian, and he smeared the rag dripping with some unidentifiable ooze down the young man's face and neck. The boy let out a scream and pulled himself away, trying to rub the crud from his face. The woman, heavyset and of indeterminable age, could only stare at Brian and the youths, who by now were beginning to back away from the scene.

"Mister, you suck!" one called out.

"If you little maggots aren't out of this alley in ten seconds, I'll run one of you down and really fuck you up," threatened Brian. The three toughs continued with an onslaught of profanity, all the while making their way away from Brian and the alley. He turned back to the woman, who was staring at him, a curious expression covering her face. She didn't speak, but simply ambled off down the street, leaving Brian to wonder who she was and about the cause of her bizarre confrontation with the youths.

"Hope I didn't hurt the little darlings' feelings," he mused through a wry smile.

It was shortly after five o'clock when Brian heard his mother's footsteps clear the second floor landing and proceed up the stairway to their third-story flat. He had returned home a short time earlier and was now stretched out on the couch in front of the television. Hopping to his feet, he bounded to the door in time to open it for his mother and usher her into the kitchen. She carried a shopping bag which she dropped onto the porcelain table top, letting out a sigh of relief as she relinquished the weight of the groceries.

"We're going to have something for supper that we've gone a long time without," she announced. Brian peeked down into the bag but could only identify a carton of milk resting at the center of the groceries. "Tell you what, sonny boy, you go back to your TV and let me start getting things going here. I'll join you once everything is boiling."

"Boiling, huh? Is that a hint? Boiling—boiling," he muttered, while trying to come up with his mother's mystery meal. "By any chance are we having lobster for supper? I mean, it is Friday and we all know how you feel about meat on Friday," joked Brian.

Elizabeth feigned a half-angry response. "Well, it's clear I can't keep a secret from you. What's more—the Kennedys are coming up from Hyannis Port and joining us for cocktails!"

"I hope Ted's not driving," retorted Brian.

"That'll be enough," said his mother, bringing their conversation to a temporary end.

Brian returned to his television program while the sounds of banging pots and chopping chimed in from the kitchen pantry. He redirected his attention to the eighteen-inch TV where a gallery of children were being entertained by a heavyset, middle-aged man in a beach hat. The sixteen-year-old sat entranced as each young member of the audience was introduced. Two or three bursts of laughter brought his mother to the doorway.

"What in the world is so funny?"

"It's called the 'Uncle Gus Show.' It must be New Hampshire's answer to 'Major Mudd.'"

"Who are those silly looking articles in the back row?" asked Elizabeth, referring to a small group of young men standing behind the overexcited youngsters.

"They're fraternity pledges from New Hampshire College—being publicly tortured and humiliated for our viewing pleasure," answered an amused Brian. His eyes shifted to his mother standing in the doorway. "So when do I find out what we're having for supper?"

"If you must know, we're having fish chowder. It's been a while, but I caught haddock on sale and couldn't pass it up."

Jumping to his feet, Brian rushed past her into the kitchen. "Don't put the haddock in the chowder until I actually see it," jested Brian. This was a reference to a pair of recent meals at which the announced fish chowder lacked evidence of anything but milk, butter, potatoes, and onions. Brian's accusations of being served fishless fish chowder had met with criticism and indignation from his mother, but not an unqualified denial. And so this evening, in full view of her son, Elizabeth unwrapped the white packing paper to reveal a fillet of haddock that weighed in at something less than a pound.

"Are you satisfied now, doubting Thomas?" she asked.

"Can't be too careful around a flimflam artist like you. There's been altogether too many potatoes and not enough of anything else fed to me. Look what you've produced, Mrs. Kelly—a son, puny and weak. But, you haven't fooled me, Elizabeth—not for a moment. I know what you do late at night when your precious baby boy is sound asleep. That's when you break out the real food, the good food, and eat to your heart's content." Brian was standing behind his mother, his hands resting on her shoulders, as he teased the only parent he had ever known.

Although she knew her son was struggling with the move to New Hampshire and a new school, Elizabeth in fact felt a guilty satisfaction from the singular importance she now played in his life. The truth was, at this place and time, the mother and son had only each other's companionship to share in this new city.

"Go back and watch Uncle Zeke," she ordered.

"It's Gus, not Zeke! If you're going to be a New Hampshire hayseed, and turn me into one along with you, at least get it right. It's 'Uncle Gus'!"

Elizabeth affectionately nudged her son back to the TV room. "Git now. Let me finish supper."

The Kellys dined at the kitchen table twenty minutes later. Elizabeth related stories from the mill and described in detail the personal appearances and mannerisms of the individuals now drifting into her inner circle at Pandora Industries. Brian could see that his mother was already developing a comfort level with a number of women at her workplace. He realized she enjoyed relating details and anecdotes from Pandora, and, therefore, made a concerted effort to keep his attention trained on her every word. Eventually, Elizabeth became aware of the amount of time she had monopolized, and shifted the conversation to Brian's progress at Southside High.

"Now, how about my handsome son? You've been close-mouthed ever since you started over there. At least tell me a little about the kids in your classes. Any cute little Manchester girls I can expect seeing you drag home to show off?"

"The girls are nothin' up here, Ma, and that's the honest truth. No interest—none! Once I'm out of school, it's back to Lowell."

"And leave your sainted mother alone?" she joked.

"I'll send for you once I've made my fortune. It shouldn't take any more than six months," boasted Brian between spoonfuls of chowder.

"So, you're trying to tell me, Brian Kelly, that there isn't even one girl in the whole school that you can fancy?"

He answered his mother in the affirmative but seemed to hesitate before replying.

"Look me deep in the eyes and say that again." Elizabeth was now playfully staring down her son with a comedic expression.

"Okay, there's one. Maybe. But she's so far out of my league it's a joke." Brian spoke with some resignation.

"No girl's out of my handsome son's league. Get that thought out of your head right now," stated the proud mother decisively. "What does she look like?"

"Well, she's blonde, dirty blonde, you know, light brown or dirty blonde, and she wears it back in a ponytail—sort of. Ma, her eyes are so friggin' blue they almost look fake. And when she smiles her mouth is like—hypnotic, and it's hard not to stare at her. On top of this, I can tell she's smart 'cause I'm in her English class and, well, she's just smart. And she always seems to be wearing expensive-looking clothes. And she's always neat and clean, you know, well groomed—classy."

Elizabeth sat back in silence, marveling at the euphoric state the very thought of this young creature from Southside High School seemed to bring to her son. It was a side of her sixteen-year-old that she had not seen before. This girl had clearly made a deep impression on her son, and she sensed he appreciated the opportunity to speak about her.

"Do you know this little thing's name?" Elizabeth urged her son to respond.

"Maggie May—Maggie May Keogh," he blurted out.

"Please tell me that's not the poor thing's real name," protested Elizabeth.

"No, Ma, I think it's probably something to do with the song. Her real name's Margaret."

"And have you broken the ice and spoken to her yet?" his mother asked.

"Yeah, we've talked—briefly. We have English class together and we sort of compared notes on some assigned work."

"Well, why don't you just see if you can build on that and get to know her a little better," she suggested.

"I get the impression she's sort of involved with someone," offered Brian.

"Sonny boy, at your age boyfriends and girlfriends come and go like downtown buses. Today she's on one boy's arm and tomorrow she's looking for someone new."

"Then, of course, there's the fact that she can probably have anyone she damn wants," he blurted out.

"Watch your language. You know I've told you about that," admonished Elizabeth.

"Come on, Ma, 'damn' is not a swear," contended the teenager.

"Maybe on the streets it's not, but it is in this house. My rules, handsome."

"Getting back to the subject—Maggie May Keogh can have just about anyone she wants at that school. What's she gonna find irresistible about a carless, friendless, penniless, ugly—"

"Whoa! Where do you get off calling yourself ugly? You're my handsome, young son."

"Oh, come on, Ma. It's not like I have all these girls coming up to me in school and handing me their phone numbers. There's the popular guys in school who get the girls and then there's the guys like me who are lucky if a girl will even talk to them. If I'm so good looking, which I know I am not, then how come girls avoid me like the plague?" exploded Brian, given the rare opportunity to express some of his frustration to an adult.

"Well, gloomy Gus, if what you say is true, and I'm saying I'm not so sure it is, then it may have something to do with the fact that you come off as fairly mature. You carry yourself as an adult. You have a bit of an air about you—not punky or anything—but an air. You come off as being sure of yourself. It's a sign of maturity, and trust me, a lot of young women need a shot of self-confidence themselves. It may be something as simple as the fact that many teenage girls are intimidated by you," theorized mother to son. Brian stared at his mom in silence, running her words over in his mind. "For all you know, your little Maggie May could be intimidated by you," his mother continued, and Brian let out a spontaneous laugh.

"Trust me, oh beautiful woman who makes my meals and washes my clothes—including my underwear—Maggie May Keogh is *not* intimidated by me. Of *that*, I am *sure*," Brian joked, speaking overdramatically to return lightness to the conversation. He briefly considered telling his mother of the incident in the alleyway downtown that afternoon but decided against sharing that story with her, and the remainder of their time at the dinner table was spent in relative silence.

The excitement created by his conversation with Maggie May Keogh on the previous Friday was tempered Monday morning when she barely acknowledged Brian in homeroom. It was already midweek when he sauntered into English class and was treated to graffiti scrawled across the blackboard. The presidential election was only days away and political ideas and feelings were on most everyone's mind. Brian took his seat and gazed up at a charged messaged chalked on the board. It read: IF GOD EXHISTED HE'D WANT YOU TO VOTE FOR GEORGE MCGOVERN. The message was met with a variety of responses from students as they took their seats. Brian stared up at the blackboard, then rose to his feet and walked to the front of the room. Picking up a piece of chalk, he quickly scratched out a message below the original.

Dear Moron,

There is no 'h' in existed.

(signed) God

His action prompted a few chuckles and unintelligible comments from the assembled students. He glanced at Miss Keogh to gauge her reaction but her mind was occupied by a book opened on her desk. Seconds later, Miss Royal breezed into the room. She paused momentarily, taking in the dueling statements scrawled at the front of her classroom.

"I want to know who is responsible for this nonsense," she commanded. There was no response from the students. "Anyone?" she asked. A hand went up. It belonged to Maggie May. The humorless teacher beckoned her to speak.

"I wasn't here when the first message was left but I was for the second one. A man with a beard, robe, and sandals left the second one, Miss Royal. He appeared to be in his early thirties." Maggie May's sarcasm brought forth a chorus of laughter and hoots from her classmates. The teacher ordered her to sit down and promptly erased the front board.

As the week rolled toward completion, all attempts by Brian to engage Miss Keogh in banter or dialogue were met with one word replies or no response at all. On Friday, Miss Royal returned the graded quizzes given on Monday. Brian was rewarded for his two hours of intense studying on Sunday afternoon by garnering a 97 on the quiz that tested the class on punctuation.

He returned to homeroom just after final period to find Maggie May sitting quietly at her desk, hands folded. It was still bothering him that she had not so much as mentioned his thoughtful act the previous Friday. He collapsed at his desk beside her while her body language warned him against approaching her in any manner. Glancing in her direction, he spotted her English quiz sitting on top of other papers. Her grade on the quiz was 95. He decided to spring to the attack.

"Get used to it," he stated matter-of-factly. Her pretty head slowly shifted sideways.

"What did you say?" she asked coldly.

"Get used to it, Keogh. Your academic standing in English has dropped down a peg. That probably means you are now a solid number two in English—nothing to be ashamed of." Brian held up his quiz with the 97 mark blazoned in red. The girl held her deadpan expression as her eyes shifted to his paper, then back to him. He knew immediately he had struck a nerve as her eyes narrowed. He had decided that this tactic might be the only way to draw this beautiful, young girl back into a conversation.

"Are you saying, Mr. Kelly—that is your name, right?—are you saying that you actually think you are brighter than I am?" she asked, seemingly in disbelief. Her blue eyes were drilling a hole in his composure, but he gathered his courage and went back on the attack.

"Well, we seem to have some objective evidence in the form of these two grades. Pray tell, Miss Keogh, are you saying you have a better basis for judging our aptitudes?" Brian could not believe he was actually pushing the conversation in this direction. But he could see, for better or worse, he had pushed all the right buttons as he now had Maggie May Keogh's undivided attention.

"Well, Mr. Kelly, if you're as smart as you seem to think you are, then perhaps you might be willing to wager on the results of our next English exam?" A glib smile appeared on the girl's face as she saw an opportunity to test this egotistical newcomer. "Five dollars to the one with the higher grade on every quiz and exam," stated the young woman, displaying total confidence.

"Whoa! There's no way I could take five bucks from you week after week—no way. Make it a buck and I can live with it. I figure you can handle a buck at a time, Maggie May," said Brian behind a grin.

"Okay—but double if the winner aces the test."

"Fair enough, Maggie May," agreed Brian, before extending his hand. Miss Keogh hesitated momentarily before grasping it and sealing the proposed wager. His heart raced as his long fingers encircled the girl's soft hand.

It was early November when Miss Royal's English class was presented with an exam promoted as a midterm. It was the first test under the wagering conditions agreed upon by Brian and Maggie May. For his part, Brian hit the books with purpose over the preceding weekend, knowing the confident Miss Keogh would expend the same effort. As promised, the midterm, which combined complex grammatical material along with an understanding of American authors Herman Melville, Jack London, and Stephen Crane, was difficult. Brian labored over the test, completing the last of a series of essay questions just ahead of the bell. Leaving the classroom in a stream of students, he caught Maggie May's eye as she jockeyed her way through the throng of teenagers attempting to escape into the hallway. He gave a shrug and motioned an invisible knife across his throat, indicating the difficulty of the test in comical fashion.

"Not until I've been paid," she cried out behind one of her familiar smirks. Moments later the girl's expression changed as she spotted someone in the hallway and exited the room in a rush to greet the same young man Brian had seen her walking with more than a week earlier.

The trance brought on by the view of Maggie May walking away dressed in a severe miniskirt was interrupted by Jerome Jefferson crashing against him from the rear, followed by a burst of laughter from Ben Turner and Josh Backman, one of his football cronies. Brian was quick to ascertain that the slightly built sophomore was merely the object of some juvenile prank by the jocks. He turned and stared coldly at the two pranksters.

"What the fuck are you looking at?" spit out Turner behind a glare designed to intimidate.

"Dog shit," muttered Brian. The response brought out an immediate reaction from the husky Turner, his body shaking with rage. Backman laughed off the new kid's act of defiance and pulled his friend away from the confrontation.

Two days later, the English exams were passed out, much to the displeasure of a majority of the students. Miss Royal called out the names of each student, requiring them, in order, to walk up to her desk where she handed them their test papers along with a personal comment or criticism. Brian trained his eyes on his academic adversary as Margaret Keogh's name was called out. The shapely sophomore strutted up to the front desk and accepted a brief word from Miss Royal. Then, after glancing down at her paper, she lifted her eyes to Brian. A smile spread across her face and her eyes widened, signaling she was pleased with her grade. A minute later when his name was called, Brian strolled to the front desk and was presented his exam. It carried the grade of 92 percent. His first instinct was to shoot Maggie May a sly smile. His eyes found her staring at him. He drew satisfaction from the circumstances he had helped to create. He was, through this silly wager with Margaret Keogh, burrowing his way into her everyday life. At the close of class Miss Keogh waited by the door, attempting to learn his grade. Brian, however, deferred sharing his grade with her until day's end in homeroom.

Returning to homeroom at the close of the school day, Brian saw Maggie May patiently awaiting his arrival. He casually walked to his desk. She looked over impatiently.

"So—show me your English paper," she ordered. He reached into a stack of papers and produced his exam. He watched her blue eyes focus on the grade. She let out a restrained giggle. This was followed by her outstretched hand demanding payment.

"May I at least see your grade before I pay off on this bet?" he asked.

"Are you calling me a cheat?" she retorted defiantly. Two female classmates, clearly privy to the circumstances, laughed at the proceedings. "Brian, I would think you'd want to get this whole thing over as quickly as possible."

"I'll pay when you produce your grade," he announced, beginning to become a little agitated with the girl's dramatization of this event. After a brief pause, she reached into her desk and produced her English exam and her 96 percent grade. After glancing at her paper, he reached into his shirt pocket and produced the dollar bill, causing Maggie May to break into a cascade of charming laughter. The payoff brought on a round of applause from onlooking female classmates.

III

OVER THE NEXT FEW WEEKS BRIAN'S ATTEMPTS to build a meaningful relationship with the Keogh girl were largely unsuccessful. While the attractive and sometimes provocatively dressed Miss Keogh did speak to him somewhat cordially and on a regular basis, it was clear to everyone, particularly Brian, that her heart was the property of an upperclassman named Skip Emerson.

Meanwhile, there was more than an undercurrent of hostility developing between Brian and the small group of jocks headed by Ben Turner. A shouting match ensued on one occasion between Brian and Ben, but this had not led to anything more serious. On another occasion, he found himself the object of some heckling from this group, leading to an obscene gesture in response from him, proving he was not in the least intimidated by the band of football jocks.

Miss Royal gave a pop quiz just before Thanksgiving break, catching Brian by surprise and enriching Maggie May by another dollar.

The long Thanksgiving weekend provided the Kellys with the opportunity to visit Lowell. Mother and son spent three nights with the Clarkes, allowing Brian to drop in on old friends, including Perez, who treated him to lunch at the Cathay Garden on the banks of the Merrimack River. During the course of the meal, Perez inquired into the status of Brian's financial situation. When he informed his friend that he still had not landed a part-time job, Perez produced a wad of bills, resulting in an uncomfortable standoff between the two old friends. Brian strongly insisted that he had looked up his friend because he missed him and not for any mercenary reason. All the while, the strong-willed Puerto Rican argued that he would be insulted if Brian would refuse his token of generosity, but it was only when he brought up the subject of Christmas gifts that his young friend ceased to resist the gift at hand. When the longtime friends emerged from the restaurant a full two hours after arriving, Brian carried sixty dollars in his wallet.

Meaning to take advantage of his short time at home, Brian spent every available hour wandering up and down Bridge Street, climbing Christian Hill, all the while running into friends from his days at Varnum School. On Saturday morning, he walked from Uncle Jimmy's house on Hildreth Street to Arthur's Diner by the bridge just to savor the taste of the finest grilled coffee rolls on the planet. He was joined by Perez for this final meal, surrounded by the people, sounds and smells familiar to him. By mid-afternoon the Kellys were seated in the back of Jimmy Clarke's sedan and driving back north to New Hampshire.

As the bitter cold of December 1972 set in, Brian Kelly was no closer to establishing any resemblance to a social life than he had been nearly two months earlier when he arrived in Manchester. In the cafeteria he sat at a table comprised exclusively of misfits and outcasts. On the positive side, his lack of any social life had him overachieving scholastically, running A's and strong B's in all subjects. Strangely enough, he had managed to forge an amiable relationship with the fascinating Maggie May Keogh. This, however, only came about through a diligent effort on his part.

On a cold, blustery morning that started out like any other, Brian's subdued routine was interrupted by an incident in English class. Arriving early, he was leaning over from his desk when a hand came down on the back of his neck, applying pressure.

"Any sign of my pencil down there, Kelly?" growled Ben Turner.

Pulling his head left in a sideways movement, Brian broke Turner's grasp and countered with a left hook that grazed the jock's cheek. A startled Turner was already pulling back from this counterattack when Brian launched a straight right hand. The second punch found Turner's cheek, but did not land flush.

Both punches had been launched with surprising quickness, catching the husky athlete off guard.

"Mr. Kelly, stop that immediately!" called out an adult voice from across the room. Brian froze, then turned to see Miss Royal standing in the doorway. "I want you to step back this instant. Pick up your books and report to administration," ordered the startled teacher.

"Better keep your faggot friends close by, Benjamin, cause if I catch you alone—"

"Mr. Kelly, I don't want another word out of your mouth. Do you understand? This is really disappointing—very disappointing," uttered the now-flustered Miss Royal.

Brian sauntered back to his desk, hooking his arm around a pile of books. He walked past the front desk which gave the teacher a final opportunity to voice her disappointment.

"I'm sure this sort of behavior isn't tolerated back in Lowell, and it certainly will not be tolerated here."

The sound of snickering was audible as Brian made his way to the door. His eyes caught Maggie May's before exiting. Her blue eyes were rounded, as if traumatized by the actions of her homeroom acquaintance. He said nothing before closing the door and making his way to the administrative offices. He had half expected someone to speak up for him. To plead his case to Miss Royal would, in his mind, have been a dishonorable act, a sign of weakness. Sitting silently, awaiting punishment for the altercation, he asked himself whether he had overreacted. There was no question that his volcanic reaction to Ben Turner's conduct was largely prompted by the presence of Miss Keogh. Brian knew he could not let himself be made the fool in front of this girl, under any circumstances.

The punishment for Brian's loss of temper in English class was stiff, but short of suspension. He would spend the rest of the week in detention class after school and would receive two demerits on his record. The demerits would automatically disqualify him from making the honor roll for the term. Brian put his time in detention to good use. School rules forbid studying during detention; however, he managed to slip loose leaf notes onto his desk in the rear of the classroom and did put the ninety minutes spent in silence to some good use.

It was for this reason that he felt confident when yet another surprise quiz was sprung on English class Thursday morning.

Thursday must have been a bad night on television because Miss Royal returned the quiz papers the following day. Brian was pleased to see a 95 percent scratched on the top of his paper. He had correctly answered nineteen of the twenty multiple choice questions. Miss Keogh appeared flustered on the one occasion she glanced over at him. He eagerly awaited the period ending bell. When it came, he quickly made his way to the door, reaching it at approximately the same instant as Maggie May. As she made a rush through the door opening, he brought his hand down on her shoulder, stopping her in her tracks.

"Oh, Miss Keogh, aren't you forgetting something?" Maggie May's body language seemed to telegraph the outcome of their ongoing wager. Head down and shoulders stooping, she seemed to have finally faltered on an exam. Brian presented his grade, pushing it to within six inches of her face.

"To be honest, Brian, I haven't even taken the time to check out my mark. Here—I'm afraid to look. How did I do?" she asked pathetically. He unfolded the quiz. His heart sank at the sight of 100%. Bringing his eyes up from the paper, he looked into the face that, by now, seem to haunt his every waking moment. Apparently, it was not enough for her to best him on every wager, she had now begun toying with him. "Now, let's see, Kelly. If memory serves me correctly, it's double money if one of us aces an exam—which means you owe me two dollars." Brian reached into his back pocket and removed his wallet, the contents of which only provided a single dollar bill. Then, with Maggie May's hand still extended, he sifted through a fist full of change, barely coming up with the additional dollar.

"For a second, I thought you weren't going to make it!" she barked. Stuffing her winnings in her purse, she flashed a deflated Brian one of her disarming smiles and strutted off.

With only a modest amount of small change, Brian picked up a single carton of milk at lunch and sat at a corner table at the edge of the cafeteria, his face buried in a textbook. The table vibrated with the idle chatter of adolescents. Meaningless conversation was being exchanged by young men, none of whom he knew. Suddenly though, the table grew silent, causing him to lift his head out of curiosity. Standing over him was Maggie May, staring down and wearing a peculiar expression on her face.

"Sorry, Keogh, you've got all my cash. I'm tapped out," he confessed, prompting the pretty sophomore to produce a sandwich wrapped in wax paper. She dropped it on the table in front of him.

"PB and J, Kelly. You're skinny enough without me adding to it." Then, through the combination of a smile and blush, he proceeded to unwrap the sandwich while his benefactor continued standing over him.

"I considered springing for the Tuna Wiggle, but then, I think I've punished you enough today."

"Wait a minute Keogh, you didn't cut the crusts off my sandwich," he cracked, still slightly overwhelmed by the turn of events.

"Kelly, if I should ever cut off anything of yours—trust me—it won't be your crusts." The table erupted in howls causing heads to turn from the surrounding tables. With that, the self-assured Maggie May turned and left the table, knowing that every male's eyes were trained on her. Brian took in her every move as she returned to her table, adorned in a white blouse and pleated, purple skirt. A redheaded fellow seated two chairs from him let his head drop to the table with a thud.

"Keogh is so—fuckin'—hot," he muttered, stating the obvious to the assembled teenagers.

As the school week drew to a close, Brian found himself rushing back to homeroom with the hope of speaking to Maggie May, even if only for a few moments. He was disappointed to find her engrossed in conversation with female classmates. There was something of importance and of a confidential nature being discussed in whispers. In ten minutes, he would be reporting to the last of his detention periods. He skipped out of class with Miss Keogh still engrossed in conversation with friends. Reaching his locker, he withdrew those books he deemed necessary for weekend studying and slammed the metal door shut. He turned to find Maggie May standing behind him.

"I hope I didn't come on too strong at lunch. You know, I wasn't really trying to show you up. It's just that I felt a little stupid bringing you the sandwich and all," she confessed.

"Listen, Keogh, I'm just happy to have someone talk to me in this place. You're one of the few. And now that I'm a criminal within the education system—going to detention day after day."

"That whole thing with Ben Turner—what were you thinking? I can't figure out if you're really, really brave or really, really dumb."

"Keogh, I am equal parts courage and stupidity."

"Do you have time to walk me to my car? My mother would like to see what you look like. I've told her about you."

"I can only imagine. Well, if you don't drag your feet, I can probably make it. What about Skip? Aren't you afraid he might get jealous?"

"He's a big boy. Oh, Brian, if you want to call a halt to our little bet, I might consent to let you squirm your way out," she called out, hurrying down the school steps.

"Go on," answered Brian.

"If you'll just admit, out loud, that you are outmatched and that I am your intellectual superior, then we can call an end to this ongoing, intellectual bloodbath."

"Forget it, Keogh, no friggin' way. Intellectual superior! Where do you get this crap from?" scoffed Brian.

Maggie May shrugged her shoulders. "As you wish." She proceeded to direct Brian to a late-model Buick on a side street. He walked up to the driver's side window and peered inside. A pretty, middle-aged woman sat behind the wheel and rolled down the window.

"Mrs. Keogh, I'm here to deny each and every lie your daughter has probably said about me," crowed Brian. The salt-and-pepper-haired woman smiled up at him.

"Mother, this is the boy I've been telling you about. The one that won't stop bothering me."

"Mr. Kelly, it's a pleasure meeting you. My daughter has a lot of interesting things to say about you," stated the woman with a gracious smile.

"I only wish I had the time to fill you in on some of your daughter's shenanigans, but unfortunately, I'm due back inside shortly."

"He's got detention, Mother," injected Maggie May.

"And I offer no apologies. Wasn't Henry Thoreau put behind bars back in his day?" reasoned Brian.

"Yes, but it wasn't for taking a swing at Ralph Waldo," countered the sharp-witted Maggie May. He shook his head and looked down at Mrs. Keogh.

"God, she's got an answer for everything," he sighed. He shot the girl a final glance, waved good-bye to both women, and jogged back into the school.

IV

O<small>N</small> S<small>ATURDAY</small> <small>MORNING</small>, Brian rose early and headed down-town. He hoped to begin, and with any luck, complete his Christmas shopping. He reasoned that a department store would provide him with the widest variety of gifts. His Christmas list was headed by his mom, followed by Uncle Jimmy, Aunt Martha and the kids, Perez, and maybe, if his cash held up, Maggie May. His mother had not dropped even the slightest hint of what she might want. He started out at Leavitt's, a department store in the center of town. There he picked up toys for his cousin Jimmy Junior, a record album for cousin Barbara, and a few kitchen odds and ends for his mother. The Fanny Farmer Candy Shop provided him with a gift for his aunt and uncle. By midday Brian found himself wandering in a semi-trance, frustrated by the chore of picking up something meaningful for the remainder of the people on his list. At Woolworth's 5 & 10, he happened upon a client and phone number organizer, something that Perez was in dire need of in his profession. With Perez out of the way, he still lacked a significant present for his mother and something for Maggie May Keogh. Strolling back into Leavitt's in search of some inspiration, he happened upon a table covered with ladies' scarves. His eyes scanned a variety of solids and prints, all in a tumbled condition from hours of inspection by countless shop-pers. However, his hazel eyes locked onto the corner of one par-ticular scarf that had gone unclaimed by scores of shoppers ear-lier. Grabbing the visible corner, he pulled the delicate, dark purple accessory from the table and examined it for defects. If his recollection was accurate, its color matched the purple skirt Maggie May had worn in school the day before. The scarf was in perfect condition. He had gotten a good feeling from this lovely piece of fabric the moment he had laid eyes on it, and the price was right. He carried it to the nearest register and paid for it from his dwindling cash. That left only a major gift for his mom to be purchased.

Brian strolled southward on Elm Street, carrying his collection of presents in an oversized bag picked up at Woolworth's. Gazing through the window of Dubois Furniture, he thought of the couch in the living room with its spring jutting upward from the left cushion. Fortunately, he and his mother had developed a sixth sense over the last year and managed to keep themselves from being penetrated by this constant danger. Most certainly, the cost of a new couch was far beyond Brian's current financial position. However, he paused a moment and imagined himself lugging a handsome living room couch home on his back—five or six blocks up Elm Street, across the Notre Dame Bridge, and up the hill onto the west side of the city. The mental image brought a smile to his face, then an audible chuckle. Instead, he continued southward to Granite Street, then turned for home over the chilly Granite Street Bridge. He had resigned himself to the fact that he would not complete his Christmas shopping on this day. His mother's major present had not been purchased and his shopping day was almost over. Granite Square was within sight when he glanced left and saw a storefront displaying religious articles. He stopped dead in his tracks, knowing he had aimlessly wandered upon the one site that, without question, could furnish him with the perfect present for his mom.

Brian's spirits began taking flight heading into the Christmas season of 1972. The long Christmas weekend would bring him and his mother back to Lowell where they would spend time with Uncle Jimmy, Aunt Martha and the kids. Throughout the week, Maggie May became preoccupied with plans for the weekend. He learned that she would be joining her friends for an overnight at Cindy Morneau's house. For his part, he began looking in earnest for a part-time job. After hitting a series of stone walls on the west side, he set his sights on Elm Street, filling out applications at Zayre's Department Store, Mister Steak, Howdy Beefburgers and The Chimes Café. As a concession to his mother, he limited his availability to weekends only.

With Christmas falling on Monday, the school week ran all the way through Friday. The Christmas break would then begin and continue through New Year's Day. One interesting development at Southside was an apparent chilling between Maggie May and Skip Emerson. Brian played the role of the concerned friend, offering himself as a sounding board as Maggie May questioned aloud her boyfriend's less than undivided attention. When Brian arrived in homeroom on Friday morning he found Maggie May seated at her desk, staring blankly out the window. The cold December morning had reddened her cheeks which brought out the blueness of her eyes. The magical face that had invaded his thoughts night after night since October seemed downcast, lost in painful thought.

"Wow, why the long face? Think of it Keogh, ten days away from me and you're only hours away. Cheer up!" he joked. She faked a weak smile. "Out with it Keogh. What is it? Did a certain spoiled brat find out she wasn't getting a new Mustang for Christmas? You're breaking my heart, Maggie May," teased Brian. She paused, then turned in her chair.

"I think things may be over with Skip. He hasn't called all week, and—I don't know, he just doesn't seem to care anymore."

"Well, let's look at this realistically. We know he hasn't found anyone in school better looking than you because—you know—you're the best. Agreed?" he asked lightheartedly.

"Agreed," she echoed. On the surface, he was acting the concerned, attentive friend. Inside, he fought back the desire to show his exhilaration. "Oh, wait a minute. I know something that might cheer you up." He reached inside his desk and produced a flat, rectangular box covered in Christmas wrapping. He gave Maggie May a shy smile and handed it to her. Her eyes widened at the sight of the small package.

"Oh, Brian, why did you go and get me something? I didn't get you anything. I didn't know," she exclaimed, embarrassed.

"Keogh, I got you something because I wanted to, not because I expected something in return. All I ask is that you think of me on Christmas morning when you're opening your gifts."

This final school day before the holiday was shortened by an early dismissal, as no classes were scheduled beyond midday. Only a handful of students even bothered to return to homeroom for the final bell. When it sounded, Brian headed to his locker to retrieve text books that he might actually open over the holidays. His uncle would be coming up from Lowell to bring them south for the long weekend. The prospect of being back home, even if it meant sharing a bed with Jimmy Junior, lifted his spirits. He would not miss much in New Hampshire over the next three days; not Southside, not Manchester, not the drafty, Montgomery Street flat. No, there was little to miss from his daily routine with the exception of Maggie May Keogh. He would be forced to endure a ten-day period without resting his eyes on her face, and this alone caused him concern.

At a few minutes after eight o'clock in the morning, Jimmy Clarke's station wagon pulled up in front of the Montgomery Street apartment house. Uncle Jimmy climbed the stairs to the third floor and knocked boldly on the back door. After joining his sister at the table over a cup of coffee, he assisted mother and son in carrying Christmas presents and luggage down to the car. On their final trip down the stairs the Kellys were stopped in the hall by Mr. Giroux. He presented Elizabeth with a small package, meticulously wrapped in paper adorned in angels. The landlord indicated that he was intending to bring the present upstairs Christmas Eve, but, seeing that the Kellys were heading out for Christmas, decided to give it to her now. The woman graciously accepted the unexpected gift, wishing her landlord a Merry Christmas while Brian looked on suspiciously.

The conversation was bright and cheery on the drive south to Lowell. At Elizabeth's request, Jimmy took Route 3A through Litchfield and Hudson. She reminded her brother of the farm she had visited with him and his parents during their childhood. She remembered the stand being set by itself in the midst of acres and acres of flat farmland. Brother and sister were not able to agree on the specific property they had visited thirty years earlier.

The ride, door to door, from the Kellys' Montgomery Street apartment to the Clarkes' modest single family house in the Centralville section of Lowell, took exactly an hour. Pulling into the driveway, the car was besieged by Jimmy Junior, a freckle-faced eight-year-old, and Barbara, the Clarkes' pretty eleven-year-old daughter. They enthusiastically greeted their aunt and cousin while Martha stood in the kitchen doorway, radiating her hospitable smile. Brian wrapped his arm around his diminutive, female cousin as Jimmy Junior hopped onto his back for a ride into the house. Martha Clarke greeted her holiday guests with a hug and an offer of eggnog. Following a few minutes of familial exchanges, Brian was sent back out to the car to retrieve the luggage. He carried his mother's things into the sewing room, which doubled as a spare bedroom. He was given the option of sacking out on the living room's convertible sofa or sharing Jimmy Junior's full-size bed. In response to his cousin's pleas, he opted to share the eight-year-old's bedroom.

The evening before, Elizabeth had addressed Brian on the matter of how his time should be spent over the visit, and he had agreed to limit his time away from his uncle's home, restricting it to daylight hours. Reminding his mother of their agreement, he snatched Perez's Christmas gift from the pile and wished the family a good day, promising to return by supper time, six o'clock sharp. His spirits soared on reaching Bridge Street as Wood Brothers Florist and Murphy and Callaghan's Pharmacy came into sight. He was home, even if only for a few, fleeting days, he was home. By the time he reached Perez's apartment house he had already exchanged greetings with two former classmates from Varnum.

Brian excitedly vaulted up the two flights of stairs to his friend's third-floor apartment and set out to make his presence known. Folding his hand into a broad fist, he forcefully pounded on the door.

"You're playing the radio too goddamn loud," he hollered into the doorway to apartment 302. There came the momentary sound of confusion from within before any response.

"Whose radio? You got the wrong door, idiot. The radio and TV's not even on! Wrong fuckin' door, moron!" called out Perez.

"Listen, creep, no one calls Big Bob Cratchet a moron." Brian had lowered his voice into a growl, and up until now, seemed to have successfully disguised it from his friend. "Why don't you open this door, chicken shit, and I'll show you what Big Bob Cratchet does to noisy neighbors," roared Brian while holding back the urge to laugh.

"What the fuck? I don't know who the fuck y' are—ya fuckin' asshole—but I'm comin' out. I need two minutes to get dressed. D'ya hear me, asshole?" threatened Perez, clearly angered by the intrusion. Brian could hear the sound of bureau drawers being opened as he kept the gag alive.

"Listen, you pile of shit, I just wanted to warn you that I just beat the living crap out of a friend of yours downstairs. Some Milquetoast faggot called Kelly." The activity from within the apartment suddenly stopped while Brian struggled to subdue a burst of laughter. Silence was followed by approaching footsteps. Finally, the door opened to the sight of Perez, red-faced with anger and only partially dressed.

"What the fuck are ya doin' to me? It's Christmas, damn it," he said quietly. Perez beckoned his friend into the apartment, embracing him immediately. "Now, if I can get some clothes on without any more of your shit."

Brian pulled out a chair from beneath the kitchen table and collapsed into it.

"Ya here for Christmas?" called out Perez from the next room. Brian answered yes while laying his gift down on the table. Looking around the familiar four-room apartment, he caught sight of no evidence of the holidays. It was a joyless place that lacked warmth and beauty.

"What about you? Are you doing anything Christmas Day?" asked Brian.

"No man, nothin'. With no family here, well, it's just a matter of gettin' through it. Christmas an' Thanksgiving, dose are the tough ones. The others are a fuckin' cinch. I'll call my mama back in Puerto Rico Monday—that'll be it." Entering the room and tucking in his shirt simultaneously, Perez spotted the gift on the table. He walked over and examined the tag, causing Brian to laugh.

"Who the hell do you think it's for—Cratchet down the hall?"

"Thanks, kid. It's gonna be my only one."

"Paid for with your money, guy. You're the reason I was able to give my mom and everyone presents this year. Did you think I was going to overlook the big guy—the man?" asked Brian.

The two friends spent the rest of the morning and better part of the afternoon together. They walked down the boulevard beside the Merrimack River, grabbing lunch at the Cathay Garden, and all the while filled each other in on the happenings in their lives. Brian told his friend of a particular New Hampshire girl that had caught his interest. He described this very special young woman in minute detail, providing his friend with clear evidence of the impact she was having on him. As the afternoon waned, Perez's spirits deteriorated. On three occasions he asked Brian if he would be dropping in on Sunday. It was becoming clear to Brian that his friend was descending into a state of holiday depression.

"Can I run something by you?" asked Brian while bundling himself into his worn, winter jacket.

"Shoot!" answered Perez.

"This is going to be a really good Christmas for me—back in Lowell, and with my family and all. Now, good could become great on Christmas if you'd come to my uncle's for dinner. Uncle Jimmy's a good shit, and you'd finally get a chance to meet my mom—and talk to her. But, I don't want to ask unless you'd really want to be there. It'll be boring, kinda. You know, either 'Scrooge' or 'It's a Wonderful Life' will be on TV. But, if I could have you and them with me on Christmas—oh man, it'd be the best."

"Come on, guy, they don't want some PR stranger in their house on Christmas," reasoned Perez.

"You're not a stranger. I talk about you all the time to Uncle Jimmy. It's not like I'd be bringing some fuckin' bum from Moody Street over. Come on, Perez, let me ask?" His friend shrugged his shoulders, throwing his hands into the air, prompting Brian to cross the room to the phone. He lifted the outdated black telephone and dialed his uncle's number from memory. With the final digit entered, there was only a brief hesitation before he spoke. "Aunt Martha, may I speak to my mom please?" Perez climbed out of his chair and paced into the next room. "Hello, Ma, it's me. Listen, I thought I'd run something by you before I asked Uncle Jimmy. I'm at Perez's house. It's about Christmas dinner. He has nowhere to go on Christmas and I thought, if it wasn't too much trouble, Uncle Jimmy and Aunt Martha might not mind too much having him over for dinner. It would really mean a lot to me. I don't want to see him alone on Christmas, but I know it's asking a lot. It's just that it would make Christmas so great. It'll really bug me if I know he's sitting here alone. Mom, it's Christmas."

"This is an awful lot to spring on your aunt and uncle at such a late date. Brian, honey, we don't really know the man at all."

"Ma, it's Christmas. I mean, think about the whole thing about no room at the inn."

"Hold on, hon, let me speak to Jimmy," Brian strained to hear the conversation at the other end of the line but his mother was evidently holding her hand over the mouthpiece. In less than a minute she said to her son. "Tell Mr. Perez to be here somewhere around noon. Dinner will be served at around two o'clock."

"Thanks, Ma. I'll be heading outta here in five minutes." Brian put down the phone and called out to his friend. "Christmas dinner at two. Try to get to my uncle's house around noon. I can give you directions later."

"Ya comin' by tomorrow?" asked Perez, emerging from the front room.

"You buying us Chinese again for lunch?" Perez nodded yes. "Count on it," said Brian as he made his way to the door. "Oh, buddy, no more giving Bob Cratchet from up the hall any more shit, okay?" kidded Brian before closing the door behind him.

Brian made the walk from Perez's apartment to the Clarkes' house in under twenty minutes, arriving just as his mother and aunt were setting the table. It was only seconds before Jimmy Junior had latched onto his big cousin and made demands for his attention. It was very much a traditional Saturday night supper. This meant franks and beans together with heated brown bread. For dessert, Martha Clarke had picked up a variety of pastries from the Yum Yum Shop. It was following this wonderful, if not healthy, meal that Jimmy invited everyone into the living room for a special movie presentation. Brian grabbed a seat at the end of the couch and was immediately joined by his cousin Barbara, who took to sitting on his lap, only to have Jimmy Junior place himself immediately to his left, arm extended around his cousin.

"Oh, you guys don't care for your cousin too much," joked Martha, bringing cups of eggnog to everyone assembled. At the moment, Jimmy Clarke was threading a movie projector which was aimed at the blank wall at the far side of the room. He explained that the eggshell-white wall paint was suitable as a movie screen. Brian and his mother were then reminded that the Clarkes had traveled to the southern coast of Maine the preceding summer where they had managed to film a portion of their vacation.

"Oh no, Brian, you're going to see me in a bathing suit," whispered Barbara. Elizabeth was seated across the room from her son. She looked on with a pleasant smile as both cousins vied for her son's attention.

The film opened with a shot of Martha Clarke and her two children standing and waving to the camera in front of a large rectangular sign reading "Timbers Motor Court and Motel." Brian stared at the action on the wall politely as the activity shifted from the side of Route 1 to Wells Harbor and a variety of recreational and lobster boats. Thirty seconds of footage of boats was followed by a sequence of shots of the family clowning in the surf in three- to four-foot waves. At one point, as the camera panned to Barbara lying on her beach blanket, Brian called out.

"Wow! No one said you guys ran into Julie Christie while you were over there!" His wisecrack brought a rumble of laughter, followed by a statement from Elizabeth that her niece was growing into a pretty, young woman.

Eventually, the screen went blank for a moment before a new picture appeared. In a shot taken from the front seat of the car and through the windshield, the vehicle was turned onto a country road lined on both sides by a series of equally sized and spaced trees. The vehicle proceeded through a tunnel of foliage for just under a minute before evidence of a beach came into sight. The Clarkes' sedan passed over a small bridge where water streamed swiftly by in the direction of the open ocean. Any view of the open sea was blocked by an extended ribbon of sand covered in long ocean grass and wild bushes. With the camera still grinding away, the car rolled to a halt, was emptied of all passengers, and the short walk to the crashing surf recorded. Access to the sandy beach was through a single break in the sand dune that ran in a perfectly perpendicular line to the sea, an opening carved by the footsteps of beachgoers through the years.

"Where is this place?" asked Brian, clearly taken with this scenic location.

"Parsons Beach," answered his uncle. "It's just off the road leading to Kennebunkport. I'm not sure our filming does it justice. It's a gorgeous place."

As Brian stared at the images reflecting off the wall he felt an almost deferential emotion take hold of him. There was something uniquely meaningful about this place, lifting his consciousness to another plane. He saw himself walking the roadway, beneath the line of trees, toward the opening in the dune. In the distance a female figure stood alone in the breach of the dune.

Brian's spell was suddenly broken by a roar from within the room as Jimmy Junior was shown peering down at a plate containing a boiled lobster. The home movies only continued for another few minutes until interrupted by the sound of film flapping wildly against the projector, signifying the end of the filmed portion of the Clarkes' vacation. The Kellys broke into applause as Jimmy jumped to his feet and turned off the machine. He was complimented by his sister and Brian again asked him for the name of the beach with the tree-lined entrance.

On Sunday, Brian dropped in on Perez, helping him put together something for his Christmas hosts. A box of chocolates from the Blue Dot Candy Store as a token gift for Elizabeth and a bottle of wine for the Clarkes. For the Clarke children, a Christmas greeting card, adorned with a crisp, ten dollar bill.

On Christmas morning the Clarkes and Kellys rose early and paraded into the living room to begin the joyful task of opening presents. It pleased Brian that he had been able to give everyone a gift, thanks to the generosity of Perez. Barbara loved her "Grassroots" album while Jimmy Junior raved over the collection of plastic military vehicles Brian had selected as his present. For his part, Brian was overjoyed to receive the denim jacket he had been hounding his mother for since the previous winter.

Christmas dinner was a complete success. Soon after his arrival, Perez was totally at ease, perched in front of the television set and picking at an assortment of munchies and appetizers. His monetary gift to the children went over splendidly as they both exclaimed how they planned spending every last cent of it. Elizabeth, too, was finally able to learn a little more about the man that had put his imprint on the character of her son over the years.

Late in the afternoon, with darkness already upon the snow-covered neighborhood, Brian walked Perez back to his home on Bridge Street, already attired in his new denim jacket worn over a thick winter sweater. The two friends wished each other good tidings, not knowing the length of time before they would again share each other's company.

A short time after his return, Brian and his mother were motoring northward, back to the quiet of their Montgomery Street apartment. Elizabeth retired to bed soon after unpacking her things. While Brian had the week off from school, she had to return to work early the next morning.

V

BRIAN ROSE EARLY THE NEXT MORNING, keeping his mother company as she went about preparing for work. The chilly air inside the house provided evidence of the frigid temperature outside. Earlier, the Kellys had heard the scraping of metal on the paved walkway beside the house, indicating that Mr. Giroux was shoveling up some overnight accumulation. With lunch bag in hand and bundled from head to toe, Elizabeth was just about to give her son a kiss good-bye when there came a series of soft knocks on the door. Responding, Elizabeth was confronted by a snow-covered Mr. Giroux.

"My car's been warming up for ten minutes now. I was about to head downtown to grab some breakfast with a couple of old friends. Could anybody use a lift in that direction?" asked the kindly old man.

"Mr. Giroux, you're heaven-sent," answered Elizabeth. "You're sure it's not a bother?" she inquired politely.

"Not in the least, Mrs. Kelly. Just watch your step when we get downstairs." The landlord turned and slowly preceded her down the two flights of stairs, remaining just ahead of the grateful Elizabeth, in a most gentlemanly manner.

The thoughtful gesture by their landlord left Brian with an uncomfortable feeling. On returning home from his breakfast downtown, Mr. Giroux found the entire sidewalk, front steps, and backyard parking area shoveled to the bare pavement.

From the moment his mother left for work until her return, Brian attempted to put his time to some useful purpose. A few weeks earlier in English class, Miss Royal had been extremely

53

critical of an author named Ayn Rand. Intrigued by an emotional tirade from his teacher, he visited the city library and withdrew a copy of *Anthem,* a work by this revolutionary writer. So, alone in the quiet of the empty apartment, Brian read the words and soaked up the philosophy of this intellectual who professed so many strong ideas, ideas foreign to anything he had ever heard discussed in school, on television, anywhere. Even with segments of the book reread three and four times, he completed the short novel by mid-afternoon. It stirred thoughts that, only hours earlier, had been outside the scope of his intellectual consideration. He longed to discuss the message delivered within the pages of this short work of fiction. He imagined his English class being informed upon their return from Christmas vacation that Miss Royal had resigned after winning the Irish sweepstakes but, through a stroke of remarkable good fortune, would be replaced by Miss Ayn Rand through the end of the term.

The next morning, Mr. Giroux again showed up at the Kellys' door just before Elizabeth was scheduled to leave for work. As his mother was graciously accepting another ride from her hospitable landlord, Brian managed to establish eye contact with the gray-haired man. It was a glance that conveyed a message, more vigilant than threatening, establishing that he was the man of the family and that his mother existed under the umbrella of his protection.

Brian had decided the previous evening that he would not be housebound the following day. So, after gulping down a bowl of corn flakes, he bundled himself in three layers of shirts and his new denim jacket, and set off for Bedford. It had been almost a week since he had set eyes on a certain Miss Keogh, and he longed to draw himself closer to her. He hoped to find her house, the house she returned to from school every day, the house she may have even grown up in. For reasons beyond his own comprehension, he craved to know everything about this outspoken, young woman. A garage attendant on South Main Street sent him south with instructions to pick up Boynton Street and then keep going straight. The cold air bit at his ears and cheeks as he walked resolutely on the path laid out for him.

He had been walking for well over thirty minutes when he ducked into a variety store, more for warmth than anything else. The man at the cash register, when asked about the distance to

Bedford center, indicated that it was approximately a mile further. Invigorated by five minutes of warmth, Brian continued on his quest with the thought that, at minimum, he would find Ministerial Road and Maggie May Keogh's neighborhood.

Eventually Brian found himself on the side of Route 101 in the town of Bedford. This state road, being the main route to the far southwest corner of the state, was traveled by large panel trucks and eighteen-wheelers that sent cold air whirling around the lone, male figure walking on its shoulder. Brian kept his eyes open for any sign directing him toward the town center, or, even better, Ministerial Road. He had been walking on the side of Route 101 for approximately ten minutes when he caught sight of a church steeple perched on a hilltop to his right. On a hunch and nothing more, he left the main road and climbed the avenue leading toward the white, picturesque place of worship. By its architecture it appeared to have been built during a different period, and by reason, probably placed near the center of the community. He hoped to find a village store near the town center, and, perhaps, someone with a knowledge of the town. By now the warmth gathered up from his variety store stop had escaped from his jacket and was little more than a pleasant memory. His extremities, hands and feet were becoming uncomfortably cold. He blew on the fingertips of his gloves as he searched for a public building of any kind. A short distance from the church and its adjacent cemetery, there was a small general store which Brian entered following a jog to the front entrance. A middle-aged man with graying hair looked up from his newspaper as Brian let out a hoot on entering.

"It sure is cold out there!" he exclaimed, proceeding to remove his gloves and blow directly on his fingers.

"Rough day to be on foot," agreed the man.

Brian walked along the aisle toward the proprietor. "I wonder if you could help me with some directions? I'm looking for Ministerial Road and I pray to God it isn't too far from here."

"You're not dressed too well for walking on a day like today," said the man, strolling toward the window. He glanced outside for a moment, then turned back toward his visitor. "The thermometer reads twenty-one degrees and it's catching some sunlight. Could be more like fifteen or sixteen."

"Yeah, no doubt it's cold. That's why I'm hoping you can point me towards Ministerial Road," answered Brian.

"You're in luck. It's maybe a couple of hundred yards from here. Go back around the corner—back up by the church—head straight toward town hall. It's on your left." The man drew his directions in the air as he pointed Brian back toward the church.

"By the way—my name's Brian Kelly," he said, extending his hand.

"I'm Charlie—that's my wife, Winnie, in the back of the store. She's the one doing all the work right now," answered the man.

"Charlie, would you happen to know whereabouts on Ministerial Road a Maggie May Keogh lives?" asked Brian.

"The Keoghs huh—you're looking for little Margaret? You know—I couldn't tell you exactly where they live—sorry."

Brian hung around the store for another few minutes, soaking up the warmth. A few minutes later he said good-bye to the two proprietors and braced himself for the winter air.

A swirl of frigid wind greeted Brian as he emerged from the superette, forcing him to pull the collar of his denim coat up to protect his ears. He headed back up the hill in the direction of the church where Charlie had told him he would find one end of Ministerial Road. Arriving at what was surely the town center, Brian caught sight of the roadway that was his original destination. Somehow the street sign had eluded his vision earlier. In the two-minute walk from the store, most of the warmth absorbed during his time inside The Wagon Wheel had dissipated. The weather was changing and it was changing for the worse. The wind began biting at his face and ears as he started up Ministerial Road. Checking the names on the mail boxes he passed, he proceeded ahead, his face angled away from the direction of the wind gusts and his hands buried in his coat pockets.

Following a relatively flat patch in the road came an abrupt incline upward. The homes in the neighborhood were, almost exclusively, single-family and well-maintained. To his amazement, and in spite of the raw, cutting wind, he found himself excited at the prospect of catching a glimpse of the house where the remarkable Miss Keogh lived. He was reminded of the old song his mother used to play on the phonograph.

People stop and stare, they don't bother me . . .
For there's nowhere else on earth that I would rather be . . .

He asked himself what was happening to him. What was he doing out here? The wind roared through the trees overhead, sending another arctic blast against the side of his face. He was now climbing the hill, still checking out the names on mail boxes, and frustrated by the ones that displayed only numerical identification. A Jack London short story about a man walking through the northern territories with his dog, slowly freezing to death, popped into his head. A car rounded the corner of the hill ahead of him, then passed by without even a glance from the driver. Fifty yards ahead, someone was walking a dog. Brian began toying with the idea of asking the stranger where the Keogh residence was located, but decided against it for fear of coming off like a criminal looking for a target. Instead, Brian decided to ask about the length of the street. For all he knew, Ministerial Road could run all the way to the Vermont line.

Glancing up through a rush of windblown snow he began to make out the figure on the roadway ahead. The individual, a female, was faced at a right angle to him as her dog, held in check by a leash, sniffed at a granite post standing at the edge of a driveway entrance. The woman's face was largely covered by a furry hood, but she now had become aware of Brian's presence, thanks to the upward movement of her cocker spaniel's head. The female turned her body toward Brian, riveting her eyes on him as her dog let out a single bark.

"Brian—Brian Kelly? Is that you?" called a familiar voice.

"I can't believe it! Maggie May, this is too much," he responded, shocked and unnerved by this sudden turn of events. Behind the cocker spaniel that was tugging in Brian's direction, strode the young girl responsible for his displacement so far from home. Framed by her synthetic bonnet, which covered all of her head save her face, her delicately feminine features seemed almost too perfect. A polite, controlled burst of laughter showcased Miss Keogh's even, white teeth.

"What are you doing out here?" she asked, smirking.

"I, uhhh, I got a little bored after breakfast and decided to go for a walk," fumbled Brian.

"Are you saying that you just decided to go for a walk—and you just happened to wind up in my neighborhood—God knows how many miles from where you live?" she asked in disbelief. It was already clear that she had her own suspicions about finding him here, leaving Brian vulnerable to her leisurely interrogation. "Now Brian, where do you live?" she followed up, prodding her friend toward some form of admission.

"The west side—on Montgomery Street."

"So, let me get this straight. You just decided—out of no-where—on a freezing cold morning—to go for a walk to Bed-ford—two or three miles away? Oh, and of course, you wound up on my street—walking aimlessly—just walking."

Embarrassed, Brian looked around sheepishly, attempting to come up with some rational explanation. None was forthcom-ing. Maggie May paused, surveying her friend.

"You look like that guy from Doctor Zhivago who walked through all the snow and ice looking for his lost love—with your face frozen and frosted over and all."

"Omar Sharif? You think I look like Omar Sharif?"

"Yeah, right!" she giggled. Brian's heart dropped as she whirled around and began walking away. "Well, enjoy your time in Bedford, Brian. Don't freeze to death, now," she called out, her back still turned away from him.

"I came just to see you, or at least where you lived," he ad-mitted, leaving his pride exposed and himself at her mercy. She paused for a moment, then spun around and looked back at him.

"I knew that. I just wanted to hear you admit it." She beck-oned him to follow her. Brian responded instantly, running up beside her. Maggie May began chattering, speaking of her dog, the neighborhood, and things back at Southside. She became animated, and remarkably overjoyed to have found someone to listen to her ongoing stream of ideas and observations. Brian barely spoke, choosing to merely look down at the face that, in his mind, eclipsed all others he had ever set eyes on in his six-teen years. If anything, at this moment she appeared more beau-tiful than back at school. Perhaps it was the rosy, healthy condi-tion of her cheeks, offset by the red, fur-trimmed bonnet that covered all but her face.

The dog turned abruptly into a driveway that ran toward a handsome, two-story home. Not as grand as a few others he had passed earlier, the house was nonetheless the residence of a fam-ily of comfortable means.

"Well, come on," she ordered as Brian fell back slightly be-hind the girl and her dog.

"Mother, look who I found going through our garbage cans!" she called out upon entering the kitchen. Brian timidly followed the fifteen-year-old into the modern, immaculately clean room, as a curious Mrs. Keogh descended the stairs.

"Now, what are you going on about?" chirped the woman, making her way toward her daughter's voice. "Why, Mr. Kelly, what an unexpected pleasure. My God, you look half frozen," exclaimed the woman. Brian stood motionless in the corner of the kitchen, taking advantage of the heat being thrown off by the oven.

"I found him wandering along our road. He claims he was just out for a walk," heckled Maggie May.

"Oh, do you live nearby?" asked the soft-spoken Mrs. Keogh.

"He lives on the west side of Manchester, but he says he was just out for a little walk when he happened upon our humble neighborhood."

"Well, I'm sure he has a good reason for being out in our neck of the woods," reasoned the gracious woman. "Mr. Kelly, may I offer you something, preferably warm?" she continued hospitably.

"Mrs. Keogh, if it wouldn't be too much trouble, I could really go for a cup of tea."

"A man after my own heart. A cup of tea it is. And how about you, crabby appleton?" asked the woman of her daughter.

"I guess that'll be okay," responded Maggie May as she pulled out a chair and gestured Brian to follow suit. Mrs. Keogh took to preparing the tea as the two teenagers peeled off their coats and deposited themselves in chairs at the corner of the table.

"You know Brian, it's good to have a little company drop in. This one's been a bear since school let out, even Christmas Day."

"It's probably just a case of withdrawal. I've been known to grow on people after a while and little Maggie May here probably just misses some of our lively discussions from school," he joked.

"Actually, I miss winning your money. You see, Mother, Brian and I have a little wager in English class on our grades. Every exam or test, the one with the lower grade has to pay the other money. I'm slowly getting rich off Brian's stupidity."

"Now that is not right! Brian, please tell me that this business isn't really going on, and she's just making this up."

"I'm afraid there's some truth to what she says. We *have* been betting on our English grades, and to date, your very intelligent daughter has managed to edge me out every time. But, on the plus side, I'm getting great grades in English so far, so it hasn't been all bad."

"Mother, I told him that if he'd just admit to being my intellectual inferior, I would let him squirm out of the wager, but he's too proud," she boasted, shooting her friend a cunning sideways glance.

"Mrs. Keogh, I know I don't have to tell you that you're raising a bad seed here," joked Brian to his hostess.

"You know, she is a bad seed, and I've told her as much," responded the woman before walking behind her daughter's chair and planting a kiss on the top of her head. "It's too bad we love her so much around here," she added with genuine affection.

Brian and the Keogh women shared a comfortable conversation over tea for the next thirty minutes before Mrs. Keogh excused herself and returned to her project upstairs. The discourse did not lag in the adult's absence as Maggie May asked Brian about his Christmas and then listened in earnest as he filled her in on his trip to Lowell and visit with relatives and friends in Massachusetts. Then, unexpectedly, she tossed out the question that sent a wave of nervous, excited energy through his body.

"Would you like to see my room?" she asked.

"Yes—I'm curious," he responded calmly, while his mind raced frantically with a spectrum of images of this very special girl's most private of places. Rising from the table, he followed her up the stairs to the second floor, his eyes trained, borderline hypnotized, on her figure. She led him to the room at the head of the stairs and pushed open the door. His eyes took in a spacious room dressed in bright, winter sunlight. The walls were lavender, showcasing the white, matching bedroom set that dominated the floor space.

"Is it what you pictured?" she asked with the hint of coyness.

"What? Do you think all I have to do all day is think about you?"

She responded with a spontaneous laugh and hopped onto the bed. Entering the room, Brian was quick to notice a group of Rod Stewart photographs taped to the wall.

"I see Rod gets to watch over his Maggie May," he commented, while depositing himself in a wicker chair by the window. As his friend untied the laces of her sneakers, the enormity of the circumstances at hand descended on his consciousness. He was sitting in the bedroom of the young woman who had, over the past two months, taken possession of his every day-dream, his every fantasy, his every romantic and sexual desire. It was true: Maggie May Keogh had pushed every other female in Massachusetts and New Hampshire from his radar screen.

"Do you want to see something I won a couple of years ago?" she asked, requiring him to focus his thoughts on their conversation. He nodded yes and she jumped up from the bed and stretched up to a shelf well over her head. As she did, her sweater rose upward from her belt line, uncovering a portion of her back. The exposed flesh and hollow contours created by her spine set Brian's mind to racing. Then, with Maggie May turning to address him, he brought his eyes up to meet hers.

"Spelling bee champion of Bedford. I won it when I was in eighth grade!" she stated proudly while bringing forth a foot-high trophy stating as much. She handed it to him to inspect.

"Pretty impressive, kid," he said while examining the award. For the next few seconds nothing was said as the young girl surveyed her friend seated familiarly in her room.

"You know, Skip's afraid of you. Did you know that?" A smile broke out on Brian's face as he continued to examine the trophy. "As a matter of fact—I think a lot of guys in school are afraid of you. Skip, well, I *know* he's afraid of you. A few weeks ago he said something to me about talking to you so much. So, I suggested that he say something to you about it, or that I'd say something for him. Well, he gets all flustered and tells me not to say anything to you. He got real serious about not saying anything to you."

"Well, Keogh, if everyone is so afraid of me, how come you're not?" he asked in a low, quiet voice. A confident smile appeared on her face as she deliberately folded her legs into a full lotus position atop the bed. She trained her eyes on him, staring boldly down on him from the edge of her bed.

"Oh, I think we both know full well why I'm not afraid of you, Brian Kelly." The young woman sitting before him was clearly discovering at this stage of her life the inherent power that accompanied her maturing as a female. Lately, the responses from young males to even her most subtle gestures had intrigued her. This was a time for experimentation, emotionally, sexually, physically, and maybe even more importantly, psychologically.

"You know—I know you think I'm some kind of popular kid in school with guys chasing after me and all, but it's not like that. Shit—three months ago it seemed like no guys would even give me a look. Then all of a sudden—God—I'm catching guys staring at me and smiling at me and coming up to me in the hall. Something just happened! I guess I'm just developing all of a sudden."

Brian sat quietly by the window, listening intently to every word that came from this girl who had, only weeks earlier, seemed such a divine mystery. "So Keogh, you're telling me that if I had transferred to Southside last year instead of this year, you would've just been some plain, little nothing instead of the stuck-up, snobby, nose-in-the-air, gorgeous, unapproachable, little punk that you are today?"

She burst out laughing. "Do you actually think I'm gorgeous Brian?" she asked, finding the only superlative buried and camouflaged within his question.

"You know damn well you're a knockout, Keogh. Don't bullshit me."

"What do boys say about me?" she asked, anxious to keep herself the center of the conversation.

"Well, for starters, boys don't say too much to me about anything, including you. Remember, they're all so, so afraid of me. But, on the few occasions that I've overheard things—like the day you brought that friggin' sandwich over to me at lunch and practically threw it at me—after you walked away, one of the guys just dropped his head down on the table—this is after admiring your backside as you walked away—he drops his head down on the table and says, "Keogh is so f—ing hot!— except he doesn't clean it up like I just did."

Maggie smiled at Brian, obviously pleased by his report. "You're good for my ego, Kelly. Not good for much else—but good for my ego." He leaned back in the chair without making a response. The conversation had reached a lull, but not an uncomfortable one. Each maintained eye contact with the other until he took it upon himself to change the topic.

"Your mother says you've been quite the little crab over the holidays. Anything in particular making you that way?" he asked, hoping to draw out the status of her relationship with Skip.

"I've got a lot on my mind right now—one thing in particular. I'm sure it'll turn out okay but, in the meantime, it has me a little on edge. Oh, and before you ask, Kelly, no—I don't want to share it with you, if I did, I already would've said something."

Without warning, Maggie May's eyes widened and fixed on something resting on the bureau beside Brian. Jumping to her feet, she raced over and snatched a brown journal from the surface of the bureau.

"What's that all about?" he asked as she hopped back onto her bed.

"It's my diary! I can't believe I left it out like that!"

"What's the matter Keogh? Afraid I was going to pick it up and start reading your innermost thoughts? You have to be the last teenager on the face of the earth that still keeps a diary! Does it have something to do with being from la-di-da Bedford?" he needled.

"That just shows how little you know about girls. No wonder none of them want to be seen dead with you. You're a jerk!" snapped Maggie May.

Brian did not respond to the attack, choosing instead to lean back in the chair, his hands clasped behind his head. She saw instantly that her minor explosion had struck a nerve. His feelings were clearly hurt. She softened her tone.

"I have a lot of personal—very personal— things written in this diary. Things about a lot of people, including you, are in here. And I know a lot of other girls who keep a diary. Most boys wouldn't understand. Brian—say something—don't be mad. I didn't mean the thing about girls not wanting to be seen dead with you."

When it was obvious that her flimsy apology was having no effect on her friend she again jumped from the bed. Approaching him in the chair, she stopped inches away and pouted down at him. "All right, Mister Sensitive, it's not true. If I was dead— and I mean really dead with rigor mortis set in and everything— then I wouldn't mind if someone saw us together. Does that make you feel better?"

"Yes, it does. The thought of you with rigor mortis does make me feel better—much, much better," stated Brian, bringing on a sigh of relief from his friend.

To the two teenagers' astonishment, the afternoon sped by as they spoke at length of their feelings about Southside High and many of the classmates with whom they shared a common experience. Brian laughed aloud when Maggie May told him of her first impressions of him back in October.

For his part, he could not be as frank with her, given the shockwave-like effect her presence had had on him right from day one. He would have liked to have told her about the frequency with which she invaded his daytime and nighttime dreams, monopolizing his consciousness for extended lengths of time before sleep overcame him in the evening. However, this he dared not do, knowing the absolute power this information would have given her. Miss Keogh was not the sort of girl you dared entrust with this amount of influence.

It was after four o'clock and beginning to get quite dark, when Mrs. Keogh poked her head into the bedroom and announced the late hour.

The teens descended the stairs minutes later and Brian went about locating his coat and gloves. Mrs. Keogh apologized for not being able to offer him a ride. The family's second car, her car, was in need of attention and she was hesitant about driving it any further than The Wagon Wheel. She told Brian that he was welcome to wait until Mr. Keogh arrived home, insisting that her husband would be happy to drive him back to Manchester. He waived this proposition off, indicating he had no problem walking back to Montgomery Street. With Brian fully dressed, in coat and gloves, and by the front door, Maggie May took up the awkward task of seeing him off.

"You actually don't look half bad in that denim jacket," she proclaimed in mock surprise.

"A poor man's James Dean," he stated, surprised by her weak admission.

"More like an impoverished, destitute man's James Dean," she retorted.

Brian suddenly stepped forward, wrapping his arms around the young woman standing before him. Momentarily frozen by surprise, she weakly returned his hug. He held the embrace for a few, fleeting seconds, his right hand sensitive to the concave curvature of her back. His emotions soared, knowing he literally held in his arms the divine creature called Maggie May Keogh. Then, reluctantly, he released the embrace and backed off.

"Do me a big favor, Keogh? Call my house a little after five and tell my ma that I'm on my way home?" he asked. She agreed, and he jotted down his telephone number. "It's almost an hour's walk from here, so tell her I'll be home between five-thirty and six." After shouting a final good-bye to Mrs. Keogh, he stole a last look at Maggie May before closing the door behind him and facing the frigid, December weather.

Brian found the walk back to Manchester tolerable, aided by the ability to play and replay his time and conversation with the now less-mysterious Miss Keogh. He basked in what he saw as the remarkable good fortune that had befallen him. Not even in his wildest of dreams could he have imagined spending private time with Maggie May during his Christmas vacation, let alone sitting with her in her bedroom! With the sun down and the wind driving the arctic air down the roads and between the houses, the walk home to Montgomery Street should have been intolerable. However, lifted by the time he had spent with Maggie May, Brian held up well under the conditions and arrived home in high spirits late in the afternoon.

VI

THE FEW REMAINING DAYS OF 1972 were uneventful, even by
Brian's downgraded standards. He instinctively knew that a
second trip out to Bedford would have worn out his welcome, so
that was not even considered. Instead, he began early preparation for midyear finals at school by poring over material that he
felt would make its way onto these exams. This was supplemented
by walks around the west side, including a few, random job inquiries, and a return downtown. On Saturday morning Elizabeth
answered the telephone and called Brian. Covering the mouthpiece, she told him that it was a male asking for Mr. Brian Kelly.

"Hello, this is Brian," he announced after grabbing the phone
from his mother. For the next few minutes he barely spoke, aside
from injecting a single word response from time to time. Finally,
following ten minutes of one word responses Brian capped off
the phone conversation with his only full, declarative sentence
since grabbing the phone.

"I'll be there on Friday afternoon at four—on the twelfth.
Thank you, Mr. Delaney." He put down the phone, made a gesture to his mother, then walked silently back to his bedroom.
Elizabeth followed him as far as the door, then waited for an
explanation.

"And?" she asked. Brian turned to her from the window, raising his arms up like a body builder.

"Elizabeth Kelly, you are now looking at the newest member
of the Howdy Beefburger weekend staff. Minimum wage and all
the burgers I can sneak out in my pockets. Ma, you'll have to
buy me some pants with rubber pockets—then I'll be able to
steal soup, too!" cried out Brian, trying to get a rise from her.

66

"I'll hear none of that talk about stealing. You know how I feel about thieves and liars!"

"I'm kidding, Ma—lighten up. They're talking about fifteen to eighteen hours a week and no school nights. So, everybody should be happy." Elizabeth congratulated her son and decided to celebrate the good news by sending out for pizza.

Unlike the prior holiday weekend, the Kellys did not visit Lowell over the three-day New Year's Eve weekend. Elizabeth would attend mass twice—once on Sunday morning as was her usual practice and again on New Year's Day, a holy day of obligation and the Feast of the Circumcision.

As for Brian, he was almost eager to return to Southside. As his Christmas vacation wound down, he found his spirits beginning to spiral upward. First, there was his new job at Howdy Beefburger and the cash that it would put in his pocket. He had already informed his mother that he would be contributing fifteen dollars a week into the house, but that would still leave him with some spending money. Secondly, his disposition brightened with the prospect of setting eyes on Maggie May again and on a regular basis.

On Sunday night the two Kellys decided to stay up and usher in 1973 together. Through the fuzzy reception on channel 9 they took in the celebratory festivities leading up to the stroke of midnight and the new year. The living room was silent for an extended period, save the merriment and festival-like celebration emanating from the Kellys' outdated black-and-white set. Brian finally broke his hypnotic gaze, addressing his mother.

"Look at these people. Look how they're acting and carrying on. To look at these idiots you'd think they had 1973 scripted and they were all heading for a happy ending. There's a friggin' war going on, for God's sake!" snapped Brian derisively.

"Now, hon, they're just trying to have a good time—and there's nothing wrong with that," cautioned Elizabeth.

"I don't get it Ma—I really don't. I see a new year coming in and I'm hoping and praying that things will be okay—hoping we'll keep our health—and stay together—and maybe save a few bucks. But in the back of my mind I know that anything can happen. People get hurt—and people get sick—and people lose their jobs—and people die. It happens all the time! So when I see a new year coming, I start thinking about this sort of stuff and wonder. It makes me meditate on these things, because that's reality. Then I look at TV here and, for God's sake, look at these morons! Watching the clock and the big ball—like 1973 means we're home free—problems solved!"

"Brian, you're a smart boy. No, you're a very smart boy. But sometimes that's not completely good. What's the point of worrying about it? You just hope and pray for the best. That's all you can do," advised Elizabeth in a soothing tone.

Brian clasped his hands behind his head, considering his mother's words for a moment. "Ma, it's not the idea of having fun that I find ridiculous. It's just that the idea of blindly and mechanically doing it on New Year's Eve seems idiotic to me."

The woman reached over and patted her son on the cheek. "You think differently than most of us. You're too smart for most of us," she surmised.

"You know what I really miss?" he asked. "I miss being down in Lowell like we were for Christmas. I don't know about you, but I had a great Christmas this year. It was great being with the Clarkes, and having you around and not having you have to go off to work. It was great seeing some of my old friends from Varnum and having Perez there on Christmas. I know he had a good time, too. I mean, it was great just getting up Sunday morning and seeing the *Lowell Sun* on the doorstep. God, I miss Lowell!" said Brian.

"I know it hasn't been all that easy for you, new school and all. But Brian, honey, I'm working regularly now and not worrying so darn much about making ends meet. I miss Lowell, too. Do you know I still listen to WCAP in the morning? I listen to Markie Poo just like I did back in Lowell. But, for my sake, see if you can make it work. Oh, now that I think of it, it hasn't been all bad up here. You have managed to make one new friend—and from the sound of her voice, she's probably a very cute one," said Elizabeth through a motherly smile.

"Oh yes—Miss Maggie May Keogh of Bedford—New Hampshire's silver lining," responded Brian sheepishly.

Although not what he intended, Brian's outburst regarding the New Year's Eve celebration triggered something inside of his mother. His uninhibited statements prompted Elizabeth to also open up and speak aloud on concerns of hers, heretofore kept hidden from her only child.

"You know what I think about this time of the year?" Her question was clearly rhetorical, so Brian did not reply but simply glanced sideways at his mother.

"From the time you were a baby I've only asked God for one, single thing—and that is that I live long enough to see you grow up and finish high school—to make sure I'm there for you until you graduate—for as long as you need me. That's all I ask," whispered the woman soberly.

"Come on, Ma, don't talk like that. You're worth a lot more than just supporting me. I want you close by until I'm an old man myself. Even when I'm still pretty young and raising a family, I want you around. I'll have a big house somewhere but there'll be an adjoining apartment where you'll live. That's the plan, Ma!" Elizabeth looked at her son seated at the far end of the couch, her eyes misting over with emotion.

"I know it's been downright hard sometimes for you and me. Parents think and worry about things like that. There are times when I feel really bad, not having been able to give you everything I wanted to. I know you have to get down sometimes, seeing other folks with more than us and me having to scrimp and save—and do without. I'm sorry, hon. You deserve better," she confessed in a state of emotionally charged regret.

"Ma, cut it out. I wouldn't trade places with anyone I know, and that's not a bunch of malarkey. Hell, I got my good looks from you. This may sound kinda hokey but a lot of times when I get home and you're making supper or fixing up, it just makes me feel good that you're there for me. That's all I need—just you being there." Brian slid across the couch, closer to Elizabeth.

"Watch out for the damn spring," she advised.

"Now who's using bad language in the house?" chided Brian.

"I'm entitled once in a while," responded Elizabeth before quietly staring at the celebration being carried out across the room on the black-and-white TV screen. Brian watched his mother from the corner of his eye as she grew quite serious.

"When you were a little boy—a very little boy—you used to ask me about your father and I would put you off or change the subject. At some point you just stopped asking. You're a smart kid, and I think you realized at some point that it bothered me having that question come up. It's been years since the last time you asked anything about him. I can't even remember the last time you asked. Well, seeing that we seemed to have picked this time to talk—I mean really talk, then maybe it's time I gave you the whole story."

"Ma, it's not going to kill me either way. Don't feel like you have to—please," cautioned Brian in a serious tone of voice.

"No, it's about time you knew, and hopefully, you won't think too much less of your mother after you do know." Elizabeth looked off into space for a moment, as if summoning back shadowy recollections long left undisturbed. Then, dropping her eyes, she began recounting the details from years earlier.

"I was still a young woman in my mid-twenties when I started joining a couple of girls from the mill on Saturday nights for dancing at the Commodore. Back in those days a lot of the guys from Devens would come over to Lowell on weekends to meet girls at the dances. Most, not all of them though, would dress in civilian clothes and mix in with the local guys. For the most part it was pretty innocent fun. Me, I'd get to dance a few times, nothing like Grace Sullivan and Doris—what's her name? I can't think of it right now. Anyway, it was a chance to get out of the house and be around fellas for a while. I wasn't seeing anyone or anything. Well, as I said, I usually spent a lot of time sitting along the wall doing my best wallflower impersonation. This one night, Grace and Doris were first to spot this fella across the room. No one had ever seen him before and he was clearly by himself—not talking to any other guys or anything. This stranger had real dark hair, shiny dark hair, just a fine-looking man. Well, all of a sudden and out of nowhere, this handsome man begins looking in my direction. I mean—I didn't know what to make of it. I think I actually looked behind me, thinking he must be staring at someone behind me. Anyway, in a few seconds he's walking across the dance floor in my general direction and I think, well, he's got to be coming over for someone else. Except—he isn't. The man with the black, shiny hair and brown eyes that can almost look right through you walks directly up to me."

There is an excitement coming from the crowd as the clock winds down on 1972 here in New York City. You can feel the electricity in the air, crackled a voice from the television. Elizabeth, having momentarily diverted her attention from her son, turned back to Brian who remained silent.

"I was shocked when this man asked me to dance and even more shocked when our conversation quickly went from the usual light topics like the weather, our jobs, and the music to much more personal things. He said he was from Oklahoma, and from what he said his work was, I gathered he was stationed at Devens. Maybe I just assumed that. His name was William Fox and he had attended college out west, somewhere in California. This man, who I would only spend twelve hours of my life with, said the things I think all young girls would love to hear, particularly one who had never heard it before, and would never hear it again. Brian, honey, your mom—well, I didn't do what a good Christian, Catholic girl should do that night. He called us a cab from the Commodore halfway through the evening, and we went to a motel where we spent the night together, this man and the foolish, stupid girl your mother was back then. In the morning, I woke up to an empty bed—not even a note or anything else left behind by this stranger that had so swept me off my feet the night before. For the next few weeks I returned to the Commodore, hoping beyond hope to see William again. It was not to be. And then, when it started to become clear that you were on the way, I even traveled out to Devens, hoping to find the man who was most certainly your father. There was no record of a William Fox on post in any capacity. They let me go through military records, photographs you know, on the chance that I could identify him that way. No luck." Brian jumped in at this point, calling a halt to his mother's confession, as the emotional strain began injecting a stressful whimper to her speech.

"It doesn't matter Ma. We don't need him—and I don't give a shit who he is!"

"Brian, don't."

"No, it's true. Look at me. I'm tall like you, and people are always saying how much I look like you. I've got your brown hair with the uncontrollable curls—and your hazel eyes. I'm your son and as far as I'm concerned, I can't see any part of him in me. I don't need him—I don't miss not having him. He's nothing."

Ten, nine, eight, seven, six, five, four, three, two, one . . . Happy New Year! erupted the voice from the television. Brian reached over and hugged his mother into 1973.

VII

IF BRIAN'S DAY TRIP TO BEDFORD over the Christmas break had elevated his relationship with Miss Maggie May Keogh, it was not in evidence on his return to school in January. It was as if he had not spent the better part of a day huddled in her room with her. From her first day back at school, Maggie May avoided any and all lengthy conversations with Brian or anyone else in homeroom. What's more, she appeared to be withdrawing not just from him, but from everyone else in her circle of friends and acquaintances. He observed her seated largely by herself on occasion after occasion, her face buried in a book or mentally detached from those around her. Suddenly, there seemed to be no interaction with Skip and only limited contact with her closest friends, Cindy and Gayle. Brian decided to temporarily stand back from the situation and provide her with the time and space to emerge from her apparent state of depression.

The second half of January hailed the midway point in the school year and a revision in students' schedules. While Brian's core classes in English and math just rolled into a second term, there were changes in other periods. In Miss Royal's English class Brian received word of his grade on the prior term's final. He got a 91 percent grade on the difficult final, probably not good enough to top Maggie May but a very respectable grade. He decided to compare grades with his academic adversary in homeroom at the end of the day. Spanish I class was replaced with world geography while a previous study hall was substituted with driver's education. Along with the new subjects came new classrooms and classmates. On the first day of Geography Brian made a point of arriving in class as early as possible in order to lay claim to a choice seat, preferably at the rear of the room by the windows.

Brian entered the nearly empty classroom, walked behind the six rows of desks, and claimed the last desk in the first row. He checked the view outside on North Main Street. Not too bad, he thought, the edge of the hill leading down to the ball field with downtown Manchester in the distance. He stretched out in a relaxed sprawl and took in his future classmates, all pretty much strangers, as they filed into the room. A basketball jock whose name Brian did not know took possession of the desk directly in front of him without an acknowledgment just before fate appeared to smile on him. With approximately half the desks filled, Gloria Sims materialized in the doorway, posing momentarily. Surveying the room behind a confident mask, she eventually spotted a familiar face within the assembly. Following an almost invisible smile, she glided across the wooden floorboards and deposited herself and an armful of books in the second row, five seats from the front desk, placing herself at a forty-five degree angle to Brian and perfectly within his line of sight. At this time Brian learned that the basketball player's name was Carl and that he and the blonde-haired, blue-eyed Miss Sims must have nothing less than a legion of mutual friends. Already Brian's mind raced with excitement as he took in every movement of the attractive young woman seated in front of him. He began to consider his good fortune; this was Gloria Sims, who believed in skirts—short skirts, and Gloria possessed two of the finest legs to stride the halls of Southside High. The young woman had only been seated sixty seconds but Brian had already been treated to the sight of Miss Sims' outstretched limbs while they were crossed, uncrossed, recrossed, extended, nylons adjusted, and then crossed a final time.

The room was nearly full except for an isolated desk near the front. The classroom vibrated with chatter from the teenagers settling in. Brian's attention was suddenly grabbed by the form of a muscular male jaunting through the doorway. Yvan "Buzz" Devereux exploded into the assembly with the same aggression as he did into opponent's linebackers. The muscularly trim athlete announced his arrival to the group while scouring the room for an empty chair befitting his status. Almost immediately, the handsome sophomore's eyes locked onto Gloria Sims who by now had turned away from basketballer Carl and whose attention was clearly riveted on Buzz. Acting on pure impulse, the handsome jock sauntered down the aisle and up to Gloria with an air of confidence.

"So, Gloria, at last I've lucked out and landed a class with you," mumbled Buzz, a devilish smile plastered across his face. By now he was half sitting on the desk adjacent to Gloria's. The young man occupying the desk sat mute, seemingly afraid to question Devereux's bad manners. Following a short period of meaningless, mindless chatter, the brash athlete turned to the timid young man seated beneath him.

"What the hell are you still doing in my desk? This desk was assigned to me weeks ago. I think you'll find your desk up front somewhere, jerk-off!" stated Buzz emphatically while pointing the overwhelmed classmate to the front of the room. To Devereux's astonishment, the young man beneath him remained seated, bringing a chorus of oohs and ahhs from the surrounding students. Devereux grew more menacing, standing erect above the visibly shaken boy.

"Move your ass," spit out Devereux while administering a controlled slap to the side of the head of his prey. The young man remained on his seat, afraid to even glance up at his tormentor but clearly resolved not to move. An instant later, his books were swept from atop the desk and scattered down the aisle toward the rear of the room.

"I draw blood in five seconds!" threatened Devereux as the room crackled with tension. However, in the next instant, the aggressive jock felt the sting of a textbook striking his shoulder. He whirled around to see Brian Kelly partially out of his seat and already involved in the confrontation.

"Mind your own business fuck face," warned Buzz, although noticeably shaken by the interruption.

"Would you kindly hand me back my book, Yvonne?" taunted Brian, while Buzz remained frozen in place.

The sound of a closing door announced the arrival of Miss Sadowski to her world geography class. She beckoned the assembled underclassmen to find vacant seats so that she might begin taking attendance. Buzz continued his attempt to stare down his antagonist but without any apparent effect on Brian's composure. Instead, Brian rose to his feet to speak.

"Miss Sadowski, I think Master Devereux appears confused, maybe even disoriented. Perhaps he is in need of more detailed instructions concerning finding a seat?" Brian's sarcasm brought a blend of snickers and subdued laughter from the room. Buzz retreated to the front of the classroom while muttering threats directed at his tormentor under his breath. Brian knew he had made a powerful enemy. Yvan Devereux ran with the same crowd as Ben Turner and was equally respected at Southside.

With attendance completed, Miss Sadowski began outlining the workload the students could expect over the next few months while Brian focused his attention between his new teacher's academic ground rules and the shapely calves and delicate ankles of Miss Gloria Sims. Forty-five minutes later, Brian emerged from class expecting a confrontation of some kind with Buzz. This did not materialize but a few steps down the hallway he was joined by the young man whom he had saved from the handsome athlete's wrath.

"Thanks for the help back there—you know, with Buzz and all. I think I was about to get the shit kicked out of me before you stepped in. Oh, and in case you didn't catch it in class, the name's Rory O'Shea." The youth extended his hand to Brian who unenthusiastically returned the favor. Rory was a pleasant-looking young man, no more than five foot, six inches with a shock of brown hair draped on his forehead. Brian continued walking to his next class, contributing nothing to the conversation while Rory chattered on about this and that, trying to strike a chord with his tall classmate.

"Listen, guy, I've got to be honest with you. What I did back in class there had almost nothing to do with you. I just saw a chance to confront that bag of shit and I took advantage of it. I haven't liked that fairy since the first time I laid eyes on him. He's a punk and he's a prick and that's all there is to it!" confided Brian before waving off his would-be friend and turning down a stairwell.

Brian was rapidly making enemies with a number of sophomore football jocks but did not cross paths with the likes of Buzz Devereux or Ben Turner the rest of the day. Back in homeroom at the close of the school day Brian brought up the subject of the English final to Maggie May as she sat withdrawn from her classmates prior to dismissal.

"This is probably only a formality, Maggie May, but don't you think we should be comparing final exam grades from English?" asked Brian good-naturedly as he produced his 91percent examination paper. Miss Keogh's eyes narrowed for an instant, unable to mask her anger. Then, following a moment's silent hesitation, she reached into her purse and produced a dollar bill which she slammed down onto his desk.

"All right, Keogh, what's wrong with you? What did I do? Why are you acting this way?" Brian had softened his voice, trying to draw Maggie May from behind her cloak of silence. She responded with a cold glance, charged with contempt. "Hey, it's pretty clear this stinkin' dollar means more to you than it does to me," he exclaimed, placing it back down on her desk.

Miss Keogh pounced on the bill, crushed it into a ball, and threw it into Brian's face. "Take your fucking dollar! Oh—and while we're at it, I don't want you talking to me in the future. Do you understand? And that includes coming anywhere near my house. Do you get it?" warned Maggie May to an astonished Brian who could only stare at her in muted disbelief.

"As you wish," he replied, as a current of depression raced through him. The dismissal bell brought the day to a close. However, Brian remained in his seat, visually following Miss Keogh from her desk to the front door and out of sight. His stomach was alive with nervous energy as his spirits plummeted at the prospect of losing his only friend at Southside, not to mention the most desirable female he had ever laid eyes on.

By this time, Brian's weekend job at Howdy Beefburgers had established itself into his routine. His chores over the first two weeks brought him nowhere near the front counter or cash registers. His assignments kept him close to the Fryolators, mops and pails, and most certainly, the Dumpsters at the rear of the Elm Street building. If it was possible, he was longing to return to Lowell even more than before. Robbed of her company and conversation, Brian had to remain content with simply resting his eyes on Maggie May at those times when he could not be detected. First period English class had developed into a predictable routine with boorish Ben Turner imposing himself on classmates, and in particular Jerome Jefferson. However, Ben's aggression was no longer directed at Brian. It was apparent he had decided upon a path of less resistance and railed on against the more passive members of the class. Geography, on the other hand, carried in it an undercurrent of tension. Buzz Devereux was prone to carry on from his perch at the front of the class and had clearly not forgotten his embarrassing confrontation with Brian on the opening day of the term. Early in the term, on a morning when Miss Sadowski was running behind schedule, Devereux swung around in his desk and addressed Brian in a venomous onslaught.

"Man, Kelly, what is it like every morning having to look in the mirror at that fucked-up, zit-scabbed face of yours?" The class exploded in a unified roar of derisive laughter as the jock mercilessly struck out at his undeclared enemy.

"Wow, Yvonne, someone must be having their period about now. Don't you go and trouble yourself about how we men are getting by. You just put on your rouge—I see the red in those cheeks—and powder your little football, faggot face before you come to school every day, and don't worry your little fairy head about us men," said Brian in a controlled, calm voice, seemingly unperturbed by Devereux's attack.

"You're fuckin' dead, Kelly!" snarled the handsome athlete.

"Well, if you're threatening me, jerk off, be sure to bring an army when you follow through, you arrogant cocksucker."

At that moment, Miss Sadowski entered the room, closing the door behind her. She called the room to order, intuitively aware of the tension overhanging the assembly. Brian became aware of the number of eyes turned on him following yet another confrontation with the popular Buzz Devereux. He sensed a degree of grudged admiration from the group. Most notable among the onlookers was Gloria Sims, who had swung around in her chair and stared directly at him, as if noticing him for the first time. She neither smiled nor showed displeasure. Instead, the pretty blonde surveyed him in the manner of a judge at an athletic event. Establishing eye contact, Brian returned her glance with his own self-assured smirk, causing Gloria to break eye contact and return her attention to the front of the room.

The following Saturday night, more damp than cold for February, Brian was promoted to the front of the fast food restaurant and behind a cash register. Howdy's had lost two employees in twenty-four hours, pressing him into service dealing with the public. He followed two hours of monitoring by the assistant manager with responsibility for one of the two active registers. Still being a relative stranger in Manchester, he had not waited on a single familiar face the entire shift when a momentary lull in customer traffic was interrupted by a group of exuberant youths bursting through the door. On entering, Gloria Sims broke free from the cluster of teenagers and walked in Brian's direction.

"Nice hat," commented Gloria, a reference to Brian's Howdy Beefburger cap complete with company logo.

"Thank you, miss. May I take your order?" he replied, unflustered by her sarcasm. Gloria shifted her eyes up to the menu board, all the while running her index finger along her lower lip, as if in deep thought but also knowingly transmitting a certain suggestive gesture.

"I'll just have a burger and an orange soda."

"One Howdy Burger and an orange soda for the pretty, sophomore from Southside," sang out Brian while entering the order into the register. He looked up from the counter to see Gloria staring admiringly at him, visibly pleased by his compliment.

"You're a lot nicer away from school than in it," she commented, maintaining hypnotic eye contact.

"Can I get you anything else with your order, Miss Sims? Extra ketchup? Extra napkins? An extra pickle?" answered Brian, returning the flirtatious girl's probing gestures. Gloria responded with a smile, showing off her flatteringly imperfect grin, showcased by a small gap between her front teeth.

"If I could have two straws, Mr. Kelly—I have a wide mouth and a single straw is not enough," she cooed, dropping her head seductively while still holding eye contact. Brian reached out and dropped two straws into her bag while chuckling aloud.

"Okay, Romeo, back to work!" cried out Mr. Delaney from beside the food preparation table. Brian followed a sheepish grin with a shrug of the shoulders.

"Till Monday," called out the statuesque Miss Sims before returning to the milling crowd she arrived with and eventually streaming out the door.

Brian concluded an uneventful night, save his encounter with the flirtatious Gloria Sims, at eleven o'clock and set out for home amid a flurry of activity by his co-workers. Two cars left the parking lot, their drivers hollering instructions back and forth about a rendezvous point somewhere at the other end of Elm Street. Brian set off on foot toward the Granite Street Bridge and ultimately the darkened streets across the river on the west side and home. The now familiar walk took just under forty minutes, taking him by Southside which was robed in darkness. He glanced up into the windows of his homeroom from North Main Street as cars cruised by. On this evening he stopped and pondered the darkness and silence in the room where he had first laid eyes on Maggie May Keogh. Her mood and demeanor from the last week seemed perfectly represented at the moment by the cold, dark, silent atmosphere behind the windows.

After unlocking the door and shuffling into the apartment, Brian found his mother asleep on the couch in front of the television. The set was off but there was a book on the floor, where she had placed it, spine up. His eyes focused on the cover of *Love Story*. The tired young man stood over his mother, taken at the moment by the total warmth of her image before him. She seemed the complete antithesis of the stark, frozen image he gazed upon only minutes earlier through the windows of Southside. There was something so reassuring, so comforting, about the sight of this woman waiting on his return. Brian bent over and nudged her, coaxing her awake.

"Okay, lady, why don't we just make our way to bed. No more passing out on me in the living room. Geez, Ma, where do you hide the bottles? Every night I come home and you're passed out on the couch, sleeping off another drunken toot—but I can never find the bottles. There's gotta be a closet full of Pabst Blue Ribbon empties somewhere in this house. You got a secret closet around here somewhere?" teased Brian as Elizabeth gradually gathered her wits about her.

"Can I make you something before you go to bed?" asked the woman.

"I'll take a Pabst, if you don't mind."

"Sorry, hon, the case is long gone. You know me once I'm on a roll." Brian reached his arm around his mother, guiding her toward her bedroom. Depositing her on her four-poster bed, he planted a kiss just above her hairline.

"Sleep it off, lady, and I'll see you in the morning. Wake me when you get back from mass."

Brian had barely emerged from his bedroom the following morning when Elizabeth returned from church, a missal tucked under one arm and a small bag clutched in her other hand.

"If you can hold your horses for a few minutes, I'll make us some corn muffins for breakfast." Brian nodded his approval through a yawn and retreated to the living room while his mother removed her coat and returned her missal to its resting place atop her bureau. The Kellys spent the morning catching each other up on developments in their respective lives, no matter how trivial or seemingly insignificant. Elizabeth learned of the deterioration of her son's friendship with Maggie May Keogh and the possible beginning of some sort of relationship with another girl, described by him as a heart-stopper, by the name of Gloria Sims. The two spent a relaxing morning over cups of tea and corn muffins before Brian had to begin preparing himself for his shift at Howdy's early in the afternoon.

VIII

MONDAY MORNING AT SOUTHSIDE saw the continued withdrawal of Miss Keogh from almost everyone around her. Certainly it bothered Brian less than it should have, offset by the blossoming relationship with the blonde, beautiful, statuesque, Gloria Sims. Gloria made a point to turn around and specifically clown around with Brian in geography class, not to mention walking with him through the corridors of the school between periods when it proved possible. Brian was quick to return her attention, going so far as to playfully bump against her in response to some of her silly exclamations. At Gloria's suggestion, they decided to meet off location after school on Thursday, late in the afternoon, and study together for a test scheduled for Friday. Gloria did not have the quick-witted, independent spirit of a Maggie May Keogh, but her radiant smile and cultivated feminine charm was proving to be a welcome addition to Brian's barren social life. In homeroom, he was careful to avoid any sort of eye contact with Miss Keogh. If she thought her behavior was carrying out some manner of psychological and emotional torture on him, he was out to prove she was quite mistaken. In truth, the attention from Gloria was proving a strong antidote to the behavior of this aloof girl from Bedford.

It was three-thirty on Thursday afternoon when Gloria Sims sauntered up to Brian in the reference section of the Manchester City Library and settled in beside him, letting her pile of school books cascade across the table in front of them. She was wearing a red dress that set off her flowing blonde hair and creamy, white complexion. Brian welcomed his new friend with unbridled enthusiasm while promising her a strong performance on the following day's geography exam. It was he who took command of their study session, sprinkling humorous stories and anecdotes together with the material likely to land somewhere on the following day's test.

Gloria accepted Brian's explanations and insight as she would have Miss Sadowski's, had she been granted a personal study session. There was a certain seriousness in her manner that Brian repeatedly attempted to dispel, hoping to make some personal progress with this very attractive girl in addition to assisting her to an acceptable grade. An hour and a half into their rendezvous, Gloria was beginning to shift her eyes upward to the clock above the reference section desk, monitoring the progress of the afternoon with almost fanatical repetition. An uncomfortable seriousness had fallen over the pretty blonde and Brian knew this did not bode well for his attempt to develop some kind of personal bond. It was almost as if this girl, who had joked and teased him at school all week, had now lost all interest in him as a friend and as a young male. It was just before five-thirty when Gloria excused herself from the table, explaining that her father would be out front shortly, waiting to drive her back home. She went on to explain that he had no knowledge she was studying with a boy, let alone one he had never met, and that it would be best if Brian waited inside until he saw that she had been picked up and driven away. Brian watched as the blonde-haired girl reached into her coat and prepared herself for the cold, February air that awaited her outside. He wished her well while she collected her things, gave him an obligatory glance, and disappeared out the door and down to the street.

It was already dark at this hour and Brian prepared for his own departure. He slipped his denim coat on over a woolen sweater, all the while watching Gloria through the window aside his table.

The elegantly dressed girl had barely been standing a full minute when a luxury car pulled up to the curb across the street and Gloria skipped over and jumped into the passenger seat. She cast a quick glance back at the building before the automobile forced its way out into the flow of traffic and quickly out of sight. That left Brian with nothing to do but collect his things and follow in Gloria's steps to the front door and out into the cold air. He descended the stairs, shuffling his way to the sidewalk and then across the street to the park. Brian followed the sidewalk along a pathway adorned with benches every twenty feet, walking toward a tall monument that dominated the snow-covered area. He was heading back to Elm Street on a straight line. A single figure stood at the base of the monument as he approached, a male whose eyes were trained on him, making no attempt to disguise his interest. Brian proceeded unperturbed, placing no significance on the male standing motionless in his path. He had closed the distance between him and the stranger when the identity of the man became apparent. It was Buzz Devereux who stood defiantly in Brian's path.

Brian's astonishment was instantly replaced with suspicion as he strode closer to his sworn enemy from Southside High. Over Buzz's shoulder on the monument was the dark image of a figure that resembled the Angel of Death. His wariness of the developing confrontation was immediately validated when Ben Turner appeared from behind the monument. The clatter of foot-steps running up from behind sent a surge of adrenaline through his body, prompting Brian to sprint to his right, hurdle a snow bank, and dash away from the group. Buzz, Ben and at least one other young male were in hot pursuit as Brian took to the road-way and ran northward beside the traffic. He was unable to put much distance between his pursuers and himself but was main-taining an approximate thirty-foot separation as his mind sped, trying to devise a way of getting to Elm Street and the hordes of shoppers downtown on a Thursday night. Lowell Street and a direct line to shoppers and grown-ups was just ahead, except another jock appeared in his path, causing him to continue run-ning due north and no closer to the safety of the city's main street. His pursuers were hollering now, sounding like rebel troops in the movies, he thought. On pure impulse, he cut in front of an oncoming vehicle and down an alleyway. This put him on a di-rect line for Elm Street. He sped down the dark, slushy alley only to spot another of Buzz's cohorts guarding his exit. Brian ran the situation through his head. He now knew of five males taking part in this pursuit—four only steps behind him and one planted at the end of the alleyway in his escape route. His heart was pounding with anxiety and fear as he played his only card.

Running directly at the jock blocking his way, he delivered a whistling right hand on impact, sending Josh Backman reeling backwards and onto his back. The impact stopped Brian in his tracks, allowing his pursuers to pounce and grab hold of him.

Swinging around, Brian delivered a jolting wallop to someone's chest before an arm reached around and locked him in a choke hold. He sensed that Ben Turner was holding him from behind just as Buzz Devereux appeared directly in front of him and let go with a roundhouse right hand, catching Brian on the cheek. The blow stung his face as his flesh was pounded between the jock's knuckle bones and his own cheekbone. Buzz let out a satisfied war cry and buried a fist into Brian's ribs. Backman was slowly rising to his feet, blood streaming from a cut above his eye. After two more hard punches to Brian's jaw from Buzz, Backman laid into Brian's body and head. Ben Turner now had Brian's arms locked behind him, allowing everyone a complementary rip at their outnumbered and overwhelmed prey.

As the pain inflicted on him began to register in his consciousness, Brian took stock of his situation, his brain still clear enough at the moment to function. Escape by any means, he thought. Two of the jocks had passed on the invitation from Buzz to whale away and Ben Turner seemed content to merely keep Brian under wraps while his friend administered a serious beating. Buzz stepped back in front of Brian, staring his enemy directly in the face.

"So, it's fuckin' Yvonne, is it? You fuckin' worthless cocksucker. Who the fuck do you think you are? Hold him up, Ben, straight up," directed the handsome jock. Turner did as he was asked and Buzz Devereux proceeded to hammer Brian's body with a dozen more punches. Still silent, Brian prayed for a passerby to come to his aid. The bodywork done, Buzz went back to peppering Brian's face with jabs, now joking with his friends as he pushed a series of lefts into Brian's puffy and bleeding face.

"I think we've made our point, Buzz it's time to quit," stated Ben abruptly.

"Tell you what—peel off the fucker's jacket and let me get a couple of clean shots at his ribs and we'll call it quits. I want to hear the sound of cracking rib—a half-dozen shots and we'll call it a night," came back Devereux. Convinced Brian was only semiconscious, Turner began pulling off his denim coat after releasing his arms. Seizing a brief opportunity, Brian broke away from his coat and dashed out of the alley with only Buzz in pursuit. Brian turned and raced toward the lights on Elm Street and was able to make his way into sidewalk traffic after a thirty-second sprint.

He stumbled southward toward city hall, already conscious of the pedestrian's reaction to his battered appearance. His face throbbed with pain and he was having a problem with the vision in his left eye. Reaching into his pocket, he pulled out a clean handkerchief and ran it forehead to chin. The crimson splotches discoloring the fabric provided grim evidence of the damage done to his face. He looked into the window of McQuade's Department Store and caught his reflection, the left side of his face swelled into a gruesome mask along with cuts above his eye and to his upper lip. Clearly the damage resulting from a series of right haymakers from Buzz. He set off for the Granite Street Bridge and a roundabout route back home. A direct route would require him to cross the Notre Dame Bridge and possibly a second confrontation with Buzz, Ben, and company.

He had walked less than a hundred yards when his ribs began to send out sharp pains. He left Elm Street and made his way through the dark alleyways of the mill yard. He did not want people seeing him this way. He was already dreading his mother's reaction to this episode and used the time walking home to come up with an account that would present her with the least amount of stress.

Over and above his appearance there was also the matter of his denim coat, the coat proudly presented to him at Christmas by his mother. It was probably lying back in the alleyway along with his geography book. Brian stopped by a set of railroad tracks on the edge of the mill yard and pondered his predicament. What to do about the coat and textbook? The shirt and light sweater he had been reduced to wearing was not keeping him warm. His only reasonable option became obvious. He turned and began the walk back to the alleyway. He would just have to risk the possibility of running into Buzz again. Arriving back at the alleyway with no sign of his attackers in sight, Brian searched the shadowy alley for his things while sounds of merriment escaped from behind the walls of the Red Onion Pub across the street. In the ten minutes he devoted hunting for his things, Brian could only locate his textbook, lying spine up along the wall. He was growing numb from the cold when he gave up the search for his denim coat and started back home.

Returning to Elm Street, he ducked into the F.W. Woolworth's long enough to drive the chill from his bones while shoppers gaped at him and his battered appearance. Brian took the long route home, crossing the Granite Street Bridge by way of the mill yard, all the while favoring a series of sore ribs on his right side.

Brian arrived home a half hour later and quickly retreated to his room before his mother caught sight of him. His bloodstained sweater was evident in the light of his bedroom lamp. Elizabeth rapped on his door.

"Everything okay in there, hon?"

"Fine, Ma, everything's fine," he responded through swollen lips.

"There's some soup left over and I can whip you up a chicken salad sandwich. Did you get some studying in at the library?" It was obvious his mother wanted some company and there was no way he would be able to keep the door closed between them all night.

At the end of an uncomfortable stretch of silence, Brian crossed the room and unhooked the lock on his door. He pulled the door open and faced his mother who stood patiently in the kitchen. Her face reacted noticeably at the sight of her son's battered face.

"What in the name of God happened to you?" she cried out.

"There was a little trouble downtown. I ran into some punks on the way home and they got a few licks in before I broke away," spoke Brian calmly, hoping to play down the incident in his mother's eyes. Elizabeth was already heading for the medicine cabinet and some disinfectant to put on her son's wounds.

"Who are the people who did this to you?" she asked, her shock swiftly being replaced by anger.

"Ma, I've never seen these people before," he answered as his mother began attending to his bruised face.

"I don't want any malarkey now, sonny boy. Are you having any problems at school or anything?"

"Ma, so help me. These were just some gutless punks from across town trying to be tough guys. I mean it was five on one," explained Brian, as Elizabeth appeared to be calming down from the shock of her son's battered appearance. She reached inside the refrigerator for more ice while he continued speaking softly to her, repeatedly stating that he was fine.

Following a fifteen-minute period working on her son's bruised face, Elizabeth put on hot water for a pot of tea, then joined Brian at the kitchen table, quietly closing out the day. Elizabeth broke from the table for her bedroom first, counseling her son not to go looking for the cowards who had preyed upon him earlier. He responded by advising her that he had no intention of crossing town and looking for them.

Following a night punctuated by restless interludes of nervous deliberations, Brian awoke the next morning dreading his upcoming day at Southside. By morning, the mild headache and ringing in his ears from punches to the head had subsided. However, if anything, his ribs were more tender eight hours after the attack than immediately following it. He purposely dragged his feet getting dressed for school, fearing his mother would question the absence of his denim jacket. Brian spent fifteen minutes slumped over his Sugar Pops planning his morning at school, knowing full well he would have to face Buzz, Ben and the others in the next few hours.

By now Mr. Giroux was faithfully driving Elizabeth to work in the mill yard every morning, leaving her by 7:30 A.M at the Commercial Street entrance of Pandora Sweaters. Brian's plan of action on this day called for him to arrive at school just before the opening bell, thereby reducing the available time for curious onlookers to survey his battered face and blackened left eye. The morning was cold, forcing him to dress himself in multilayered sweaters, given his lack of a presentable winter coat. He found the prospect of presenting himself in this manner depressing. Although she was no longer on speaking terms with him, Brian nonetheless cared about how he appeared before Maggie May Keogh. He decided to attempt to find his coat after school. He would hoof it downtown to the alleyway off Elm Street then make his way south to Howdy Beefburgers before his four o'clock shift.

It was not a pleasant walk to school on this day. He was poorly dressed, both fashionably and for the cold, and his ribs hurt from the pounding the night before. Brian approached the entrance to Southside with his head lowered, his line of sight dragging along the cement sidewalk. Fortunately, this spared him the sight of his denim coat unceremoniously tied to the flag pole on the roof, high above the entrance to the school.

His prized denim jacket, the Christmas gift from his mother less than two months earlier, was on display six feet up the pole, saturated in the urine of his attackers.

Brian gingerly climbed the stairs to Southside with shockwaves of pain shooting from his rib cage, looking straight ahead as he made his way through the corridors and to his homeroom.

"What happened to you, Mr. Kelly? Been back to Lowell?" joked Mr. Sullivan, mercifully trying to make light of Brian's situation on his entrance.

"Debating team tryouts. You've got some pretty tough nerds in this school," answered Brian while continuing to his desk.

"No, seriously—trouble at home?" asked the concerned teacher. Brian answered without turning.

"No big deal, Mr. Sullivan. It's nothing." He walked toward his desk. A wide-eyed and unsettled Maggie May stared at him as he made his way down the aisle, collapsing into his desk.

"What have they done to you?" she exclaimed, speaking to Brian for the first time in over a week.

"No one did anything to me," answered Brian lifelessly.

"Everyone in the school knows Buzz and Ben jumped you last night. They're bragging about how they worked you over."

"Oh, and did they mention the other three dirtbags with them?" he snapped back.

"Have you gotten your coat back from the roof?" asked Maggie May, all the while surveying her friend's battered face at close range.

"Keogh, what are you talking about?"

"Brian, your coat is up on the roof hanging from the flagpole. You didn't see it coming in?" Brian did not respond, feeling a pulse of rage flare up inside him. The opening bell sounded, calling the two to first period English. They rose from their desks in unison.

"Are we on speaking terms again, Keogh?" She nodded her head in the affirmative and the two set out for their first period class.

"I don't see you and Skip walking together or anything anymore. Don't tell me there's trouble in paradise?" She turned her blue eyes on him, a sad expression momentarily appearing on her face.

"The last time I checked, you and that bitch Gloria Sims were all chummy-wummy. Has romance come to Brian Kelly?" she asked sarcastically.

"Take a long look at my face, Keogh. That's what's come of my involvement with Miss Sims."

"What are you saying?" she questioned.

"What I'm saying is that it seems awfully funny that Sims excuses herself from our study date at the library at five-thirty, and by five-forty-five I'm bleeding in five places and running for my goddamn life. I'm saying she set me up."

Their friendship completely re-bonded, Brian and Maggie May reached the door to English class and entered. His arrival brought about an immediate hush followed by sporadic pockets of giggling. He walked to his seat, noticing Ben Turner was already present in the room. He was surprised when Turner did not so much as turn his head on Brian's arrival.

As the bell sounded the end to class, Brian nodded at Maggie May and hurried to the roof in search of his coat. Racing to the flagpole, he could find no evidence of the denim coat. He scurried over much of the school's rooftop in vain, then retreated back into the building for his next class.

Ben Turner's passive behavior in English class would prove the exception on this day. Brian was the target of a number of taunts from male classmates throughout the morning. For his part, he would shoot a cold glance at his tormentor in each instance, making a mental note of their identity. Just before his lunch period he was called to the vice principal's office and questioned on the circumstances surrounding his battered appearance. A certain code of honor learned on the streets of Lowell over his sixteen years prompted him to not divulge the identity of his attackers. He simply parroted the story presented to his mother the night before to the school administrators and was quickly dismissed. He reported to Miss Sadowski's geography class to the kind of reception he had expected earlier.

Entering the classroom, Brian was quick to notice that Buzz had confiscated the desk beside Gloria Sims formerly occupied by Rory O'Shea, the student he had tormented a few weeks earlier. Brian was met with immediate eye contact from Buzz the moment he passed through the doorway. Devereux gave him a sadistic grin, then whispered a few words to Gloria Sims, who did not raise her eyes from her desk. Easing himself down onto his chair, Brian half expected Gloria to swivel around and address him. She did not, therefore confirming his assumption that she was privy to the plans to assault him the night before.

"You know, Kelly, I can't say I've ever seen you looking better," scoffed Buzz in a voice loud enough for the entire class to hear. His remark was met with a weak chorus of laughs. "Oh, by the way, I just love what you're wearing today. The whole sweater thing and all—I mean, you're making a certain statement—like, here I am, world—a useless, rag-picking fuck and proud of it. What's the matter, Kelly, Goodwill's prices too expensive for you?"

While the handsome jock delivered his words of torment, Brian sat expressionless, staring directly at his tormentor without uttering a word.

"One more thing, fuck face! If you have any problem with our kicking the shit out of you last night, keep in mind, I'll be heading down to Dunkin' Doughnuts after school. Feel free to meet me down at the square after school you skinny sack of shit."

Buzz's challenge did not draw even the slightest gesture from Brian, who chose to break eye contact and focus on his notes spread out on the desk before him. He raised his head a few seconds later when Miss Sadowski entered the room, catching sight of Rory O'Shea glancing back in his direction. Soon the entire class was struggling with the challenging exam scheduled that day.

Brian did his best to avoid the jocks, and particularly Buzz, in the hallway for the rest of the day. After final bell, Brian was delighted when Maggie May caught up with him at the door and asked him if he would walk her to her mother's car. A subdued Brian walked beside his chattering friend, unable to figure out the unexpected change in her demeanor but delighted with his good fortune.

"Any sign of your coat yet?" she asked politely.

"None—and I mean none. It's like the damn thing just vanished from the face of the . . . ." The attractive girl looked up at him, breaking in on his words.

"Is there any chance you might want to come by the house tomorrow—like you did at Christmas time? It was fun having you before and I'm thinking maybe we could talk again like before. I really could use someone to chat with and my mother likes you and all."

"Your mother likes me? Then, why doesn't your mother ask me herself instead of having her daughter do the dirty work?" cracked Brian, smiling through swollen lips.

"God, Brian, you can be such a smart ass. Is that a yes or a no?"

"Listen, Keogh, I'm working three to closing at Howdy's tomorrow. I'm going to have to walk or hitch out to your house on Saturday and then again to work by three o'clock or so. Will that be enough time?"

"I can have my father drive you to work in the afternoon so you can hang around until two-thirty or so. How does that sound?"

"Will I get to hang around your bedroom again?" he asked guardedly.

"God, you sound like a dirty, old man! Yes, I'll invite you up to my room, if that's what turns you on."

"What time do you want me at your door in the morning?"

"Nine will be good," she answered as they reached her mother's car.

"Brian, what happened to you?" called out a wide-eyed Mrs. Keogh from behind the wheel.

"Mrs. Keogh, I just happened to walk into a series of doors last night—a long series of doors. I really have to begin working on my motor skills a little harder."

"Mother, I've invited Brian over to the house tomorrow morning. I'm sorry I couldn't find anyone smarter or more charming but he'll just have to do."

Mrs. Keogh extended Brian a warm glance, then motioned her daughter into the car. "We'll hold breakfast until your arrival," she added, then pulled the Oldsmobile away from the curb and back toward Bedford.

Brian made his way back inside the school, checking with the office in the event someone had found his jacket and returned it to school officials. However, the office reported no word on his coat.

Mindful of Buzz Devereux's challenge earlier in the day, Brian avoided Granite Square and any crowd that might be loitering in that vicinity after school. He had time to take the long route to work this day, backtracking across the Notre Dame Bridge before heading south on Elm Street to Howdy Beefburgers. After catching sight of Brian, Mr. Delaney, the manager, assigned his bruised employee to food preparation duties, out of sight of the customers. The shift sped by as Brian mechanically prepared food while thinking about his time the next day in Bedford. He left work a few minutes after ten o'clock and headed straight home to bed. He burst through the door, into the kitchen and quickly into his bedroom, only to emerge stripped of his sweaters before his mom had laid eyes on him. He hoped to keep word of his missing denim coat from his mother as long as humanly possible. He bolted into the living room and threw himself down on the couch in one motion next to his mother.

"So, what are you watching, my beautiful stranger?" he joked.

"'Love, American Style.'"

"Where's our lovesick landlord? Or did you send our aging Casanova downstairs to cry in his beer?"

"Now, don't you make fun of that nice man," cautioned Elizabeth.

"Heck no, Ma—he's perfect. Harmless—got a few bucks in his pocket—will do anything you say—and finally, you can probably kick the crap out of him in a pinch and so your devoted son doesn't have to worry about his drop-dead, gorgeous mother. I'd say he's perfect," teased Brian.

"You got any plans, besides work, this weekend?"

"Well, Ma, as a matter of fact I do. I'm heading out to Bedford early tomorrow morning. Maggie May Keogh invited me out for breakfast."

"Wait a minute, hon. Weren't you just telling me how she was ignoring you and how you were interested in another, even prettier girl, only a few days ago?" quizzed an amused Elizabeth.

"That didn't pan out. Boy, that didn't pan out!" he exclaimed.

"Make sure that girl doesn't go and play you for the fool. She seems to be a bit flighty, not talking to you one minute and then inviting you to her house the next. That's not how nice girls operate."

"Ma, trust me, she's a great girl—smart and gorgeous."

Elizabeth gave her son a skeptical glance then returned her attention to the television screen. After only a few minutes on the couch, Brian informed his mother that she would find his paycheck on the kitchen table, endorsed over to her. He asked her to cash it at her earliest convenience, keep fifteen dollars for room and board, and return the rest to him. Brian pecked his mother's cheek before heading off to bed.

IX

B RIAN AROSE WITH THE SUN ON SATURDAY MORNING while the balance of Montgomery Street residents slept in on this February weekend. He made himself a cup of instant coffee, but held off preparing any food, knowing the Keogh's would be expecting him to join them for their morning meal. It was not even seven o'clock when he crept into his mother's room, planted a kiss on her forehead, and informed her he was leaving for Bedford. It was already over twenty degrees when he descended the stairs at the rear of the three family building and began the long walk to the suburbs. Unlike on his journey two months earlier, he was not confronted by the frigid, roaring wind and made appreciably better time.

Aided by a light tail wind, reasonable February temperatures, and two or three interludes of running, Brian reached the bottom of Ministerial Road in Bedford at seven forty-five, long before his expected arrival time of nine o'clock. From there, it took less that five minutes for him to plant himself on the Keogh family's front porch. He stood motionless for a moment, listening for the slightest sound from inside the house. There was none. He began to feel self-conscious, afraid the family dog would sense his presence and begin barking. Stepping back off the porch, he scooped up a handful of soft snow, pressured a snowball together in the palms of his hands, and scanned the windows a floor above him. He surmised that the window directly above his head had to be one of Maggie May's two bedroom windows. So, with a bit of apprehension, he took aim and bounced the snowball off the pane of glass above. Following a cautious thirty-second interlude, a second snowball was hurled against the same window, this time causing a more audible thud. He heard some scurrying above, then the sound of two sets of windows being pushed up. Finally, a sleepy-eyed Maggie May jutted her head through the opening, her disheveled, dirty blonde hair hanging down over her face.

"What the hell are you doing down there?" she questioned, her long hair now cascading over the window sill.

"I'm a little early, Keogh. Can you let me in?" asked an embarrassed Brian.

"What time is it, Kelly? Did I oversleep?" The girl pulled her head inside, presumably to check the time on her alarm clock.

"I may be a bit early," he called up. His friend's head reappeared in the bedroom window. The sleep appeared to be clearing out of her eyes which were now wide and locked on her visitor.

"You're over an hour early, Kelly. I told you nine—not eight." He shrugged his shoulders and looked up pathetically. "Oh, please, and you're wearing those ratty sweaters again today. What's with you and those damn sweaters?" she snapped.

"I told you my jacket was still missing. It's these sweaters or freeze. And besides, how do you know I'm not just making a statement by wearing these things? If the long-haired freaks at school can get away with looking like sub-humans and say they're making a social statement, why can't a nice, conservative boy from Lowell do the same?"

"And, pray tell, what statement are you and your ratty, moth-eaten sweaters making?"

"My sweaters are saying there are poor people in third-world nations that need our help."

Maggie May reached her hand to her mouth and yawned as if bored. "And your third-world friends are, no doubt, dressed better than you. But, enough about the third world—you see, Brian, I know the real reason you're here early today."

"And that is?" he answered warily.

"You just thought if you came early, you might get to see me in my pajamas—and that makes you some kind of pervert." Down below, Brian dropped his head, an exaggerated grimace on his face. Maggie May grabbed a handful of snow and tossed it down at her friend. The makeshift snowball broke in midair, the larger portion falling on Brian's exposed head.

"Thanks for the snow, Keogh, very refreshing. Now, are you going to let me in out of the cold?"

"It's not nine, Brian—and I invited you for breakfast at nine. If I were you I'd walk back to The Wagon Wheel. I'm sure Charlie and Winnie will let you hang out for a while until it's time for me to receive you," she chirped.

"Time for you to receive me? Who are you, Queen Elizabeth?"

"Okay, if you'll admit, out loud, that you only came early so you could see me in my pajamas, then I'll let you in early. But, only if you admit it," she stated boldly.

"I see you in school in miniskirts all the time! Why would I be so hepped up about seeing you in your pj's?"

She looked down crossly at her male friend in mock anger. "You've heard my terms, Kelly—take them or leave them!"

Brian raised his eyes to heaven in total frustration. "Okay, Keogh, you figured me out. I came out to Bedford early for the sole purpose of seeing you in your pajamas," he recited in a false, monotone manner.

"Then you are a pervert!" she cried out before disappearing inside and pulling down the windows. Brian stood outside patiently for a few moments before his friend appeared in the doorway, her long hair still mussed in a heap and resting on one shoulder. She directed him to follow her upstairs and he obliged, watching her round, petite backside as she climbed the stairs—and at eye level.

Thirty minutes later when Maggie May heard her mother pass by her room, she quickly informed her that their breakfast guest had already arrived. Mrs. Keogh stuck her head inside the bedroom, greeted Brian, then made her way downstairs. Shortly after nine, the teenagers were called down to breakfast, at which time Brian got his first look at Mr. Keogh. Howard Keogh was a stern, cheerless man with thin lips, cold eyes, and a receding hairline. He acknowledged Brian with an almost imperceptible nod as they were introduced, taking in the boy's facial bruises but not commenting on them. Brian, conversely, extended his hand behind an enthusiastic hello. Mr. Keogh shook hands in silence before burying his face back in the morning newspaper. Over the course of the meal, both Maggie May and Brian told entertaining stories from Southside, including her gift of a peanut butter and jelly sandwich to him, the message from God regarding the candidacy of George McGovern scrawled on the board by Brian, and the strange case of his sideways leaning locker named Eileen. As breakfast was winding down, she asked him if he would join her for a walk. Her manner seemed to grow more serious as they prepared to venture outdoors. The two proceeded upstairs where Brian grabbed his sweaters, only to be cut short by Maggie May.

"Oh, please, tell me you're not going to wear those on our walk?" she asked in earnest.

"What? You want me to go out in my shirt and freeze to death?" responded an embarrassed Brian.

"My father has at least three heavy coats in the downstairs closet. Will you wear one of them for me?" Brian's feelings were hurt but he understood her request. He nodded yes and followed her downstairs, where he slipped on a brown, woolen jacket. Maggie May slipped the leash and collar on Funnel, her cocker spaniel, and they proceeded out the front door and onto the porch. Funnel, eager to extend his sniffing out onto the road, pulled on the leash, yanking his mistress off of the porch ahead of Brian. Following a period of momentary laughter, she grew serious and seemed to mentally drift off. Finally, Brian broke an extended period of silence.

"By the way, Keogh, you look gorgeous today—if you don't mind me saying."

She looked back at him, a sad smile lifting the corners of her mouth. "If nothing else, Kelly, you're good for my ego."

Brian was unaccustomed to the quiet demeanor of his friend. It was making him apprehensively curious. "Are you okay, Keogh? You don't seem yourself."

She returned his words with a sad, cautious glance, then stepped up directly in front of him, placing her head on his chest. She spoke with her face buried in her father's borrowed coat. "There is a lot going on in my life right now that practically nobody knows about. That's part of the reason I invited you out here today."

"That's bullshit, Keogh. You invited me out here because my Irish good looks are finally getting to you and you couldn't stand the idea of a weekend away from me. I think my bruises turn you on, you little sicko," he joked, a bit taken aback by Maggie May's serious tone.

"All kidding aside, Brian, I have a serious problem." She looked to see his face stricken with fear, his eyes rounded and riveted on her.

"Please—tell me you're not seriously ill or anything. Tell me it's not anything like that," he insisted.

"No, I'm not seriously ill or dying or anything, Brian—I'm pregnant." She lifted her eyes to his and the two stood staring at each other for a full ten seconds. She could see the news had shocked him.

"It was Skip, right?" he asked.

"Yes."

"Well, thank God it's only that!" he stated while exhaling.

Her blue eyes rounded in anger. "Oh, that's fucking easy for you to say. It's only that, is it? Well it's plenty fucking serious to me," she spit out angrily.

"Keogh, I'm not saying it isn't serious, but being pregnant is a pimple on the ass of say, dying or being paralyzed, or something like that. God, for a second I thought you were going to tell me you were dying. Jesus Christ, you scared me!"

"And what would it be to you if I were dying? You barely know me."

"That's exactly the reason, Keogh—I barely know you," he whispered tenderly.

"What are you saying, Brian?"

"I think you know what I'm saying," he added before turning his attention back to the dog. He leaned over and patted the cocker spaniel, then jerked upward and spun around back to his friend. "Damnit, please tell me you're not going to marry that bag of shit!"

"If you must know—and I'm not sure it's any of your damn business—Skip and I are past tense. I will not be socializing or anything else with him in the future," she said behind a blank expression.

"Man, I hate that prick! Pardon my French. Be sure to let me know if you ever want the shit kicked out of the bastard," snarled Brian, prompting an affirmative nod from Maggie May.

"I'm in the mood for a candy bar. Let's take a walk down to The Wagon Wheel. You're a working man, Kelly. How about treating me to a pack of Chuckles?" Brian laughed out loud.

"I haven't had Chuckles since I was five."

"Well, they're not for you. They're for the drop-dead beautiful girl who's letting you walk with her," she snapped back.

"You're going to have to see a lot of Skip once the baby comes. There won't be any avoiding that," said Brian.

The girl stopped in her tracks and stared straight ahead for a brief moment. Her eyes were narrowed into slits, an expression Brian had come to recognize as a sign of consequence in Miss Keogh. She turned to her friend wearing a look of grim seriousness.

"I'm going to share something with you which I do not want repeated to anyone else. Is that clear?" she stated emphatically. Brian nodded his head yes. She started again down the hill. "A few weeks back, after we learned that I was definitely pregnant, the Emersons were invited over to discuss the whole matter. They had been advised in advance of the nature of the meeting. Well, we weren't too far into the discussion when it became perfectly clear that they saw only one resolution to the problem—and that would have meant ending the pregnancy. I got pretty upset because no one harms my baby—no one! My parents and I had pretty much anticipated this from them, just from some of the comments they had thrown out in our brief, earlier conversations. Anyway, as it was worked out and left, we agreed that the Emersons would not be bothered with any of the expense or trouble surrounding the pregnancy. Skip and his parents could just go back to their pathetic little lives and not be concerned with my baby."

"Are you kidding? You just let them walk away like that?" asked an astonished Brian.

"In exchange for their being released from all responsibility and care for my son or daughter, they were obliged to sign a document—a legal document—requiring them to never contact my child, in any manner, directly or indirectly, until it reaches the age of twenty-one. The agreement stipulates that if they should contact my son or daughter, even if by mistake, they will be forced to pay a cash penalty to the family. They have already signed the document, and I intend to make sure they abide by it." She turned to Brian, who appeared stunned by the revelation.

"Keogh, did you come up with this yourself?"

"My dad and I did."

"Be sure and remind me never to cross the Keogh's, okay?" uttered a perplexed Brian.

"I'll make a note of it," replied the deadly serious girl.

They continued down Ministerial Road, reaching the intersection by the town assembly hall, cemetery, and library in about ten minutes. The air was refreshingly cool, far more bearable than the arctic blast that had greeted Brian on his first visit during the prior Christmas vacation. Brian observed a mood swing in his friend as they continued down the hill toward the store. Maggie May broke into a comical series of pants, causing Funnel to turn and take in his usually serious mistress.

"Hha—hha—hha, sugar, Brian, sugar. I need sugar and fast. Get me Chuckles!" commanded the girl. Both laughing aloud, they came to the front of The Wagon Wheel. "I'll wait outside in the fresh air—which is making my already perfect complexion even more perfect. You—Kelly, inside with you and don't return unless you have a package of Chuckles for me. Is that understood?"

His eyes were twinkling with merriment when he entered the store. Behind the counter Charlie could be seen accepting payment from Brian as he quickly found what he was sent in to purchase. A bell sounded as the tall, teenage boy exited the store and returned to his friend.

"I hope my little Maggie May is planning on sharing her candy with me," said Brian as he approached his friend.

"You can have one, but not the black one. That's my favorite," she answered.

"They all taste the same, Keogh. What are you talking about?"

"No, they don't, you moron. No two taste the same. God, you're stupid," she called out.

"Okay, Keogh, why don't you close your eyes and I'll put one in your mouth. We'll see if you can tell one from another." Maggie May stepped back, sizing up her friend, then accepted Brian's challenge.

"Okay, close your eyes and I'll put a Chuckles in your mouth—just a bit. You nibble off the end and tell me the color. Agreed?"

"Agreed, but no funny business, Kelly."

The two stepped back against the building and Brian proceeded to unwrap the package of candy.

"Eyes closed tight!" he called out while she stood motionless against the store window.

"Don't try any funny business, Kelly, or so help me, you'll be sorry." She stood, mouth open and hands by her side, although still holding the leash to the dog.

"Here goes, Keogh. Now, nibble off the end and tell me what color," Brian commanded as he pushed his forefinger by her sparkling, white teeth and onto her tongue. Her eyes opened in an instant as she forcibly bit down on his finger, causing him to cry out.

"Ow, ow, ow, Keogh, cut it out!" he cried out.

"Apologize," she demanded while applying considerable pressure on his finger. Her teeth had a strong hold on his forefinger.

"Cut it out! It was only a joke," he exclaimed.

"Apologize," she insisted.

"I apologize, Keogh. You're going to break the skin. Enough, I give up!" he cried out. She immediately separated her teeth, allowing him to pull his finger free. The marks from her teeth were visible, although there was no apparent break in the skin.

"It was only a joke, Keogh. You almost took my finger off, for God's sake."

"Brian, you're going to have to learn that I am not to be trifled with."

"Damn it, you almost took off my finger!" he protested, while surveying the deep marks left by her teeth.

"Stop being a baby, Kelly, and feed me—feed me, I say!" Brian removed one of the candies from its wrapper and carefully placed it in her mouth. She began eating the sugary treat through exaggerated chomping sounds, then cried out for more, making Brian burst out in laughter. This was a side of the refined, subdued Miss Keogh that he had never seen before. She reached around him and snatched the remainder of the candy, mimicking a starving child. She pulled the remaining candies from their packaging, forced one into Brian's mouth, then eagerly devoured the remaining pieces.

"I can't believe what I'm seeing here, Keogh. I had no idea you could act like this." She looked up at him through a playful smile, saying nothing. He had the sense that, for this fleeting moment, she had managed to drive the thoughts of her problem from her mind. The dog had started to bark, reacting to his mistress's antics.

Brian reached out, grabbed her, then pulled her against him. The top of her head crested just below his chin. Involuntarily, he placed his lips against her head and kissed her sweet-smelling hair.

"I don't believe in public shows of affection," she cautioned.

"Who's going to see us?" he asked.

"Well, Charlie for one. He could look outside and see you mauling me here."

"So, a little peck on the top of the head is considered mauling out here in Bedford. Is that it?"

"It's a mauling when a roughneck like you is doing it," she answered before turning away and heading back toward home. Finding no purpose in forwarding the argument, Brian jogged up to her and started the walk back to the Keogh residence.

The matter of the innocent kiss was dropped and replaced with a conversation about school. Brian detailed the circumstances leading up to his beating downtown but offered no information on any future actions against his tormentors. Maggie May offered further insight into the difficult period she was in the midst of. It was as if the two had been magically drawn back together, to find comfort in each other while sharing their current roles of underdogs. Halfway back to the house, Maggie May flabbergasted Brian by reaching out and putting her arm around his waist, finishing the walk up Ministerial Road in an embrace. Reaching the end of the family driveway, she turned to her friend.

"Boy, I could sure go for some more candy about now," she uttered.

Immediately, he reached into his pocket and produced another package of candy. Spotting the colorful bar of Chuckles candies, she pounced upon him, sending him backwards onto the snowpile by the road.

"They're mine, Kelly! Hand them over!" she hollered, all the while pulling herself on top of her friend who had already broke out in a fit of uncontrolled laughter. Brian found his back squarely on the cold snow as Maggie May straddled his chest, pinning his arms down with her knees. She ripped at his hand, trying to loosen his fingers from around the package of candy.

"Kelly, I'm ten seconds from biting your hand off at the wrist. Now, hand them over," she ordered through a burst of her own laughter. Brian offered no resistance. The sight and feel of this magnificent, young female perched on top of him was more pleasurable than anything he had ever experienced before in his life. This lovely young woman, the one he had admired from afar, the one he had fantasized about on countless occasions, was resting her body on his. It mattered not that it was part of some silly, juvenile routine she carried out. All that mattered to him was that the flesh—and bones—and blood, yes, everything that constituted the physical entity named Maggie May Keogh was resting atop him, Brian Kelly—and at this moment he felt that he surely must be the luckiest guy in the world.

"I can't believe Buzz and Ben had to have half the football team with them before they'd go after you! You're nothing, Kelly—a pushover. Now I'm just going to eat each, individual candy in full sight of you, knowing that you want one," she taunted through a beautiful, mischievous grin.

"Oh please, kind lady, may I have just one?" he asked in a playful whimper.

"One?"

"Yes, just one. Perhaps the black one?"

"The black one is mine! To the victor belong the spoils—and I'm the one sitting on top of you. Tell me, Brian, is the snow cold on your back?"

In truth, the snow was cold on his back and his bruised ribs throbbed, but he was reveling in his comical predicament and offered no clue of any discomfort.

"Tell you what, Kelly, I will give you one Chuckle—the yellow one. It will be the yellow one, a tribute to your yellow belly," she mocked, outwardly enjoying her tumble in the snow with him. Through the entire confrontation, Funnel kept up an ongoing series of barks.

The front door opened and Mrs. Keogh called out to her daughter. "I hope you're not hurting that boy, Margaret." The comment brought another burst of laughter from the fifteen-year-old girl.

"So, Kelly, does that make you feel stupid enough?" She took the yellow candy from the package and carefully placed it on Brian's lips. He took it into his mouth in an instant but also made a point of allowing his tongue to run across Maggie May's outstretched fingers. The gesture caught her by surprise but did not elicit any negative response. She raised herself from his body and motioned him to follow her back into the house.

The two classmates spent the next two hours up in Maggie May's bedroom, during which she broke out every class picture, yearbook, and the like she could locate. Maggie's mother delivered sandwiches and milk to the room somewhere around midday, as calculated by Brian's internal clock. He was halfway through reading one of her English compositions from Miss Royal's class when the silence in the room was broken.

"So, when are you going to ask my father for a ride to Howdy's?"

"Me ask him? I thought you were going to ask him," he exclaimed in horror.

"I'm not asking that old crab to take you into town. Are you kidding?" He jumped to his feet.

"Shit, I'm going to be late for work if I've got to walk." Maggie May broke out into laughter.

"You're so gullible, Brian. Relax. I'll take care of Daddy."

He gathered up his things and was escorted downstairs by his hostess who sought out her father in the living room. She walked across the shag carpeted room and deposited herself on the arm rest of her father's easy chair.

"Daddy, my dear, greatest father in the entire world and patriarch of the Keogh family, I need to ask you the smallest of favors. Oh please, tell me you'll say yes to what I am forced to ask for," she rattled off in an overdramatic style with an almost Scarlett O'Hara-like delivery. Her father dropped his newspaper to his lap and looked directly into his daughter's eyes.

"My stupid guest has overspent his time with me and now needs a ride to Elm Street to be at work on time. Please say you'll give him a lift—for me?"

Mr. Keogh shifted his eyes to the doorway where Brian stood silently. He frowned with irritation at Brian, but rose to his feet immediately and walked toward the hallway closet. "I'll have the car out front in five minutes," he said, addressing his daughter, but for Brian's benefit.

Brian began putting on his layers of sweaters with Maggie May looking on disapprovingly. "I'm sure my father wouldn't mind if you kept his coat. He never wears it."

"No, no handouts," snapped Brian. The offer clearly had wounded his pride. "No handouts—get it? But, there is something you could give me before I leave."

"And what's that?" she asked, standing by him in the doorway.

In one quick motion, he put his hand behind her head, then pulled her to him. He placed his lips firmly on hers and gently drew upon them, a charge of intimate passion descending on him immediately. For two, perhaps three seconds, she did not resist. Then, she pulled herself back, slightly breathless from the experience.

"Lucky for you, you kept your tongue in your own mouth. That's all I'm going to say. Good-bye, Brian," she said in a huff before closing the door behind him.

"Good-bye, Chuckles breath," he called out through the door. He walked to the driveway and waited for Mr. Keogh to emerge from the garage.

The drive to Manchester with the reserved Mr. Keogh was uncomfortable, as Brian expected. Howard Keogh did not say a word when Brian climbed into the car and the silence was maintained for the first five minutes of the fifteen-minute ride downtown. Brian wanted desperately to break the silence and inject some manner of witticism or point of conversation. However, the truth was he was intimidated by the dignified gentleman. Having had no father of his own to communicate with, he was afraid that most anything he might say would sound forced, or worse, inappropriate. In addition, this was Mr. Keogh, the individual fifty percent responsible for Maggie May Keogh, the young woman totally in control of his future happiness or misery. Finally, Brian was unable to bear the silence any longer.

"Mr. Keogh, I'm real sorry if this drive to town was sprung on you at the last minute. I thought Mag—Margaret had said something to you earlier." The well-groomed, middle-aged man glanced over at his passenger and granted him a weak smile.

"Whether or not you know it, you earned this ride into town," he said.

"How's that?" questioned Brian.

"It's been a long time since her mother and I have heard Margaret laugh the way she did with you today. The family's been through a lot over the last couple of months. It was good to hear my daughter enjoying herself again," he stated soberly, while never taking his eyes from the road.

The drive to Howdy's took them through Manchester's west side, across the Queen City Bridge, and finally onto Elm Street. Once again, the hum of the vehicle's tires on the roadway was the only sound to pierce the inside of the car. Mr. Keogh pulled his Oldsmobile up to the front door of the fast-food joint as Brian fiddled with his gloves before exiting. Standing outside the car, he looked back at Mr. Keogh before closing the door.

"You have an incredible daughter, Mr. Keogh—but I suppose you already know that." That said, Brian swung the door of the Oldsmobile shut and rushed inside.

Brian's shift ended at six o'clock on Sunday night, allowing him to get home at a reasonable hour, finish any undone homework from Friday, and spend some relaxing time with his mother in front of the television. Clearing the door, he rushed to his bedroom, trying to peel the sweaters off his back before Elizabeth Kelly had time to react. However, this evening his mother was already in transit to the kitchen at the moment he cleared the door. She caught sight of him ripping off his sweater and followed him across the kitchen floor to his bedroom.

"Brian, why aren't you wearing the denim coat?" she asked pointedly. The question was direct and to the point, providing him with no wiggle room. He was faced with the choice between lying to his mother or confessing the circumstances regarding his missing coat. He chose the latter, explaining how the coat had been ripped from his back during the assault a few days earlier. He still did not offer his mother a full explanation of the attack, allowing her to continue to believe that he did not know the identity of his assailants. Elizabeth remained calm throughout Brian's partial confession as she took in the new account of her son's attack the previous Thursday.

"I'll say a prayer to Saint Anthony tonight. I'll ask him to give you a hand locating the coat," she uttered quietly.

"Ma, the coat is gone!" responded Brian, irritated at having had his secret partially revealed.

"You think whatever you want, mister smart aleck. I'll let Saint Anthony do my work for me." Brian gestured to his mother that she was free to do whatever pleased her. "Now, if my big, handsome son will agree to sit down and watch the 'FBI' with me, I'll pop us some popcorn,"

"Are you kidding? Freshly popped popcorn, the gorgeous Elizabeth Kelly beside me on the couch, and Efren Zimbalist Jr. on the tube—it doesn't get any better than this!"

"Better than having your little Maggie May by your side?" she jested.

"A poor second to you, Ma—a poor second."

X

THE BITTER COLD WEATHER was back on Monday morning as Brian readied himself for the half-mile walk to Southside. He hated having to don his ratty sweaters again. However, the only alternative was a stained winter coat with tears by the shoulders that exposed some of the inner lining. He opted for the sweaters. He timed his arrival just before opening bell, quickly stuffed the sweaters away in Eileen, and made his way to homeroom. Maggie May looked up from her desk the moment he cleared the doorway, staring stonefaced at him as he made his way to the back of the room.

In the course of his morning classes he caught certain students staring at his bruised face, but nothing was said. Following lunch, he reported to geography class where Gloria Sims sat in the practically empty classroom. Brian took his desk in total silence, careful to not even make any noise laying down his books. On this day Gloria was wearing a fabulous red and black outfit, her slender waist set off by a wide, black belt. Brian's eyes were involuntarily drawn to her. Her long, blonde hair flowed down her back, set off by the crimson blouse while her long, shapely legs sprang out from beneath her pleated black skirt. Moments later she turned her head as Buzz entered the room. His eyes, too, were quick to catch sight of Gloria on this day.

"Oh, wow, you look great," he called out. "You must have picked this up over the weekend, cause I'd have remembered you in this—wow!" Gloria responded with a catty smile, basking in the flattery and attention. "Okay, we gotta be talkin' McQuade's or Pariseau's here." Gloria laughed but did not offer any information on the subject. Then, Devereux made eye contact with Brian, who was taking in the flirtation behind a blank expression. "Oh, and look what else we got here. The dapper Brian Kelly, once again adorned in the same, fucked up army shirt, complete with soup stains. And the question again—from where? Tell us, Kelly, where did you buy this shirt—which you no doubt love—cause you wear it so fuckin' much. Share your secret with us. I've narrowed it down to two—Salvation Army or Goodwill? Which is it? The whole fuckin' fashion world is waiting to know," taunted Buzz.

"Devereux, you suck!" called out Rory O'Shea from the front of the room. Buzz spun around in his seat and glared at the small, studious, young man at the front of the classroom. The jock catapulted over his desk and was already halfway to Rory when Miss Sadowski breezed through the door.

"Okay, everyone, back in your seats. We're already a couple of minutes late starting class," she chirped.

Devereux pointed ominously in Rory O'Shea's direction. "You've signed your death warrant," he muttered.

At the close of geography class Rory O'Shea was careful to avoid meeting Buzz anywhere near the doorway. He held back, noticing that Brian was taking an extended time organizing his notes and textbooks on the top of his desk. As he rose from his chair Rory stepped in front of him.

"I'd like to take a couple minutes of your time, maybe at final bell today?" Expressionless, Brian peered down at the young man who stood at least a half foot shorter than him. "Tell you what, hang around a couple of minutes at final bell, I'll meet up with you in front of your homeroom. I have something for you."

Following a moment's hesitation, Brian responded. "I'm walking someone to their car after school. Give me about ten minutes and I'll meet you back at homeroom."

O'Shea nodded his head in agreement before turning and quickly retreating out into the hallway. Following dismissal, Brian delivered an uncharacteristically quiet Maggie May Keogh to her mother's car and footed it back into the school building to meet with Rory O'Shea, whom he found leaning against the lockers by his homeroom. As he approached his classmate from geography class, Rory motioned for Brian to follow him. Brian stared at him with suspicion but followed nonetheless.

"I've something in my locker that you might find interesting," exclaimed O'Shea excitedly.

"If you've dragged me back in here to check out your porn collection, then you're wasting my time," warned Brian warily. Rory gave off a nervous laugh and continued up the hall, a step in front of Brian.

"Hey, O'Shea, how's your health insurance? You've pissed Buzz off good," cried out a voice from a circle of young men surrounding a biker magazine.

"Screw him," said Rory, but with little authority. A few seconds later, he stopped in front of a locker and directed a key into the lock. The door swung open and Rory removed a folded denim coat. Turning to Brian, he held it out for him to inspect. "It's been through the wash cycle twice—hot water. My mom mended it. It was torn along the seam so you can't even tell where it got ripped. I figured, it was the least I could do."

Brian just stared down at the slightly faded jacket, then took it from his classmate.

"I know it's faded a little from the hot water washings but, I mean, I had to get the piss stains out of it."

Brian remained silent, gazing down at his garment in disbelief. "You took it off the roof?" he asked.

"Yeah, I picked it up with a stick, 'cause of the piss and all, and put it in a plastic bag I had in my desk. God, it stunk. I washed it at home on Saturday when no one else was around. It's perfect now, though, no smell at all."

Brian was not outwardly responding to his gesture which began to make O'Shea a little nervous.

"Well, I just thought I'd get this back to you as quickly as I could. I'll see you in geography tomorrow—I guess." The boy turned away, closing his locker.

"Your name is Rory?"

"Yeah, Rory," answered the boy without turning.

"Thank you, Rory. You really didn't have to do all this—but thank you. I appreciate it."

There was a sincerity in Brian's voice. As he walked away and back to his own locker, Rory O'Shea's voice called out.

"Why don't you join some of us guys at lunch tomorrow?" Brian knew immediately that "some of us guys" meant Jerome Jefferson, Marc Cote, and a few, nameless-to-him, brainy types who he had seen O'Shea hanging out with.

"Let me think about it," Brian called back before turning the corner of the hallway.

It was just after six-thirty when Brian was called to the dinner table by his mother. He immediately made out the fare, tomato soup and grilled cheese sandwiches. Elizabeth led them in a short prayer of thanks. Mother and son customarily joined hands at the supper table and thanked the Lord for the food before them. Brian poured a generous quantity of oysterette crackers from the box and into his soup before opening the dinner conversation.

"Ma, thanks for making the soup with milk and not water. It makes a difference."

Elizabeth nodded. "Well, it's not like we can't afford a few extras, with my handsome son kicking in his fifteen dollars every week. It makes a difference."

"Oh, it seems I got some news to drop on you—and I'm wondering if you want the good news or the bad news first," he said.

His mother's expression turned serious instantly. "Oh dear. Are you okay? Give me the bad news first."

"Well, it seems I'm going to have to eat some crow this evening—practice a little humility," stated Brian while still gazing down into his soup.

"In front of me?" asked Elizabeth.

"Exactly."

"And what does this concern?" she asked, her serious expression already giving way to a smile. Brian pushed back his chair from the table, stepped back into his bedroom, then emerged with the denim jacket over his arm. Elizabeth gave a cry of delight.

"It was returned to me today at school. A guy at school picked it up, had it mended and cleaned, and gave it back after school. Wild, huh?"

He resumed eating, his eyes riveted on the food and the table before him while his mother looked on, waiting for her son to engage her in eye contact. A few seconds later, he did.

"Don't give me that look!" he exploded through half-subdued laughter. "I know what you're thinking! You're thinking I got it back because of you and your prayer to Saint Anthony last night," howled Brian in a good-natured roar.

"And what's your explanation?" asked his mother calmly.

"A certain Rory O'Shea found the coat and returned it to me. No big deal, Ma."

"And you don't find this slightly coincidental?" she asked.

"In all honesty? In all honesty—I find it friggin' spooky. As I see it, my voodoo woman mother says a prayer to a saint who's probably been dead for eight hundred years, asking for his help, and twelve hours later I've got my coat back—mended and cleaned. Friggin' spooky! All I can come up with is that you must have a private line to heaven, and when you call, I don't care if the pope's on another line, the Big Guy puts him on hold and takes your call."

Elizabeth just smiled back at her son, a certain contented expression beaming from her face.

Brian had his denim coat back on the following morning. His arrival at Southside caused no comment. Few, if anyone, remembered that this very coat had hung limply from the flagpole only a few days earlier, awash in the urine of Buzz, Ben, and friends. Through the week he continued to keep a low profile in class, particularly around members of the football team. The week's only incident saw Buzz calling out to him at dismissal on Thursday, making a reference to the recent history of his jacket in the presence of Gloria Sims.

On that occasion, Brian did turn around and cast his tormentor a strange, ominous smile.

On Friday in the cafeteria, Brian approached Rory O'Shea and asked for his phone number, indicating that he would like the opportunity of discussing something with him over the weekend. They exchanged numbers with the understanding that Brian would call on Sunday evening.

On Sunday night Brian asked his mother for a measure of privacy and pulled the black phone into his bedroom and to the end of its long cord. With the door closed, he dialed Rory and proceeded to inform him of a plan of action—directed toward the jocks involved in his attack, most particularly, Buzz Devereux—the following week. He explained that anything he did would need the assistance of another, and the most logical individual was Rory. He emphasized and reemphasized that Rory should not feel pressured into doing anything. As Brian explained his plan, Rory was quick to ask questions and voice concerns over various aspects of what appeared to be a brazen scheme.

With the strategy completely laid out and the risks honestly discussed, Brian pledged his uncompromising protection and support to his smaller, less physical, classmate. The thirty-minute conversation ended with a promise from Rory to give Brian a definitive answer the following day. Brian construed this response as a probable rejection.

Monday morning, during the first full week in March, Brian approached his locker, noticing a small piece of yellow paper taped to the door. His first thought was that Maggie May was playing some sort of silly joke. However, reaching the locker, he pulled down the paper and unfolded it. It read: "I'm in," and was signed by Rory. With no visible reaction, he stuffed the note in his pocket and made his way to homeroom.

Tuesday morning found Rory waiting for Brian in front of homeroom. He fidgeted just outside the doorway, afraid Mr. Sullivan would ask him to explain his presence. As Brian approached, Rory ran up to him, pulling him aside.

"I'd like to run something by you. You know, about Thursday night." Brian nodded, beckoning his friend to go on. "I was talking to Jerry Jefferson—you know—about everything. . . ."

Brian's eyes widened in anger and he clutched at Rory's shirt. "You told who? Didn't I say this was between us—and only us?" He spoke in a low voice, visibly holding back his exasperation.

"Brian, listen to me. You're going to need an alibi if you pull this off. Jerry can put you somewhere else. Believe me, you can trust him. He's a good guy. You've got to trust me on this. It's his idea and it's a good one. He'll put you in the library on Thursday night, when all the shit is coming down. What could be better than pulling this thing off—and then completely getting away with it?"

Brian released his hand from Rory's sleeve as he ran this new twist over in his head.

"All he expects from you is the same understanding that we have. You know, support your friends."

Brian made no attempt to mask his displeasure with the revelation that a third person was now privy to his plan. He expressed neither his acceptance to the plan's modification nor rejection. For the remainder of the week, through Thursday's dismissal, he spoke socially to no one at Southside High School outside of Maggie May Keogh.

XI

LATE IN THE AFTERNOON ON THURSDAY, Rory O'Shea waited at the side of the street near the liquor store parking lot. The sidewalk and roadway were illuminated by street lights and by the headlights of passing cars. In the parking lot before him was the orange colored, 1970 Corvette owned by Buzz Devereux, a gift from his prosperous father on his sixteenth birthday. Rory kept his eyes focused on the front door of the store where Buzz held a part-time job. On information provided by Brian, he was told to expect Buzz to emerge from the building and make his way to the car shortly after six o'clock. It would then be his task to walk somewhere in the football player's line of sight. Once spotted, Rory was to flee toward the alleyway and back of the building, presumably with the speedy halfback giving chase. It would be imperative to not let the able athlete haul him down before reaching the darkness afforded by the alleyway. He was frightened by the prospect of what might be about to unfold. He had it on Brian Kelly's word, whom he hardly knew, that he would be waiting somewhere near the rear of the building.

The clock struck six o'clock in the main floor hallway of the Manchester City Library while Jerome Jefferson sat at a table a short distance away in the fiction section. The studious young man turned his head to the window behind him, wondering if the particulars of a certain scheme were in the process of unfolding less than a mile away on the other side of the Merrimack River. Suddenly, and for the first time, he was apprehensive about what might occur. He had completed his homework nearly an hour earlier, and now was simply placing himself at this location for purposes of an alibi for an almost complete stranger, Brian Kelly.

Brian pulled a black ski mask from the pocket of a shredded fatigue jacket and made his way from Montgomery Street to Notre Dame Avenue and down the hill to the rear of the strip mall. At home, a note placed on the kitchen table advised his mother that he would be studying at the library on this evening but should return home no later than seven-thirty. His plan was to arrive at the back of the mall at approximately five minutes to six, then wait in the shadows for the arrival of Rory, hopefully with Buzz in hot pursuit. Realistically, he knew that there was less than a fifty-fifty chance of his plan coming off, at least on this first try. There were many things that potentially could go wrong. However, he did have faith that Rory would keep his promise and serve as bait for Devereux. In addition to the ski mask, Brian wore a shabby pair of sweat pants together with a pair of leather sparring gloves, the latter to avoid any possible injury to his hands. He had decided to take Rory O'Shea's advice and use Jerome Jefferson's alibi in the event he was questioned following this altercation, and bruised, swollen hands would go a long way to erase the believability of Jefferson's testimony.

As he waited by the side of the building, Brian caught himself growing impatient with anticipation. This told him that he was mentally prepared to confront his arch enemy.

Rory heard the sound of bells from a nearby church indicating the stroke of six o'clock. During the next few minutes he continuously shifted his eyes from the door of the liquor store to his watch, monitoring the passage of time against the possible appearance of the handsome, popular teenager who had single-handedly made his sophomore year at Southside High School miserable. His watch read four minutes past six when he lifted his eyes to see Buzz Devereux standing in the doorway of the store, bidding a young female good-bye.

Rory began the slow, calculated walk obliquely toward Buzz's Corvette as Devereux adjusted the hood of his coat and made his way across the parking lot. It was Rory's task to pass behind the Corvette within sight of Buzz, and after assuring himself that he had been recognized, sprint toward the back of the building and the steep hillside behind it. He carefully kept himself from sight until the moment he was sure he could not be overtaken beneath the parking lot's bright lights. He had just passed behind the orange Vette when he perceived a sudden head movement by

Devereux, indicating that he had been recognized. Immediately, Rory dashed toward the side of the building. From the corner of his eye he saw Buzz stop, then take off in a direct line toward him. Rory, saddled with two schoolbooks, made for the dark shadows beside and beyond the side of the mall building.

"You're fuckin' dead, you little maggot!" hollered Devereux excitedly while rapidly closing the distance between the two.

By the time Rory reached the shadows beside the building he could clearly hear the football player's panting from the burst of speed. Then, for a brief second, Rory considered the possibility that he might be alone, practically within arm's reach, of this menacing young man. His trepidation was short-lived.

At the precise moment Rory reached the base of the hill there came the sound of a confrontation. The sound was followed by a series of sickening thuds, producing groans and eventually the crash of overturned garbage cans. Rory stopped in his tracks and turned back, but was unable to make out even images from within the unlit rear of the building. Another series of horrifying thuds was followed by moaning and whimpering.

The confrontation was mercifully over, having lasted no more than thirty seconds. Rory had not heard so much as a single word spoken or called out during the entire unnerving event. He turned from the site of the confrontation, climbed the hill to Notre Dame Avenue, and legged his way home.

At six-thirty Jerome Jefferson closed his science book, collected his things, and made his way to the front door of the library. Fifteen minutes earlier he had checked out a book as evidence of his presence on this day. He descended the stairs of the Manchester City Library, praying that the planned showdown had not taken place. Less than an hour later, thanks to a phone call from Rory O'Shea, he would learn that this was not the case.

It was just past seven o'clock when Brian pushed in the door to the apartment and hastily made his way toward his bedroom. His progress was interrupted by his mother who appeared in the doorway to the living room.

"How was your time at the library? And—what on earth are you doing dressed like that?"

Brian had hoped to barricade himself in the bedroom before detection but now was faced with the prospect of an explanation. "It went fine Ma, just fine," he blurted out.

"All right now, what's with the old clothes and all? Are you keeping something from me, son? No malarkey, now. You know I can't stand a liar. What's this all about?"

"Please, Ma, don't. I think it's best if I keep this little matter to myself. I'm okay and it's not like I was out stealing or something. I just had to take care of something tonight and it was best if I wasn't recognized doing it."

Elizabeth Kelly closed her eyes, seemingly in thought or prayer. "You're a good boy, that I know. I trust you and I know you wouldn't be out there up to no good."

Brian crossed the room and embraced his mother. "Please, Ma, relax. Everything's all taken care of and things will be fine starting tomorrow. Now, I don't want you losing any sleep an' worrying all night. Everything is fine."

Brian guided his mother back into the living room to the corner of the couch where a book rested under a reading lamp. The matter of Brian's clothing and his whereabouts for the last two hours was dropped.

On the Friday morning following the carefully planned altercation, Brian, Rory O'Shea, and Jerome Jefferson avoided contact with each other. Arriving in first period English, Brian never so much as glanced at Jerome, a student he had had no interaction with during his first four months at Southside. During third period, Brian was summoned without explanation to the administrative office. There he was confronted with the accusation that he had attacked a fellow student, Yvan Devereux, requiring him to receive medical attention the night before and, in all probability, causing him to miss a number of school days. Brian claimed total ignorance of the attack, advising the authority that he had spent three or four hours at the library downtown, not leaving until a short time after six-thirty and arriving home just after seven o'clock. When asked about possible witnesses that might attest to his whereabouts the evening before, Brian stated that he was studying alone.

A short time after Brian was hauled off to the office of administration, Rory O'Shea was called from class. Once seated before a vice principal, he explained the circumstances from the prior evening as they related to him. It was then, for the first time, that school officials were made aware that Yvan Devereux was not out for an innocent stroll or running an errand for a sick friend on the evening in question. Rory explained, in perfect detail, the events leading up to the altercation. Emotionally, he told of running for his life from the charging football player after being spotted by him in the parking lot. Rory spoke of his terror the evening before, fully expecting a horrific beating at the hands of the popular high school athlete. The honor roll student indicated that his pursuer had been intercepted by someone behind the mall building but he had no knowledge of the individual's identity.

Brian was still being detained a full thirty minutes after Rory had been sent back to class when he offered his accusers a fragment of evidence to support his claim. "There may have been someone at the library who saw me and could vouch that I was there last night. The black kid in my English class. He might have seen me."

"Are you talking about Ben Turner?" asked the vice principal.

"No, not Turner. The other black kid. The little one."

"Jerome Jefferson, is that who you're referring to?" asked a deadly serious administrator.

"I guess it would have to be. It's not like we have that many blacks in the school," answered Brian, and with that, the call went out for Jerome Jefferson to report to the office.

Brian had sat isolated in a remote administration office for no more than ten minutes when he heard Jerome Jefferson being ushered into the adjoining room. He sat quietly as the vice principal and another male teacher inquired into Jerome's whereabouts the prior evening, and Jefferson told them that he had been downtown at the library from about three-thirty until just after six-thirty. They went on to ask him if he had seen anyone he knew from Southside during this three-hour period and Jefferson feigned confusion, then stated that he had sat alone the entire time.

"Okay, let me make this a little clearer," stated the teacher. "Did you happen to see Brian Kelly there last night?" he asked.

Brian strained his ears through a prolonged silence following the question until Jefferson finally responded to the point-blank inquiry.

"Yeah, as a matter of fact I did notice him there, sitting over in the corner."

"And at what time was this?"

"He was there quite a while because I remember him getting up and moving around some. And I do know he was still there when I left," Jefferson stated emphatically.

"And why is that, that you remember he was still there when you left?"

"Well, first of all, I think it was downtown, near the library, where he got beaten up a few weeks ago. I thought it was weird that he'd be back there, knowing what happened. And, I kinda thought that—well, maybe — "

"Maybe what?" asked the man conducting the questioning.

"Well, he seems to come from a poor family, you know, by the way he dresses; I was wondering if he had any place to go for supper, it being after six-thirty and all."

The last statement seemed to set the men to shuffling papers and, shortly after, Jefferson was dismissed and told to return to class. Brian sat in silence, in awe of the brilliant series of lies from the mouth of Jerome Jefferson. A few minutes passed, then the vice principal addressed Brian alone. He was told that this would not be the end of the matter but, for the time being, he was to return to his class schedule until further notice.

Brian sat alone during lunch as the word of the assault on Buzz Devereux spread through the student body in whispers and undertones. He reported to geography class to find Rory O'Shea seated at his old desk, to the right of Gloria Sims. The two young men glanced at each other as Brian strolled to his seat. On her arrival, Gloria was dumbfounded to see Rory seated at Buzz's desk.

"I'd get my ass out of that chair before Buzz gets here," she scoffed.

Rory responded with a wide grin. "Oh, I'll take my chances," he answered.

The young man seated to her left leaned over and whispered in her ear for about thirty seconds. Her eyes widened, then glassed over. She whirled around and flashed Brian a piercing look, her hatred for him at the moment on total display.

"Don't look at me, princess. I've been cleared by the powers that be in the main office. I was nowhere near the cowardly attack on Yvonne. I was at the library—you know—the scene of our dream date," said Brian mockingly.

"I hate you. I hate everything about you. You're a low life—
a Massachusetts low life. You look like a low life—you dress
like a low life—you are a low life," she bit out between gritted
teeth.

Miss Sadowski entered the room before Brian could muster
a response.

Back in homeroom at the close of the school day, Maggie
May told Brian that he was invited to the house the following
morning and that she expected a complete accounting of the
events surrounding him, Buzz Devereux, Rory O'Shea, and anyone else involved in the mysterious happenings on Thursday
night. On the way out of school, Brian hailed down Rory and
asked if the two could meet sometime the following week. He
also suggested that Jerome might be invited to an informal meeting, perhaps at someone's home. Rory offered his house as a
meeting place and proposed Monday evening after dinner. The
two promised to touch base with each other over the weekend
and Rory indicated he would try to convince Jerome to attend.

XII

AFTER GULPING DOWN HIS SUPPER on Monday evening Brian took off for Rory O'Shea's house, which turned out to be a handsome colonial on Coolidge Avenue, a mostly well-maintained street that followed a ridge, paralleling the west side of the Merrimack River. After knocking at the front door, he was greeted and sent to the basement by Mrs. O'Shea, a pleasant, heavyset woman with a plain round face, where Rory and Jerome were engrossed in a Ping-Pong game.

They had much to talk about. For one thing, Buzz still had not returned to school from the incident the week before. There was no shortage of stories making their way around the school about the attack on the football player. Among the rumors circulated were that Buzz had suffered both a broken jaw and nose and that he had spent the prior Thursday night at Notre Dame Hospital as a precaution for a possible concussion. On Monday, as they did the prior Friday, the three boys had kept their distance from one another at Southside. Brian ushered his two friends to the far corner of the basement game room, lowering his voice in the process.

"First of all, Jerome, may I say that you were damn brilliant last Friday when you were questioned. Damn brilliant." Jefferson flashed a smile, shrugging his shoulders.

"That crap about wondering if I was going to have any supper and all that night—goddamn brilliant. It made the whole thing sound so real! God, you almost had me in tears," joked Brian. "The reason I thought it might be a good idea if we all got together is that there could be some real shit ahead for us. I'm not so sure that these guys, you know, Buzz and Ben Turner and all, are going to just roll over after this. They're liable to be real pissed!"

"What do you think we can do, Brian?" asked Rory, some concern showing on his face.

"Well—what I see as the best course of action here is for the three of us to just band together. I mean really band together. Think of it as a matter of mutual protection and support. If someone jerks any one of us around, they jerk all of us around. We stand together—we fall together. If you're with me on this then from this day on I stand behind you—no one screws around with you without me getting involved. At the same time, you've got to stand with me. Do you know what I mean?" The two boys nodded their heads in agreement.

"Realistically though—Jerome and I can't fight anything like you. How much help can we be, really?" asked Rory.

"I just need to know that you guys'll be there. Plus, we'll find other guys to join us—smart guys like us—no jerks or clowns—smart guys. I want you guys to think about it—and let me know." Brian sat back in the lounger where he had positioned himself. His two new friends stared at him in silence, Jerome reaching down to take a swig from his root beer.

"I don't need any time to think it over. I'm in," stated Rory emphatically.

"You don't have to make up your mind now," cautioned Brian.

"Screw it, I'm in. All I got to think about is last Friday and taking my desk back from Buzz. That bastard humiliated me in front of a lot of kids I know. God damn it, it felt good sitting back at my desk, having Sims warn me—and me just sitting there grinning." The boy's eyes shifted to Jefferson, who was obviously thinking through the possibilities, and possible drawbacks, of the proposed alliance.

"I don't need any more time to think it through. I mean—if I don't join you guys then I'm out there alone. Screw that!"

"I want to make sure you guys know what I'm talking about here before you say you're in. I'm talking absolute loyalty to each other, not some half-ass pledge." Brian's tone was serious, putting his two companions on notice.

"What? Do you want us to sign something, you know, put it in writing?" asked Jerome.

"To be honest, I'm thinking about something a little stronger than that," answered Brian. Rory and Jerome glanced sideways at each other, catching a glimpse of concern on each other's faces. Then, Brian took an envelope from his coat pocket and removed a razor blade.

"If we're going to pledge loyalty to each other then it'll mean more if it's done in blood. Either of you two see a problem with that?" The two sat frozen in their chairs, speechless.

"How much blood are we talking about?" asked Rory tentatively.

"No big deal—I'm thinking we carve a cross on the top of our wrists, the three of us. We break the skin enough to leave a faint scar and draw some blood. Then we mix our blood, like the Indians used to, you know—like blood brothers. If you want, I'll go first."

He removed a lighter from his other pocket, struck a flame, and ran it under the razor blade. Following this step, intended to eradicate germs from the razor, he turned it to an angle and scraped the skin deep enough until blood could be seen surfacing along the break in the skin. Adding a second cut to complete the symbol of a cross, he passed the blade along to Jerome. Following a moment's hesitation, Jerome matched the mark left by Brian, utilizing the same scratching technique. When an insufficient amount of blood evidenced itself on his wrist, Jefferson bore down on a second pass, causing a small eruption and a crimson stream down onto his hand.

"Come quick, nurse, we've got a bleeder!" called out Brian through a burst of laughter.

"Shit!" called out Jefferson before passing the razor on to Rory.

"Not on the rug, Jerry," called out Rory, afraid he would stain the basement floor.

"Forget the rug, O'Shea—carve!" laughed Brian. Rory took a deep breath, bit his lip, and proceeded to make the two incisions.

With the blood of each teenager moist on the backs of their hands, they leaned forward across the card table and mingled their fluid of life, pledging mutual protection and support for each other—no matter what. When the ceremony was played out, Brian grew serious again. "You're a couple of bright guys. I don't think I have to remind you that we may be facing some real shit over the next few weeks. Don't forget—if one of us is struck at, we all are struck at! We react as one. And of absolute importance is the need to go out and recruit. We've got to add to our numbers. No assholes, just guys we can count on. Okay?" The two other boys nodded in agreement.

"Rory, do you think we can start meeting here every week, if we keep it down, I mean?" asked Brian.

"No problem. My folks have been bugging me for quite a while for being too much of a loner. They'll love the fact that I have a bunch of guys coming over. How about every Tuesday night around seven?" Brian and Jerome agreed and a meeting was set for the following week.

The three boys clowned around for the next hour as Rory and Jerome began to relax more in Brian's company. At approximately eight-thirty, the boys had put on their coats and were about to climb the basement stairs and head home when Brian grew serious again with his friends.

"Guys, I hope you feel as pumped up as I do right now. Think of it this way. When we came here tonight we were nothing but three jerk-offs with a lot of balls—considering what we pulled off last week. Three jerk-offs who had better watch their asses. But now, we're a six-armed, six-legged, four-hundred-and-fifty-pound monster. Do you understand? Mutual support and protection!" The three boys swung their arms around each other's shoulders. Nothing else had to be said. The gesture said it all. As they reached the front door, Jerome stopped in his tracks and addressed the others.

"You know, there's something I've never figured out. It's Ben Turner and how he puts me down and treats me like shit. You'd think I'd be the last one he'd screw around with. I've never done anything to him. I don't get it," confessed Jefferson.

Brian shook his head in disbelief. "Jefferson, you've got to be kidding. It's nothing personal—it's Ben covering his ass. He figures that if he treats the only other black kid in the school like dogshit, he's free to treat everyone else, except his rodent friends, like dogshit. As I see it, Ben has no problem being an absolute prick—but what he doesn't want to be seen as is a racist prick. Subsequently, you get treated worse than anyone else and Ben's home free," theorized Brian.

Jefferson stared up at him in silence before shaking his head and opening the door.

Jerome made a hasty retreat for home after clearing the O'Shea's front door while Brian loitered out front, seemingly interested in talking to his newfound comrade. However, it was Rory who broke a brief period of silence.

"Can I ask you something Brian? It's about the whole thing with Buzz and all."

"Fire away."

"After the whole thing at the library a few weeks back—I mean, why did you wait so long to do something—especially after all the shit you were taking in school?" Rory looked up, a puzzled expression blanketing his face.

"Self-preservation, my man, self-preservation. There was no way I could have held my own with Buzz, or any of them, with the way my ribs felt. I had to give myself time to mend. Hence, I had to take a lot of crap. It's that simple."

"Man, guy, the stories about Buzz. Is his jaw and nose really broken, do you think?"

"It's definitely possible. I mean, I didn't hold back."

"Damn, Brian, how do you do something like that to somebody, really?"

"Jesus, Rory, put yourself in my place! The guy beats the crap out of me, rubs my face in it in school, in front of everyone. He pisses all over my coat, he and the rest of those cockroaches— the coat my mother scrimped and saved to buy me for Christmas—and I end up wearing friggin' moth-eaten sweaters in its place, looking like dog shit in front of people—people like Keogh. Man, there's something friggin' wrong with me if I can't get myself up for a little revenge."

Rory studied Brian's eyes, then nodded his head.

"But I'm sure there's a little more when it comes to Buzz— and I'll admit it," Brian continued. "Doesn't it sometimes strike you as a little unfair? I'm mean, this bastard seems to have everything! His old man buys him a Corvette—a Corvette! He's the big jock who walks around like he owns the school. He seems to be able to have any friggin' girl he wants! He's got looks, and popularity, and money. Meanwhile, guys like me can't get most girls to give them a second look. I mean, man—how about a little justice in the world! So I guess that was sort of in the back of my head when I finally got—*Yvonne*—the other night. It's nothing I'm too friggin' proud of—but it was there."

"What's this shit about no girls giving you the time of day? Aren't you and friggin' Maggie May Keogh sort of, you know— friends?"

"Well, I'm working on it, buddy. But, I'll tell you, it's slow—friggin'—going," he called out in a laugh. Rory's face turned from amusement to concern.

"Uh, Brian, now don't take this the wrong way but, you have heard the stories about Keogh and being—possibly—knocked up?" He asked the question tentatively.

"Where'd you hear that?" responded Brian seriously.

"Listen, I'm only mentioning this because we're brothers—blood brothers—and, I mean, the story's all over the school."

"For how long?" quizzed Brian.

"I heard it late last week. Jesus, guy, don't take this the wrong way and turn on me."

"Of course not. Rory, of course not. It's just that Keogh's been totally honest with me, but it sounds like the cat's out of the bag. Probably that scumbag, Skip. No, it's good that we know if the story is out," reasoned Brian, out loud. Rory let out an audible shiver, reacting to the March night air and said good night. Brian lifted the collar on his jacket and headed back to Montgomery Street.

On Tuesday morning Brian walked with his arm loosely resting on Maggie May's shoulder as they both made their way to the far end of the school and Miss Royal's English class. He half expected her to say something about her dislike for public shows of affection but instead, she seemed oblivious to his gesture. He had just seated himself when the sound of Ben Turner's voice grew louder as he approached. He cleared the doorway, walking by way of the front of the room toward his chair. Purposely brushing over Jerome Jefferson's desk on the way by, he sent a couple of ballpoint pens and a stack of textbooks crashing to the floor.

"The kid's an accident waiting to happen," he blurted out to the amusement of some of those in the room. "Oh, Jerome, I forgot to ask yesterday. How did your romantic weekend with Miss Royal come off. Get much?" Turner drew big laughs from the usual subjects.

"It was okay. And how was your weekend with every homo in Provincetown?" responded the usually timid Jefferson. The class squealed with surprise and anticipation.

"What the fuck did you say to me?" spit out a startled Turner.

"You heard what I said, you muscle-bound pile of shit." There was an audible gasp from the assembled youths. Turner rose from his desk and started toward Jerome. Instantly, Brian jumped to his feet. "Jerome, I think an apology is in order here."

Jefferson gazed back at Brian in astonishment as Turner stopped in his tracks, looking back in Kelly's direction. "I mean, Jerome, you have just insulted the dignity of every manure pile and mound of excrement in the country, maybe even the world. Comparing excrement to Benjamin here, well, it's insulting to the entire fertilizer industry."

Turner did not respond to Brian's witticism, choosing instead to turn back to Jefferson. "Your ass is mine. Get it!" he threatened.

"Careful, Ben, it's a new world out there now. Jerome's got friends—lots of friends—and the West Side's got lots of alleyways—maybe one with your name on it."

Miss Royal entered the room at that moment and set things in motion, and away from the confrontation that was taking shape. When the atmosphere had returned to something resembling normalcy, Brian glanced over to see Maggie May staring at him thoughtfully. She had no way of knowing what had taken place the evening before in Rory O'Shea's basement. The evolving relationship with his two new friends would no doubt be a topic of conversation during his now perfunctory Saturday morning visit to the Keogh residence. Later the same week, the rumor was confirmed that Buzz Devereux had transferred across the city to Northern Catholic High.

Elizabeth Kelly was standing in the pantry washing the supper dishes Tuesday evening when a series of loud knocks shook the back door to the apartment. Drying her hands, she laid down the red and white towel and stepped across the kitchen to the back door. Releasing the lock, she swung it open to see two men standing before her. Each wore a serious face along with their knee-length overcoats. They introduced themselves as Sergeants Guerin and LaMothe and asked if they could come in and speak to Brian. Elizabeth hesitated momentarily, then stepped aside and guided the men to the kitchen table. Brian had overheard the brief conversation and was already standing in the doorway to his room.

"Ma, did you turn me in? You know, for taking those tags off of pillows that said, 'Do not remove under penalty of law.' Ma, I was only a kid." Brian made light of the circumstances that were already making his mother look terribly nervous.

"We'd like you to answer a few questions for us, son," stated Officer Guerin, the older of the two officers. He had a bulldog face set off by a ruddy complexion.

"Absolutely, go right ahead, sir. What's on your mind?" said Brian while offering his mother a reassuring smile.

"Well, as you might suspect, we're here to follow up on the matter of the attack on Mr. Devereux last week. Mr. Devereux has stated that you were definitely the individual who jumped him behind the mall building last Thursday night."

"Well, he's wrong. I've been over this whole thing with the people at school. I was at the library on the other side of town that night. I walked home from there without even going near the building."

"He's identified you, son."

"Then its gotta be someone who looks something like me—'cause it wasn't me," he argued. Brian had a good idea what the two policemen were trying to force out of him. There was no way Buzz could have identified him with his ski mask on. They were hoping to catch him at an unguarded moment when he might question the validity of the identification. He knew it was imperative for him to feign that he had no knowledge of the details of the attack.

"Admit it, son, you wanted to get revenge for a little scuffle a few weeks back and this was your chance. It's understandable."

"Officers, in all honesty, I wish it had been me, but it wasn't."

"Gentlemen, I think my son has been more than forthright with you. But now, if you don't mind, I'd like him to get back to his homework and I'd like to get my dishes done. So, if you don't have anything more than this boy's clouded recollection of the whole ugly matter, then I'd appreciate it if you'd leave now," stated Elizabeth, quietly, but firmly.

The policemen got up and made their way toward the door.

"Can anyone confirm you were at the library on the night of the attack?" asked Guerin.

"As it turns out, someone did see me there. His name's Jerome Jefferson and you could get his phone number and all from the people at Southside, I'm sure."

LaMothe scribbled down the name on a small pad of white paper, stuffed it in his coat, and the two men descended the stairway and made their way back out into the cold March air.

When Elizabeth was satisfied that the two cops were tucked back into their car and on their way out of the neighborhood, she left the front window and walked back to her son, who by now was back in his room at his desk. "Son, you know I love you dearly and would do anything for you, but I don't want to be put in a position to have to lie for you ever again. Is that clear?" Brian lowered his head and answered almost under his breath. "You know how I feel about liars, so you can imagine what I'm feeling like about myself after that little episode." Elizabeth shuffled over to her son and gave him a peck on the cheek. "No more."

"I'm sorry, Ma, I'm really sorry. It won't happen again—I promise," he answered apologetically.

XIII

ELIZABETH ROSE FROM BED early enough on Saturday morning to spend some time with her son before his long walk out to Bedford. Brian passed on her offer of porridge but did join her in a cup of tea. His mother prepared the tea while he washed and dressed for his weekly visit with the Keogh's.

"This Mary Margaret must be quite the little dish for you to haul yourself out of bed every Saturday and walk out to Bedford," she observed.

"It's Maggie May, not Mary Margaret, Ma. And she is worth it. And how about you? What is it? Dinner and a movie with old man Giroux? I couldn't be happier. There's something very reassuring knowing your mother, your beautiful and charming mother, is out with a man that she's capable of beating to within an inch of his life. No worrying about any funny business going on and not having to watch the clock if it starts getting late. Yes, I'm very happy with this arrangement."

"Keep your voice down, Brian. What if the poor man overheard you?" she warned.

Brian responded with a hearty laugh and kissed his mother while pulling on his denim jacket.

To Brian, the walk to Bedford and Ministerial Road had seemed to grow increasingly shorter as the weeks progressed. He successfully hitched a ride on Boynton Street that brought him to Bedford's town center by twenty minutes past eight. This had him at the Keogh's door by half past the hour. The barking Funnel forewarned Mrs. Keogh that her regular Saturday morning guest had arrived. The pretty, middle-aged woman ushered

Brian inside, all the while subduing her overprotective, yet harmless, dog.

"Little Miss High and Mighty is still upstairs in bed. Please feel free to go knock on her door, Brian." He gave a grin and bolted up the stairs to Maggie's bedroom. He applied three raps on the white door and waited for a response.

"Who is it?" cried out a voice from beneath a pillow.

"Your handsome Irish friend and confidant."

"Did you bring me anything?" she asked in a brattish tone of voice.

"Ahhh—I've got a couple of gift certificates to Howdy's," he answered faintheartedly.

"Oh God, I'm going to puke," she countered.

"Can I come in?"

"May I come in, you mean. Jesus, Kelly, your Lowell upbringing is showing," wisecracked Maggie May.

"May I come in?" repeated Brian.

"I'm practically naked, which rules out letting Irish perverts in my room," she snapped back.

"Shall I wait downstairs, Maggie May?"

"No, Kelly, you can come in," she called out lightheartedly.

Brian pushed open the door to find his friend under the covers with the exception of her head. Her hair was wild and tumbling over her face, which he found extremely sensual. "Practically naked, huh?" he scoffed as he made his way to the window, seating himself on the sill.

"Yes, no doubt the way you envision me in all of your depraved male fantasies."

Brian burst out laughing, shaking his head at the girl's shameless, verbal jousting. "There is positively no one else like you, Keogh. You are the most exciting, beautiful, and unpredictable girl in the world." The statement caused her to pause for a moment, staring wistfully at the young man who had, in a remarkably short time, crafted an incredibly personal relationship with her.

"I'm glad someone in this town can see me for what I am. As a reward for recognizing me for the goddess that I am, I am going to let you stay in the room as I come out from under the covers. Brian, this is what you've been dreaming about for such a long, long time."

"I can't tell if you're serious or not," he answered, cynical yet intrigued.

Maggie May stepped out onto the floor behind the bedspread, which was still pulled up to her chin. She lifted her left hand high above her head, leaving only her right hand to hold up bedspread. "Behold your goddess," she proclaimed, and released her grip on the bedding, allowing it to fall into a pile at her feet.

Brian gasped in mock excitement. "My goddess—in Doctor Denton pajamas no less!"

"Think of me as your little Lolita, Kelly," she said.

Mrs. Keogh's voice rang out from the stairway landing, calling the two to breakfast. Funnel, his tail wagging at the first sight of his mistress, greeted them in the kitchen. Following a breakfast of blueberry pancakes, Brian and Maggie May took the dog for a walk into the village, discussing more serious matters away from the house. The mid-March sun was beginning to bring down the piles of plowed snow that bordered the road, causing pools of water to develop in depressions and low lying areas.

"I've started to show, the baby I mean," admitted Maggie May wistfully.

"Well, I haven't seen any sign of it, Keogh, so you can't be showing too much."

She grew more serious as they walked down the road toward the Bedford Library building. "Brian, I want you to be straight with me, okay? Is the word out at school yet, about me and the baby?"

He hesitated, looking upward into the bare, leafless tree branches that creaked with the rush of the wind above their heads. "Yeah, kid, I'm afraid it is," he answered apologetically. He glanced down at his friend as her eyes began filling with tears. She turned herself to him, burying her face into his chest to shield everyone but Brian Kelly from this vulnerable side of her. Seconds later she was sobbing uncontrollably, propped up by the boy who only months before was a total stranger.

"It'll be okay, Keogh. We'll get through this whole thing a lot easier than you think," he said, trying to comfort her.

"Will you still be around when I'm fat?" she asked.

"That's a given, Keogh. The question is, will I still be around after you're no longer fat and every male slug for a hundred miles is beating down your door? Will you still be there for me?"

"I can't believe you can even ask that question!" she exploded, already recovering from her teary breakdown. Turning around, she started back toward her house. "You know, I thought people were acting funny around me last week, but I kept telling myself I was just imagining it."

Brian jogged up behind her, placing his hands on her shoulders. "That was a short walk," he commented.

"I'm suddenly not in the mood," she snapped back. "You haven't told me yet. What, don't you trust me?" Maggie May asked, suddenly coy.

He lifted his right hand and began rubbing the base of her neck. "Tell you what, Keogh?"

"If you were the one who jumped Buzz Devereux."

"The people at Southside have concluded that it couldn't have been me. Why can't everyone else?"

"That's not a denial, Kelly, it's a statement. You're being evasive with me. I thought we were friends—and friends trust each other."

Brian remained silent while continuing to rub the girl's neck. "If you must know, it was me," he uttered.

"Well, I advise you to keep your mouth shut around my parents. They're friends with the Devereux. My father plays golf with Buzz's dad."

They reached the house minutes later, retreating to Maggie May's room immediately. Brian collapsed into the white wicker chair in the corner while his hostess, perched at the foot of her bed, began removing her wet sneakers.

"Have you started thinking of names for the baby yet?" asked Brian.

"If it's a girl, I'm naming her either Victoria or Jenny."

"Jenny's cute. Victoria sounds like some dried-up old prune sitting on her porch wolfing down bonbons," joked Brian. "And if it's a boy?"

"Reginald, my maternal grandfather's name. Reginald B. Keogh," she stated proudly.

Brian lifted his eyes from the floor. "What's the 'B' for?"

"Barnstead—a proud English name," she snapped.

He shrugged and dropped his glance back to the floor in front of him. A second later, a wet, cotton stocking flew from the bottom of the bed, striking him above the right eye before dropping onto his lap.

"Don't be so gullible, Kelly! The 'B' is for Brian. Are you satisfied?"

"Hey, never mind throwing your stinky socks at me!"

"I'll have you know my stockings don't stink! And incidentally—for your information—I don't have any kind of a body odor problem. None! You can ask my mother," she boasted.

"So, let me get this straight. Your mother can vouch for you not having any odor problems, so, like she walks around the house all day sniffing after you? Some moms wash clothes, and cook, and iron, but Bedford moms sniff," commented Brian through laughter.

"I don't smell," repeated Maggie May.

"You're really going to give your son the middle name Brian?"

"It's not a bad name, and it goes well with Reginald," she answered. Brian smiled. "Now, I want you to say I don't smell, right now," she ordered.

"Then why is there deodorant sitting on your bureau?"

Maggie May reached down for her other stocking and hurled it across the room at him. Now they were both laughing, she in spite of herself and Brian from the joy of sharing time with this girl who was so special to him.

"It means a lot to me, you know," he uttered after the laughter subsided. She looked up from the bed for clarification. "The Reginald-Brian thing—it means a lot."

XIV

THE TUESDAY NIGHT MEETING of the group formed by Brian, Rory, and Jerome saw two new recruits, a long-haired, serious kid named Marc Cote, and Chris Riggas, a tall, exceedingly thin lad who appeared quite nervous. Both were acquaintances of Rory's who had overheard Rory and Jerome discussing the alliance with Brian Kelly during lunch in the cafeteria. After the introductions, it was Brian who addressed the two potential members.

"All we're doing here is putting a fraternity together, of sorts, to cover each other's asses. If you're here because you think that tomorrow you can go into school and start pushing people around, well, forget it. I'm not going to spend my time backing up a bunch of arrogant punks out picking fights. We're forming to keep jerks from busting our balls—mutual protection and support. But, if you decide to come in, and we unanimously decide to take you in, you better not ever turn your back on one of your blood brothers. If you do—you're screwed. Am I being clear here?" he asked the two boys seated down the table from him.

They nodded their heads in unison.

Brian went on to explain the initiation ritual, how their blood would have to be mixed with one member of the present group's blood. Following a brief question and answer period, Brian, Jerome and Rory indicated that both boys were acceptable. Cote and Riggas, along with Brian's razor blade, retreated to the corner of the basement where they carved the required crosses on the back of their wrists. Both chose Rory as their direct brother within the group which required him to break the skin along his scar and mix blood with the two boys. With the ceremony drawing to a close, Brian spoke out.

133

"Cote, Rory did tell you that that friggin' mop of hair of yours will have to go, right?"

The boy's mouth dropped open in surprise and horror, causing Brian to burst out laughing.

"Just jerking you around," he piped in, clearly pleased to have added two more bodies to their ranks.

"I'm wondering if anyone besides me has seen today's paper. There's an article on the sports page that a few of us should find amusing," said Jefferson. Brian gestured him to continue. "Let me read a couple of paragraphs and see if anyone can keep down their dinners," said Jerome. "Ahem—*The football program at Northern Catholic High pulled off a major recruitment when they coaxed Yvan 'Buzz' Devereux to transfer over from Southside after two outstanding seasons on the city's west side. "We're not only getting an outstanding football player, we're getting a great, great kid," said head football coach Danny Shanahan of Northern Catholic.*—Brian sends Buzz across town in a body bag, jaw wired from ear to ear, and they get credit for recruiting him. Oh, and Rory, I bet you didn't know that Buzz wasn't just a great kid—he was a great—great kid!" Jefferson needled.

"Well, I'm going to sleep better knowing I had nothing to do with driving that rich, pretty boy prick across town," added Brian sarcastically.

The next hour was spent playing Ping-Pong and darts as well as discussing various girls at Southside. On more than one occasion Brian noticed the two recruits looking at their wounds. As the boys collected their coats and gulped down the last of the refreshments served by Mrs. O'Shea, Brian spoke again to the group.

"Remember guys, we're not just a bunch of jerks putting our time in at Southside anymore. We are all part of a ten-armed, ten-legged, seven-hundred-and-twenty-pound monster! We act as one!" The boys roared their support in unison. "And don't forget—more recruits," called out Brian to conclude the meeting.

Elizabeth Kelly was startled Thursday evening by a series of knocks on the back door. She turned from the kitchen table and opened the door. Standing before her was a smallish young man with a winsome grin.

"Is Brian ready?" he asked while surveying the tall woman in the doorway.

"So, I finally get to put a face with the name. You're Rory O'Shea, I imagine." The woman stepped aside and directed the well-groomed teenager into the kitchen as Brian emerged from his bedroom.

"I see you've met her royal highness," needled Brian, throwing on his denim jacket and making a ducking gesture as he passed his mother, as though reflexive from years of parental beatings. It was a long-running joke, started years before at family and church gatherings.

"Oh, and Rory's supposed to believe that I'm beating on a big fella like you." Brian retreated from the doorway long enough to plant a kiss on the top of Elizabeth's head. "I don't want any shenanigans from you two tonight," ordered the woman from her kitchen chair. "It's a school night, so no late-night stuff."

The duo rumbled down the stairs to Montgomery Street where a shiny, green, 1972 Ford Pinto waited at the curb.

"So am I first to go on a joy ride with my buddy?" asked Brian, while depositing himself in the passenger seat.

"Lots more than a joy ride buddy—lots more. We'll have to swing by Howdy's first, though." Rory made his way toward the Granite Street Bridge and downtown while Brian merely took in the sensation of being taxied around by his friend.

"We're going to be meeting up with someone famous—well, famous around here," teased Rory.

"Let me guess, O'Shea. You've got Raquel Welch and Faye Dunaway waiting on us at the library but we're going to have to bring them burgers—is that it?"

"Reality, man! Reality!" laughed Rory as he hopped out of the car and ran inside Howdy's. Two minutes later the excited teenager trotted out of the burger joint, a bag in one hand. Jumping back behind the wheel, he sped out of the parking lot onto Elm Street and headed south.

"Where the frig are we going?" hollered Brian over the sound of the car engine.

"We're going out to Merrimack. 'FEA's studios are out in the boonies and that's where we're going. We're going to see Johnny Tripp. I spoke to him last night and he said it would be okay to come out to visit, but that I should bring something for him to eat. You do listen to him, don't you?"

Brian nodded his head yes, his mouth open in mock surprise. Rory guided the Pinto onto Route 3 and began the five-mile trip to the rock radio station. The two young men bantered for a few minutes, trading inconsequential observations as they continued to build the foundation of the friendship that was rapidly developing. Eventually, Rory's voice grew mildly serious.

"Can I ask you something a little personal, Brian, with the understanding that it stays between you and me?" Brian looked over at his friend and nodded. "Well, I was wondering, do you ever picture yourself with girls, you know, in your head, and do really—really wild things? I mean—pretty bad things—like really dirty things." Rory's eyes shifted across the front seat to Brian, who seemed to be reflecting on the question.

"Like what?" he asked.

"Oh man, I'm afraid to go into it. I'm afraid you'll think I'm sick or something. Shit, I mean, since freshman year I've been having thoughts about some of the girls in school that are pretty far out. Jesus, I start wondering if I'm some kind of pervert or something. And if I'm going to confession or something—oh man, what do you say?"

This comment brought a burst of laughter from Brian. "Anything but the truth—the whole truth—and nothing but the truth," wisecracked Brian. But he knew that his friend was really searching for reassurance of some kind. "Listen, Rory, I can't come out and tell you about what I think about—but trust me, the things I do with, and to, Keogh, in my head—and some of the things that go through my mind when I'm with her—it's whacked out— really way out."

His friend answered with a nervous laugh.

The car had traveled south on old Route 3 for about five minutes when the Pinto took an abrupt right onto a driveway that led up to a huge, star-shaped tower. Beneath it, a small, austere building sat in the middle of an open field. It was almost eight o'clock when Rory led his friend up the walkway to the studios of WFEA. Brian felt a twinge of anxiety as Rory pounded on the heavy, red, wooden door. A few seconds passed before a youngish-looking fellow in bleached jeans raced to the door.

"Rory and company—enter," cried out the man before turning and jogging back to the control room. The boys followed just behind, with Brian taking in the surroundings with keen interest. The office area, newsroom, and production studio were all in darkness, leaving the main studio ablaze in light at the center of the building. The disc jockey was already back sitting at the control panel when his visitors pushed open the sound-insulated door and shuffled into the studio. To Brian, Johnny Tripp looked younger than he had imagined, having pictured this outrageously aggressive jock to approximate the ages of the radio people he had seen back in Lowell. Tripp raised his hand to the two, signaling them not to speak as he flicked open the microphone switch.

"Jim Morrison and the Doors and 'Light My Fire'—short version, for Goffstown, by request. Now I know you Goffstown losers asked for the long version but—forget it! You're unworthy! Do you understand? John deems you unworthy!" He pressed a button and there ensued the sound of a woman hellishly screaming. "Besides, too many stinkin' pizza joint and speed shop commercials to fit in the long version." With that said, Tripp popped on a speed shop spot and turned to his guests.

"I see a bag in your hand, O'Shea. You're a good man." Rory placed the bag of burgers down on the counter. The disc jockey glanced up at Brian. "So, you got a name? O'Shea here's showing his usual lack of manners and just letting you stand here like a nonentity."

"Oh, I'm sorry. Johnny, this is Brian Kelly—a friend of mine from Southside."

"Oh great, O'Shea and now Kelly. What the hell—suddenly I have a hit squad from the Irish Republican Army in my studio!" joked the talkative radio man.

"How come you look familiar?" answered Brian as the boys stood over the jock, now downing his first burger.

"I think I know why," blurted out Rory. "Johnny, you screw around sometime about how you come from Lowell, Mass, and so's Brian here."

"That's a relief. When Kelly here starts in with the look familiar crap, it almost sounds like I've got a fruitcake in the building— and a Lowell one at that—the worst kind. Whereabouts in Lowell you from?" asked the vaguely familiar adult.

"Centerville, Read Street," answered Brian.

"You're shittin' me! I'm from First Street. We must have been almost neighbors." Abruptly Tripp raised his hand for silence and directed his attention back to the microphone. He rattled out the weather forecast and a plug for the morning show before starting the next record, a dedication of love to a girl in

Pinardville. "Which end of Read Street? The St. Michael's end or the Hell's Angels end?" he asked Brian in the next breath.

"The Hell's Angel's End."

"What's this about Hell's Angels?" asked a curious Rory.

Brian turned to his friend. "The New England Chapter of the Hell's Angels lives on Second Street in Lowell, in our neighborhood," replied Brian.

"Hey, you guys want to be part of my next bit?" The boys broke out in smiles, giving a thumbs up.

"Just go along with whatever I say during the next break. This is radio, gentlemen—I can do anything!" crowed the jock as he cued his next record and set up a series of tape cartridges. Once again he raised his hand as the sound of Creedence Clearwater Revival faded through the studio. "It's seven-fifty-two on WFEA and you, the unworthy, are with Johnny Tripp—and—two guests, witnesses to what's about to happen. Here with me are Rory O'Shea and Brian Kelly, both of Manchester's Southside High, the school where old teachers go to die." A flip of his finger, and the sexy sound of a woman laughing filled the studio. "Now, unbeknownst to the bottom feeders that constitute my audience, there has been a beautiful, naked woman sitting silently in the corner of my studio since seven o'clock with an envelope addressed to me taped to her forehead. Gentlemen, is this indeed a fact?" he asked, half turning to Rory and Brian.

"Yes, it is," they answered in unison.

"She's very pretty, John," added Brian timidly.

"Never mind the ad libbing, Kelly. If I want any more crap from you I'll squeeze your head," wisecracked the disc jockey. "I will now reach over and remove the envelope from the lovely lady's forehead. The envelope, addressed to me, is in WFEA afternoon man and my roommate, Lee Gordon's, handwriting." Tripp proceeded to tear a piece of paper directly in front of the microphone, creating the sound of an envelope being ripped open. "Hmmm, a message addressed to me. It reads: Dear John—I have kissed her two, sweet lips—and left her *beeee-hind* for you!" The sound of a dozen drunken men at a strip joint emanated from another one of Tripp's toys, then he followed the punch line of his bit with a WFEA jingle and the Rolling Stones' "Jumpin' Jack Flash."

Over the next hour the three males bonded as they exchanged stories about the only three subjects that meant anything to them:

girls, music, and sports, in that specific order. The disc jockey inquired into the dateability of either of the boys' sisters, then displayed mock rage on hearing that neither had sisters between the ages of thirteen and fifty-nine. When the deejay's workload became more and more hectic in the next hour, Brian and Rory began the process of excusing themselves. The jock thanked both boys for coming by and for the burgers before Brian spoke up.

"Johnny, I wonder if I could ask you for a small favor?" Tripp motioned him to go ahead. "A girl I know is having her sixteenth birthday on Friday night. Could you wish her a happy birthday for me?"

"What's her name?"

"Maggie May Keogh, from Bedford."

"All right—the kid from Lowell's moving up in the world," joked the deejay as he jotted down the information. "I know you keep her amused, but I feel Kelly's being used," sang out Tripp to the tune of the Rod Stewart classic. Rory roared with delight.

"You won't forget?" cautioned Brian.

"What do I look like?—some brain-dead Read Street homo?"

"No, you're definitely a First Street homo," retorted Brian, causing Tripp to jump to his feet in mock anger, and Brian and Rory to scurry back to the front door and out into the parking area.

The two boys excitedly relived their on-air experience with the popular rock jock all the way back to the west side of Manchester. The next day at school, they were approached by a number of classmates who had heard them on WFEA the night before. True to his word, Tripp dedicated "Maggie May" by Rod Stewart to Maggie May Keogh, "the original Bedford heartbreaker," on Friday night, her sixteenth birthday.

XV

ON THE SATURDAY MORNING FOLLOWING Margaret Keogh's birthday, Brian dragged himself out of bed early, as was his custom, and set out for Bedford. However, on this morning he carried a shopping bag. Its contents caused it to flair out on the sides, making the journey to the suburbs somewhat more difficult than on other occasions. Also, hitchhiking proved to be fruitless, probably due to the unknown contents of Brian's shopping bag and the impression it made on potential good Samaritans. So, it was after nine when Brian puffed his way up to the Keogh front door and rang the bell. He was greeted by Mrs. Keogh and invited in.

"I'm afraid her royal highness is in one of her moods this morning and refuses to come down," she apologized. Brian turned and looked to the stairway in the next room. "Brian, I don't want you to have walked all the way out here for nothing. Why don't you join Howard and me for breakfast?"

Brian could not disguise his disappointment. "I brought her a birthday present. Would you mind if I took it upstairs to her?"

Mrs. Keogh responded with a embarrassed smile. "Not at all, dear, but keep in mind, she's in a dreadful mood."

He nodded, took an exaggerated deep breath, and headed up the stairs. Reaching the door, he wasted no time in engaging Maggie May. "Hey, you inside. The boy you've been fantasizing about all night is just outside your door."

"Screw you! Go away!" she answered in a no-nonsense tone.

"Come on, Keogh, I walked all the way out here from Montgomery Street."

"And you can walk all the way back. No one asked you to come."

"I brought you a birthday present."

"Slide it under the door and leave."

"It won't fit under the door and besides, if I leave it alone it might get in trouble and start tearing up the house."

"Please tell me you weren't stupid enough to get me an animal. I already have a dog, you moron."

"But Maggie May, you can never have enough animals in the house," answered Brian, now pretending to hold back the tears.

"God, if you knew how stupid you sounded you wouldn't do that," she warned through light, reluctant laughter.

"Can I come in?" he asked meekly.

"*May* I come in?" she corrected.

"May I come in?"

"All right, come on in and bring me my present," she relented.

He turned the handle of the door and pushed himself in, catching sight of Maggie May sitting defiantly in the middle of her bed. She motioned for him to present her with the birthday gift. He placed the shopping bag on the bed in front of her and made his way to his now familiar chair in the corner. She wasted no time removing his gift from the bag. Lifting it out, she stared at it at arm's length. It was a large, white gorilla. The oversized stuffed animal had extended arms and stood approximately two feet high. Following a few moments of silence she pulled it up against her body, cuddling it.

"With all the daydreaming you must do about me, Keogh, I thought it'd be nice if you had something to cuddle in my absence. So, happy birthday."

She looked up from the gorilla and wrinkled her nose. "You know Kelly, there is a resemblance. I'll give you that."

"Your mother said you're a little stinker this morning."

The now sixteen-year-old did not lift her eyes from the animal. "I heard my dedication on 'FEA last night. Bedford heartbreaker, huh? Tell me Brian—am I breaking your heart?"

"Not even close, Keogh—not even close. Now, are you going to join me downstairs for breakfast, 'cause your parents are ready to have breakfast without you—with me."

A slightly devious look came over Maggie May's face. "You think they like you, but do you know what they call you when you're not around?" she asked. At her question, Brian's eyes riveted on hers, a serious expression replacing his amused one. "My father refers to you as the mackerel snapper, you being a Catholic and all. And my mother, well, she has her own name for us. She calls us Lady and the Tramp."

Brian's facial expression transformed from serious to wounded. If it was her intent to strike a nerve, she had scored a direct hit. All at once, Brian seemed quite uncomfortable and ill at ease. Maggie May jumped up from the bed and raced across the room to him.

"They love you, Brian, they really do. I'm sorry. I don't know why I said that. Sometimes I lash out at people and it's always the people that I care for. Please forgive me," she pleaded. He sat in silence momentarily, seemingly poring over what she had told him. She leaned forward and kissed him on the lips. His hand reached behind the back of her head, holding the kiss in place and at length. Finally, she pulled back from him.

"Am I forgiven?"

"Of course," he replied.

"And not a word about me and my big mouth downstairs?" Brian nodded his agreement and rose from the chair. Maggie May reached for his hand and began leading him to the door.

"Then let's go downstairs and show my parents the new man in my life—Jake the gorilla."

XVI

THE MONTH OF APRIL ROLLED IN with Brian Kelly's life definitely on the rise while Maggie May was feeling increased social pressure and stress associated with her "condition."

Brian, Rory, and Jerome were taking in recruits weekly and their numbers were swelling. On successive weeks in April, The Band, as they now called themselves, had brought in Emile "Percy" Provencher and Bruce Sloan, two young men who had experienced their fair share of taunting at Southside since their freshman year. Offsetting these two were Pete Mars and Rich D'Eredita, a couple of ruggedly built young men whom Brian saw as welcome additions to the crew. By the last week of the month, the assorted coffee and card tables could barely provide adequate space for the Tuesday night meeting.

By this time Brian Kelly had been unanimously elected president by voice vote. It was he who sat at the end of the table for each meeting, flanked by Rory O'Shea and Jerome Jefferson. The last Tuesday of the month had two more sophomores vying for membership in The Band. They were led in by Rory and Jerome and were explained the rules, expectations, and conditions. Rory's prospect, a good-looking lad named Jack Polidoro, nodded his head in agreement as Brian ran down the details and consequences of membership. Finally, and without questions, the youth took the razor from Brian and headed to the corner to carve his acceptance in blood. The second candidate, Nathan Roth, was recruited by Jerome. He stopped short of full acceptance of the terms explained by Brian and beckoned to Jerome to intervene.

"There's a little problem here with the blood oath," explained Jerome to the assembly.

"Problem?" asked Brian.

"Well, Nate has asked me if this part of the ceremony might be modified. Being Jewish, you can see how this would create a problem—the religious thing and all. We're wondering if the blood thing with the cross can just be done symbolically in Nate's case. Nate's in full agreement with the conditions and all, it's just the cross thing." The room was silent as, one by one, each member glanced up at Brian for direction.

"I don't see where we have a problem here," stated Brian, his eyes shifting between Jerome and Nathan Roth. "The blood oath is absolutely critical, so that stays. I think we can make an exception here for Mr. Roth, and allow him to waive on the symbol of the cross. However, this is serious, and I, for one, don't want some friggin' peace symbol, or shit like that, put in its place. To me, the answer is obvious."

Silently, Roth looked to Jerome, then to Brian. "Star of David?" he asked tentatively.

Brian smiled and nodded yes.

Roth stepped forward and took a razor blade from Jerome. "Have a tourniquet ready, this means a fuckin' lot of cutting," snapped Roth as he proceeded to the back of the room. Polidoro, the night's other candidate, was already through marking himself and chose Rory to complete the ceremony.

During the next few minutes Band members exchanged stories on how their membership in the group was changing things for them at Southside. On no less than a half-dozen occasions, the sound of gasps, curses, and half-muted cries filtered through the conversation from the back of the cellar where Roth gingerly carved out his ritualistic symbol. A full fifteen minutes after retreating to the back of the room, Nathan Roth returned to the table and displayed the back of his wrist to the charter members.

"Holy shit! Where'd you get the chain saw, Roth?" kidded Brian, a reference to the bloody, gory mess that constituted the back of the newest member's hand. A hand went up at the table and Brian motioned Marc Cote to speak.

"You know, it just hit me that we may be running amuck of the law in some way by using religious symbols as part of our ritual. The supreme court's been pretty clear on how they feel about religion in schools and we're a school club—or fraternity— or something. Maybe we should be looking for some other kind of symbol?" suggested Cote.

"Oh, thanks, Cote. In case you haven't noticed, I'm already down a pint—and now you start worrying about the goddamn supreme court!" snapped Roth.

The members, almost in unison, turned back to their president.

"I make a motion that, if challenged on the religious symbol thing, we tell the supreme court to kiss our collective asses," stated Brian. The motion was seconded by Jefferson.

"All in favor, say aye," instructed Brian. The room erupted with ayes. "Any no's?" Silence. "End of matter," said Brian emphatically.

"I could use a few paper towels," Roth added while dabbing at himself with a single tissue. Rory ran upstairs laughing while the other members gathered around Roth, the soon-to-be thirteenth member of The Band.

"Quick, Jerry, draw some blood before we lose this one on the operating table. He's a bleeder," heckled Brian to a round of laughter.

"No, wait! Don't I get to pick my blood partner?" asked the bespectacled Roth.

"That's right," answered Jerome.

"Then I want Kelly," stated Nathan emphatically.

Brian nodded and promptly opened up a corner of his existing symbol of the cross and the two mingled their blood. Following Rory's return from upstairs, the meeting resumed with clowning and story telling. At the close of the meeting, Brian broke in with his usual statement of unity.

"And don't forget, all of you here are part of something special now—mutual protection and support. We're The Band, and we're a twenty-six armed, twenty-six legged, friggin' one-ton monster!" The statement was greeted with a roar of support as they made their way toward the bulkhead.

"Oh, and one more thing—more recruits!" shouted Brian.

XVII

B Y MAY, THE RAPID TURNOVER OF HELP at Howdy Beefburgers had left Brian high up in seniority among the non-supervisory employees. Using this as leverage, he had asked for, and received, Mother's Day off. By taking driver education, he had earned his New Hampshire driver's license and had already begun to save money toward the purchase of a car, but realization of this dream was still many months away so he approached Mr. Giroux and asked if he would rent him his Buick for two or three hours on Sunday, Mother's Day. His landlord dismissed the idea of taking payment for the use of the car and told Brian to come downstairs late Sunday morning and pick up the keys. So it was, on Mother's Day morning of 1973, Elizabeth Kelly returned home from mass to find her son already up with a shabbily wrapped gift sitting on the kitchen table.

"I would rather of had you with me at mass than any present you could give me," she lamented.

"Ma, as soon as they stop changing everything every other week, then I'll be back."

"That's no excuse, baby boy, and you know it," she chastised, then immediately dropped the subject and focused on her gift. Her face was beaming as she removed the wrapping paper and found a decorative box of exotic soaps and fragrances, laid out painstakingly. In the center of the box was a cassette tape of Tony Bennett. As his mother focused on the cassette at the center of the layout, Brian broke out into song:

"I wanna be around to pick up the pieces
When somebody breaks your heart,
Some somebody twice as smart as I . . ."

With tears welling up, Elizabeth reached out and embraced her son.

"Don't cry, Ma, there is nobody twice as smart as I," he joked, while she continued to hold him against her. "I want you to know that you have me all to yourself for the entire day. What's more, I've a surprise for you later today. You've mentioned more than once that you've heard people at work talking about going to Verani's. Well, I want you to know that your devoted son will be escorting you to the very same Verani's for your afternoon meal. I have acquired the use of Mr. Giroux's car for that purpose. And so, Mrs. Kelly, your son Brian, of Southside High School honor roll fame, will be transporting you downtown on this day. Happy Mother's Day, Ma."

Mother and son spent the morning sharing a light breakfast and sipping on tea. The two also sat with Mr. Giroux until well after noon, at which time the elderly gentleman handed his car keys over to Brian. Minutes later, mother and son were making their way to the small garage on the alleyway at the rear of the house and the oversized Buick. From there, Brian motored them across the Notre Dame Bridge to Verani's Restaurant on downtown Elm Street.

Elizabeth and Brian were promptly seated in a bluish, vinyl-covered booth a short distance from the front door. Brian impressed on his mother that cost and money were of no concern, that she should order whatever on the menu that struck her fancy. Following an extended period during which her eyes darted back and forth between descriptions and prices, she decided.

"I'll have the spaghetti and meatballs dinner, along with a glass of red wine," she finally announced to the waitress.

"Ma, you can have anything on the menu. You don't have to order the spaghetti and meatballs. I think I can afford a little more than two forty-five. What about the boneless breast of chicken a la parmigiana?" he suggested, trying to pronounce the words with a semblance of Italian flair.

"I'm not having my son pay four dollars and forty-five cents on dinner for me. I don't care how good it may be. It's my Mother's Day dinner and I think I can order what I please," she responded.

Brian backed off immediately and duplicated her order, aside from the wine. As they waited for their meals, the Kellys relived some of the events that had shaped their lives in New Hampshire over the preceding seven months. Reminiscing naturally brought up stories and memories from Lowell. For the first time, Elizabeth admitted missing her Massachusetts roots, but was quick to add that, in retrospect, the move north to New Hampshire had proven to be a wise one, at least economically. The open, frank conversation continued beyond the arrival of the main course.

As if by calculation, his mother shifted the conversation to Maggie May Keogh.

"You know, hon, for a girl who seems to have my son's unwavering attention and devotion, I know hide nor hair of your little Bedford friend."

Brian went on chewing his food, his eyes searching the wall behind his mother for a response. "Not much to say Ma—she's gorgeous—and smart—and I'm incredibly happy every minute I'm with her."

"How come I've never met her? She's got to be in Manchester sometime? Why doesn't she come by the house and say hello?"

Brian debated as to how much information he should share with his mother about Maggie May's condition. "She just turned sixteen, Ma. She just began taking driving lessons a week ago."

"Don't take this the wrong way, baby boy, but when your little Maggie May calls for you and you're not home, she's always so short with me. I suppose it could be because she's a little nervous talking with grown-ups, but it comes off as being a little snooty."

He stopped eating for a moment, looking his mother deeply in the eyes. "Ma, Maggie May's got a lot of things going on in her life," he stated seriously.

"Such as?" asked Elizabeth.

"Ma, Maggie May's pregnant."

Elizabeth's eyes opened wide and she let her fork drop back onto her plate. Momentarily, the prospect that her son might be involved in this serious situation registered on her face.

"Ma, I don't have anything to do with the pregnancy. I'm just her friend," explained Brian quickly.

"Brian, please tell me you'll be very careful around this girl. I'm sure she's a nice girl and all, but a young female in her predicament, they might be tempted to do anything," she cautioned.

"Trust me, Ma, there's nothing like that going on. Her family's helping her with things and all—everything's fine."

The Kellys resumed their meal and the name of Maggie May Keogh was not reintroduced.

Minutes later, Brian looked up from his plate to see Ben Turner round a corner and make his way toward the exit to the restaurant. However, in the next instant, he noticed Turner was not alone, but was in the company of a heavyset, black woman, in all likelihood his mother. A smiling Ben's demeanor changed instantly when he noticed Brian Kelly seated almost directly in his path.

"Do you see someone you know?" asked Elizabeth, seeing her son's attention pulled from the table. The Turners drew closer as Brian stared in silence. Elizabeth turned toward the approaching mother and son, conscious that Brian was distracted. Ben's mother, now also aware of the uneasiness in her son, established eye contact with Elizabeth. As the two reached the Kellys' table, the impeccably dressed woman came to a complete stop and smiled down on the Kellys.

"A couple of pretty nice young men we have here—taking their mothers to dinner and all," commented Elizabeth, addressing Ben's mother directly. She shifted her eyes to Brian and gestured for him to speak.

"Ma, this is Ben Turner, a friend of mine from Southside," said Brian unenthusiastically.

Ben's mother gave him a visible nudge. "Mom, this is Brian Kelly—we have English class together."

"And I guess that leaves us to introduce ourselves. I'm sorry, I'm Loretta Turner," she said, extending her hand to Elizabeth.

"Elizabeth Kelly, mother of the young man of so few words across the table." The two women smiled and shook hands while their sons remained frozen, taking in this incredibly unlikely development.

"Mrs. Turner, why don't you and Ben join us," said Elizabeth, already pulling over in the booth.

"Oh, we couldn't impose—and besides, we've been here for over an hour, and I think we've both overeaten as it is. More importantly, I've just had a wonderful meal with my son, just the two of us, and, Mrs. Kelly, I wouldn't want to deprive you of the same. But, thank you so much for the invitation."

Brian breathed an inward sigh of relief at Mrs. Turner's decline. The two women wished each other a happy Mother's Day, and the Turners made for the front door. The Kellys sat in silence while enjoying their meals. Finally, Brian looked up to see his mother staring across the table at him. She wore a contented expression.

"You know, you teenagers are all alike—so embarrassed to be seen in public with your parents. I guess that's not exactly a cool thing to do," she needled, bringing a short burst of laughter from Brian.

"Ben looked like he wanted to crawl under the table."

"Oh, and you didn't?" countered his mother.

Brian threw up his hands, gesturing that this was not the case.

This leisurely Mother's Day dinner at Verani's Restaurant would be the one and only time the Kellys would dine out together in Manchester. The frank, earnest, yet warm conversation between mother and son on this day would prove to be a treasured memory that Brian Kelly would carry with him into adult life.

XVIII

THE WEEK FOLLOWING MOTHER'S DAY proved to be a good one for Brian. On Monday morning, Brian was hurriedly throwing a few personal belongings in "Eileen," when someone called out to him from down the hall.

"Kelly!" echoed a familiar voice. He turned to see Ben Turner halted in the hallway. "You got a pretty nice mom," he shouted.

"We came away with the same impression of your mom. Not you, Turner—just your mom," said Brian. The tall, husky athlete smiled, shrugged his shoulders knowingly, and turned into his homeroom.

While the two would never evolve into lifelong friends, the hostility that seemed to habitually be present when they were in the same room was largely gone.

The Band's weekly meeting proved to be a lively one. Marc Cote brought a situation to the attention of the group that caused members, particularly Brian, to become enraged. Cote reported that he had heard that one of their members, "Percy" Provencher, was being harassed by a recent transfer to the school. On hearing this, Brian asked Provencher to comment on the report.

"There's a guy in my homeroom who's been a little sarcastic around me. I didn't think that much about it, really. I've heard worse," explained the bookish sophomore. The explanation did not play well with Brian.

"You're one of us for a reason—you don't take shit from anyone. In case it hasn't dawned on you, when you take shit it reflects on all of us. We all look like jerk-offs! Who is this prick who's bothering you? What's his name?" asked Brian in a roar.

"His name is Duke. I'm not even sure what his last name is. I think it's Porter."

"Okay, here's how we'll handle this. Roth, Mars and D'Eredita, you go with Provencher, who'll point out this Duke clown. Roth, you do all the talking—tell this jerk-off that if Provencher reports any more shit from him, then he suffers the consequences. Feel free to tell him what they are—the consequences I mean. Don't make them too hideous because if the moron screws up, we follow through on your threat. D'Eredita and Mars, just stare this bastard down—scare the shit out of him but don't say a word. Roth does all the talking. Roth, I want this guy's pantyliner filled to capacity by the time you're done with him. Everybody clear on this?" asked Brian.

The three boys nodded their heads, grins all around. Provencher looked nervous but accepted Brian's orders. Everyone in the room listened and watched, the realization striking them that it was not all talk anymore, The Band was growing teeth. Near the end of this week's meeting, Rory dropped something of a bombshell on the gathering.

"I wanted to take a second to tell everyone that next week we will have at least one new recruit putting their name in for membership. Dolores Drapeau asked me if I would bring her to the next meeting so she could ask to be a member—and I said yes." There was more than one surprised expression on the faces of the attendees.

"Are you shittin' me?" cried out Roth from across the table.

"She asked, and as far as I know there's no rule against girls being members," Rory said defensively.

"O'Shea, what is it with you and the collection of losers you bring in here every week?" he asked sarcastically.

"Who the hell are you calling a loser?" asked Mars.

"Okay, okay—maybe not all losers. As a matter of fact, Mr. President, may I have my last statement stricken from the record?" he called out laughingly to Brian.

"I would, if we had a record," Brian responded.

"Anyway, all kidding aside. Rory, tell her to save her breath 'cause there's no way I'm voting a broad into The Band. And all votes have to be unanimous. Nothing personal—just no broads," said Roth, sounding deadly serious.

If the week had any negative properties it was in the disposition of Maggie May who appeared mired in depression. All attempts by Brian to jolt her out of her blue mood were met with deadpan responses. However, when the dismissal bell rang on Friday afternoon, he nonetheless eagerly volunteered to walk her to the family car. On a sunny Friday, Southside was emptying out even more rapidly than usual, leaving the teenagers a deserted stairwell as they reached the front of the building. On the top stairwell landing, he ushered her up against the wall.

"You know I hate seeing you mope around."

"I'm sorry, Brian, I can't help it."

"You know, Keogh, there's been something on my mind for a while now and this may be a good time to get it out." She lifted her blue eyes upward from an expressionless gaze. "This probably isn't gonna come as any big surprise, I mean, you've been around me so much since last Christmas and all. And—well, you can read me like a book anyway," he said, his eyes now shifted down onto the floor.

"I take it this conversation is leading somewhere, right?" she countered.

"Anyway, in case you haven't figured it out already—I'm madly in love with you." Her eyes widened as she took in his state of total vulnerability.

"I know you are. I guess I've always known," she said slowly, almost sadly. They stood speechless until Maggie May broke from him and headed down the stairs.

"My mother's waiting," she called out without turning back.

Brian's walk downtown to Howdy's was consumed with his thoughts of the abbreviated conversation with Maggie May and her totally unenthusiastic reply. He had hoped for some form of spirited response. In his wildest, most optimistic dreams he envisioned her saying that his love was not in vain, that she, too, had feelings for him—romantic feelings. But there had been nothing in her response to give him even a glimmer of hope that she harbored any intimate feelings for him. Consumed by depression, he made the long walk to work. He arrived at three, listless and withdrawn. Three hours into his shift, the manager observed signs that his employee was not well. Taking Brian's temperature, he found him running in excess of one hundred and one degrees and immediately assigned an employee to bring him home. Brian left without argument, and was bedridden before seven.

Elizabeth took on the role of nurse for her son, filling him with liquids like ginger ale and cold water. Brian complained of general weakness along with mild nausea, headache and an accompanying fever. He did, however, drag himself out of bed while his mother ventured to the store for ginger ale and called the Keogh residence the next morning, informing Mrs. Keogh of his condition. The kindly woman told him to heed his mother and get himself healthy as soon as possible. He had his mother call Howdy Beefburgers later, advising them of his inability to go to work this day. During the day, Brian drifted in and out of sleep through the morning and into the early afternoon. He was remotely conscious of the phone ringing on two or three occasions. Finally, his mother appeared at the side of his bed.

"I've got a certain little pest from Bedford waiting on the phone in the other room. Do you feel up to taking her call?" she asked impatiently.

"Maggie May's on the phone?"

"Yes, and this is her third call. You'd think it were life or death the way she's pushing me to get you to the phone."

"Tell her I'll be right there," he mumbled, then began pulling himself up out of bed. He shuffled across the room, threw on his bathrobe, and made his way to the phone in the kitchen. "Hello," he uttered listlessly.

"Brian, I hope you're all right. I'm sorry if I'm bothering you. Your mother sounded a little put out with me. I guess I was a little scared you were mad at me and that's why you didn't come to the house today."

"No Keogh, I'm really sick and just couldn't make it. I'm not going to work, either."

"Brian, I guess it has something to do with what you said yesterday and how I acted. I can't bear to have you mad at me and I want you to know that. I don't know what I'd do if I lost you right now. It's hard for me to express myself, but you have to know there's no one else. You mean more to me than any other boy I know. You have to believe me."

"I believe you, Keogh, I really do. Don't worry, nothing has changed. I'm not going anywhere. But, it's nice to hear you so concerned about what I do and how I feel. I must be getting to you, Keogh."

"You know, Kelly, in some sick, bizarre way you seem to be. So we're back to where we were yesterday?" she asked.

"No, Keogh, we're not. I think I love you the tiniest bit more today than I did yesterday," he said in a whisper. The statement prompted a giggle from her end of the line.

"I'm glad," she answered. Brian then wrapped up the call, explaining his weakened condition, but promised to make it back to school on Monday. As he hung up the phone Elizabeth appeared in the living room doorway.

"Be careful with that one, hon. I can see and hear how you feel about her, but be careful with that one," cautioned his mother.

It took the entire weekend to bring Brian's health back. Nursed and pampered by his mother, he began regaining his strength in the late afternoon on Sunday and was back in school the following morning. Maggie May brought him a package of Chuckles candies, presenting it to him first thing in the morning. She instructed him to eat them as early as possible, for the energy.

"Open your mouth and close your eyes," he instructed just before the opening bell of the school day.

"I hope you've learned your lesson on this count," she warned, then followed his instructions. He carefully placed the black candy from the package in her mouth. Both started the day knowing the agitation from the week before was behind them.

It had been an uneventful Tuesday in May at Southside as Brian negotiated his way between classes. The school year was winding down and the whole school day routine had grown sluggish, owing to the increasingly warm days. Following a Tuna Wiggle lunch, a Southside specialty, Brian's mind was already projected ahead to the evening's meeting of The Band. Dolores Drapeau would presumably be there to pitch her candidacy for acceptance into the group. He saw little chance for the girl's admittance based on statements from the prior week's meeting, particularly those from Roth. Some of the members had expressed their own concerns about Dolores, citing that the admission of a female, particularly this female, would reduce the group to laughing stock. Dolores Drapeau was, in all honesty, one of the least popular girls in the sophomore class. Not particularly attractive and possessing a prominent speech impediment, she was prone to speak too loudly at times. Add to this a boyish swagger and an aptitude for putting her foot in her mouth, and you had the profile of a young woman who remained in a social vacuum throughout her freshman and sophomore years. Brian envisioned a quick and painful rejection for the girl.

Turning a corridor corner, Brian's attention was removed from thoughts of the forthcoming meeting as an explosion of activity erupted in the hallway ahead. As he grew nearer to the shouting and students began parting, he caught sight of a disheveled, angry Gloria Sims. She appeared to be soaking wet, her blonde hair matted against her scalp and mascara running down her face in a clownish fashion. As Brian and Gloria drew nearer their eyes met.

"I know you're behind this, Kelly, you fucker," spat out the usually elegant Miss Sims.

"Princess, I don't think I've ever seen you looking lovelier. Don't be so hard on yourself," admonished an amused Brian.

"You're dead, you prick," she called out, reaching the stairwell and disappearing from sight.

At precisely the stroke of seven that evening, Brian called the meeting of The Band to order. He called upon Roth to report on the whole matter of Provencher and his problems with the student named Duke.

"When I was done threatening that douchebag, I swear to God, there was a wet spot in the hallway that they'll never dry out," bragged Roth to everyone's amusement. Following the brief report and a round of congratulations from other members, Brian announced that Dolores Drapeau's name would now be introduced for induction. Dolores would not be present, which transferred responsibility for entering her name to Brian. He stood up and addressed the twelve other members in a serious voice.

"Guys, Dolores can't be here tonight to plead her case but has asked me to do it for her." The statement drew more than one groan from the assembly. Brian asked for quiet. "Just after lunch today Dolores walked into the ladies' room at school and filled a bucket full of water. She then took the bucket and searched the stalls for an old friend of mine—and she found her. Dolores found Gloria Sims sitting on the throne behind a locked door. When Gloria wouldn't open the door, Dolores pulled a stepladder over to the stall, climbed the ladder, and drenched her. Not only that, she told Sims that it was payback for setting me up at the library last winter and for tormenting Maggie May Keogh in school about being pregnant and all. Needless to say, Dolores's been suspended for the rest of the week and grounded at home for God knows how long. She snuck a call to my house this afternoon to fill me in on this stuff. I had already seen Sims in the hallway this afternoon and, man, she was pissed."

A chorus of cheers broke out in the basement which Brian laughingly gestured to a halt. "Guys, I know some of you have a real problem with Dolores trying to get in, and she can be a pain in the ass sometimes, but I'm asking you, as a favor to me, to vote her in."

"Come on, Bri, we don't need broads in the group. It'll fuck things up," injected Roth.

"Guys, having a female in the group gives us some flexibility as Dolores just proved. It can get us in places to do things we can't do now. And besides, she's made some real enemies today—for my sake. I'm asking you to let her in for my sake, if for nothing else."

"Come on, Bri, how about me? I'm on record as against this whole Drapeau shit." Half the heads in the room swung around to Roth. He dropped his head, staring down at his glass of Kool-Aid on the table. The room sat in silence for a full thirty seconds. "Can I bum a butt from someone? I have this sudden urge to go outside and work on my lung cancer." Mars punched him out a smoke from his pack and slid it and a book of matches across the table.

"Thanks, buddy," added Brian as Roth closed the door behind him. Less than a minute later, Dolores Drapeau became the fourteenth member of The Band, pending her blood initiation. Following Roth's return the members discussed the matter of curtailment of meetings over the summer vacation. After a lengthy discussion it was unanimously agreed to suspend Tuesday meetings from mid-June to early September. This left Brian to bring the meeting to a close with his usual bravado.

"Remember, more recruits—mutual protection and support— and no shit from anyone. Because you are all part of a twenty-eight armed, twenty-eight legged monster!"

"With two titties!" cried out Roth to a roar of laughter.

XIX

WITH THE ARRIVAL OF SUMMER came expanded hours for Brian at Howdy's. Members of The Band exchanged phone numbers at their final meeting of the school year and penciled in September 11th for their next meeting. Dolores Drapeau, owing to her grounding, was only able to attend the final meeting of the spring where she was greeted with restrained acknowledgment. Burdened by his full-time hours, Brian was limited to seeing Maggie May twice a week, Saturday morning and all day Tuesday, his only day off. He delivered on his promise of jobs for members, getting Jefferson, Roth, and Riggas positions at Howdy Beefburgers. Various friendships blossomed between members of The Band but none stronger than Brian's with Rory. So strong was the developing bond between the two that Brian, on Rory's insistence, had use of his friend's Pinto on Tuesdays. This allowed Brian to escort Maggie May out of Bedford and get her away from the house on Ministerial Road, which had evolved into her prison during the summer. He had brought her to the beach in Maine, to Pinkham Notch in the White Mountains, and to a number of movies and art shows. However, late in August and in her final month of pregnancy, she gave him his most difficult task. She made a request of her friend that, on the surface, seemed impossible.

"I want to go back to the ocean one more time before the baby comes, but I don't want people staring at me in my condition." This was the challenge presented to Brian on a Saturday morning, leaving him three short days to come up with a solution. On Monday morning he called the Keogh house, telling Maggie May to prepare a picnic lunch for them for the following day. She consented, but warned him that she did not want to be gawked at in public.

The green Pinto rolled to a stop in the Keogh driveway early Tuesday morning. Brian hopped from the car and bounded to the front door. He relieved his friend of the weight of her picnic basket and escorted her to the passenger seat of the car. With passenger and cargo safely on board, he backed the vehicle out onto the road and pointed machinery and passengers due east for the Atlantic.

"Don't look at me, I'm fat and ugly," she complained.

"Not true, you're fat and gorgeous."

"Where are we going? Remember, no crowds and no people."

"We're going back to Maine."

"Brian, I told you no people and Parsons Beach means people," referring to the beach in Kennebunk where he had brought her the previous month.

"We're not going to Parsons. Trust me Keogh. No people—but we're going to the ocean."

She glared across the front seat while he harbored thoughts of how incredibly beautiful she looked on this day. Reaching Portsmouth, they cruised across the drawbridge and began snaking their way up Route 1.

"You are so gorgeous today," he confessed, breaking minutes of complete silence.

"You're drunk or blind," she responded, although seemingly amused by his statement. After a pleasant drive northward they left Route 1 and followed signs to Long Sands Beach, an extended beachfront collaring the Atlantic in York, Maine.

"Brian, there are thousands of people here," she barked while gazing to her right out the window.

"Where are we going?"

"Somewhere Johnny Tripp told me about."

"So you don't know where we're going? You're taking directions from some idiot disc jockey, sight unseen? I don't want people to see me looking like this," she shouted.

"Johnny says there's a place up here where you can sit and look at the ocean in complete privacy."

"I don't like this," she muttered, folding her arms and pouting.

Eventually the beach gave way to a rocky outcropping where Brian turned right onto a roadway that followed an arm of land that jutted eastward into the Atlantic Ocean. He drove the car up an incline, his attention focused on the right side of the road.

"Watch for an empty lot somewhere up here on the right," he directed. Maggie May turned to the side window, her arms remaining folded in defiance. The Pinto crawled along the road as both took in a series of weathered beach houses perched along an abrupt cliff.

"I think your radio friend is full of shit," she snapped in her next breath.

"There!" trumpeted Brian, pointing to a grassy lot tucked behind a small cluster of vegetation. Pulling the car ahead and off the road, he yanked on the emergency brake and pushed open his door. After running around the car, he opened the passenger door, ushering his Maggie May out onto the flattened grass. She stepped away from the car and walked toward the edge of the lot. In silence she moved to within two feet of the precipitous drop down to the rocks and crashing surf below. The two teenagers looked out over the open ocean, water uninterrupted to the horizon. From this vantage point, the glistening ocean seemed a flat, blue table below and before them. The sun was peeking between a layer of puffy, white clouds. To their right and far below, the beach was dotted with bathers and sun worshippers. Maggie May turned back to Brian.

"I want to stay here all day," she said, but in the form of a request. He had already begun unloading the picnic basket and oversized thermos. "You did it, Kelly, you really did it. I love this place." He smiled while lying down the blanket atop the trampled grass. Maggie May's face abruptly showed a sign of concern. "What if someone comes and tries to throw us out?"

"Well, if it's the owner, we reason with him and point out your delicate condition. We play our trump card. If it's anyone but the owner, then, let's just say you'll have to step over my lifeless body as they lead you out."

"Will you pull it closer to the edge?" she asked, pointing down at the blanket. Brian responded, dragging it to within inches of the steep decline. He assisted her as she lowered herself onto the blanket, her feet extended just over the lip of the cliff. He removed her shoes before positioning himself directly behind her, allowing her to lean back against him and comfortably take in the dramatic vista. He began playing with her light brown hair while intermittently planting pecks on her shoulders and sides of her face.

"Will you bring me back here after the baby's born?"

"I'll bring you here for as long as humanly possible. I'm just not sure how long that'll be," he responded.

"What do you mean?"

"I mean, you know, it's only a matter of time till some rich guy buys this piece of land and puts a house on it. A month from now, maybe a year from now. It's gonna happen," he uttered thoughtfully.

"Look at the sailboat out there!" she called out, pointing southeastward toward the horizon. His eyes, trained on her, did not respond. "The baby's kicking. Do you want to feel?" He laughed and slid his hand onto her extended belly. She looked back at him wistfully.

"I love you madly, Keogh, and every day it gets worse."

"I'm glad," she responded, then looked back out to sea.

"So, Keogh, answer me this. If I bought this land and built you a house on it, would you marry me?" he laughed.

"No, but I'd definitely sleep with you," she said through a charming burst of giggles. He was now rubbing the back of her neck, causing her to give off periodic sounds of contentment. When she complained of not bringing a pillow, he retreated to the Pinto and returned with a jacket, which he folded and placed on the blanket. Easing her body down onto the cushioned ground, Brian then gently brought her head down to rest on the folded jacket.

"In a lot of ways, you're too good for me," she admitted in an offhanded manner. The statement brought no response from him. "You know, as the baby's coming gets closer, I'm really starting to get scared. I'm not real brave anyway, and then I start thinking about something going wrong. It happens!"

"Keogh, everthing is going to be fine. I'll have you know my mother's already praying for you and the baby every day. And, believe me, God listens to her. Ma's really holy and He listens to her. Me, on the other hand, He pretty much ignores. But her— whoa!"

"I know it's going to hurt, really hurt," she stated pensively.

"Keogh, if there was any way I could take the pain and bullshit for you, I would, in an instant."

"Trust me, Kelly, if there was any way of passing the labor pains and shit on to you, I would take you up on your offer in an instant. You can bet your ass on that!"

They both broke out in laughter before Brian brought himself over her, his arms suspending his weight. Her laughter was interrupted when his mouth came down on hers and their lips joined. She lay motionless beneath him, his lips drawing upon hers, unifying them. Maggie May had neither the strength nor inclination to resist this male who so coveted her attention and approval. So it was, for the first time, she returned in full the affection that, until now, she had only been the recipient of.

Pulling back from the intimate entanglement, Brian was pleased to see a look of numbed passion drawn across Maggie May's face.

Following a gradual cooling down period they slowly began preparing the food and drink, picnicking just before noon as a sea breeze off the Atlantic picked up. Maggie May brought out a deck of cards from her handbag and relieved Brian of nearly three dollars over a two-hour period as they intermittently dined and gambled. He was kept amused by his companion's mood swings as she periodically broke out in frustrated tirades followed by bursts of laughter, depending on her success at poker. At the conclusion of the final game, she dropped her winnings on the blanket before them and slowly, painstakingly counted each coin, out loud, under Brian's nose.

By mid-afternoon, a bank of clouds appeared on the southern horizon and pushed its way northward toward the spit of land where Brian and Maggie May sat.

"Looks like rain, kid. What do you think, shall we call it a day?" he asked.

"I'm not ready to leave, Brian. Make it go away." Her intentionally juvenile remark caused him to laugh. They felt the air grow cooler as the wall of dark, threatening clouds approached. At the far end of Long Sands Beach, sunbathers could be seen scurrying to their cars parked along the edge of the shore.

Brian jumped to his feet and jogged to the car. Pulling the keys from his pocket, he opened the trunk. "Rory, I love you!" he shouted, then pulled a plastic, olive drab tarp from the back of the vehicle. Running back to the edge of the cliff he sat behind Maggie May, cradling her against his chest, and pulling the tarp over their heads, providing a tent-like covering. Within seconds they heard the sound of rain droplets hitting the plastic above them. The patter of rain grew more intense by the second as they took in this mild assault of nature.

"I'm jealous, Kelly," she said without turning.

"Of what?"

"You said you loved Rory. An hour ago you said you loved me. Which is it?"

He pulled her backward, shifting her head to the side. In seconds his lips were covering hers and he felt her warm breath mix with his own. He followed this with a single kiss to the bridge of her nose.

"Now, as much as O'Shea would love having me do that to him, I belong to you, Keogh, and you alone." She did not respond to his humor.

"Brian, there's something I haven't told you yet because I was afraid it would bother you."

"What is it?"

"After the baby's born and I go back to school, it's not going to be Southside." He did not respond. "I'm going to need a fresh start and I can only get that away from Southside and Manchester. I'm going to be going to Bishop Primeau in Nashua. New school, new friends, new start, everything new except you. We'll still see each other all the time, just not every day. I told you my folks will raise the baby, for the most part, till I'm out of college. I'm going to stay local for college, New Hampshire College or Saint A's. That way I'll be able to stay near the baby and my family— and you." Below them Long Sands Beach was virtually clear as the rain continued to pour down around them.

"What if you meet someone at Bishop Primeau you like better than me?"

"I'll warn the guys there in advance that I have someone up in Manchester who'll come down and kick their asses if they even look at me. I'll tell them if he won't do anything, then his band of losers will do it for him."

"They're not losers," objected Brian, albeit weakly.

"Percy Provencher, Dolores Drapeau, Nathan Roth, Jerome Jefferson—Brian, they're losers—all losers."

"Keogh, they're my friends."

"Enough said. Life's too short to talk about losers. Besides, Brian, you'll have your own car soon—I hope. How much have you saved?"

"Over five hundred dollars," he answered.

"Once you have your car you'll be able to drive out to Bedford to see me any time you want. Everything'll be okay."

It was nearly five o'clock when Brian packed up the provisions, blanket, and tarp and closed out a very full day in York.

On the last Thursday prior to the start of their junior year at Southside, Brian, Jerome Jefferson, and Nathan Roth rumbled into the lobby of the Amoskeag National Bank in downtown Manchester. It was payday and the trio had picked up their checks hours before their shifts and made for the bank. As his friends splintered off and immediately jumped in lines to cash their checks, Brian found an available customer service representative and took a seat at her desk.

"I was hoping to open a savings account. Can you help me with that?" he asked politely.

"There's a ten-dollar minimum on all savings accounts," responded the smartly dressed woman in a direct, businesslike tone.

"I have five hundred dollars that I'd like to put in today," he answered, causing the woman to raise one eyebrow.

Reaching inside her desk, she produced a five by seven index card, then filled it in with the information he provided. With the process nearing completion Brian produced a stack of ten and twenty dollar bills, which the professional woman, a Mrs. Teresa Wheeler, counted on the surface of her desk.

"Mrs. Wheeler, this is a lot of money to me and I've worked very, very hard to get it. I just want to make sure my money's safe here. I mean, this bank's not going anywhere, right?"

The attractive woman's face broke out in a patronizing smile. "Mr. Kelly, the Amoskeag National Bank is one of the financial rocks that Manchester is built on. It is a corporate entity which means it can live forever. Trust me, young man, I dare say that long after Brian C. Kelly of Montgomery Street is dead and six feet under, there will still be an Amoskeag National Bank."

"You sound very sure of that so I guess it must be true," conceded Brian, accepting this grown-up's superior knowledge of the financial world. He thanked her for her time as he accepted a passbook attesting to the existence of his five hundred dollars. He left the bank that day hoping he would soon be able to convert this cash into the car his social life most certainly needed.

XX

MAGGIE MAY GAVE BIRTH to a daughter, Jenny, on September 11th. For the following ten days or so, Brian's access to Maggie May was limited to impersonal conversations at the hospital and later at home on the phone.

In mid-September Elizabeth Kelly began experiencing serious headaches, a few of such intensity that she missed work. On the recommendation of a doctor and at her son's insistence she consulted a specialist who strongly urged a series of extensive tests. The Kellys' health insurance from work carried a two hundred and fifty dollar deductible, which Brian covered, putting a severe dent in his savings account. The tests proved negative, leading the specialist to speculate that the woman was experiencing migraine headaches and was probably destined to battle these the rest of her life. The medical expenses were not the only thing driving Brian to the doors of the Amoskeag National Bank. Elizabeth's absenteeism for medical reasons caused partial paychecks and Brian's funds were needed to meet the expense of weekly necessities. By mid-October, his savings account was barely one hundred dollars and all thoughts of purchasing a car had been temporarily abandoned.

Starting on the day of Jenny Keogh's birth, all communications between Brian and Maggie May were initiated by him. As weeks passed he found it increasingly difficult to reach her on the phone. On those occasions when he was successful, she responded to most of his proposals and suggestions with disinterest. On the two nights he was able to coax her from Bedford and out on a date, she mercilessly reminded him that it was her ve-

165

hicle they were driving, badgering him to provide her with a specific date when his car would become a reality. Finally, on a weekday evening in mid-October, she would put an end to the lingering death that was their relationship.

Brian called the Keogh residence early in the evening. Maggie May took the call in the privacy of her bedroom.

"Listen, Keogh, I wanted to run something by you. Rory can get his hands on four Bruins tickets next weekend—and how would you like to go to Boston next Friday night—have dinner—then go to the Garden and see the Bruins—all expenses paid—in Rory's car—and you get a night out with me?" Brian was hard pressed to restrain his enthusiasm.

"Brian, there's been something I've been meaning to talk to you about—and this may be a good time to do it." There was a foreboding tone in her voice, causing his stomach to knot up. "Trying to get together has become a real hassle. I guess what I'm saying is—if you want to call me once in a while—that'll be okay—but I want to put an end to the idea that we have to get together on weekends and go out. I would have thought by now that you might have gotten the hint. Do you follow what I'm saying?" she asked.

"I think so—I mean—" he mumbled, fumbling with the words. "Keogh, you must know that—that I have this problem. I'm madly in love with you," he confessed.

"Then, I'd say you have a real problem," she answered coldly. Her statement was followed by silence at both ends of the telephone, the seconds ticking off toward the end of their relationship.

"Is there anything else, Brian?" she asked impatiently.

"No, I guess not," he responded listlessly. His words were followed by a click on the phone followed by the dial tone.

The late autumn brought a decrease in the severity and number of Elizabeth's headaches. The loss of Maggie May threw Brian into an emotional tailspin. His customary jovial disposition was replaced by a thoughtful, measured one. The Band, now numbering more than twenty members, was recognized as a legitimate force within the school, a group not to be trifled with. Rory, more than anyone at Southside, saw the change in his friend and encouraged him to talk it out. But Brian clung to the hope that Maggie May would have a change of heart and reestablish contact with him. So it was, with winter bearing down on New

Hampshire and Brian's spirits grounded in a state of discontent, he would face a crisis that would dislodge the memory of Maggie May Keogh from his daily thoughts.

Once again, Elizabeth and Brian Kelly planned to spend the Christmas of 1973 at the Clarkes' residence in Lowell. The thought of spending more time back in Centralville visiting family and friends lifted Brian's spirits, albeit slightly. He had not spoken to Perez in months and planned dropping by his Bridge Street apartment on arrival. It was on a Sunday morning a short time before Christmas that Brian awoke to an unusually quiet house. With one eye he checked out the alarm clock which read nearly nine-thirty.

"Ma, are you home?" he called out, thinking his mother must certainly have returned from mass at this hour. St. Patrick's was less than a ten-minute walk from the house and the eight o'clock mass seldom ran over an hour. The apartment remained perfectly still as he searched his mind for anything that might have delayed his mother's return.

Brian slowly climbed out of bed, reaching for his robe laid across the chair in front of his desk. A strong sense of apprehension was overtaking him, causing him to rush from his bedroom and into his mother's adjoining room. Entering her bedroom, he hoped and expected to be confronted with an empty bed. This would mean that Elizabeth must be talking with someone at the convenience store on Kelley Street or perhaps praying inside the now empty church. However, he looked down and beheld his mother beneath her bedding.

"Ma, wake up!" he called out as he raced around the bed. There was no movement or response. "Ma!" he cried, falling to his knees beside the bed and looking into the peaceful face of the woman. Placing his hand on her shoulder, he shook her, hoping to trigger a response. "No—please!" he roared, breaking out in tears. Brian wrapped his arms around his mother, pulling her lifeless body up and against his own. With tears running down his face he called out for her to return to him. "I can't go on without you, Ma—oh, please don't do this to me!" he implored, while cradling her body. A few minutes later, Brian ran downstairs and pounded on Mr. Giroux's door as tears streamed uncontrollably down his face.

XXI

CLIMBING BEHIND THE WHEEL of his uncle's car, Brian sensed that this assuredly would be his last visit to Manchester. It had been more than a week since his mother's funeral. Throughout the drive northward, paralleling the Merrimack River, Brian was lost in thoughts of his fourteen months spent in New Hampshire. He would have to face, actually confront, the Montgomery Street apartment a final time, an apartment now largely stripped of any evidence of Elizabeth Kelly. He would have to officially remove himself from the last place he had spoken to, looked upon, and touched the human being who had given him life seventeen years earlier. Then, too, there would be many other good-byes.

He left the Everett Turnpike at the Queen City Bridge and snaked through the now familiar back streets that made up Manchester's west side until he pulled up to the familiar three-family on Montgomery Street. Plodding up the stairway he stopped before the wooden door at the top of the stairs and turned the key. The kitchen, bathed in the winter's late afternoon sunlight, was stripped bare, save the white stove and refrigerator. Brian stepped into the pantry, finding a cabinet filled with dishes, cups, silverware and assorted kitchen items. He put aside a few more personal items, a cookie jar and tea cups, then piled the remaining objects in boxes. The packing process took slightly over an hour. Brian followed six or seven trips to the car with a last pass through each room with a broom. The brief time spent in his mother's bedroom proved most painful. Finishing the large, corner bedroom, Brian's spirits plummeted as he closed the door behind him. As his eyes passed through the empty living room, they caught sight of the telephone resting on the floor. A surge of bitterness shot through his body. A final call to Bedford, he thought. He picked up the phone, only to find the absence of a dial tone. Perhaps it was for the best. No angry words to regret at a later date.

Brian knocked on his former landlord's door on his last trip out of the building. When Mr. Giroux answered the door, Brian thought he looked older than he remembered. He thanked the man for all his kindness and told him of his mother's affection for him. The elderly gentleman was in tears as Brian broke off the conversation and retreated back to the sidewalk. He felt some consolation, observing another human being dealing with the passing of Elizabeth Kelly.

Next, Brian made the short hop to Rory's house. Mrs. O'Shea answered the door, immediately extending her condolences. Rory threw on his coat and invited his friend outside, sensing the conversation would become emotional. With the front door closed behind them they embraced.

"It's hard to say when I might be getting back to see you again," acknowledged Brian.

"Hey, Bri, I've got a car. It's not like Lowell's on the other side of the world."

"I'll try to get back every once in a while, I promise."

"What the hell are we going to do without you? I mean, you held us together," asserted Rory.

"You and Jerry assume command. You've still got two-thirds of the original base. God, it seems like a thousand years ago the three of us made the pledge together. Member—the three of us that first night in your basement?" joked Brian.

Rory smiled and nodded his head in the affirmative.

"I'll miss you, buddy, I really will. And every time I put on the denim coat I'll think of you." Brian descended the porch stairs, leaving his friend standing by the door, his breath visible in the cold, December air. "It's painful saying good-bye and I'm not going to drag it out. So long, buddy. I promise I'll try to get back to see you. Tell the guys I'll miss them and I love them, all of them."

"You've got my number Bri, call," hollered Rory as Brian reached the car. With a final wave of Brian's hand, the vehicle pulled away and disappeared down Coolidge Avenue.

Brian hastily drove away from the emotional good-bye and sped south toward the turnpike. Unconsciously, his route took him past Southside. Stopping the car near the front entrance, he remembered the first time he had set eyes on the building. He had jokingly informed his mother that a naked man and woman were posed above the front entrance. The only other thought that came to him now was of his former friend, Maggie May Keogh.

Turning the key in the ignition, he proceeded from Southside with the turnpike home his immediate goal. However, Brian would put one final stop on his itinerary this evening. So, instead of rejoining the Everett Turnpike, he turned the vehicle along the route that he had walked so many times. It was a short drive out of Manchester to Bedford and a certain house on Ministerial Road. With the car parked safely in the town center, Brian hiked up the cold, dark roadway until he reached the familiar structure. The Keogh house was edged in Christmas lights as it had been one year earlier when he ventured within the domain of Miss Keogh. For a time he had penetrated the fortress she had warily constructed around herself. But now, as he shivered in the cold, he genuinely felt the disparity in their lives. Wasn't it only a few months before that Brian Kelly was a welcome guest inside those walls? What had caused him to fall from grace? In the end, Maggie May Keogh had not even felt compelled to return his last phone call. He had called her home shortly after his mother's death, hoping to speak to her. He had apparently interrupted a party or something, given the sound of shouting in the background. It was at that time that she promised to call him back the next day. The call was never made. Certainly she knew of his mother's passing. And what if she knew that he was standing on the roadway by her home this very moment? Would she send her father out to drive him away, or perhaps call the Bedford Police Department? "Officer, there is a man standing on the street outside our house on Ministerial Road. Could you see that he is told to move on?"

Brian longed to set eyes on her one final time. Already the face of Maggie May Keogh was beginning to blur in his memory. Only the pain from their brief relationship remained securely in place. He turned from the house, walked to his uncle's car, and drove south to Lowell.

Brian arrived home just before seven-thirty. He was greeted by his aunt and uncle and escorted upstairs to the attic. There, the Clarkes had put together a makeshift bedroom. Until now, he had been asked to sleep with his young cousin.

"We certainly wouldn't expect you to sleep up here in the summer, with the heat and all, but it shouldn't be too bad the rest of the year," suggested Uncle Jimmy. Jimmy Clarke joined Brian seated on the bed, which was placed by an octagonal window at the front of the house.

"You know, your mother's death has hit me pretty hard too. Between you and me, the night of the funeral I couldn't sleep. I went for a walk and let it all out. I cried over by the Polish Club. I mean, I grew up with your mom. It still hurts, a lot. Don't hold anything in, Brian. It's good to let it out." Jimmy Clarke was concerned about the absence of any overt emotion from his nephew. The words had barely passed through his lips when Brian slumped sideways against his uncle. Finally, Brian was weeping aloud, tears streaming down his face. He leaned forward, burying his face in his hands.

"I miss her so much. I barely have any pictures of her. She left me. She went away so quickly, so suddenly. I never had a chance to say good-bye, and she never said good-bye to me." His uncle remained seated beside him, clutching his forearm in a display of reassurance. The man reached around his nephew, pulling Brian toward him and literally felt the grief locked up inside the young man. Finally, Jimmy Clarke rose from the bed, crossed the room, then returned to his nephew carrying an object.

"Brian, this is from the funeral parlor. It's the guest register from the wake. I'm not sure you realize how many friends you have and who was there to pay their respects. Take a look. Then I'll call you down in a few minutes. Don't come down till I call. I've got something I want you to see but it's going to take a few minutes to set it up." Brian nodded and took the book from his uncle.

Although puzzled by Jimmy Clarke's request, Brian followed his uncle's wishes and flipped open the white, hardbound book. He skimmed the pages mechanically until he reached the first page containing signatures. His memories of the wake and funeral at St. Michael's were badly clouded. He had been under the influence of antidepressants for the most part. He could recall staring over at Perez who sat quietly in the back of the room, and of a visit and prayers given by a priest, but largely the rest of the time was spent staring at his mother, laid out peacefully in the casket in front of him. It was Uncle Jimmy and Aunt Martha who had taken to greeting the arriving visitors. The funeral was little more than a blurred memory. His eyes scanned over a series of vaguely familiar names, no doubt his mother's acquaintances from St. Michael's Parish and former jobs around Lowell. Then, abruptly, the names took on a distinct, New Hampshire ring—Armand Giroux, Emile Provencher, Peter Mars, Bruce Sloan, Richard D'Eredita, Chris Riggas, Marc Cote, Jack Polidoro, Benjamin Turner, Josh Backman, Nathan Roth, Dolores Drapeau, Jerome Jefferson, Rory O'Shea. Over the next few minutes he relived some of the experiences of the past year. Could he have ever imagined that two of his assailants from outside the library less than a year ago would travel all the way to Lowell to show respect for his mother?

"Brian, can you join us downstairs?" called out his uncle. Brian responded, closing the book on Manchester for what probably would be the rest of his life.

Brian rumbled down two flights and joined the Clarkes who were gathered in a darkened living room. He quickly noticed that the film projector was set up, the white bedsheet draped across the far wall.

"When you mentioned not having any new pictures of your mother, I remembered something from last Christmas. You weren't here a lot of the time, so you missed some of what went on," said Jimmy before flicking the switch on the projector.

Brian fell back into a living room chair left empty for him. The film started off with Martha Clarke chopping vegetables in the kitchen and hollering something at the camera. There was no sound to go with the film, so Brian did his best to read lips as the footage rolled on. The action continued with Jimmy Junior and Barbara placing ornaments on the tree and smiling knowingly at their father who, no doubt, was capturing the scene. A few seconds later Aunt Martha inserted a plug into the wall and the Christmas tree was aglow. With the tree illuminated and young Jimmy clapping his hands hysterically, the camera went into a slow pan around the room, finally settling on the image of Elizabeth Kelly seated in the same chair where her son found himself at the moment. Brian felt his senses assaulted by a convergence of emotions—shock, exuberance, sorrow, gratitude, loneliness, all descended upon him as his eyes gazed at her image in near

disbelief. At first looking away, Elizabeth quickly righted herself and smiled gently toward the lens. Seconds later she added a
wave, as if at the prompting of someone in the room. Brian
watched in amazement as his mother spoke, clearly saying,
"Hello, Brian," into the lens just before the eight millimeter
moved back in the direction of the Clarke children. Brian sat
frozen and speechless as his uncle switched off the projector and
flipped on the lights in the room.

"You have something far more precious than a few pictures
of your mother. Brian, I'll have a copy of this footage made for
you in the next couple of weeks. We can't chance having just
one copy in case something should happen to it." The four Clarkes
stepped forward, gathering around him. Misty-eyed and astonished, Brian reached out individually for each member of what
surely was his family.

After an understandably subdued Christmas vacation, Brian
was back at Lowell High School in January. He was reunited
with many of his friends from Centralville and Varnum School.
However, it was a far more introspective Brian Kelly than was
snatched away fifteen months earlier. Brian applied himself scholastically, but kept largely to himself. Over the winter he tried in
vain to find a part-time job. He was driven by a desire to repay
his uncle for funeral expenses he had been forced to absorb after
his sister's death.

XXII

A T THE COMING OF SPRING, Brian went to his uncle and asked
for permission to join a friend from school to look for a
summer job. The plan was to travel over to Maine during April
vacation and line up a job for the summer. While the plan to
search for work in Maine was factual, the existence of a friend
from school to transport him there was not. Brian knew Jimmy
Clarke would not allow his seventeen-year-old nephew to hitch-
hike his way out of state, placing himself at the mercy of perfect
strangers. And so, when spring vacation arrived, Brian arranged
to kick off his adventure on a Monday morning, just after his
aunt and uncle left for work. The weekend before his trip to
Maine, Brian visited Perez at his Bridge Street apartment to borrow an army knapsack. Perez was glad to lend his young friend
the olive-drab carrier.

"I suppose I should tell someone what I'm up to," confessed
Brian as Perez poured the contents of the sack onto the floor.
"I'm going to hitch-hike up to Maine next week and find a summer job. It's too tough finding a job around here, everything's
taken."

"You got some cash for the trip?" questioned Perez.

"Yeah, Uncle Jimmy advanced me some."

"How much?"

"Enough."

"How much, Bri?"

Brian hesitated a moment before answering. "Ten bucks
oughta do it."

"Ten bucks! You won't reach the border on ten bucks. What
are you thinkin'?" admonished his friend.

"I'm bringing some food with me in the knapsack. I can stretch ten bucks a long way."

"Wait a minute. Are ya telling me your uncle is letting ya go all the way to Maine on just ten bucks?"

"My uncle thinks I have some cash of my own, and that I'm getting a ride from someone. I had to lie through my friggin' teeth to get him to let me go. I really want to do this." Brian made an exasperated gesture as Perez reached for his wallet.

"How long you gonna be gone?" he asked.

"I figure three days. A half a day up, two days job hunting, a half a day back."

"I'll kick in fifty bucks. Spend it wisely. You gotta get two nights o' motel rooms on it and some food to keep you going. Just bring me back anything you don't spend," he counseled.

"I'll pay you back every cent, buddy," promised Brian, folding the ten dollar bills and stuffing them in his pocket. Perez nodded but did not add anything to Brian's statement.

Following his plan to the letter, Brian left the house on Monday morning immediately after the Clarkes drove down the driveway, and made his way to the Bridge Street Bridge. He met up with Perez at Arthur's Diner where they had a bon voyage breakfast. Brian scarfed down two grilled coffee rolls, enough to keep the hunger pains away until supper time. Finally, a short time before nine o'clock, Brian stood by the side of Route 110 and began his journey to Maine. Route 110 pretty much followed the Merrimack River. It would carry him through Methuen, Lawrence, Haverhill, and Amesbury, eventually leading him to Route 1 in Salisbury. He made remarkable time as he traveled northeastward toward the sea. Employing a tactic explained to him by Perez, Brian carried a textbook in plain sight, casting the impression of a student in need of transportation to school. Brian disembarked a VW bus in Salisbury before eleven o'clock and joined Route 1 for the journey due north.

Not one to merely sit and wait, Brian continued northward on foot, his thumb extended. After spending less than five minutes beside Route 1, an eggshell-white Ford Falcon rolled to a stop and Brian hurried up to the passenger door.

"I'm going practically to Wells up in Maine," called out the elderly man behind the wheel.

"Sounds good to me," answered Brian through the window before being gestured in. Tossing his pack into the back seat, Brian made himself comfortable beside the jovial senior citizen.

"My daughter gets upset with me when I tell her I pick up hitchhikers, but I just like having someone to talk to."

"Don't worry, your secret's safe with me," answered Brian with a laugh as the two set off for the New Hampshire line. True to his word, Jack Allen, a retired milkman, bent his young passenger's ear for the next forty-five minutes. Brian saw this as a small price to pay for a chauffeured ride through the narrow neck of New Hampshire, over a drawbridge at the mouth of the Piscataqua River, and ultimately into Kittery and the state of Maine. It was at the drawbridge in Portsmouth that the route began to take on a familiar face. All the while Jack Allen chattered, Brian listened, while his eyes darted from side to side at the road ahead. He had been on Route 1 in Maine the previous summer, escorting Maggie May to the Maine seashore on two occasions. But, as a passenger, he was now able to take in many more wonderful details, details lost to anyone behind the wheel. The Falcon soon sped out of Kittery and into York. They passed a highway sign that read: 13 MILES TO WELLS.

"See that little shack there on the right? Flo's?"

"Yeah?"

"Best hot dogs in the world, son!"

"In the world, Jack?" laughed Brian.

"In the world, and if you don't believe me, give it a try some day. I'd stop right now but the ball and chain was expecting me at eleven. I'm in enough hot water as it is."

A few minutes later the car was crawling through Ogunquit and Jack began preparing his passenger for the end of his lift. A short distance up the road the Falcon coasted to a stop at the side of the pavement. A sign post read Eldridge Road. Brian reached into the back seat and retrieved his pack.

"Wells' town center is a couple of miles ahead. Sorry I couldn't take you further," apologized the congenial man.

"No, this is great, Jack. Thanks to you I've made incredible time. How far's the ocean from here?"

"A mile up the road. Can I take you there?" he offered.

"No, just asking. I'm going to keep going a little farther. Thanks again!" Brian gave the man a wave and watched the Ford chug away.

He stood at the corner of the road for a moment, getting his bearings. Brian was already aware of a difference in the area from the prior summer when he drove this same road in search of Parsons Beach. In July the cars literally crawled along Route 1, the tourists clogging the roadway with station wagons packed to capacity with luggage, beach paraphernalia, and children. On this April morning, just before noon, there was only a moderate stream of passenger and commercial vehicles to contend with. Following a brief interlude spent leaning against an iron fence, Brian threw his knapsack over his shoulder and proceeded north on foot, content to walk for a period. Minutes later the sound of rushing water prompted him to cross Route 1 and inspect a waterfall a few dozen feet from the road. The spring thaw was feeding torrents of fresh water over and through a rock formation, causing foam from the current as it crashed to the river bed below. After sampling the water, Brian returned to the pavement above and continued north. When he reached a major intersection and saw the prominent sign for Mile Road a painfully familiar sight sprang up before him. It was Howard Johnson's, the same restaurant where he and Maggie May Keogh had dined nine months earlier, and although six months had passed since he had seen or spoken to her, the pain left from this broken relationship persisted, albeit diminished.

Brian knew it was time to face his pain. Crossing back to the ocean side of Route 1, the ocean being visible a mile due east, he walked up to the twenty-foot-high sign that read, HOWARD JOHNSON'S HOME MADE ICE CREAM, 28 FLAVORS, and thought of happier times. While the cars passed by him, he made a promise to himself. He would confront any and all demons left by the past and strike out on an adventure. He would return to Lowell with a job secured for the summer, whether it took four hours or four days. Incredibly, in spite of his monstrous breakfast four hours earlier, Brian was already getting hungry. HoJo's parking lot was already overflowing with cars and he knew he must do everything in his power to conserve his money. Therefore, he reasoned that his plan of action might be to find something to snack on before purchasing a local paper and following up on classified ads. Brian trotted across the street and joined the back of a line at Congdon's Doughnuts. After purchasing a cup of coffee and two doughnuts, he leaned against the side of the take-out stand and methodically sipped on his drink between bites.

Directly across the street from the doughnut stand was a cottage and motel complex. At the center of the complex stood a large, white house where a man and woman labored, scraping paint from the front of the building. He watched the couple work on the building while he wolfed down the doughnuts and finished the coffee. Finally, he pulled himself up from the ground and made his way across the road. The sign at the front of the property read ATLANTIC COAST MOTEL AND COTTAGES.

As Brian drew closer to the white house the man turned around and spotted his approach.

"Can I help you with anything, young fella?" called out the stocky, bald-headed man.

"I'm not sure. I'm up in the area looking for work. Are you folks looking for help by any chance?" answered Brian.

"No, not really, but I'm sure there'll be jobs opening up in a few weeks. A lot of us are just getting back from out of state, you see. And besides, aside from chambermaids, we don't take on any people here."

"Now wait a minute, Lou. Don't be so quick to send this young man off," said the woman who by now had turned and begun sizing up the young stranger standing on her driveway.

"What? Do you think this kid's looking to make beds and clean toilets?"

The woman gave Lou a sideways glance. "You know what we went through last summer. You haven't forgot I hope?" quizzed the petite, middle-aged woman.

"We don't have the traffic to afford taking someone on this early," countered the man. The couple, whom Brian perceived to be husband and wife, engaged each other in a discussion about staffing while Brian, a perfect stranger, stood silently in their midst. The woman turned to Brian.

"Last summer this one almost worked himself into the ground. All I ever heard was, 'Why did I ever get into this business?' and, 'I must've been out of my mind to buy this place!' It didn't make for a pleasant summer."

"We can't afford to be putting anyone on the payroll in April when there's no money comin' in," argued Lou.

"Well, I'm not putting up with another summer of you moaning and groaning like last year," stated the woman defiantly.

Brian saw an opportunity to break into the discussion. "To be honest, I wasn't looking for a job right away. I'm still in high school. It's spring vacation. I'm up here to line up a job for mid-June, you know, through Labor Day." The woman peeled a pair of work gloves from her hands and approached Brian.

"Do you have any experience in the motel business?" she asked.

"Absolutely none," confessed Brian.

"Good, no bad habits to break! I say we hire him," barked the woman.

"Do I get to put my two cents in here?" asked the man.

"I like his face, Lou. I say we take him on for the summer. Are you above making beds and cleaning toilets in a pinch?" questioned the woman.

"Ma'am, I'm not above anything. I do it at home for nothing. I'm a hard worker, really I am. I just need a chance to show you."

"I'm hiring him, Lou."

"No references or anything. You're hiring someone just like that," answered Lou.

"He's got a good face and I like his way."

"You got a name?" asked the man in a lightly sarcastic manner.

"Brian Kelly, from Lowell, Massachusetts, junior at Lowell High School, and I'm on the honor roll."

"Oh, a know-it-all!" kidded Lou behind a straight face. Brian laughed but said nothing. "Where you staying?" asked the man.

"To be honest, I just got here so I haven't found a place yet."

"For twelve bucks we can put you in one of the cottages," offered the man.

"God, you old miser, you're not going to charge the boy for staying in one of the places when we haven't even had a chance to clean them from over the winter," scoffed the woman.

"Boy, Lou, your word's really law around here," quipped Brian behind a smile.

"Yeah, the old battle-ax really jumps every time I open my mouth, doesn't she?"

The woman stepped forward. "Brian Kelly, I'm Bella, Bella Russo, and you already know Lou's name. Would you be interested in earning your night's stay?" When Brian nodded yes, he was directed across the lawn toward the back of the complex. She led Brian by a row of motel units to the edge of a grassy incline. Below him and behind a row of trees was Wells Harbor with the Atlantic Ocean in the distance. A swimming pool with a fence around it sat in the middle of an extended lawn twenty yards down the slope.

"This is really nice, Bella," Brian said admiringly.

The woman did not answer. She led him onto the porch of a small cottage that sat at the top of the hill and pushed open the door. Inside the small, knotty pine cabin was an assortment of corrugated boxes, broken furniture, tools, and assorted fixtures. "It's a mess, a real mess. But there's a pretty decent mattress in the loft above our heads and a working fridge with a couple of burners. You can make it home if you want to. There's a utility shed over by the house where most of Lou's junk could be stored. If you feel like cleaning the place up, and giving Lou a hand in the shed, then you will have more than earned your keep. We'll provide you with clean sheets and towels for tonight."

"Bella, this is great, really," said Brian enthusiastically. The woman closed the door behind her, leaving him in the dusty, cluttered cabin. After opening the windows and allowing some fresh air to overcome a smell of closeness, he set to organizing the array of supplies strewn about the single room. Throughout the afternoon he moved boxes of supplies and assorted objects to the utility shed. This work was only interrupted when he assisted Lou moving heavy or bulky items. With all extraneous objects moved from his cabin, #14, Brian set about cleaning the tiny studio, washing down the bathroom, sweeping the floor and loft, cleaning the windows, and polishing the meager furniture. The sun was low in the sky when he stopped long enough to sit back and survey his work. The little cabin at the top of the hill was ready to be lived in. He was seated contentedly on the couch, surveying his work, when the screen door to the porch opened and someone knocked at his door.

"It's open," he responded. Bella stuck her head inside the half opened door.

"Brian, it looks terrific, really! You hungry?"

"I couldn't impose," he replied.

"Nonsense, we have more lasagna than we could possibly eat in a week. Come join us."

Brian shared dinner with the Russos and began to learn more about the couple. During dinner it was decided that #14 would be his home over the summer. The cabin had long been a difficult unit to rent to tourists, due to its small size. Brian accepted a reduced salary in exchange for free room, an arrangement beneficial to both parties. It was after eight o'clock when he returned to the cabin. The curtains from the loft window were soaking in the sink, leaving the pane of glass by his head uncovered as he lay awake on his first night in Maine. He looked out through the row of trees below toward the harbor and Atlantic Ocean. Lights from the row of cottages along Wells Beach peeked through the tree line. What a wonderful sight this was!

He lay awake in bed considering his good fortune, mulling over the events of the day. It was only this morning that he had stood on the side of Route 110 back in Lowell, thumb extended, hoping for a ride in the general direction of Maine. In one day he had found a job and a place to live over the summer!

His thoughts also brought him back to Lowell, to the Clarkes and Perez and ultimately his mother. He considered this place that would be his home for a few months. Just up the street was Howard Johnson's, the very place he and Maggie May had dined not so long ago. How ironic this seemed.

Brian slipped off to sleep minutes later.

A stream of sunlight coming through the window woke Brian just after sunrise. His sleep had been undisturbed, the sound of cars from nearby Route 1 partially muted by the hundred-yard distance. Moments after awakening, he rolled over on his stomach and took in the vista below. There was a layer of dew on the lawn which extended down the hillside to just before the tree line. The distant harbor was partially shrouded in fog, but he caught sight of a lobster boat chugging away from the others a short distance from the dock. Energized by a sound night's sleep, he carefully made his way down the ladder and into the bathroom. He dressed quickly after showering and made his way back to Route 1 and Congdon's. Breakfast would be the same as the prior day's lunch, coffee and doughnuts. Brian brought his food back to the cabin, content to sit on the porch in the chilly morning air and sip on his coffee in these new surroundings.

It was almost two hours after rising that Brian approached the main house to speak to the Russos. He had already mapped out what would be his schedule for the next two days. He told his future employers that he would put in a full day's work at no cost in exchange for using their phone for two minutes to call home in Lowell and advise his uncle of his plans. The Russos, a little flabbergasted by the generous offer, agreed and the day was spent attacking a long list of small, repair items throughout the complex. That evening, Brian again dined with the Russos, retiring to his cabin well before nine. However, he had left Wednesday free to explore Wells and the surrounding area. Before climbing up into the loft, he removed the cash from his wallet and laid it on the table. He counted out fifty-six dollars. Next, he dug his hand into his back pocket and produced fifty-five cents. In two days he had limited his spending to three dollars and forty-five cents! Thanks to the generosity of the Russos and a steady diet of coffee and doughnuts, he was sure to return to Lowell with a large portion of his original sixty dollars. Climbing up into the loft he pulled the covers back and slipped in between the sheets. He went to bed excited about the day ahead—a day to roam and explore the town.

Brian awoke to a landscape draped in fog Wednesday morning. However, this did little to diminish his enthusiasm as he showered, dressed, and made his way out to Route 1 by eight o'clock. Backtracking his steps from Monday, he trooped the short distance back to Mile Road and turned east toward the ocean. He followed a gentle incline down the road, eventually reaching the marshlands that separated Wells from Wells Beach. As he walked, vehicles, their headlights on for guidance through the gray air, passed him from both directions and motored back into the foggy ground cover. Crossing a bridge, a single building emerged from the grayness in the midst of marshland. It sat dark and unattended.

Brian's face was wet from the moisture-laden air as he continued on. He eventually detected the roar of ocean water in the distance before him. He had left the marshland behind, buildings now visible on both sides of the roadway. He sensed the proximity of the Atlantic as he reached a street corner. The sign above his head proclaimed ATLANTIC AVENUE.

Brian stopped to gain his bearings, made more difficult by the fog. Stepping back from the building to his immediate left, he read the block letters blazoned across its front: BEACHCOMBER. The shop obviously dealt with beach merchandise, evidenced by the items displayed in its windows. Unlike most of the structures and signage back on Route 1, this store reflected an air of a bygone period, an almost World War II ambiance.

Following a full minute of contemplation, he turned from the building only to lay eyes on the structure that, most certainly, dominated the face of Wells Beach. Stepping off the sidewalk, he walked back onto Mile Road in the direction of an expansive, two story, green and white building. Identified simply as CASINO, the building was capped with an immense, gently sloping roof along with an awning that covered a second-floor walkway facing out onto the Atlantic Ocean. Brian's eyes took in a modest movie marquee, identified as the Wells Beach Casino Theatre. He reasoned, with good cause, that this building and general locale would be the hub of the area's entertainment during the coming summer. He circled the building before proceeding down the steps and onto the beach sand.

The fog was rapidly burning off. Climbing the stairs up from the beach and back to the parking area, Brian decided to follow Atlantic Avenue northward along the coast. He would explore the extended finger of land visible in the distance from his loft window back at the cabin. He had skipped breakfast this morning and was growing hungry. A short way down the road was a store, which proved to be open. He stepped inside Lee's Market and purchased breakfast, an eight-ounce bottle of Royal Crown Cola and a variety of candy bars.

"Not exactly the breakfast of champions," he thought to himself as he strode from the store, the first of the candy bars already half gone.

Continuing northward, his eyes scanned left and right as he took in the beach houses that lined the street. On the ocean side of Atlantic Avenue many of the homes sported huge, wraparound porches. He was spellbound by the architecture of many of these buildings, clearly built in another, more grand, era. There was a charm and grace to these structures that spoke of prior generations of inhabitants, something he found mentally stimulating in a most profound, nostalgic manner. He found himself picturing men and women frolicking in dated, full-body bathing suits in some of the yards of these weather-beaten, yet elegant, houses. The image brought a smile.

He walked on. Eventually he reached a parking lot and channel of water. Before him was the entrance to Wells Harbor, a waterway defined by two jetties which extended outward from the entrance to the harbor into the Atlantic. Unable to proceed any further north, Brian stepped along the walkway of massive, uneven rock slabs, out to the tip of the jetty where the waves surged past him on both sides. Here, he sat and rested, hypnotized by the ocean's actions as it pounded against the boulders beneath him. Slightly less than a hundred yards across the water, an identical jetty sat due north of his position. He spent the next hour perched at the end of this man-made peninsula, considering his choice of summer jobs and locations. A sense of complete satisfaction had descended upon him. He was already comfortable with the Russos, both as future employers and human beings, and the complex itself and his tiny cabin seemed to him like something out of a fairy tale. But more than this, he found himself embracing this stretch of the Maine coast, this wonderful area of earth and sea, as his own.

He felt like he had come home.

Brian did not return to his cabin until late afternoon on this day. Anxious to explore as much of immediate York County as possible, he headed south from the jetty on foot, hugging the coastline. His travels directed him toward Ogunquit. After a seal spotting at Fisherman's Cove, he wound around Moody Point, eventually reaching the sand dunes at the northern end of Ogunquit at around eleven o'clock. From there, by way of the footbridge behind the dunes, he found his way into Ogunquit Village where lunch, two packages of Sno Balls and another Royal Crown were gulped down, directly across the street from L'Auberge Bretonne, an upscale restaurant on Main Street.

Invigorated by this high-energy snack masquerading as lunch, he picked up a pathway identified as Marginal Way, a scenic walkway that ribboned along the rocky shoreline from Ogunquit Village to Perkin's Cove. En route, Brian was continually taken aback by the number and variety of beautiful vistas, overlooks, and settings. Amazed, almost overwhelmed, by his surroundings, he arrived in Perkin's Cove convinced that he had wandered into a picture-book world almost too picturesque to be real.

Nothing in his sixteen years in Lowell or one year in Manchester had prepared him for this. He found the snug, rustic cove largely quiet, except for the working lobstermen and fishermen bustling along the wharf and aboard their boats. Perkin's Cove would be the farthest point from home, home being the Atlantic Coast Cottages and Motel, he would reach this day.

At three o'clock he set out from the cove and traced his steps back to Wells and Route 1. After dining with the Russos at six, Brian was asleep in his loft by nine, exhausted by his day's explorations.

On Thursday morning, Brian packed his gear, cleaned cottage #14, bid good-bye to the Russos, and was extended a hug from both Bella and Lou. He turned down their offer for breakfast, as he was now addicted to Congdon's doughnuts and would purchase a half dozen for the trip back to Lowell.

So, with a bag of doughnuts in his pack, a textbook under his arm, and the thought of his cabin and job waiting for him in two months, Brian stepped back onto Route 1 and headed home.

His first of many rides would materialize even before reaching Howard Johnson's, a stone's throw down the road. By early afternoon he was already back in Lowell and climbing the steps to Perez's apartment. He found his friend at home, taking a call from a client, and settled into an easy chair while his friend completed jotting down the details of a wager on an upcoming horse race.

Brian let the backpack fall to the floor as he went about counting his available cash. Before him on a coffee table laid a stack of bills and small pile of change. Perez finally wrapped up his call and placed the receiver down.

"Fifty-three dollars and thirty-five cents," stated Brian proudly.

"An' how much didja leave with again?"

"Sixty bucks—fifty from you and ten from Uncle Jimmy."

"You're shittin' me!" cried out his flabbergasted friend. Brian laughed and counted out fifty dollars.

"Here, buddy, it was great knowing I had it but I pinched my pennies and made do."

"Come on, Bri, you didn't sleep outside or anythin', didja?" Brian flashed a proud smile and related the events of the last three days to his friend. When he was through, Perez removed a ten dollar bill from the pile and handed it back.

"Your uncle's got a family to support. Give'm back his ten spot an' keep the change, ya earned it," acknowledged Perez to his young, enterprising friend.

XXIII

THE SUMMER OF 1974 saw a full season of activity in the Wells Beach area, over and above the boating, bathing and sun worshipping along the miles of sandy beaches. W.T. Grant opened a Grant City store in the Wells Plaza while the Ogunquit Playhouse brought in celebrities such as Sandy Dennis, Barbara Bel Geddes, David McCallum and Gary Merrill. A few miles north of town, the Kennebunk Drive-In Theatre offered tourists *The Last Detail* and *American Graffiti,* saving them the drive to Sanford and the Jerry Lewis Cinema.

However, Brian was afforded little free time to enjoy his summer in York County. For him, the summer of 1974 was a time for learning the hospitality trade, and this was done through hard, diversified work. It was not uncommon for him to put in eighty-plus hours a week and he did so cheerfully and with a seemingly unlimited amount of energy. By the time Labor Day rolled around, Uncle Jimmy had been repaid for the expenses incurred at the time of Elizabeth's death. Brian had always insisted that he would pay the full cost of putting his mother to rest, and he followed through on that pledge. He also brought home a back seat full of presents for the Clarkes and a pair of powerful binoculars for Perez, a gift well received by his friend and immediately hung in his Bridge Street apartment window.

Brian had learned a great deal from the Russos but had already begun to develop ideas of his own through observation and paperwork analysis. However, it was knowledge he would become privy to regarding a very unusual set of circumstances that would ultimately play a major role in his life during the following year.

It would be naive for anyone to think that establishments in the business of providing overnight accommodations could not harbor secrets. It is also true that, in these times of plummeting values and mores, the only thing that should surprise us is that we can still be surprised!

In mid-August Lou Russo pulled Brian aside and explained the circumstances surrounding some unconventional guests that he would be dealing with later in the month. The unconventional guests were Dr. William McShane, a dentist with a magnificent, oceanfront home in Ogunquit and an extraordinarily successful practice in Portsmouth, New Hampshire, and Ruth Davenport, an actress of considerable fame and recognizability brought about by a long-running role in a network soap opera. Brian was told how these two were college flames who, as a result of misguided choices from their youth, became star-crossed lovers, doomed by bad timing and fate to carry on their tragic romance over the years through periodic, secret rendezvous away from the prying eyes of the public. The meetings, seldom more than twice a year and largely of the weekend variety, had been carried out for the past six years at Atlantic Coast Cottages and Motel, and always in cottage #17. This cottage was selected because of its location at the far end of the complex, invisible from the road due to the thick vegetation surrounding it and situated at the very end of the driveway, providing maximum privacy.

Brian was advised that it was of the utmost importance that this situation and the principals involved in it be kept absolutely confidential. The doctor's second wife had entered the marriage years earlier with full knowledge of the circumstances, under the assumption that she would be spared the scandal of this long-running arrangement becoming public knowledge. Until Brian's arrival, word of these quietly orchestrated meetings had only been privy to the Russos and the individuals directly involved. By necessity, Brian, by virtue of his full-time position and total involvement in daily affairs, had to be added to this short list of confidants.

Brian Kelly spent his senior year at Lowell High School totally focused on his education, resulting in an academic year on the honor roll. His romantic life remained largely dormant, although he did manage to develop friendships with a handful of girls from his graduating class, the most prominent being the tall and attractive Edel Kenny, whose fiancé was on active duty with the United States Marines. In his absence, it was Brian who escorted her to their senior prom, each knowing that their lives were about to draw them apart. Brian's forthcoming relocation to Maine and Edel's October wedding plans had set the course of their lives on diametrically opposite paths, allowing them a sense of absolute freedom with each other. On graduation night they drove to the coast, discussing their dreams, fears, and aspirations as they walked the sands at Hampton Beach, finally watching the sun rise on their adulthood. When Edel left Brian off that morning in front of his uncle's house, they both knew it was with a certain finality.

Such are the painful realities of graduation. They are best not looked upon or contemplated at length. They are sobering, disheartening events masqueraded in celebration.

XXIV

TWO DAYS AFTER HIS GRADUATION a large portion of Brian's worldly belongings were piled into the back seat and trunk of Jimmy Clarke's car and driven, along with Brian, to Wells, Maine. On arrival, Uncle Jimmy was introduced to the Russos who immediately encouraged him to reserve a week at the complex that summer, thanks in part to a generous discount. Brian and his uncle unloaded the contents of the car into cottage #14 before final good-byes and a promise to see each other the following month. It was only seconds after his uncle's departure that Brian climbed the ladder up into the loft, pulled back the curtains, and took in the expansive view of the harbor and distant ocean.

He was home.

Brian set right to work the next day. Immediately, he put to use everything he had learned the summer before. The Russos anticipated another busy year, much like the previous one, even though the price of gasoline had risen to nearly sixty cents per gallon! Less than two weeks after arriving, Brian was unexpectedly called upon to take over the running of business. Bella Russo's brother took ill and died in mid-June, requiring her and Lou to travel to Florida to attend to the funeral and an elderly parent. It was with some degree of trepidation that the Russos were forced to turn over the entire, day-to-day operations of the Atlantic Coast Motel and Cottages to Brian, an eighteen-year-old with limited experience. However, there were no other options.

So, for nine days in June, Brian attempted to do the work of three people and, for the most part, succeeded. A lawn crew was called in for grass cutting, a task usually handled in house by Brian. Thankfully, the family emergency had occurred prior to peak season, leaving the complex's young manager to deal with only seventy-five percent occupancy. However, his major challenge would come in the form of a phone call from New York City and a reservation for cottage #17. With a mere three days notice, he had to coordinate the arrival of Miss Ruth Davenport in Wells, with no assistance from anyone.

It was just before eight o'clock in the evening on a Friday when a sedan rolled passed Brian who was seated in the office, and proceeded down the hill and out of sight. His suspicions that his celebrity guest from New York City had arrived were confirmed when the phone at his desk rang and Ruth Davenport announced her arrival. This called for him to walk down to cottage #17 and place a covering over her vehicle, hiding its identity throughout her stay. Customarily, Dr. McShane was on hand to greet his longtime love but, on this evening, he was missing. After covering her car, a slightly apprehensive Brian approached the door and knocked. Footsteps were heard approaching before a latch was unfastened and the door swung partially open.

There, standing a foot beneath him, was the television actress the Russos had spoken of the preceding summer. The pretty brunette looked up at him tentatively and spoke. "Mr. Kelly, I presume."

"That's right, ma'am. Just checking in on you to make sure you got everything like you want it."

"Everything appears fine—and Bill?" she asked, surprised by her friend and lover's absence.

"No word of any problems at his end. You're a little early, I think. I'm sure he's on his way." Brian continued standing in the doorway, taking in the sight of the first celebrity he had ever set eyes on—the first female celebrity anyway. He had seen a few Red Sox players at store openings and the like, but the image of an attractive woman of note was far more impressive and intimidating. Ruth Davenport appeared older in the flesh than she did on the screen. However, there was no arguing that, probably in her late thirties, she still possessed the beauty to carry off her role as daytime TV vixen.

"Please, come in," she said, stepping away from the doorway. Brian proceeded into the cottage but remained silent. "And why aren't Lou and Bella around again?" questioned the woman, possibly just to keep conversation alive in the room.

"Bella's brother passed away unexpectedly about a week ago. They're back in Florida taking care of all the details including Bella's mom. I expect them back in a few days."

"And who's running the place in the meantime? Certainly not just you?"

"Just me, Miss Davenport—just me."

"Please, it's Ruth. I feel like someone's grandmother when you call me Miss Davenport," answered the woman through a contrived chuckle. Outside, the lights from an approaching vehicle flashed through the row of back windows. Seconds later came the sound of footsteps on the deck before the door swung open, and Brian observed the sight of two human beings in love. Brian quickly retreated from the cottage, covered the doctor's car, and returned to the office. He would not see Ruth Davenport for the remainder of the weekend while Dr. McShane only stopped by the office long enough to advise him of his departure early Monday morning.

During the summer 1975 Brian's social life remained as stagnant as it had the previous year as a result of his ponderous work schedule. However, he was able to purchase his first car, a beat-up Chevrolet Biscayne.

The financial position of the Atlantic Coast Cottages and Motel took another step forward in 1975. From an analysis put together over the off-season, Brian had convinced the Russos to raise their rates, citing that even after the increase they remained the lowest-priced complex on Route 1. The rate increase dropped directly to the bottom line while Brian, during his winter and spring vacations, coordinated a promotional campaign pushing the fact that their prices were the lowest in the area. The complex experienced less than one percent vacancy from mid-June to Labor Day, fattening the bottom line and allowing Brian to draw a salary through Columbus Day, when the cottages and motel were closed.

The Russos left for Florida early, in late September, handing over their house at the center of the complex to Brian. With effectively no job until the following spring, he began to search for another position to carry him through to May.

XXV

A NYONE WHO LIVED IN YORK COUNTY, MAINE, through the 1970s will concede that Columbus Day ushered in an economic hibernation for its year-round residents, save for the professionals and city and state workers. With the majority of restaurants, motels, attractions, and retailers boarded up for the winter, there was little hope of finding a job for blue collar and unskilled labor until the next spring, and Brian Kelly was no exception. By late October Brian found himself in line at the unemployment office in Sanford, one of many out of work since the flow of tourists had dwindled to a trickle.

It was on his first visit to the state agency that he made the acquaintance of Bobby Copeland, a man his age from Wells. Bobby, he learned, rented a mobile home off of Route 9B and had worked for a lawn and pool care contractor for the past six months. The two hit it off immediately and wound up having lunch together in Sanford before returning to Wells. Through the meal, they shared their individual plans for surviving the oncoming winter. Brian was already attending college two nights a week in Portland. He had salted away a considerable sum over the summer and would now live off of unemployment compensation and his savings account until April. Bobby, on the other hand, had managed to save nothing from his wages over the summer and would be forced to sell firewood, perform odd jobs, and the like, in order to pay his rent and meet other expenses.

On the following afternoon Brian drove his Biscayne west on 9B in search of his new friend's home. A short distance from a driveway leading into two mobile home lots a young child abruptly sprang up out of the ditch alongside the road. Brian slowed the car to a crawl, then brought it to a halt. The child, a boy no more than three years old, was attempting to climb the incline of the ditch onto the roadway. Jumping from his vehicle, Brian addressed the boy before hoisting him into the front seat. He proceeded to direct his car up the driveway, parking it between the two mobile homes. With the Biscayne's engine turned off and the emergency brake on, he jokingly tucked the child under one arm, to the youngster's amusement, and made his way to Bobby's front door. His friend opened the door before Brian reached the steps.

"Don't bring the little crumbgrabber in here. This is a bachelor pad—not a nursery. About face and twenty steps forward," instructed his friend, pointing him in the direction of his neighbor's home. With the young boy under his arm laughing hysterically, Brian walked the short distance to the other mobile home and knocked. There was no sound from within for a few moments, then came the shuffle of footsteps.

"Who is it?" called out a female voice with a hint of wariness.

"Actually, no one you know, but I do have a delivery for you," answered Brian.

"What kind of delivery?" she asked skeptically.

"Oh, I'd say a two- to two-and-a-half-year-old-dirty face-runny-nose kind." The door opened immediately and an anxious mother's face registered surprise.

"Trevor!" called out the woman from beneath a full head of uncombed, auburn hair. The mother of the child had a pretty face that once might have been beautiful. Although her features showed symptoms of needing sleep, her recessed, brown eyes nonetheless displayed a haunting quality that Brian immediately found intriguing. The woman leaned forward around Brian in the direction of a fenced-in play area.

"Don't tell me I didn't lock that thing," exclaimed the woman in disbelief. She reached down, lifting the child to her hip before turning back to Brian. "Thank you so very much. He must have jiggled the lock to the gate somehow. Smart little bugger!" Brian broke out laughing, and the woman followed suit.

"You a friend of Bobby's?"

"That's right, Brian Kelly at your service," he responded, extending his hand. The woman returned a guarded smile.

"Linda Birch, Trevor's mom," she stated as two additional children, a boy and girl, bounded up to the woman, attaching themselves to her legs. Brian continued to smile at the woman, until an awkward silence prompted him to excuse himself.

"You seem to have your hands full. I'll get out of your hair." Brian gave a little tug at Trevor's leg, then turned and made his way over to Bobby Copeland's mobile home. Bobby met his friend at the door, throwing a football at him.

"Toss the ball around for a while?" he asked. Brian reacted immediately, sprinting up the driveway.

"Going long," he called out just as Bobby heaved a spiral in his direction.

Brian had already begun to feel a bonding develop between himself and this local fellow. Judging from Bobby's speech and personal belongings, he sensed that his new friend was not well educated. However, their common status as unemployed locals seemed to be forging a genuine affinity. They continued to toss the football for a while, pitching comments at each other about everything from female relationships to the bleak job market.

Linda Birch had put Trevor back in his play area by now, double-checking the lock mechanism after closing the gate. She emerged from the house a short time later, bringing her son a snack.

On this occasion she and Brian exchanged glances.

The October air was quite pleasant as the young men played on, switching from passing to kicking the football. As one of Bobby's kicks sailed over his head, Brian observed Trevor straddling the top of his play area fence. The mystery was solved. He walked over to the boy as he laid precariously half way over the wooden and wire fence, pulling him up and off. Signaling to his friend for a break, he carried the youngster back to his front door and knocked. Linda Birch pulled the door open

"Is Trevor being a pest out there?" she asked.

"No, but he's given you a new problem. You see, Linda, your son's not getting out through the gate, he's going over the fence."

The woman shook her head in mock disbelief. "Give me the brat," she joked, reaching for her son.

"One more thing, Linda, do you mind if I ask where you got those turnovers you gave to Trevor? They look like peanut-butter-and-jelly turnovers." Brian pointed to a half-eaten one sitting in the grass behind them.

"Don't get 'em anywhere. I make 'em myself."

"Could I buy one from you, just to try them?"

"Buy one? Don't be silly! You've had to drag my little monster back to me twice in the last half hour. The least I can do is give you a turnover, if there's any left." She disappeared inside the house, then emerged with a doughy lump in her hand. "Last one," she called out, handing Brian the pastry on a napkin. "I'd invite you in but the house's a mess. Three kids'll do that."

Brian bit into the turnover, then closed his eyes in an expression of pleasure. "Mmm—just as I remember. My mom used to make these for me when I was a little kid. I can't believe someone else makes them, too."

"Some flour, peanut butter, and jelly—that's about all it takes to make the darn things."

"Linda, I'd like you to make me some more. Of course, I'll pay you for them."

"I can't take your money for this. I'll just make you some."

"No, it takes money for the ingredients and all, plus your time." Brian took out his wallet and removed a bill. "Here's ten bucks to buy the ingredients. It means a lot to me. It reminds me of when I was a kid and my mom was alive. Please—make them." Sensing Brian's sincerity, she took the ten dollars from his hand.

"I'll have some ready by the weekend. Meanwhile—" She gave her son a push back through the doorway. "It was nice meeting you, Brian," she said quietly, closing the door behind her. Brian walked back toward Bobby who had been taking in the scene from a short distance.

"What—the fuck—was that all about?" Bobby asked under his breath. Brian walked by his new friend in silence.

"Want to take a ride and check out where I live?" he finally asked. His friend lobbed the football toward the house and the two scrambled down the driveway to the Biscayne.

Following the short ride back to Route 1, Brian gave Bobby a cursory tour of the complex, including the inside of the main house, before directing him down to cottage #14. Ushering Bobby through the front door he gestured him to take a seat on the couch.

"Beer?" Brian asked.

"You don't have to ask twice," was the reply, given while taking in the interior of the small, studio cottage.

"Check out the sleeping loft," instructed Brian, pulling the ladder to the middle of the room. Bobby jumped to his feet, then carefully climbed the rungs. "Oh, wow! Is this where you sleep? What a view!"

"Not for too much longer. Got to drain the pipes for the winter in a few weeks. Most of the complex's already been drained. Then I'll move to the main house."

"What are they gettin' from you for this?"

"Nothing, they're letting me stay for free. I get less salary in return but it works out good for both of us," confessed Brian.

After a couple of minutes more in the window Bobby descended the ladder and returned to the couch.

"Out of curiosity, have you had any broads in here or in the loft yet?" questioned Bobby behind a mischievous grin.

"None—zero—the big goose egg," admitted Brian.

"That's because you didn't know Bobby Copeland. Course, all that's changed. Next spring we'll head up to Old Orchard when the French-Canadian babes start comin' down lookin' for their summer cottages. Bri, we'll be golden," he chuckled.

"Sounds like a plan and a half," retorted Brian before taking a slug from his beer. With a mouthful of brew down his own throat Bobby lurched forward, trying not to choke.

"Imagine the view climbing up to the loft, a cute little Canadian gal three steps above you. Wow! Forget the friggin' view from the window!" The boys laughed out loud at the comment, then stepped back outside. There were two plastic chairs on the small, screened porch and they deposited themselves onto them. Sitting in silence for a moment, swigging from their bottles, Bobby broke the quiet.

"You know Brian, your nice view here would be friggin' spectacular if it weren't for those damn trees down below."

"Yeah, I've thought the same thing. I've even mentioned it to Lou, but he just waves me off."

"Who owns the land the trees are on?"

"Lou and Bella."

"Wait a minute! Your bosses own the land and they just leave the trees there? That's crazy."

"I know, but they're all spooked about the town and the environmentalists and God knows who else. I guess they've been told not to screw around with the trees and they don't want to make any waves," explained Brian with a sigh.

"They're fuckin' nuts!" spat out Bobby before bringing his bottle up to his mouth.

"Robert, my man, not to change the subject but, tell me a little about your neighbor Linda's husband."

"You're still thinkin' about her, are you!" exclaimed an astonished Bobby. *"Those oldies but goodies remind me of you,"* he sang out, causing Brian to reach over and playfully slug him on the shoulder. "You're asking me about Bubba Birch?"

"Linda's husband's name is *Bubba*? Bubba Birch!?"

"That's right."

"Does he walk erect?" wisecracked Brian.

"When he hasn't been drinking, but Bubba likes his beer. I went to school with his little sister, Barbie." The admission caused Brian to break out in laughter.

"Barbie was damn cute," Bobby protested. "Haven't seen her, in a while, though. All kidding aside, Linda Birch is a little past her prime—not to mention—married!"

Brian shrugged his shoulders. "I find her—interesting—and appealing."

"Yeah, appealing in a used up, burned out way, maybe," answered Bobby, causing Brian to feign anger. "No more arm punches, man—they hurt. I'm just saying that if a thirty-year-old woman in curlers, bathrobe, and moth-eaten slippers lights your fire, then fine. But wait till you get a load of some of those girls from Quebec next year. Stay close to me, buddy, we're goin' to have a great summer next year."

Brian looked down, noticing his friend's beer was gone. Bobby accepted an offer for a second and they both sat back, their feet resting on the porch railing.

"Enough talk about beautiful women," said Brian.

"We weren't talking about beautiful women. We were talking about Linda Birch," retorted Bobby before covering his arm in jest.

"You know, if those damn trees were down, the land would probably be worth a hundred grand more—'cause of the view," sighed Brian.

"If they ever decide to cut the friggin' things down, I'll do it for them for nothin'—'cept the wood, of course. I'd want the wood to sell."

Brian considered Bobby's words and gazed thoughtfully on the tree line below them. "With the trees down the view would be, like, twice as good as anybody else's along Route 1," reasoned Brian aloud.

"Brian, how about this? You give me a hand, cutting and hauling, and I'll have the stumps removed for nothing. A couple of guys I know from Lyman owe me a favor. I'll call it in. They have the equipment to remove the stumps."

Brian stared over at his friend as a smile spread over his face. He extended his hand. "Let's do it," he said.

"You gonna call your boss first?"

"I'll surprise them. Besides, if I ask him—he'll say no."

After an early breakfast on Saturday morning, Brian drove over to visit Bobby. As he pulled into the driveway, he observed a pickup truck parked close to Linda's house and immediately theorized it belonged to her husband. Knocking on Bobby's trailer door, he was invited in and offered a cup of coffee. This was the day the two would finalize plans to remove the trees bordering the wildlife reserve back at the complex. While discussing the schedule for tree cutting, they were interrupted by a knock at the door. When Bobby opened the door Brian spotted Linda Birch standing below him.

"I have a delivery for Brian," she announced.

"All right, Linda, you met the deadline," Brian joked, jumping up from the couch.

"I can't stay long. Bub's not in the best of moods this morning." She sat down and presented Brian his turnovers on a tray. "When you're done just return the tray—oh, and here's your change." The woman handed him seven dollars.

"Don't be silly. That's for your labor and a little profit," chided Brian, placing the bills back in her hand. She smiled appreciatively and accepted them.

"Oh, before I forget, Bobby—do you have any aspirin or Anacin I can borrow?" Linda asked.

"Again? I think I've got some—somewhere," answered Bobby, before disappearing into the kitchen.

"Headache?" Brian asked.

"No, toothache. I've gotta have it looked at soon."

Bobby reentered the room with a small tin of tablets. "This is the last of what I've got, Linda. Use it wisely," cautioned her neighbor. She thanked him and immediately made her way to the sink, downing a pair of tablets.

Brian observed her closely as she took the medication. She was dressed in a blouse and loose-fitting jeans. However, she appeared to be wearing makeup, partly obscuring darkness from under her eyes, the result of apparent, insufficient rest.

"I'd better be goin'. Thanks, both of you. Anytime you want more, Brian, just ask. Don't feel like you have to pay me all the time for them."

"Don't be silly, Linda. I'll be back for more of your turn-overs, you can count on it," he promised.

He proceeded to walk Linda back to her door, but had taken only a few steps toward the Birch residence when the family pickup truck whirled into the driveway and sped in. Brian and Linda watched as the rusty-fendered vehicle screeched to a halt and a man with thinning, blonde hair emerged from the front seat, glanced disapprovingly at the two, and pounded into the house.

"Your dad looks a little out of sorts," Brian jested.

"That's my husband, Bubba, but thanks for the compliment anyway. Bye, Brian," she said before scurrying back to the mobile home.

The following week brought the matter of the great tree removal. On Monday, and half of Tuesday, Bobby and Brian cut and sawed tree after tree, limb after limb, at the bottom of the property. Bobby loaded truckloads of split logs and transported them back to his yard. On Wednesday, the last of the fallen trees were carried off, leaving only stumps below. Finally, on Saturday, two surly-looking young men from Lyman, answering to the names of Steve and Gary, came by and removed and carried away the tree stumps. Bobby and Brian assisted in the day-long project that drew to a close just as the sun began setting behind Mt. Agamenticus. With the last stump placed in the back of a hauler, Brian offered the men a beer but they declined. Instead, one yelled out something to Bobby about a "debt paid in full," and drove away. Brian and Bobby walked toward the main house together, both physically exhausted. Bobby turned to Brian as they reached the back door.

"You know what I could go for right now?"

"No—I'm stumped!" said Brian with a deadpan face.

"Stumped, huh? If you weren't nearly a foot taller than me I'd make you pay for that friggin' comment. But instead, I'll settle for a beer," he answered before collapsing onto the couch.

XXVI

B Y NOVEMBER ONLY THE MAIN HOUSE and a few remaining cottages had not had the water drained from the pipes in preparation for winter. In the main house, the second floor had been closed to save on heating costs. Although officially unemployed and not receiving a paycheck, Brian continued to handle a trickle of guests at Atlantic Coast Cottages and Motel, putting them up in the few cottages not closed for the season. On the Sunday morning following the stump removal, Brian leisurely strolled to the top of the hill with his coffee and took in the sight of the new view of Wells Harbor, the estuary, and the Atlantic Ocean from the complex.

He was now temporarily staying in cottage #15 which had a single bedroom. He had needed a rest from the low ceiling in the loft at his studio cabin. Not far above the ocean horizon, the sun lit up the harbor and estuary below him. He could make out Kennebunkport in the outlying distance, so clear was the morning. He was very pleased with what he saw and looked forward to the Russos' reaction on their return.

When Brian and Bobby met the following week at the unemployment office, each had good news to share. Bobby had sold his first cord of wood and was now officially part of the underground economy. Brian had learned that he was running A's in both his college courses, based on grades from his midterm exams. The boys decided to celebrate by attending a dance Friday night in Portland.

One advantage of being unemployed is the ability to get an early start on the weekend. Hence, it was just after three o'clock when Brian pulled into Bobby Copeland's driveway. Their plans were to travel up to Portland for dinner, then attend the dance at a social club later on. Brian was a little nervous about the prospect of the dance.

The Birch household appeared deadly quiet as Brian scanned the mobile home from behind the wheel. Grabbing Linda Birch's cookie platter from the back seat, he jumped from the car and walked up to the prefabricated home. He knocked at the front door and was actually surprised to hear footsteps shuffling from inside. Seconds later, the door swung open to reveal a tired, beleaguered Linda standing before him.

"Oh Brian, oh, that's right, the platter," she muttered.

"Are you okay?" asked Brian, taken aback by the woman's peaked appearance.

"I'd invite you in but—my mouth is killing me, you see. That tooth I've been nursing has just gone real bad on me."

"Can't you see a dentist or get something from the drugstore?" he asked.

"Bub's gone for the weekend—hunting with his buddies up north—so I'm left with no set of wheels and no money either. The kids are over in Sanford with their grandparents till Sunday—thank God. I'm stuck here in the middle of nowhere. I don't have a dentist over here and even if I did have one, I got no way to pay him."

Brian stood in silence, looking down at her. She was a human being approaching the end of her rope. She was a woman in pain with no options. She looked up at him pathetically.

"Is there any way you could advance me a few dollars to get something for this tooth at the drugstore?"

Brian could see that it was humiliating for her to ask for help. "There's a chance I may be able to get someone to help you," he answered kindly. "We can get you something from the drugstore if this doesn't work out. May I use your phone?"

She gestured yes. He pulled a business card from his wallet and took a seat beside her on the couch. Dialing the operator, he asked to make a person-to-person call to Dr. William McShane in Portsmouth. Brian asked to have the call charged to a third number, his phone number back at the complex. The call went through and after verbally jousting with a receptionist, William McShane was put on the line.

"Doctor, this is Brian Kelly from Atlantic Coast Cottages. Do you remember me?"

"I know who you are," came the guarded response.

"I need to ask you for a favor. I have a friend in a great deal of pain from a bad tooth. I was hoping you could see her and see what you could do for her," said Brian apologetically.

"I'll switch you back to the front desk. We can probably schedule something for next week."

"No, doctor, you don't understand. She's in a great deal of pain right now. She can't wait till next week. I'm not asking for some freebie here. I'll be paying."

"If it's as serious as you say, it may require extraction, and we do not perform them here. You might have her call her own dentist and proceed from there," answered the man, sounding slightly agitated.

Brian was growing impatient.

"Dr. McShane, I'm asking you to help me in this matter. My friend needs some relief from the pain." For the first time, Brian's voice had an edge to it, not present earlier in the conversation. His tone of voice carried an implied threat, not lost on the dentist. Following a short pause, Dr. McShane changed the tone of the discussion.

"Let me make a call. There may be someone I can get you in touch with who could see you this afternoon. Are you at the cottages?" Brian explained he was not and gave the dentist the Birch's phone number. Dr. McShane promised Brian he would get back to him within fifteen minutes.

Hanging up, Brian turned to the woman who now sat, eyes closed, with her head leaning against the back of the couch. "We'll hear something in a few minutes. They'll call us back," comforted Brian just as she broke out in a dreadful series of sobs. Linda turned her face toward him. She was unable to mask the throbbing pain she was experiencing. Her body slid limply sideways, eventually falling against him. Her head was resting on his shoulder. The next five minutes found no sound from within the room, save the occasional whimper from the woman. The silence was finally broken by a double ring from the telephone. Linda leaned forward and picked up the receiver.

"Hello," she recited listlessly.

"Brian Kelly, please," came a no-nonsense, female voice at the other end. Linda handed the phone to her friend.

"Yes?"

"Mr. Kelly, this is Dr. McShane's office. We are putting you in contact with Dr. Brunelle in Biddeford, which is a little closer to where you are. Dr. Brunelle has agreed to see your friend this afternoon. Can you be there by five o'clock?"

Brian answered in the affirmative and the woman provided him with the Biddeford address, indicating that she would call back the Biddeford dentist and confirm the five o'clock appointment. Brian thanked the woman, but did not receive a response. Hanging up the phone, he turned to Linda.

"Get dressed, I'm taking you to Biddeford. We have an appointment to take care of your tooth." Linda breathed a sigh of relief, rose to her feet, and made her way out of the room to shower and change. "I've got to go tell Bobby I can't make the dance tonight," Brian shouted before leaving the house and walking next door.

Bobby did not take word of his friend's change in plans well. Following a brief argument, he gave up the battle and departed for Portland. Brian returned to Linda's living room and waited. She eventually emerged from her bedroom, her hair wet, but appearing ready to travel.

"Getting yourself gorgeous for the dentist?" teased Brian.

"I got absolutely no sleep last night. I hate having people seeing me like this," she complained.

"Aren't I people?" asked Brian.

"No—you're something better. Jesus, I haven't slept for almost three days now that I think of it! God, I must look like hell!"

"It won't take long and this bullshit will be all behind you."

Brian put Linda in his car and sped north on Route 1, ahead of schedule for the five o'clock appointment.

Dr. Brunelle's office, it turned out, was in a dated office building in downtown Biddeford. Maurice Brunelle was a young dentist, probably not too long out of school. Brian sat with Linda in a poorly lit waiting room for nearly a half hour before Brunelle ushered his referral in. Brian sent her off with a smile, then began digging through a pile of woefully dated magazines.

A full hour after disappearing into the dentist's office, Linda Birch stepped back into the waiting room. Her face was already reflecting the absence of the pain that had distorted it an hour earlier. Making a few wavering steps to a chair, she dropped into it immediately. Dr. Brunelle, now alone in the office, summoned Brian in. He explained that the problem tooth had been extracted following an X ray, which had indicated that it was beyond saving. Brian was then presented with a bill for one hundred and fifteen dollars. In addition, he was given a prescription for a pain-killer to prevent discomfort during the next forty-eight hours. After thanking the dentist, Brian paid the bill from his checkbook.

The drive back to Wells found Linda Birch asleep in the front seat of the car beside Brian, her head resting on his shoulder. At age nineteen, Brian found these circumstances odd. After all, here was a married woman asleep on his shoulder while her husband was off hunting in the Maine north woods. The woman, exhausted from days of pain and limited sleep, could not be awakened after Brian pulled the car to a halt in front of the house. After propping the woman up in his front seat, he raced around to the other side of the car, then hoisted her out and carried her first into the house, then into the bedroom.

Brian awkwardly flipped on the light while continuing to cradle the sleeping woman in his arms, then placed her carefully onto the bed. He looked down at Linda, her unkempt hair framing her face. She was fully dressed. Brian leaned over, unbuttoning her coat and clumsily removing it first from her arms and eventually extracting her body from the garment. His actions did not even cause the woman to react, so sound was her sleep. Next, he moved to the bottom of the bed and removed her boots. Two toes on her right foot protruded through a well-worn pair of panty hose, still pressed into action beyond its normal life cycle. He returned to the head of the bed, where he gazed down at the woman again.

He began entertaining the idea of undressing her, at least down to her undergarments. There seemed little chance of her regaining consciousness during such a process. His motives, he knew, were not noble. The thought of seeing this mature woman, God, she had to be thirty if not a little older, even only partially clothed, was exciting him. What could she say? He could say he didn't want to leave her sleeping in her clothes like a bum. God, that was weak! Brian reasoned to himself that opportunities like this did not come along every day.

But she had kids! He'd be doing this to someone's mother! Wait a minute, he'd given up a dance to help this woman—and paid her dentist bill! Why was he feeling guilty?

He stood above the bed, aroused by the circumstances. He was attracted to this woman, he had been since the day he dragged Trevor back to the house, but he liked her too. He'd been standing above the bed for no less than ten minutes when he leaned down and kissed her on the mouth.

She kissed back, probably unconsciously, instinctively.

He turned from the bed and made his way out. He was careful to lock the front door as he left Linda Birch, mother of three, in a sound sleep. Bobby's house was in darkness.

Brian awoke Saturday morning to the sound of wind swirling through the trees and between the cottages outside his window. The last remaining leaves from the trees lining the complex could be seen flying horizontally by the glass panes. Not surprisingly, his initial thoughts centered on the sight of Linda Birch in bed the night before. It was seven-thirty before he lifted himself from the mattress and stumbled into the combination living room and kitchen. Following coffee and toast, he stripped the bed and added the linens to a half-filled laundry basket. Walking to the main house, he braved the biting, autumn wind before depositing his laundry in one of the commercial washers.

The wind was gradually joined by precipitation, a sign that inclement weather was coming in off the Atlantic. This prompted Brian to pull out a project assigned his marketing class. His concentration was broken when the phone rang at the front desk. He rose from the kitchen table and lifted the telephone after the second ring.

"Good morning, Brian here," he answered.

"I'm trying to reach the Florence Nightingale School for the Sick—Volunteer Department," sang out an unfamiliar woman's voice.

"Uhhh—I think you've got the wrong number, Miss," muttered Brian.

"No, I think this is the right number all right. Is volunteer Kelly there?" she pressed.

"Who is this?" quizzed a suspicious Brian. Laughter in the background was followed by a male voice hollering into the phone.

"Hey, Kelly, my grandmother has a boil on her ass that needs lancing. You up for taking her to Biddeford for me? Better yet—do the lancing yourself!" needled Bobby, to the amusement of the young woman in his company.

"Go ahead, Bobby—I've got it coming to me. I'm sorry about leaving you high and dry last night."

"No apology necessary. It turned out to be a great night in Portland—and now a great day back here. Brian, say hello to Carol. Brian—Carol, Carol—Brian."

Bobby quickly explained that he and his new female friend would be occupied right through the weekend. Before ending the phone call, he and Bobby arranged to hook up for breakfast Monday morning at the Maine Diner.

As Brian hung up the phone, he knew that all thoughts of driving to Bobby's house, and accidentally running into Linda, were now dashed. There had been no subtlety in his friend's wishes to have complete privacy over the weekend.

It was nearly five o'clock when a pair of headlights turned up the driveway. With its windshield wipers at full speed, Bobby Copeland's pickup truck made its way through blowing sheets of rain and toward the house. The slam of the pickup's door was followed in seconds by a knock at the back door.

"Just come in," called out Brian. The door flung open and a woman rushed in, her chestnut hair dripping water onto the floor as she held a tray out in front of her. The woman was Linda Birch. Brian stood in the middle of the room speechless.

"What are you doing here?" he asked.

"Well, as you can see, I made you some more of your favorite pastry, and when Bobby wouldn't drive me over to deliver them to you, he did the next best thing. He loaned me his truck." She placed the tray down on the table in the office where they both stood.

"Can you stay a while or do you have to run right off? How are you feeling?" he asked. Linda was dressed in jeans, a pink and white blouse and a rain jacket.

"I'm feeling great, thanks to you. Thank you for everything last night—everything."

"That's what friends are for," answered Brian. The two looked at each other through an awkward silence before Brian spoke. "I'll make us some coffee or tea—if you can stay awhile."

Linda nodded and followed Brian into the kitchen. He prepared the coffeemaker for six cups and the two returned to the sitting room. Before settling in, he flicked off the television.

"The coffee'll come in handy washing down these dry old things," commented Linda, pointing at the turnovers.

"Lin, I told you, these things are special to me. I actually feel closer to my mother—she died a couple of years ago—when I eat them. Hokey, huh? I miss her a lot."

"Don't get me wrong, I'm happy to make them for you—anytime. It just seems a pitiful way to repay somebody who's done so much for you. Have you ever had a toothache?"

"Never," replied Brian.

"Well, pray you never do. It's awful. I mean, I wanted to literally die. I can't describe the pain."

"I could tell it was bad. I just couldn't stand watching you suffer like that." Brian rose and left the room to check on the coffee while Linda checked the weather outside through the window. Moments later, he returned with the coffee, cream and sugar.

"I'm guessing it was you who put me into bed last night," she said.

"Yeah, you were out." He joined her on the couch, preparing both of their beverages. Responding to questions about the complex, Brian told his guest the story of how he arrived in Wells and how he came to work for the Russos. Eventually, the two were sitting shoulder to shoulder, with Linda, on occasion, resting her head against his.

"You know, not all men would have behaved like gentlemen under those circumstances last night. That probably has something to do with me being an old lady—compared to you, anyway," she confided, and perhaps to some extent, probed. Brian paused before his reply.

"I kissed you, you know. You were totally out—and before I left I kissed you," he admitted.

Linda's hand came up, turning his head toward her. She leaned forward and pressed her lips to his. He returned the kiss. It was she who broke it off, but continued to rest her body against him. "I was actually beautiful once, everybody said so. Now, there is a part of me that wishes I could be that way again—for you. I'm very afraid of making a total fool of myself right now. Do you know what I'm trying to say, Brian? What would a young, healthy boy in his prime want with some dowdy housewife?"

"I've been thinking about you ever since the day I first saw you, when I brought back Trevor."

"That's funny, 'cause I thought about you, too. 'Course, I chided myself for thinking that a teenage boy could see anything in an over-the-hill mother of three."

"Stop putting yourself down," Brian ordered before pulling the woman forward and kissing her again. He literally felt her go limp in his embrace.

"If I'm off the mark, tell me, but is there someplace we can go with a little more privacy and to lie down?" she asked.

"The door's open at cottage #15, where I'm staying." Brian jumped up, grabbing an umbrella from behind the front desk. "Take this and go to #15. I'll be along in five minutes. There's no one else in the entire complex. I'll shut everything down."

At the cottage, Linda had already turned up the heat and pulled back the covers on the bed when Brian bounded onto the porch and through the door.

"I really didn't expect to find a young man's place looking so tidy—bed made and all."

Brian half blushed. "My mom trained me well—she insisted. I caught hell if I didn't make my bed in the morning."

"The bedsheets look reasonably clean," she commented.

"Never mind reasonably clean! I just did a laundry this morning and put them back on the bed," Brian protested. Their brief banter was followed by a span of uncomfortable silence.

"By the way, Brian, I do intend to pay you back every penny it cost you last night. How much was it exactly?"

"It's okay Linda—whatever!" he stated, embarrassed by the talk of money.

"How much?"

"One hundred and fifteen dollars," he answered, leaving off the cost of the prescription.

"I will pay you back every cent." The woman walked up to him and began pushing him backwards toward the bedroom. "But right now, I intend to show you how much last night meant to me." She pushed him toward the bed until the backs of his legs were touching the edge of the mattress. It only took a slight nudge to cause him to fall backwards onto the full-sized bed.

"From this point on I want you to just relax—and enjoy. We have all night together, if you want. We don't need to hurry anything. Do you follow what I'm saying?" she asked. "The more you relax, the more pleasure I can give you." She hoisted herself on top of him, and he sighed audibly.

"Now listen—you can't leave any marks on me. Bub could notice something like that. But you're a single guy, and unless you tell me not to, I intend to leave marks all over you. Is that okay?" Brian consented through a stream of apprehensive, boyish laughter. The woman removed her blouse, tossing it onto a chair in the corner of the bedroom. She leaned down and kissed him, with purpose, then dropped her mouth to his neck, drawing on the skin, teeth lightly tearing on his flesh. His breathing quickened, heightened by her sensual directness along with the feel of her thighs tightening around his waist. He was lying helpless, her auburn curls strewn over his face.

"Don't move," she ordered, and rose to her feet. After unbuttoning her jeans, she kicked off her shoes, heaving her jeans to the corner of the room, then remounted him. "Pleasure comes from the mind, not just the body," she whispered.

Brian looked up intently at this woman called Linda Birch. The warm, maternal countenance present on her face only minutes earlier had been replaced by something quite different. There was a property in her behavior, an exhilarating, bestial property that sent a shockwave of excitement through him, mind and body. She proceeded to undress him, button by button, all the while describing in detail her plans for him for the next few hours. With Brian's clothes completely off and strewn across the floor, Linda began tantalizing her teenage lover, running her hands, feet and tongue across his erogenous zones. Only stroking long enough to cause his body to grow rigid with excitement, she would then retreat to less inflammatory regions, working his body like an instrument, always under her control.

Brian continued to lie on his back, paralyzed by the pleasure shooting through his body. Glancing up at her through her cascading hair, dressed only in undergarments, he thought how incredibly beautiful she looked. How could this be the same helpless woman slumped against him in the front seat of his car only the day before? This woman, who now utterly controlled him through sexual manipulation, had been his powerless ward only a day earlier. Brian's mind was racing through a series of random thoughts, instigated by an intensifying level of stimulation by the woman. He became aware that her breathing, too, was growing louder.

"I want to taste you," she whispered, breaking the silence. Totally beyond any resistance, Brian lay in anticipation. Seconds later, his body was involuntarily jolted by a series of repetitive manipulations to his genitals. A wave of pleasure surged in his body, building, rolling, and finally crashing.

Brian lay, weakened and drained, his body temporarily depleted of its masculine capacity. Barely gathering the strength, he pulled Linda up toward him. "I want you naked beside me," he said, then flicked open the clasp on her bra. Seconds later she had removed her undergarments. He cradled the woman's head against his chest, then ran his hands lightly over her aroused breasts, running his index finger in a tight circle around her hardened nipple. The tempo of the rain and wind picked up outside the cottage window, sending droplets against the pane of glass.

"I can't even begin to react to what just happened here. You are just so great," he uttered, causing Linda to laugh but not respond. "I mean, what you just did for me and I barely know anything about you," he stumbled on.

"What do you want to know?" she asked.

"Everything."

"Okay, I was born and brought up in New Hampshire."

"You're from New Hampshire! Manchester?" he blurted out.

"No, Berlin, up in the mountains. I've got two brothers and my folks still live there."

"How'd you get all the way down here?"

"I worked here a couple of summers while I was in school. That's when I met Bub. We went out—you know the routine. 'Course, back then I went out with a lot of boys. I mean, you wouldn't know it but I was drop-dead gorgeous once."

"You're still gorgeous. Stop putting yourself down like that."

"Anyway, after I graduated from high school I moved here— made good money waitressing. Eventually, in a moment of weakness, Bub proposed and I accepted. He had a good job at the time as a chef. But he sort of drank himself out of that job, and a few more."

"I'll bet you were a cheerleader in high school."

Linda laughed, then shook her head in disbelief. "Yeah, as a matter of fact I was."

"What was your school's mascot? I'm trying to picture you in your cheerleading outfit."

"Mountaineers—the Berlin High Mountaineers."

"So you're kind of like Heidi—growing up in the mountains—yodeling a lot," teased Brian.

"Hardly—Berlin's like a working town with a paper mill where most of the people who actually stay around go to work."

"And you can see the mountains, must be the White Mountains, from town?" Linda nodded yes.

"What's your real name, you know, your name before you married Bub?"

"Pelletier, almost everyone in town's French."

A contented expression came upon Brian's face as he settled his head back on the pillow. The two continued to talk a short while longer until one, then the other, drifted off to sleep.

Brian opened his eyes, then swiveled his head toward an illuminated alarm clock resting on the dresser. It was one of the wind-up models that clicks out the seconds monotonously until the spring runs down. It was ten minutes past four.

In the next second, he picked up on Linda's breathing beside him. He rolled his body against hers, felt her warmth, then brought his mouth down over her nipple. The realization that this woman was still sharing his bed brought forth a wave of excitement and sexual energy. She was still naked. She awoke, opening her eyes, smiling, full of invitation.

Brian lifted himself up and carefully lowered himself on top of her. The very feel of her beneath him sent his spirits soaring. He was already rigid. Slowly, he directed himself inside her, making them, for the moment, one being. One being in perfect rhythm, in perfect motion. Their sexual unity, so compliant with the laws of nature, brought a rapid climax to the proceedings. The woman arched her back in response, suspending the two lovers on a euphoric plateau for an additional few moments.

"You are perfect, do you know that?" whispered Brian, when his breath returned. She did not answer, instead holding the boy against her. They lay and listened to the noisy clock run down their precious time together.

"Maybe you could make us something before I have to leave," she suggested. Brian climbed from the bed, making his way toward the kitchen area.

"Please don't put your clothes back on—not just yet," he requested. She did not answer.

"Brian, you do realize that we're not going to be able to get together like this in the future—well, near future anyway?" There was no response. "I'm married, Brian—with kids. It's not like I have all this free time to come running over here. This was like once in a lifetime."

"There's got to be sometime you can get away?"

"Brian, I've got a husband and three kids. My life isn't mine anymore," pleaded the woman, now obviously begging for his understanding.

"I'm telling you, Linda, you can call me anytime you want me. I'll be here for you." Brian brought a pot of tea over to where she was sitting, placing it down on the coffee table.

"Oh, Brian, you just don't see it. My life is already over. Do you understand? You just don't walk away or mess around with your life when it's like mine. You're single—nobody depends on you. You don't have things weighing you down." He sat on the floor in front of her. "I'm trapped with no way out. One minute you're young and carefree and then, wham, everything's over." Linda's eyes were now wet with restrained tears. She rose from the couch and walked to the bedroom where she dressed. She retrieved a few articles of clothing for Brian as he poured their tea. They drank the tea in silence, taking in each other's faces during these last, fleeting moments.

It was still dark as Linda Birch stood in the doorway to leave. The two extended the moment through an embrace before she kissed him one final time, then hurried back to Bobby's truck.

Over the ensuing weeks, Brian was only able to speak to Linda for brief periods, always while visiting Bobby. Bub found himself drawing unemployment compensation a short time before Christmas. When Brian returned from Lowell after spending the holidays with the Clarkes, Bobby gave him a handwritten note:

Brian,

By the time you get this we'll be gone. Bub's got a job all the way down in Hartford, Connecticut. We had to leave on short notice. Of all the things I'll miss in Maine, I will miss you the most. I'm sorry I couldn't say good-bye in person. Please take care of yourself and don't worry about me. Please know I will miss you.

Love,
Linda

XXVII

THROUGH THE FOLLOWING WINTER the friendship between Brian and Bobby continued to grow. The young men routinely went in search of parties, willing to travel anywhere from Kittery to Portland in their quest. Through Bobby, Brian learned that the Birchs moved from their trailer in the middle of the night. The news left Brian heartsick, imagining Linda hurriedly throwing her worldly possessions in the back of Bub's truck during the holidays.

Brian received definitive word from the Russos that they would arrive back in Wells in early May. He looked forward with anticipation to their return, primarily for their reaction to the new view from their hilltop over the estuary below. The Russos' fears about retaliation from the town or environmentalists had proved unwarranted. Secondly, he had managed to amass nearly six hundred dollars worth of rentals from mid-October to early November. This money had been deposited in an old Christmas Club savings account of Bella's he had found in the bottom of a drawer.

When the Russos' station wagon turned onto the driveway, Brian was painting trim on the motel building. Taking advantage of the ever-increasing May daylight, he was working right into the late afternoon. He descended the ladder and began making his way to their car. The Russos had been absent since September and Brian looked forward to having their company over the coming summer season. Their vehicle parked in the opening between the motel and one line of cottages, where they caught their first sight of the transformed view of the estuary and distant ocean. Lou had already stepped from the car, gazing out over the landscape, his mouth literally hung open. Bella remained in the car's passenger seat. She, too, stared out over the transformed terrain.

"When the hell did this happen?" snapped Lou, his voice edged in rage.

"Last fall, Lou, what do you think?" asked Brian enthusiastically.

"And who told you you could go ahead with something like this?"

"No one. I just did it—and it didn't cost a cent."

"No, Brian—when the hell did I or anyone else give you permission to do something like this? You just don't take down trees in an area like this with government land so close by and a million environmentalists just waiting to jump on you," hollered Lou, his anger now openly visible.

"It's your goddamn land, Lou, and it's been down over six months. No one's said jack shit. It's okay, Lou."

"It's not okay. You could have cost me a fortune in fines. You could still cost me!" barked the man.

"Well, I'm sorry for turning your dog-shit view into this! My goddamn mistake!" spat out Brian.

Bella finally emerged from the station wagon. "I think someone is very tired from the drive today, and probably very hungry, too. Lou, I suggest we get back in the car—I'll drive. Maybe we head over to Suzelle's. You've been talking about going there all week. It'll give you time to cool off. You're tired and hungry, Lou."

"This guy's gone over the line," argued Lou, his tone beginning to moderate.

"Brian, enough's been said here already. Go back to your cottage. Let's let everyone cool off a little. Lou—dinner— Suzelle's," instructed the woman. "Brian, why don't you come over for breakfast in the morning? Everyone will be calmer by then."

"Welcome back, Bella," muttered Brian before wheeling around and returning to his painting. Angry, he only worked for another five minutes before putting his supplies away. Returning to cottage #15 he hurriedly loaded all his possessions into the Biscayne, left his key in the door, and sped away from the complex. It had taken him less than one hour to pack away most of his worldly possessions. Upset, disappointed, discouraged, he headed south on Route 1, the first leg of his trip back to Lowell.

On Saturday morning Brian sat at the Clarkes' kitchen table, picking at his scrambled eggs and attempting to shed the best possible light on his situation. The night before he had shown up at his aunt and uncle's door, visibly upset and in need of sympathetic ears. The Clarkes were quick to open their door to him. The entire family listened intently as Brian explained the circumstances that brought him back to Lowell—his first visit since the previous Christmas. Jimmy Junior, for one, was overjoyed at having his older cousin home. The two were in the backyard tossing a baseball when Martha Clarke appeared at the door.

"Phone call for you, Brian," she called out, causing a look of astonishment to break out on his face. He signaled for little Jimmy to hold the baseball and bounded into the house. The phone laid on its side atop the kitchen counter.

"Hello?" he said tentatively.

"Thank God we've tracked you down. What's this all about, you running off last night without a word?" It was Bella.

"Oh, hi, Bella. How did you know I was here? As you can see, I decided to come back home after everything that went on last night. I got the distinct feeling I wasn't wanted anymore."

"Brian, that isn't true. Did you hear that, big mouth? Thanks to you and your big mouth, Brian thinks he's not wanted anymore," she called out, evidently directed at Lou somewhere within shouting distance. "Brian, I don't want any more of this talk about us not wanting you anymore. My God, we got back from Suzelle's last night and Lou heads down to your cottage to apologize and we find you gone. Brian—listen to me—we don't just want you back, we need you back. Lou flew off the handle 'cause he was overtired, and hungry, and the shock down below just set him off. Now please tell me you're going to turn around and come back." Bella's words were followed by momentary silence from Brian.

"I'll head back up Monday morning."

"Thank you, Brian. Oh—we found the money you left in my Christmas Club. How'd you manage that? Anyway—it's half yours," said Bella, her voice already expressing relief at Brian's decision to return.

"You're giving him half?" exclaimed Lou from across the room.

"Brian, we'll be expecting you Monday sometime. Have a nice stay with your family," Bella chirped before bringing the phone call to an end. Brian placed the receiver down and smiled at his aunt.

"I guess they want me after all," he proclaimed triumphantly. "Listen, Aunt Martha, before I go outside and dazzle your son with my curveball, I want you to be thinking about where you guys would like to go out to dinner tonight. I'm treating the family! They're giving me half the money I made for them last fall and suddenly I'm in a generous mood," exclaimed a jubilant Brian.

Brian rose early Monday morning with the family, sharing breakfast with everyone before heading back to Maine. He had made the most of his weekend, dining out with the Clarkes Saturday and surprising Perez with Chinese takeout at his apartment Sunday afternoon.

It was a revitalized Brian Kelly who retraced his path from two years earlier, following Route 110 eastward to Salisbury where he banked the Biscayne off an easterly ocean breeze and motored north to York County, Maine. He had only been back at the complex a few minutes when he was joined by Lou in front of his cottage at the crest of the hill.

"It's magnificent, you know—with the trees down. We're going to make all new brochures and show off our new view. You did good. All I ask though, please—in the future—no more surprises."

"No more surprises, Lou, I promise."

XXVIII

IN 1976, BRIAN MANAGED to put together his most enjoyable Maine summer yet, thanks in part to his friendship with Bobby Copeland. The summer of the bicentennial saw the popularity of disco music and bikinis in full swing. The young men never seemed to be at a loss for female companionship, whether it was cramming four into the Biscayne at the Kennebunk Drive-In Theatre where the summer saw an endless stream of horror movies come and go, or getting their coveted back row seats at the E. M. Loew's Casino Theatre at Wells Beach where they took in *One Flew Over the Cuckoo's Nest* and *Taxi Driver*. On one occasion, when Brian had managed to arrange a double date with a pair of sophisticated college juniors from Radcliffe, he was able to convince Bobby to escort the girls to the Wells Beach Casino Ballroom where they faked their ways on the dance floor to the music of Dr. Provencher and his Heartbeats Orchestra.

The evening wound up being a prolonged one, finally playing itself out at Bobby's place where the four paired off and shared impersonal intimacy, the kind common in summer, beach community romances. The following morning, as the pretty coed combed her hair in Bobby's tiny guest bedroom, Brian looked on from the bed. This young woman, whom he barely knew, seemed almost oblivious to his presence.

"We don't know too much about each other, do we?" suggested Brian.

"What's there to know?" she answered as she applied lipstick in front of the bureau mirror.

"I mean—we made love last night and I know hardly anything about you," he explained.

"Made love! Who are you, Cary Grant? Are those two up?" asked the black-haired coed as she walked from the congested bedroom, seemingly uninterested in keeping up any manner of discourse with him. Apparently having heard the sound of her friend's voice, the second Radcliffe girl appeared in Bobby's bedroom door, fully dressed, and the two prepared to leave. The black-haired girl took a second to look back to Brian, who by now was standing in his bedroom doorway, covered only in a sheet from the bed.

"It's been real," quipped the girl, who then disappeared out the door, not even waiting for a reply. Bobby then emerged from his room, dressed only in briefs, arms outstretched and yawning.

"Good-bye, girls, don't forget to write," he called out.

"Is it me, or was that pathetic?" asked Brian, twirling the bedsheet around him like a toga.

"Are you kidding? That was great! Wham, bam, thank you ma'am. No friggin' strings, my man, no friggin' strings. No lovey dovey bullshit."

"Okay, now their names were Judy and Julie, right?" asked Brian.

"I thought it was Judy and Janet? You did that screwy Cary Grant impression—Jewdee—Jewdee—Jewdee, so we definitely know one of their names was Judy," reasoned Bobby. Brian shook his head in disbelief.

"Man, that whole thing was beneath pitiful. What name did you call the girl you slept with?"

"Judy!" announced Bobby.

"So did I! Christ, they couldn't both be Judys!" exclaimed Brian, shaking his head in disbelief.

"Hey, we dated disposable Judys!" Bobby cried out.

"Man, it'd be funny if it weren't so goddamn pathetic. I swear, there's got to be something better out there than this. Do you know what I mean, Bobby?—a little less crass."

"Brian, life's not some romance novel. That was back with Queen Victoria. This is what life is now—disposable Judys. Loosen up and make the most of it," joked Bobby.

"I hope you're wrong, dirtbag, I hope you're wrong," chanted Brian, shaking his head.

It is certainly true that every summer day is a workday in the Maine hospitality business, but Saturdays are generally the most hectic of the week, and this was certainly true at Atlantic Coast Cottages and Motel.

On July 2nd, in the summer of 1977, Brian rose before dawn on a Saturday, and set work schedules in motion on this day of the week when the majority of weekly renters would be checking in and out. Just before the sun broke the horizon, Brian was inspecting the inventories of clean towels and linens along with a host of other duties. After printing up billing statements for each of the guests, he joined forces with the small cadre of chambermaids to assist in cleaning the nearly two dozen housing units within the complex. At noon, he thoroughly cleaned the pool area, adding chemicals to the chlorinated water and raising the water level back to its proper depth. From the pool it was back to helping the chambermaids until, at approximately two-thirty, his duties for the day were completed.

With Lou Russo behind the office desk and Bella downstairs sorting and cleaning towels and linens, Brian entered the main house and staggered toward the television room where he collapsed into an overstuffed chair by the far wall. He rose to his feet only long enough to drag a matching hassock close enough for his tired legs. The fatigue from his extended morning duties caused him to drop off to sleep, a light slumber where he was vaguely conscious of the happenings around him and in the adjoining room.

However, he was abruptly jolted from his catnap by the sound of Lou's boisterous greeting to an arriving group of tourists. Hearing his boss hollering something in French, Brian opened his eyes and took in a family of four crowded by the front desk. Brian thought these must surely be returning guests, as Lou stepped forward and embraced first the man and then the woman. In addition to the two adults, there was a boy perhaps ten or eleven years old, and a teenage girl of indeterminable age. Lou, the only member of the staff who spoke French, was obviously enjoying the opportunity to practice his second language. Although slightly halting, he showed a remarkable aptitude for putting together sentences as the French couple rattled off statement after statement, prompting his responses.

During a short break in the conversation the boy excused himself in French and made his way outside. Brian was now able to get his first clear view of the teenage daughter who stood quietly behind her parents. She had long, straight, brown hair that flowed down over her shoulders. Dressed in white shorts and a blouse that set off her tanned arms and legs, the sight of this young girl pulled his attention away from the adult conversation. Her parents, as Brian assumed, introduced her to Lou and the two exchanged greetings in French.

Moments later, with the adults again embroiled in conversation, the girl drifted away from the adults and slowly stepped into the television room. It was just as she cleared the doorway that the girl lifted her eyes, a pair of dark, brown eyes, and gazed upon Brian across the room. Following only the briefest of glances, she turned to the side wall and began admiring the first of a series of framed, colored photographs of early Wells. With apparent keen interest, the teenage girl stepped up to one, then the next, of these photographs, staring intently at each one as if taking in each minute detail portrayed. She followed the sequence of pictures in a counterclockwise direction around the room, slowly making her way closer to Brian, who sat beneath a picture of Mile Road at the turn of the century.

As this beautiful little creature drew closer to his chair, he felt anxiety building within him. He glanced sideways as she moved to the next photograph, again stepping right up to the photo before her as if studying it in great detail.

She was now at the picture on his immediate left, allowing him to observe her features at close range. He could see that her face carried the same light-brown color as her tanned body. She did not appear to be wearing makeup of any kind, allowing a sprinkle of freckles to show across her nose.

The girl made no attempt to return Brian's glance. A small pulse of nervous energy shot through his stomach as she drew back from the photograph and stepped over directly in front of his chair. Now, unlike with the preceding half-dozen pictures, there was an object between her and the photos. Expressionless, she looked up at the photograph then down at Brian. He said nothing, rendered speechless and in awe of this beautiful, young woman. He searched for something to say, but could not come up with anything even mildly amusing. Finally, the teenage girl removed her sandals, stepped over the hassock, and stepped up onto the chair, her feet resting on either side of Brian's lap. His head was at the girl's belt level as he sat frozen in the chair.

Looking up, she appeared totally focused on the photograph, seemingly oblivious to him, pinned in the chair below her.

Shocked, mortified, mesmerized, Brian finally managed to utter a sentence.

"Miss, if you would like to stand on my shoulders, you could examine the top of the frame better," he blurted out.

"*Pardonnes-moi?*" she replied. Brian broke out in nervous laughter.

"Is it just me or are we in a very awkward position here?" He could feel his heart racing inside his chest from the circumstances, the close proximity of this strange girl.

"*Que dis tu? Tu veuz que je te quitte?*" she asked, looking down on the embarrassed stranger.

"Christ, do you speak any English at all?" The girl responded to his question with a look of total bewilderment. "Come on, you must speak some English?" Her expression registered no comprehension of his words. "Oh my God, it's like talking to a rock—an adorable, gorgeous, nutty-as-a-fruitcake rock. Is it me or is this little dope totally lost? I mean—come on!" he muttered out loud. The girl simply continued to look down at him, apparently not understanding a word he said.

"*Sais-tu comment drôle, comment fou, tu sembles a ce moment?*" asked the girl.

"What kind of nutcase just steps up on a chair with a total stranger sitting in it?" asked Brian rhetorically.

"Angelique! What are you doing to that poor man?" called out the woman from the next room.

"I wanted to see if American men are as stupid as they appear on television. It does appear that they are," answered the girl in impeccable English, flavored with a French accent.

"Angelique, get down off of Mr. Russo's furniture. You were not raised to walk on furniture. And what are you doing to that poor man?" The pretty girl stared down at Brian, a foxy smile now spread across her face. Stepping down from the chair, she slipped her feet back into her sandals and rejoined her parents in the next room. Brian remained seated, staring in trancelike fashion at the brown-haired girl. With her parents having concluded their conversation with Lou, the girl turned to leave but did glance back at Brian before clearing the doorway.

Attempting to be as nonchalant as possible, Brian made a pass by the front desk a few minutes later, taking in a few details of the French-Canadian family who had just checked in. They were the LaChapelles of Quebec City and would be staying in the three-bedroom cottage close to the pool for the next two weeks. He returned to his cabin, pulled a Royal Crown from the fridge, and parked himself on the porch. He riveted his eyes on the cottage that the LaChapelle family, most notably Angelique, would be occupying. The family was unpacking their belongings, transporting them from the family wagon to the cottage. He strained his eyes at the delicate teenager as she made trip after trip between vehicle and cottage. He tried to come up with an excuse, any reasonable excuse, to approach them. He was drawing a blank. All he could do was sit tight, watch the door from afar, and hope to catch Angelique on her way out. He continued his vigil for what seemed like the entire afternoon, but actually was forty-five minutes.

It was then that Angelique left the cottage and walked toward the swimming pool. There were only a handful of guests at poolside at this time, none of whom were in the water. After closing the gate behind her, Angelique removed the towel draped over her shoulders and promptly dove into the water with hardly a splash. Brian jumped to his feet and made his way down the hill toward the girl. Making his way through the assorted pool furniture, he set himself down on a chair directly aside the lounger where Miss LaChapelle had tossed her towel. After swimming a half-dozen laps the girl ascended the ladder from the water, giving Brian his first true glimpse of her. She walked toward him, dripping from every part of her body. Her bright orange one-piece bathing suit clung to her dark, willowy body, showcasing her athletically muscled form. Her eyes widened as they focused on him. She had not seen him arrive and take the chair beside her own.

"Perhaps you'd like me to move to the other side—being the little dope that I am?" she said. Brian's head was swimming, so great was this girl's effect on him.

"No, don't—I'm really quite fond of little dopes. You can ask anyone." The girl smiled, then began drying her legs. He took the next few seconds to search for something, anything, to say. "Can I get you anything?"

"I'd like my own car," she replied.

"Well, you know, not anything anything."

"I'm thirsty. Would you get me something to drink?" He jumped to his feet, hustled back to the cabin, then returned with a bottle of soda. The girl took a long series of gulps from the bottle, offered Brian a sip, then placed it down by her lounger. After a prolonged silence, she caught him off guard with, "So, you actually believe I'm gorgeous and adorable?"

"I said that, huh?" She smiled and nodded yes. "Well, put it this way. I don't make a habit of running around and fetching sodas for all our guests. Does that tell you something?" She giggled and reached down for her drink.

"It's been five years since I've been here," she confided. "My parents and my brother have come every year but I've gone to a summer camp instead. This year I came—I think I'm getting a little old for camp, don't you?"

"Definitely, now I'm guessing you're twenty-six, maybe twenty-eight, which means you're definitely getting a little long in the tooth for summer camp," he teased.

The girl burst out laughing. "What does that mean? Long in the tooth?" she asked, now turned and facing him.

"You know—uh—I think it means that when people get old—like you—their gums recede and it makes their teeth look longer," he answered.

"So, you think I'm twenty-six or twenty-eight?"

"I was only kidding."

"Well, then, how old do you think I am?" she asked.

"Eighteen?" guessed Brian. His estimate made her laugh aloud.

"Then that's all that matters." With that, she rose to her feet, wrapping her towel about her shoulders. "It's been very enjoyable speaking to you," she said as she began walking off.

"I hope I'll see you again—around the pool or somewhere," said Brian hopefully.

"It would be nice if I knew your name," responded the girl.

"The name's Brian."

"And do you have a last name?"

"Kelly."

The girl stood at the gate to the pool, her hair cascading over one shoulder. "And do you want to learn my name?" she asked flirtatiously.

"Don't worry, Angelique, I already know your name," Brian answered. The girl tossed him a look of amusement and marched back to her cottage.

Brian would not set eyes on the intriguing Miss LaChapelle for the remainder of the day. She and her family dined out on

Saturday night, not returning until sometime after 10:00 P.M. Curious about the family, Brian spent time lending Lou some help Saturday evening, all the while pumping him for information about the LaChapelles, particularly Angelique. He was astonished to learn that the girl was extremely intellectual, her test scores indicating that she was a borderline genius, and that she was somewhat of a loner, slow to make friends, particularly with other females. Curious personality traits, perhaps the result of her advanced intellect, had caused her parents to send her for psychological therapy. This had gone on for more than three years without any trace of results. The pretty teenager was prone to play outlandish practical jokes, with a few resulting in the need for punishment by her shocked and mortified parents. The LaChapelles were also quite concerned that, to date, their daughter had shown little interest in boys, but instead was content to sit at home on weekends, reading or watching old movies on television.

"Bella and I have known the LaChapelles for almost ten years now. They are a wonderful family and Angel is a special little girl. Listen to me—little girl! Why, she has to be fourteen or fifteen by now."

"Fifteen? She's fifteen?" exclaimed Brian.

XXIX

SUNDAY CALLED FOR BRIAN TO WORK a full day—full meaning twelve hours. He was only able to catch brief glimpses of the LaChapelles and that was as they left and returned from church. However, his spirits soared when Angelique stuck her head inside the door long enough to tell him she would be spending the afternoon with her family on the beach by the jetty. She wanted him to know that if he was able to break away from work that he was invited to join them. He assured her that he would attempt to get off early and join her family. He then went about quick-stepping his way through his chores, laboring feverishly to complete every task expected of him in as short a time as possible. Just before two-thirty he approached Bella and asked to be dismissed for the day.

Within ten minutes he was pumping his bicycle down Mile Road and onto Atlantic Avenue, reaching Wells Harbor and the jetty just before three o'clock. After fastening his bike to a telephone pole, Brian made his way up the path and onto the beach, scanning the sea of faces for Angelique's. He searched and searched, walking nearly a quarter of a mile southward looking for her. After thirty minutes, frustrated and despondent, he climbed up onto the jetty and viewed the throng from atop the pile of boulders. She and her family were simply not there.

He looked away in disgust, disappointed beyond belief. It was then that a young female wearing a bright orange bathing suit came into view across the channel at Drake's Island approximately a hundred yards away. She had just climbed up onto the rocks of the jetty that ran parallel to the one that he himself was standing on. Instantly he realized that he had mistakenly concluded that Angelique had meant the Wells Beach jetty while extending him her invitation.

He began flailing his arms and bellowing across to the girl who, at this moment, was so close yet so far away. Although unable to hear him, Brian's arm-waving did catch her eye. The two stared across the water at each other for the next minute while their body language telegraphed their mutual disappointment and frustration. Finally, Angelique slumped down onto the rock, folding her legs in front of her and resting her chin on her knees.

Brian assessed the situation: to bicycle around from his current position to Drake's Island would take nearly an hour, and that was much too long. The channel of water between them was approximately a hundred yards wide. He made his decision in an instant. Pulling off his sneakers, he stepped onto the seaweed-covered jetty rocks and dove into the cold Atlantic water.

Brian felt his body recoil on impact, the cold ocean water dropping his body temperature in seconds. Putting his head down he set out to cross the channel through a burst of aggressive long strokes. He had only been in the water seconds when he felt the influence of the tide as it receded, drawing the water from the estuary out through the narrow, man-made channel. While only drawing in air after every other stroke he looked up to get his bearings after approximately thirty seconds in the water. He caught himself veering to the right, being dragged by the tide running outward. At the same time, he caught sight of Angelique's orange bathing suit against the rocks on the far side. He was no further than halfway across when, in the next instant, he was struck by a wave on his right, pushing him back toward his original line.

The thought struck him that this crossing might be beyond his swimming capability. Forcing himself to think positive, he pressed on. His body felt cold, causing his muscles to tighten. Grabbing a second peek at the far jetty, he could now make out Angelique halfway down the rocks and seemingly in a state of panic. By now his body was aching, but he knew he was only perhaps twenty yards from the other side. Willing himself to continue despite pain in his arms and legs, he put together another series of strokes, then another, until finally he felt the slimy edge of the seaweed laden rocks. Wrapping his arms around a sharp stone, he was washed over by a wave breaking into the channel. He held onto the rock, coughing up sea water for a few seconds, before being joined by Angelique.

"Was that stupid or what?" he asked. A few spectators were standing on the jetty above them clapping.

"Why did you do such a thing?" she asked, still stunned by the stunt.

"I wanted to ask you if you'd have dinner with me some night next week? If you say no, I swear to God, I'll turn around and swim right back—and you'll have my floating, dead body on your conscience the rest of your life."

"I would have said yes to you without any of this craziness," she answered, then projected a smile that caused Brian to gaze up at her in amazement. There was no denying his state of mind, his reckless behavior, or his total lack of concern for what anyone thought of his deportment. It did not matter if Angelique LaChapelle was fifteen or fifty years old.

He was in love.

Brian knocked on the LaChapelles' cottage door just after six o'clock on Tuesday evening, and was urged to come in by Mrs. LaChapelle, a tall, slender woman with a pretty face set behind a pair of rather plain eyeglasses. She told him that Angelique was almost ready and for him to make himself comfortable in the meantime. Brian, dressed in a three-piece suit, was visibly nervous in her presence. The woman tried to put him at ease.

"I hope you know what you are getting yourself in for. My daughter can be a handful," remarked Mrs. LaChapelle. Brian laughed but did not respond. "The Russos have nothing but wonderful things to say about you, Brian. My husband asked, Angel being only fifteen. You *did* know that she is only fifteen?"

"Yes, Mrs. LaChapelle. I'll be a perfect gentleman, you can count on that. And, of course, I'll take good care of her while we're out. She'll be perfectly safe."

"It sounds like you two are going to a very nice restaurant, and very expensive," commented the woman.

"I sort of wanted our first date to be something special. She wanted to go to the drive-in but I told her we could go there sometime before you guys go home. I figured some place classy for our first date." The two heard the sound of a door opening and seconds later Angelique walked into the kitchen. She was wearing a medium-length red dress with matching heels. Her long hair flowed down her back, stopping just before her waist. Brian could only stare, words escaping him until the young woman spoke.

"You look very nice, Mr. Kelly, but it still isn't too late to go to the drive-in."

"You look beautiful, Angel," offered Mrs. LaChapelle.

"You really do," added Brian, tongue-tied.

Brian escorted his young date to the car and headed south to Ogunquit. He did not even entertain Angelique's suggestion that they head up to Kennebunk and the drive-in movie. Instead, he would attempt to dazzle his Canadian companion at one of southern Maine's most exclusive restaurants, one featuring French cuisine, no less. After burying his banged up Biscayne in the far end of the establishment's parking lot, he proudly walked his date through the front door. Heads turned as he approached the *maitre d'*. They were shown to a corner table where their middle-aged host pulled out an opulent, lavishly upholstered chair for the young woman. Brian was pleased to see his reservation had been honored and the two had been seated without a hitch. The candle burning atop the table cast a radiant light upon the girl's face, causing him to stop in mid-sentence at one point in the conversation and simply admire her.

"I don't suppose I could order a hamburger here?" she asked playfully.

"You could, but it'd still cost me twenty bucks in this place, so why don't you order something on the menu that they feature."

"My shoes are too tight, may I take them off, Mr. Kelly?"

"As long as you don't put them on the table—and what's with this 'Mr. Kelly' business?"

"Well, I am just a child and you are a grown-up. I call you 'Mr. Kelly' out of respect."

"I'll be twenty-one in September—and you'll be sixteen?"

"Next year, I'll be sixteen next year. Right now I'm what you Americans call jail bait."

Brian laughed at her frankness. A waitress approached the table and asked Brian if he would care to order drinks before the meal.

"I'll just have a ginger ale. How about you, Angel?" inquired Brian.

"Whatever you think is best, Mr. Kelly."

"Two ginger ales, please. We'll need a few minutes to decide on our dinners," instructed Brian, sending the waitress back in the direction of the kitchen.

"Mr. Kelly, have you noticed—not only hasn't the waitress spoken to me, she hasn't even looked at me."

"Please, Angel, cut out the 'Mr. Kelly' stuff. It makes me feel like your father. As far as the waitress is concerned, she's probably overwhelmed by your beauty—I know I am."

Angelique flashed a bashful smile and glanced down at the menu. "Mr. Kelly, I'm afraid I have a problem. I need to go to the ladies' room and I cannot locate my shoes. They are under the table somewhere. Would you be a gentleman and bend down and get them for me?"

"You're asking me to crawl around on the floor and pick up your shoes? I'll look like a fool."

"The table cloth is very long. No one will even notice. I made myself beautiful tonight just for you. This isn't so much to ask, is it?"

"Where did you kick them?"

"They are probably right under my chair, but I just can't reach them."

Brian glanced around the room, then climbed down under the table, hidden from view by the long tablecloth. "I don't see them, Angel," whispered Brian from beneath the table.

"Look way under my chair," she instructed, to which Brian lowered his back and continued the search. Seconds later he felt the girl's feet come to rest on his shoulders.

"What are you doing?" he inquired, panic in his voice.

"Mr. Kelly, you must not move. My knees are resting just under the table—any sudden movement by you and everything might go flying, including the candle—besides, the waitress is on the way over." Brian looked to his left and saw a pair of woman's shoes approaching the table.

"Are you ready to order?" asked the waitress.

"I'm afraid my boyfriend and I have had a quarrel. It seems he found you very attractive and that led to words between us." Brian felt his jaw drop.

The waitress, too, seemed at a loss for words. "I'll give you two a little more time to decide," said the embarrassed waitress before scurrying away from the table.

"May I come up now?"

"Mr. Kelly, there is an elderly couple across the room who keeps looking over our way. They may have seen you go under the table looking for my shoes. Mr. Kelly, they are looking very disapprovingly at me. Do you have any idea what they could be thinking?"

"Pass me down a sharp steak knife. I'm cutting my own throat and putting myself out of my misery."

"I'll let you back up if you promise you'll never make me go somewhere I do not want to go again."

"Are they still looking over here?"

"Yes, they are. Do you promise?"

"I promise." Angelique let her feet slide down from his shoulders.

"You know, the view down here is pretty nice—it's the circumstances I object to," cracked Brian.

"Are they looking?"

"No, hurry, they're looking away." Brian scrambled back into his chair, hair disheveled and his face red with embarrassment. Before he could speak the waitress approached. She had seen him come up from below the table.

"Are you ready to order?" she asked awkwardly.

"We'll need more time, I'm afraid," Brian confessed apologetically.

"As you wish," answered the waitress before sauntering off.

"You do know what that couple thinks was going on under this table, don't you?" asked Brian.

"Mr. Kelly, I am only a child. How could I possibly know about such things?"

"Those people think I'm a degenerate!"

"But I know you are not." Brian could only stare into her magnificent brown eyes. "Will you take me to the drive-in tomorrow night?" she asked.

"Sunday night," he answered.

"Will you go to mass with me next Sunday—with my family?"

"If it means that much to you I will."

"It does."

"Will you behave like a big girl for the rest of the meal? A big, fifteen-year-old girl?" Her eyes widened and she nodded.

There were no further shenanigans through the appetizers and main course. As a matter of fact, as the meal progressed, Brian began to catch glimpses of the girl's superior intellect that Lou had spoken of on the day of the LaChapelles' arrival. Pretending to have no knowledge of his date's intellectual prowess, he probed into her academic background, seemingly for conversational purposes only. She neither boasted of nor tried to disguise her exceptional mental abilities.

When the waitress came by the table and inquired about dessert, Angelique passed while Brian ordered strawberry shortcake. Still hungry due to the measured portions of gourmet food, he was pleased to see his dessert piled high with whipped cream. He thought he detected evidence of regret in his date's face as the shortcake was placed in front of him.

"We can share," he offered, prompting an immediate acceptance. "I'll even give you first bite."

Brian scooped a small portion of cake and strawberries onto his spoon along with a generous cap of whipped cream. Reaching across the table, he carefully delivered the cake and strawberries into Angel's mouth but purposely lifted a portion of the whipped cream upward, leaving a large dab on the end of her nose. Brian's face lit up in a broad grin as he stared across the table at Angelique, who made no effort to remove the cream.

The waitress came back to inquire about his reaction to his dessert. "Is the strawberry shortcake to your liking?" asked the waitress.

"I'll tell you in a second. I'm about to take my first bite," he answered lightheartedly. The waitress glanced down at Angelique, only to see the girl staring up at her pathetically, the dab of whipped cream still balanced at the end of her nose. Still staring at the waitress, she rolled her lower lip downward into a pitiable pout while maintaining her deadpan expression and absolute silence. Brian buried his face in his hands, trying in vain to subdue his laughter.

"I'll come back in a few minutes after you've had a chance to try your shortcake," stated the waitress before walking off to another table. Brian separated his fingers and peeked through them at his date.

"You're insane, you know," he said. Angelique would only stare across the table at him, expressionless. He lifted himself from his chair, leaned across the table and licked the whipped cream from her face. He then used his napkin to wipe her nose dry. Picking up his spoon, he fed a second portion of his dessert to the girl, this time carefully directing all of it into her mouth.

"I will never—ever—forget this date," he acknowledged before taking his first bite. Angelique grew quiet, thoughtful, as the two finished their meal. Her silence made Brian uncomfortable.

"Mr. Kelly, please give the waitress a generous tip, I think she earned it." Brian agreed and settled the bill before they made their way out to the car.

On the four-mile trip back to Wells they said little, suddenly and inexplicably ill at ease in each other's company. He drove the Biscayne up behind the LaChapelle family's cottage. Brian found the silence in the car deafening. He wondered if she had had a mood swing and was angry at him.

"You don't have to walk me to the door, I will be okay," she announced. Brian's heart plummeted with despair. She climbed out of the car, prompting him to roll down his window.

"No matter what tonight was to you—I just want you to know, it was the best date of my pathetic life, and I think I will, all my life, have to compare every date to this one. And you know what? It'll always be the best. I don't know what I might have done wrong tonight, but I want you to know I didn't do it on purpose," confessed Brian, a certain desperation present in his voice.

Angelique stopped in her tracks, hesitated for just an instant, then raced around to his side of the car. Pulling open the door, she sprung inside the vehicle, landing in a straddling position atop his lap. Without any hesitation, she pressed her mouth over his. Brian's mind swam eagerly as his body responded with euphoric arousal, gladly submitting to this passionate outburst. He returned her kiss with equal intensity.

"I acted like a silly child at the restaurant," she whispered.

"You were funny—really, really funny!"

"I acted immature."

"You're only fifteen." She continued to press her lips against his, her tongue probing inside his willing mouth. The feel of her legs wrapped against him fueled and inflamed his blood. He could barely think straight, his heart was pounding so hard.

"Will you still take me to the drive-in movie, Mr. Kelly?"

"Of course."

"And to church on Sunday?"

"Angel, I'd march into hell on a rescue mission for you."

"I did not ask you to do that. Will you take me to mass on Sunday?"

"Yes."

"Was I really, really funny?"

"Really funny—and incredibly beautiful."

She leaned back from him, her eyes searching his for sincerity. Leaning down, she kissed him a final time then raced for the house.

"*Bon soir,* Mr. Kelly," she called out before rounding the corner of the cottage and bounding onto the deck.

For Brian, the LaChapelles' two weeks in Wells raced by in an instant. He kept his promises, taking Angelique not once, but twice, to the drive-in theatre. He also attended mass with the LaChapelles, sitting proudly beside Angelique throughout the service. In return, he asked a single favor of her.

On the Thursday afternoon prior to her family's departure, Angelique accompanied Brian and spent the afternoon at Parsons Beach in Kennebunk. He had been unable to return to this particular beach over the past few years, owing to the painful memories of Maggie May Keogh and her visit to this beach with him years earlier. He saw bringing Angelique to this wonderful, private beach as a form of exorcism, ridding him of the tormenting recollections from the summer of 1973. It took only two hours of frolicking in the surf with this magnificent child and lying together below the dunes to ease the pain in his remembrance of the past.

On the Friday evening before their trip back to Quebec City, Brian spent the evening with the LaChapelle family. By this time he had developed an amiable relationship with Angel's parents and a good-natured, rough-and-tumble connection with her younger brother, Henri. As the hour grew late, Brian set out to excuse himself from the gathering, citing his early working hours the next day. He and Angelique embraced on the deck outside the cottage, knowing they would have the opportunity for a final good-bye the following morning. As the two kissed, Brian felt Angelique's hands uncharacteristically drop down his back and onto his buttocks. His head grew light from the mild massage and patting action carried out by her delicate hands. Abruptly, she slipped her fingers back up to the small of his back and applied a last, purposeful kiss. He descended the steps and began the walk across the lawn back to #14.

Halfway across the lawn, Angelique's voice cried out. "Brian!"

He turned back to her and saw the entire LaChapelle family standing outside on the deck. Glancing down, he saw a ten-foot stream of toilet paper flowing from behind him, extending from the adhesive tape stuck on his pants just above his buttocks.

"*Bon soir*, Mr. Kelly," Angel called out.

"You'll pay for this one," he called back, relaying a good-natured threat.

"Please, sir, I am only a child," she heckled before leading her family inside.

On Saturday morning the LaChapelles made it a point to stop by the office before heading back to Quebec. There were hugs and good-byes with the Russos and a promise to return the following year, same time, same cottage. Brian and Angelique broke away from the chorus of well wishes and meandered by the pool and down the slope to the edge of the property.

"This is only good-bye until just after Labor Day. Angel, I promise I'll take a week off right after Labor Day when things slow down a little and come up to Quebec City to see you."

There was a forlorn expression on the young girl's face that served to comfort him. "I'm afraid you'll forget me," she confessed sadly.

He pulled her against his body, then allowed himself to slowly slump to his knees. He showered the exposed skin above her belt line with kisses. "You own me, Angel, I'm your helpless slave."

"Tell me you love me," she requested.

"I love you, Angelique—and I will till the day I die. I just know it." She beckoned him to return to his feet.

"For two years, every night I have prayed to meet someone I didn't know but I knew I would love. Sometimes you came to me in dreams but I could never clearly see your face. But I had a sense of who you were. When I saw you sitting in the television room the day we arrived—I knew it was you immediately. I was already in love with you."

"There'll be no one else, no girl, between now and when I visit you in September. Do you understand?"

"You will call me often?"

"Every day if that's what you want," replied Brian.

"Twice a week will be good," she suggested. The two walked back to the office where Brian and Angelique kissed a final time before the family began its return trip to Canada. His heart sank as he watched the station wagon disappear onto Route 1, Angelique waving dispiritedly out the back window until the vehicle wheeled out into traffic.

XXX

TRUE TO HIS WORD, Brian visited Quebec City no less than three times between Labor Day and December 1st. His last two visits were limited to long weekends where he arrived on Friday morning, returning to Maine late in the day on Sunday. Following a week spent with the LaChapelles just after Labor Day, the next extended visit was scheduled to coincide with Angelique's entire Christmas vacation from high school. Her last day of classes would land on Thursday, December 22nd, and Brian planned to leave for Canada Friday morning the 23rd, permitting him to settle into the LaChapelles' guest room well before Christmas Day and accompany Angelique on any last-minute shopping she might have on Christmas Eve. However, her plans were jolted by a phone call from him on the Tuesday prior to Christmas.

On that evening the phone rang and her mother called her to the telephone.

"Hello," she answered, not having been told who was on the line.

"Hi, kid, how's everything up there near the North Pole?"

"It gets better and better as Friday gets nearer," she answered.

"I'm afraid that's what I'm calling about. I've had to make a small change in plans." The line went silent for a moment.

"What kind of change?"

"I'll still be coming up—it's just that I'm going to have to spend Christmas in Lowell this year. It just can't be avoided."

"Oh, Brian," she blurted out, somewhat shaken.

"Kid, I'll be on the road right after Christmas, next Monday morning. It's a family thing and can't be avoided."

"But you'll still come?" she asked.

"Of course—it's just going to be a day late. I'll be like the wise men, you know, getting there after everybody else."

"I'm not going to pretend that I'm not disappointed. Are you going to tell me the reason you can't come for Christmas, why you need to go to Lowell?" she inquired, sounding more suspicious than hurt.

"I'm afraid I'll have to keep it secret for a little while."

"It better not be some old girlfriend from Lowell that is causing this."

"You'll have to trust me, Angel," Brian responded.

Dejected, Angelique dropped the subject and caught Brian up at the latest goings-on at *l'Academie de Sacre Coeur*. The twenty-minute phone call ended with a promise from Brian to leave Lowell for Quebec City early Monday morning, the day after Christmas.

Angelique descended the front steps and began the five-block walk home following dismissal from school on the last school day of 1977. The frigid Quebec City air numbed her legs as she strode through her neighborhood, dressed in the parochial school uniform that she could now hang out of sight in her closet until classes convened in January. All month she had been eagerly anticipating the Christmas holiday. Her spirits had been dampened by the news that Brian would not arrive until the day after Christmas but it was still her favorite holiday and, after all, he would still be coming soon after. The temperature was hovering near zero as the girl quick-stepped her way through the neighborhood and finally up the porch steps, pushing open the door to the house. At the far end of the hallway, Angelique could see her mother working at the sink. Tossing her books onto a hallway chair, she walked directly into the kitchen.

"Shhhh, no noise," instructed her mother as she passed a door leading to the living room.

"Why? What's the matter?" questioned the girl in a whisper.

"Your Uncle Hermas is resting on the couch." Angelique turned to the doorway, eyeing a figure lying on the couch, draped in one of the family's patchwork quilts.

"Who?" asked the astonished teenager.

"Angel, I'm afraid we've had a lot going on here since you left for school this morning. Your father's Uncle Hermas, that would make him your great uncle, showed up at our door this morning, very ill and weak. He asked your father if there was any way we could put him up for the holidays, as he was quite sick, and your father has agreed."

"Uncle Hermas? I don't remember ever hearing his name before."

"He's Pepere's brother, but really the black sheep of the family. The doctors have told him that he probably only has a few months to live. I know your father feels obligated to help him— he is family, after all."

"Mama, are you saying he's going to be here for Christmas?" asked a bewildered Angelique.

"Darling, it's not like we can turn him out. It's Christmas." The teenager walked to the far end of the kitchen, staring out the window in disbelief. "Uncle Hermas will probably be with us until he is just too sick to stay out of the hospital." Angelique whirled around.

"And where is he sleeping?" she asked in a state of near panic.

"He's already moved most of his things into the guest bedroom," answered Mrs. LaChapelle.

"But that is where we put Brian."

"We will have to somehow make do. Perhaps Brian can share with Hermas, or we can bring in a cot and he can sleep in the hall or downstairs somewhere." Speechless, Angelique could only stare across the kitchen at her mother.

"I cannot believe how this Christmas is working out! We cannot ask Brian to sleep in the same bed with a stranger—one who could die in bed overnight beside him. Mother!" exclaimed the girl in a hushed voice.

"Dear, none of us planned this. I think Brian will understand. Now in the meantime, why don't you go into the living room and say hello to your uncle. He was asking about you this morning when he arrived. He saw you in the family picture and repeated over and over how pretty you are." An apprehensive expression appeared on the girl's face. "I think it would mean the world to him," added her mother, sending Angelique out of the kitchen and into the living room where her uncle lay beneath a quilt.

The teenager moved toward the couch, eventually picking up the sound of breathing from the man. Each breath from beneath the quilt sounded labored, as if forced through a pair of lungs congested and clogged. She was reminded of descriptions in novels of dying men, and the accompanying death rattles present in their last, final breaths. She looked back to the kitchen. "He is asleep," she whispered to her mother.   .

"It will be all right to wake him," instructed Mrs. LaChapelle, gesturing her daughter to stir the stranger. Angelique looked down on her elderly uncle, her heart beating frantically inside her chest. She knelt down by the end of the couch and touched the man on the shoulder through the quilt.

"Uncle Hermas?" she said softly. The breathing from under the quilt was arrested, replaced by a painful sounding series of bronchial coughs. Angelique pulled back for a moment, then gained her composure and addressed her uncle a second time.

"Uncle Hermas, it is Angelique. I wanted to welcome you to the house." From under the blanket the man seemed to recoil, then resumed breathing.

"Mother said you wanted to say hello," the girl said timidly.

In the next instant the quilt came flying up from the couch and over Angelique's head, causing her to fall back. She let out a scream as the man came catapulting off the couch and onto her, trapping her blindly beneath the quilt as his weight came down, at least partially, onto her body. She screamed a second time, then called to her mother for help while the man's hands grasped her, pulling her toward him. Overcoming her fear, she flailed away at the man, still unseen by her from behind the quilt.

She screamed again, but now heard her own voice partially drowned out by the sound of laughter. From the doorway, her mother laughed out loud at the frantic scene unfolding on the floor before her. The second source of laughter came from directly above her. She ripped the quilt from her face to see Brian kneeling above her, laughing hysterically at the reaction his practical joke had managed to elicit.

"Mrs. LaChapelle, you were fantastic!" he cried out.

"You two," blurted out Angelique, still in a mild state of shock.

"We thought we'd teach you a lesson. How does it feel being on the receiving end of one of these little jokes?"

Angelique looked up at Brian for a second, then wrapped her arms around his neck and drew him down to the floor. Moments later their lips joined, and their hearts raced with the joy that each brought to the other. Following a full minute's embrace,

Brian looked up to see that Mrs. LaChapelle had left the room. He took this opportunity to lightly run his teeth and lips over Angelique's exposed knee.

"God, the sight of you in your little Catholic school uniform drives me wild."

"If my uniform does this to you, what will happen when you see me in my little baby-girl pajamas?" she added teasingly. They both fell over onto the floor.

"Oh, my God, ten days with you. How will I ever survive this?" questioned Brian.

"Christmas with my family—at home—in front of the fireplace—presents under the tree—with Mr. Kelly. I think this will be the best Christmas of my life," she said, her head resting on his shoulder.

At two-thirty on Christmas morning Angelique and Brian sat alone in the living room in front of the dying flames in the fireplace. Fresh from midnight mass, Brian's long frame lay extended across the couch, his head resting in the girl's lap. She looked down on him while her fingers played with his thick, shaggy hair. They had remained together through every waking hour since his arrival.

"Do you have any idea how much I love you, Brian?" she asked following a quiet interlude.

"You've probably already forgotten this but last summer I told you that I thought I'd probably love you forever. Well, that's changed," he said. "I think it's now safe to remove the word 'probably.' I now know I will love you forever," he explained dreamily. She leaned down and planted an innocent kiss on his lips.

"Some of the girls at school tease me and say my American boyfriend is probably fooling around on me back in Maine. I know it must be hard on you having a fifteen, almost sixteen-year-old girlfriend. It makes me feel guilty knowing you may be giving up having lots of fun with girls back home," she commented. He glanced up at her, smiling.

"Well, first of all, Frenchy—you noticed that I went to communion tonight—and I haven't been to confession since I got here—that tells you something, right? Secondly, it's not like all the girls back in Maine are battering down my doors, trying to go to bed with me. I'm not as good looking as you seem to think," he joked.

"Oh, but you are. Brian, if I was not a good girl and I lived down in Maine, I would batter down your door and take you every night. I swear I would."

"Against my will?"

"That is right. I would not take 'no' for an answer. I would ignore your cries for mercy," she added laughingly.

"Enough with this kind of talk—you're getting me all hot and bothered! It's a good thing I'm not sleeping with your poor, dying uncle. Even he wouldn't be safe after hearing you talk like this."

A few minutes passed before Brian finally was able to close the flue on the fireplace and escort Angelique upstairs to her bedroom. With no work or school duties to come between them, the two were inseparable through his ten-day visit.

He returned home to Maine just after New Year's Day, dispirited at having to leave the side of his Angelique.

XXXI

WITH THE NEW YEAR CAME Brian's desire for an elevated sense of independence. This meant finding an apartment away from Atlantic Coast Motel and Cottages. Arriving back in Maine, he had picked up a copy of the *York County Coast Star* and began his search. Initially interested in something in Wells or Ogunquit, his curiosity was raised by an ad for an apartment a short distance away in Kennebunkport. The second-floor apartment was situated directly above Julia's Gift Shoppe in Dock Square, included major appliances, and was year-round. He had learned on arriving in York County that many apartments and homes in beach communities could be rented at a reasonable price, but only eight months a year. A problem arose around June 1st when the tourist season began and properties had to be vacated so tourists could pay the greatly inflated rate these properties commanded in warm weather. It was Brian's intent to establish a permanent residence in the area and Kennebunkport seemed like an ideal place to do so. Ten days after speaking with his potential landlord, and after his personal and professional references checked out without a hitch, he and Bobby lugged an assortment of used furniture and dated accessories up the stairway to his second-story apartment. Moving in had proven to be an all-day affair, carried out in the cold, January air.

With the last of Brian's possessions dropped, stacked, leaned, or placed inside the apartment, the young men collapsed onto a couch conveniently placed in front of a window overlooking Dock Square. Across the street, the sign for Alisson's Restaurant told him that it would be a short walk indeed on nights when he did not have the energy or inclination to cook. The two young men,

Brian now twenty-one, sipped on cans of beer and celebrated the day's accomplishment.

"Man, Kelly, you've got it made in the shade! Think of all the great-looking babes that come through this place every year—and you're up here on Cloud 9 able to check 'em out. Shit! Meanwhile, I'm out in nowheresville in my friggin' trailer. You just got it made." Brian smiled at his friend, took a swig of beer, but did not respond. "Listen buddy, this is your pal speaking—the one who just spent the day helping you move—and I didn't see anybody else helping you lug your furniture up those friggin' stairs. Anyway, I know how great you're gonna have this place lookin'—well clean anyway—what I'm sayin' is, sometime you're workin' and ain't comin' back here and I have a hot date—."

"It's yours Bobby, don't sweat it! No Radcliffe girls though—those are my rules."

"No Disposable Judy?" laughed Bobby, sharing their private joke.

Two days after the move Brian's phone line was activated. That evening he called Angelique and told her about his new living arrangements.

"Angel, I am so looking forward to when you get down here and I can bring you here and show you everything. First of all, and being a friggin' genius this'll really mean something to you, the Kennebunk Book Port, the local bookstore, is in the next building to me. You'll be able to fill your gorgeous little egghead with anything you want to read—right next door. There's a movie theater around the corner, a gift shop downstairs, and Alisson's Restaurant is across the street—I mean, you're going to love it here."

"Can you see the ocean?" she asked.

"Well, not quite. But from the back windows you can see where they dock boats and the water comes in behind the building and under some of the buildings," exclaimed an excited Brian.

"If I dive out the back window when the tide is in, will I land in the water?" asked the girl.

"Yeah, but you'll go down about two feet into the mud with just your feet and legs kicking above the water," answered Brian, causing the sixteen year old to laugh.

"And will you be inviting girls up to see your apartment when I'm not there?"

"I only allow in sixteen-year-old girls in Catholic school uniforms. You know how they turn me on—those uniforms."

"There had better not be any Catholic schools close by, Mr. Kelly."

"I haven't even checked yet, but thank you for reminding me," laughed Brian.

"Are you still in Wells?"

"No, LaChapelle, haven't you been listening? I'm in ritzy, snooty, classy, noses-in-the-air Kennebunkport. God, I can't wait for you to get down here and see it!" he exclaimed.

"Well, how about this? Why don't you take some pictures and bring them with you up here next weekend?"

"It's a deal, Angel—and I'll bring Uncle Hermas with me, too."

Angelique laughed. "I miss you, Brian, more than you can know—and I love you."

"And I miss you too, Angel—but I love you more."

Following his January weekend up in Quebec City, Brian began settling in his Kennebunkport apartment. On the first Saturday in February, he sat in front of his television as the folks on channel 13 began speculating on the severity of a storm roaring up the Atlantic seaboard and beginning to bear down on New England. As a precaution, he loaded up on provisions in the unlikely event that this northeaster packed anything even close to the punch the weathermen were speculating on. He would spend the better part of this February weekend buried in his college texts. He was beginning to close in on his associate's degree, lacking only twelve more credits. His college courses had to be set within the framework of the complex's off-season months. Sitting on the living room couch, a textbook balanced on his lap, the sound of a steady breeze shearing its way between the Dock Square buildings relaxed him.

He was back on unemployment compensation, but was now drawing a salary from the Russos nine months a year. He thought how, in a little over a month's time, he would again begin the task of slowly awakening the motel and cottages from their winter sleep. For the last few years, Brian had lived at the complex over the winter, shutting down all but the main house from Thanksgiving Day through mid-March. It was in late winter or early spring as he reopened cottages that a sobering, almost mystical, sensation would wash over him. At the precise moment he would push in a cottage door and break the extended, frigid silence, he was sure there came an almost spiritual rush throughout the building. It was, he thought, as if each cottage might be inhabited during the long, hushed winter by other spiritual beings, they being content to reside in the building in the absence of the living. Occasionally, in the spring, having pushed in a cottage door, he would stand motionless in the doorway, seeming to feel the memory of past owners and inhabitants flow by him, content simply to return with the cold and the silence months later. He shared these feelings with no one, not even Angelique, for fear of being ridiculed.

On Monday morning Brian awoke to a stiffening wind blowing in from the Atlantic. Flicking on the TV, he was quick to learn that a storm was bearing down on New England. With lots of nonperishable food and a quantity of candles and batteries on hand, he felt secure that he could ride out even the worst of storms. He had moved the Biscayne to higher ground in the event of rising tides and would now simply ride out the northeaster within the comfort of his apartment.

The Storm of '78 roared into Maine just after sundown on Monday evening. With all his supplies and an insulated sleeping bag good for temperatures down to twenty below, Brian was braced and ready to take on anything Mother Nature could throw at him. He was standing at the window looking down on Dock Square just before nine o'clock when the phone rang.

"Hello, Kelly's Storm Central," he joked, thinking Angel was calling to check up on his well-being.

"Hey, buddy, it's Bobby. I'm in need of a very big favor," sounded his energized friend.

"You're calling from home, I hope," commented Brian.

"I wish. Bri, I know this is asking a lot, but I'm really screwed at the moment. I'm somewhere on—I should say off—Route 9 between Goose Rocks and Cape Porpoise. I've hydroplaned off the friggin' road—the car's nose down in a ditch. I'm calling from someone's house over here. The weather is bad! Annie's with me. Jesus, Bri, can you come and get us? The people whose phone I'm using want us out. Is there any way?"

"Bobby, there's a goddamn lake forming in the square here and it's snowing like hell. This storm is going to be bad shit!"

"I wouldn't ask if my back wasn't to the wall," said Bobby.

"Okay, I'll get dressed and try to find you," relented Brian.

"Don't come through Cape Porpoise. I think the road's completely under water!"

"Okay, I'll be coming at you from the Goose Rocks direction. I'll hook around from here. Be out on the road with a flashlight or something," instructed Brian.

After throwing on his waterproof boots and a poncho, Brian descended the stairs to the sidewalk on the square. Water had already seeped under the outside door with two inches collected on the landing. He stepped out into a shallow sea of slush and water. He turned and headed up toward Temple Street where his car was parked for the night. Crossing the square, he looked back toward the Saxony Theatre, only to see a wave of tidewater, looking like molten lava, pushing its way toward him from the overflowed Kennebunk River. The wind howled through the trees above his head as he made his way up the hill to Temple Street and his car. The car started, first try, and he backed it out of the yard and headed out on his rescue mission. His own eyes told him that the bridge over the Kennebunk River was impassable and Bobby had advised against driving through Cape Porpoise. With the main routes beyond use, Brian snaked his way through a series of back roads as the wind pushed the Biscayne all over the slippery streets. It was thirty minutes before he reached Route 9 near Goose Rocks and headed south to where he deduced Bobby and Annie were stranded. Five minutes later, a waving flashlight by the side of the road turned out to be in the hand of Bobby Copeland and the first part of the rescue was complete.

Cautiously, Brian turned the car around with Bobby acting as traffic cop outside and the three started back. Annie sat shivering in the back seat, a blanket wrapped around her.

"God, you saved our asses, Bri," stated a drenched Bobby beside him in the front seat.

"What the hell were you guys doing out here?"

"We've been up in Camden since Friday—you know, a little romantic getaway. As you know, my pickup radio's on the blink and we were in this shit before we knew it. I was detoured onto 9 back in Biddeford and the rest is history—hydroplaned off the road into the ditch. I think the truck's had it. I think I heard the whole front end give when we crashed into the gully."

"I figure you two should stay at my place till this blows out to sea. Dock Square's practically under water but I'm on the second floor."

"Man, it didn't take long for me to call in my favor after helping you move," joked Bobby.

"The water's so deep in the square that I don't want to drive down into it. You'll have to hoof it with me from Temple Street once we get there," instructed Brian to his passengers.

Arriving back in Kennebunkport, Brian drove the car back to a friend's driveway and let out Bobby and Annie. Neither was dressed for the walk back to his apartment but Bobby volunteered to carry his date through the cold, slushy tidewater. Brian grabbed a piece of their luggage salvaged from the pickup and followed behind. The wind was gusting over fifty as the three lowered their heads and made their way toward the warm apartment. Brian reached the door first, pushing it in, then stepped aside so Bobby could bring Annie up the stairs. Given the condition of the road and the ferocity of the wind, they were all amazed that the power had remained on. Bobby and Annie were quick to begin peeling off their saturated clothing while Brian decided some warm drinks were in order. Within ten minutes the three were sitting on the couch, the visitors wrapped in warm, dry blankets and Brian in a dry set of clothes. They stared out the window as the wind played havoc with the telephone wires and the swollen ocean and river water sat a foot deep in Dock Square below them.

Being the gracious host, Brian extended Bobby and Annie his bedroom, pointing out that the couch could not accommodate two adults. The couple thanked him apologetically and within an hour were behind closed doors. A second apartment bedroom was still unfurnished, making it useless. Brian sat alone in the living room, sipping on his tea and listening to the wind outside. It did not take long for his guests to succumb to the romantic setting that fate had provided them, as sounds of passion could now be heard through the walls. After a couple of minutes of this psychological torture, Brian walked to the phone and lifted the receiver. There was a dial tone. He dialed up Quebec City.

"*Bonjour, residence LaChappelle,*" answered Angelique.

"Hey kid, it's the guy from under the restaurant table. I needed someone to talk to."

"Mr. Kelly, what a surprise."

"I started getting lonely, very lonely, and you came to mind. We've got a hell of a storm going on down here right now. How about you?"

"Nothing at all. Where are you calling from?" An instant later Annie let out a howl from the next room. "What was that?" asked Angelique.

"I've got company. Bobby and his latest got stranded in the storm and guess who had to bail them out?" Brian found himself talking over a series of moans from the bedroom.

"Are they doing what I think they are doing?" she asked, almost in disbelief.

"The answer is yes."

"It sounds as if they are in the room with you."

"No, it's not quite that bad," answered Brian.

"I cannot believe someone could be that crude."

"You don't know Bobby."

"I'm sorry, Brian—for not being there and getting you through this. I feel guilty. Your friend is in the next room enjoying himself and you're stuck talking to your underage girlfriend."

"I'm fine. It doesn't take much to keep me going—trust me. All I have to do is think of you in your *Academy day Sacray Cur* uniform, that's all it takes," admitted Brian.

Angelique laughed at Brian's bad French accent, then observed, "God, you men are so strange. Well, then, if that is all it takes, I will be sure to bring one of my uniforms with me next summer," she said, laughing. Her tone grew serious. "Brian, you know, I think about it—but always with you. No one but you," she admitted.

"You're still a kid—sixteen's a kid. Our time'll come."

"Are you jealous of Bobby?—with a girl there in the next room and you alone?"

"I'm not alone. I have you. Angel, listen to me. I would rather be just sitting around thinking of you than be with another woman—and that's the honest-to-goodness truth."

Bobby and Annie strode from the bedroom, catching sight of Brian slumped against the wall, the phone cradled against his ear. "Is that Angelique, by any chance?" shouted Bobby. Brian gestured yes and his friend ran over covered only in a towel. He took the phone from his friend. "Listen, gorgeous—and you must be a real French-Canadian dish. I'm looking forward to meeting you next summer. Do you know what a lovesick basket case you've turned my best friend into? Do you?"

A flustered Angelique found it hard to respond.

"Are you there, Angelique?" asked Bobby.

"I'm here. I just do not know how to answer you," she replied.

"Oh, that accent, that sexy, French accent!" called out Bobby before being tackled by Annie and dragged from the phone.

"You made quite an impression on my friend, Angel."

"When I heard him speak to me I could only think of him moaning in bed from before," she admitted. Brian laughed.

"I'm afraid I should wrap up the conversation, kid. Thank you for helping me through the night here. Say hi to your parents and Henri and know I'll be thinking of you all week."

"Good night, my love. Please know I miss you and I love you," added Angelique.

"But I love you more. *Bone swore*," concluded Brian, in a poor imitation of French, then hung up the phone. Outside the wind blew a sheet of frozen snow against the window as it howled through the square. Brian was glad he had company on this evening to keep his mind occupied, so great was the craving within him for Angelique.

It was another full day before the storm of the century subsided. Brian played host to his house guests until late Tuesday when he drove Bobby and Annie back to Wells. Although Maine was spared the snowfall depths dropped on nearby Massachusetts, there was considerable damage up and down York County. The evacuation of shore houses was commonplace as structures all along the coast were damaged or washed out to sea. Wells and York reported hip-deep water as the combination high tides induced by a new moon and winds up to seventy miles per hour blasted the coast for thirty-six hours straight. Herbert Walker's house on Walker Point in Kennebunkport suffered extensive damage and residents of York reported waves at Nubble Light washing over the lighthouse keeper's house on the island, a sight not seen in recent years.

Brian himself could attest to the water level in Kennebunkport's Dock Square, as the slushy saltwater left its mark outside and inside the exclusive shops and establishments.

XXXII

THE SUMMER OF 1979 SAW PROFITS continue to rise. It was a spring and summer that saw Dr. McShane and Ruth Davenport rendezvous twice within a three-month period. After Brian took expanded time off during the LaChapelle's vacation in late July, he worked around the clock for a week in mid-August, enabling the Russos to spend a week away in Nova Scotia during the heart of tourist season.

It was just after Labor Day when the Russos asked Brian to have dinner with them at the house. He had the distinct impression there was some issue that they needed to discuss with him. It was a relaxed and lighthearted meal, reminiscent of the early days spent with the owners years before. With the dinner dishes already cleared and back in the kitchen, Brian and the Russos sat at the table with only coffee in front of them. Brian would not have long to wait before learning the purpose of the get-together.

"Brian, do you know that we've just come through our sixth summer season together, you, Bella and me?" indicated Lou. "Your contribution to the success of this place has not gone unnoticed, and that's the damn truth. That's why we want to keep you fully informed on something that's going on right now, 'cause it concerns us—and you—and the place itself. Bella and I aren't kids anymore and we've been looking at taking it easy and maybe selling. We've been talking to someone here is town, Peter Dawes, who owns the Tidewater Restaurant—and, well, he's interested in maybe buying the place from us," explained Lou calmly. Brian felt his heart and spirit plummet at the announcement. "We've had a long discussion about you—to the extent that Peter's come to see you as an integral part of any deal."

Lou was interrupted by an anxious Brian. "Listen, Lou, thanks for the consideration, but I'm not interested in working for someone else—but thank you anyway," he stated, already starting to rise from his chair.

"Brian, hear me out. Peter's not interested in you as just a manager. He's thinking more in line with whether you'd be interested in joining him and his partner as a part owner. His partner's an attorney from Portland and neither of them has any interest in running the place. I just think that this might be a great opportunity for you—and it would mean a lot to Bella and me to know the place was being handed over to you and not just some strangers. Plus, I happen to know that Peter Dawes is a good man—a fair man. Would you be willing to meet with him and his partner and discuss something along these lines?"

Brian looked across the table at his friends' faces. After bouncing a short series of questions off the Russos, he agreed to meet with his potential partners.

A few days later Brian, the Russos, Peter Dawes, and attorney Christopher Schumer sat around Lou and Bella's living room table going over the merits and specifics of the proposed sale of Atlantic Coast Motel and Cottages. In brief, the understanding was that the property would be sold to a closely held corporation owned by Dawes, Schumer, and Brian. Dawes and Schumer would put up fifty thousand dollars each for an eighty percent share of the business. Brian would be required to put up twenty thousand dollars for an initial twenty percent of the ownership. In addition to the cash, the Russos would accept paper on the remainder of the selling price with this to be financed over twenty years. Brian would be required to sign an employment contract calling for him to stay on and manage the complex over the next five years. In exchange for his contracted services, Dawes and Schumer would relinquish a percentage of their shares in the property each year until all became thirty-three-and-a-third percent owners at the end of five years. It was understood that Brian would take full control of the daily operations right from day one. His two potential partners left him with a copy of the proposed corporate agreement for his review, asking him to get back to them within seven days with a decision.

The Russos had inquired as to whether the twenty thousand dollar investment was workable, and Brian had indicated that it was. Lou and Bella were aware of their assistant manager's habit of saving money. When they asked him point blank about his financial situation, he had indicated that his savings were sufficient to meet this requirement of the contract. In reality, he had slightly more than seventeen thousand dollars in savings and would have to somehow dredge up the other three thousand. He knew of only one place he could turn.

The day after the meeting with his two potential partners he placed a call to Perez back in Lowell. He asked if it would be possible to have lunch the following day; that he was in need of a big favor and there was no one else he could turn to for help. Perez agreed to meet him for lunch. Brian would drop by his Bridge Street apartment and the two would proceed from there.

Brian arrived in Lowell late the next morning and parked his road-weary Biscayne on Second Street, around the corner from Perez's apartment. He had not seen his friend since spring and felt somewhat uncomfortable about dropping in now for the single purpose of borrowing money.

His friend's face lit up upon opening the door and seeing Brian standing before him. The two men wrapped each other in a bear hug, Brian forced to lean down to complete the embrace. He looked around the apartment, same kitchen set, same stove, same couch. There was something reassuring, he thought, about the lack of change.

"Okay, let's get the stinkin' favor outta the way so we can both have a relaxed lunch," ordered Perez. Brian's eyes darted around the room from anxiety.

"I want you to know that if what I'm asking is too much—well, that's all right. We're still friends."

"Whatta ya need, Brian?"

"I have this chance to buy the—"

"Whatta ya need, Brian?" interrupted Perez.

"I need three thousand dollars," he blurted out.

"No problem," answered Perez immediately.

"I'll pay you back."

"I know."

"I'll pay you interest," added Brian.

"Like fuck ya will." The two men stared at each other for a second. "I think y'oughta be the one to buy us Chinese today," suggested Perez.

"Hey, we'll go in my car. I'm parked around the corner."

"Whatta ya drivin' these days?" asked Perez.

"The shitbox."

"Not that blue Biscayne piece-a-shit," laughed Perez.

"I'm waiting for some asshole to steal it so I can collect on the insurance," answered Brian, now relieved, a result of his friend's generosity and trust. He returned that evening to Kennebunkport with three thousand dollars in cash, Perez not believing in checking accounts.

Ten days after receiving a copy of the corporate agreement to review, Brian sat in Schumer's law office in downtown Portland, waiting on Peter Dawes to arrive so that the three partners could sign documents and hand over the cash investments as called for in the agreement. Brian had been led to a seventh-floor conference room looking out on the Portland skyline and down on the business district. He was standing at the window when Dawes arrived. Peter apologized for being a few minutes late and the three men took their places at a large conference table. The lawyer placed a copy of the corporate ownership agreement down in front of each of them and offered both the opportunity to review the document a final time before signing off.

"I'm assuming we all have brought a check covering our initial investments. As treasurer, I'll be responsible for getting this deposited in our corporate account," injected Schumer.

Brian reached down and withdrew his copy of the corporate agreement from a briefcase. He proceeded to place the two agreements side by side and began comparing the two documents.

"I think you'll find everything in order," stated Schumer from the other side of the table.

"I'm sure it is," responded Brian. "It's just that twenty grand is a lot of money—to me, anyway."

Directly across the table from Brian, Dawes was casually reviewing the paperwork, certainly not putting the same emphasis on the detail as his young, future partner. The agreement ran fifteen pages and Brian was only on page four when the lawyer spoke up.

"Brian, I don't know about Peter but I, for one, have a lot of things on my plate at the moment. Can you give me an idea how long you see your review taking? You've had this agreement for over a week. This is not the time for rethinking the whole matter," chastised Schumer, attempting to move the whole process along at a faster pace.

"Please—feel free to go off and work on something else. I'll come and get you when I get through this thing."

Peter Dawes rose from the table and strolled out into the hall with Schumer, the two discussing another matter. Meanwhile, Brian continued·on, comparing his copy of the agreement, the copy he had poured over for the last seven days, with the copy produced for signing ten minutes earlier.

Dawes and Schumer returned to the conference room after a twenty-minute absence. They found Brian leaning back in his chair, displaying an icy countenance.

"So, partner, are we ready to sign the dotted lines?" asked Dawes lightheartedly.

Brian did not answer the man at first, instead moving his eyes back and forth between the men.

"Is there something wrong?" asked Schumer, uneasily.

"Are these two agreements supposed to be identical?" asked Brian, already knowing the answer.

"There may have been a little fine tuning—ironing out the wrinkles," answered Schumer.

Brian's eyes were now riveted on the lawyer. "Is that what you two were doing on page fourteen—ironing out a fucking wrinkle?" spat out Brian, barely holding his temper.

"What are we talking about here?" cried out Peter Dawes, appearing to be unclear about what was being implied.

Brian gave him a menacing glance. "I'm talking about paragraph twenty-six, which reads quite differently in my original from this piece of shit you tried to have me sign." Brian pulled himself up out of the chair and walked toward Schumer. Both men, but particularly Schumer, were now unsettled. They flipped the pages of their agreement to page fourteen and read the offending paragraph.

As written, the paragraph set a stipulation that any stockholder with less than thirty-three-and-a-third-percent ownership at the time of sale or dissolution would not share in any gain or accumulated profits but would be entitled to only his or her original investment back.

"I'm not sure how this paragraph got included in the final draft of the agreement. Someone out front has made an error here," explained a flustered Schumer.

"So I work my ass off for three or four years—build the business—and then you two cocksuckers sell it and just give me back my twenty grand. Is that how it was supposed to work?" Brian took his copy of the agreement and tossed it directly in the lawyer's face.

"Brian, listen—" called out Peter Dawes, jumping to his feet.

"Stick your deal up your ass—both of you!" Brian strode back to his side of the table and picked up his briefcase. He turned and made for the door.

"We'll talk again when you've calmed down," uttered Peter Dawes.

"Don't fucking bet on it!" Brian cried out before slamming the conference room door behind him.

Brian did not return to Wells after his disastrous meeting in Portland. Driving directly back to Kennebunkport, he holed himself up in his apartment for the next few hours, slowly defusing himself from the explosion that simmered within him. By late afternoon he was calm enough to visit the bookstore and walk through a few of the shops, content to mingle with the tourists. He was not looking forward to hearing from the Russos, who only that morning saw the sale of the complex as a done deal. He tried to stay away from the apartment as long as possible, dreading his next conversation with Lou or Bella. At Alisson's he nursed a sandwich and a beer for over an hour, but finally returned to the apartment at seven o'clock. The phone was ringing as he pushed open the door.

"Hello," he muttered into the receiver.

"Am I speaking to Kennebunkport's newest real estate tycoon?" joked Angelique.

"Hi, Angel, as a matter of fact, you're not," he answered flatly.

"What's the matter? How did things go today?" she asked, sounding concerned.

"It turned out to be nothing like what I was told. These two slugs I was supposed to be going into business with tried to pull a fast one at the last minute. I guess they thought they had a real fish on the line."

"Are you sure?"

"Angel, of course I'm sure! They modified the agreement at the last second, then hoped I wouldn't catch it."

"Did you call them slugs to their face?"

Brian burst out laughing. "Oh, I called them a lot worse than slugs—words I wouldn't even repeat to you."

"Have you spoken to the Russos about this?" she asked.

"No, I'm sure they're going to be disappointed. They have their hearts set on selling soon and this is going to set them back. The thing is, I can't be signing on with a couple of pukes who are just waiting to screw me at the first opportunity," responded Brian, sounding equally angry and disappointed. "By the way, where are you calling from?"

"Clarkson, from the dorm." Angelique had begun her freshman year in college.

"How's it going so far?" he inquired.

"This will make me sound like a baby but I miss my family, even Henri. I am always missing you, so that is nothing strange, but missing my family is a new feeling."

"Well, you knew it wasn't going to be easy when you made your mind up to become a doctor. This is just the beginning of a long, tough road, Angel," counseled Brian.

"My biggest fear is losing you during the wait," she acknowledged.

"Angel, I've told you a thousand times—I'm in for the duration. There can be no one else for me; you've done me in, I'm yours," he added reassuringly.

He kept her on the phone for another twenty minutes before they were able to pull themselves apart. The receiver was barely down when the phone rang out again.

"Yeah," he answered shortly.

"Brian, I've heard about everything that happened today. We have to talk." It was Lou.

"Lou, I don't know what kind of horseshit those two clowns have thrown at you but the deal is dead. They're pricks and I don't trust them," he stated firmly.

"Brian, Peter's here with Bella and me right now. You're absolutely right about the horseshit— he's already been real clear about that. Peter says he had no idea, and I believe him. I'm asking you to hear him out. Schumer's out. He did try to screw you over. Peter wants a chance to sit down with you—work everything out—like the original agreement. Brian, Bella and I have known Peter for some time. If he says he didn't know what was going on, then, you can believe him. Let me put him on," suggested Lou.

Brian remained silent at his end of the line.

"Brian, I want a chance to work this fucking mess out. You and me—talk things through. I'm thinking we bring in a new partner. Phil Snow up in Saco is interested. You must have heard of Dr. Snow, right? Everything just as we talked about before Schumer screwed things up royally. Will you hear me out?"

Eventually, Brian agreed, and the two men met over lobster at Billy's Chowder House the following week. The meeting started out cautiously with Brian venting a residue of anger held over from the prior week. However, before long, the two men were sharing visions of where they saw the region going through the next decade and how they could build Atlantic Coast Motel and Cottages into a major player in Wells.

By the end of the meal they had reached a gentleman's agreement. The specifics would remain the same as in the original arrangement except Dr. Snow would replace Christopher Schumer, and an outside attorney would be brought in to draw up the paperwork.

The agreement also allowed the hiring of an assistant manager the following spring, the selection process being carried out exclusively by Brian. The corporate agreement was signed by the three owner-stockholders before the end of September and ownership of the Atlantic Coast Motel and Cottages was transferred to the corporation by the close of October.

His contract called for Brian to draw a salary from the corporation year-round. For this year, he had already decided to push the closing date for the complex back until after the Prelude Christmas celebration in Kennebunkport was over. A majority of the cottages within the complex were closed in early November but the motel units remained open, thanks to the deep-water pipes servicing these units. With minimum promotion he was able to fill all of his units at Prelude this Christmas season, drawing overnight visitors away from Kennebunkport with lower rates. However, by Christmas Day, the complex was closed and boarded up for the winter.

Christmas season, like the last two, was spent with Angelique and her family in Quebec City.

XXXIII

THE NEW DECADE CAME IN WITH A BANG! On New Year's Eve Bobby Copeland proposed to Annie and was accepted. Interest rates, inflation, and unemployment were climbing out of control. Americans were being held hostage in Iran and the run for the White House promised to be an all-out war right from the New Hampshire primary on. Jimmy Carter would face a challenge from Ted Kennedy for his party's nomination and there seemed to be a million Republicans running, most notably Ronald Reagan and George Bush. However, in the winter of 1980, as in other years, York County, Maine, went to sleep beneath the ice and snow.

It was during this time that Brian recharged his batteries, rested up for the hectic spring, summer, and fall seasons ahead. The typical morning found him lounging around his apartment until ten, sometimes getting dressed only to visit the bookstore to pick up some light reading, then stretching breakfast out for an hour at a local diner. His relentless summer hours were his dues, paid to allow him the comfort of this low-stress season.

It was Thursday evening and Brian was treating Bobby to a dinner out at the Maine Diner. Bobby and Annie's wedding had already been set for September and Brian sensed that his friend might like to run a few things by his best man. Over the past few months Annie had monopolized a large part of Bobby's time, meaning the two had a great deal of catching up to do. After answering the perfunctory questions concerning the status of their businesses the conversation turned to more personal items.

"You'll never guess what I got in the mail yesterday?" exclaimed Brian.

"A love letter from Disposable Judy," answered Bobby.

"Wise-ass! No, I open the mail yesterday and there's a money order for one hundred and fifteen dollars—made out to me. And guess who it's from?"

"Disposable Judy!" kidded Bobby.

"Jerk off! Will you get off of that?" retorted Brian, "No, it's from Linda Birch."

"Wow, there's a friggin' blast from the past," said Bobby.

"Keep in mind, I haven't seen her in four or five years."

"She sends you money?" asked a bewildered Bobby.

"Back when she lived next to you—she needed some work done on her teeth and I wound up paying for it," explained Brian.

"That's right, I remember now. You japed me at the last minute and took her to the dentist—leaving your buddy screwed."

"If I recall, you made out all right that weekend," said Brian.

"Hey, did you ever get it on with her? Man, Bri, you were going through a weird period back then. Shit—how old would she be now—like ninety or something?" teased Bobby.

"Man, you're in rare form tonight, Copeland—and, if you must know, I didn't get it on with her," fibbed Brian, protecting the woman's good name.

"Anyway, I was thinking that maybe we could talk about something a little more serious than Linda Birch," stated Bobby.

"It's Linda Turcotte now. I think she's remarried."

"Buddy—back to me. I needed to run something by you. I'm hoping you can point me in the right direction." Brian leaned back in his chair and gestured his friend to continue. "I may be getting cold feet about this marriage business. I mean, I'm starting to get real antsy about getting tied down—and if Annie's the one. It doesn't help when I see the way you and Angel act around each other. I start thinking—well, like if that's what love looks like, and I don't think there's any question to the answer to that—then what do Annie and I have? What if she's not the one?"

"Well, first of all, you guys get along great. From my vantage point it looks friggin' real. But, then there's the other question you ask when you start going through this crap; how would I feel if, all of a sudden, somebody else came along and he has her and you don't? Think about having to live without her and how it'd feel," suggested Brian. Bobby looked at his friend, mulling over his words.

"At this point, I think it'd kill me—not having her," Bobby confided.

"That, to me, means you're probably going through some normal, cold-feet phase. You're in love, jerk-off! You'll be fine."

"She also wants us to move to Ogunquit, so she can be closer to her job. She's supposedly getting this great waitressing gig in town and wants to live close by."

"Big deal—so you're four miles away," responded Brian.

Seated by a window looking out onto Route 1, the two friends stretched their sixty-minute dinner to two hours, talking and reminiscing on a few of their crazy adventures. It was after seven-thirty when they gulped down the last of their coffee, paid their tab, and made their way to the parking lot.

Brian stretched out the ride back to his apartment by leaving Route 9 and cruising by Gooch's Beach. It still wasn't eight o'clock when he arrived back at Dock Square. The center of Kennebunkport was quiet this particular evening, as it was most any February evening. He unlocked the front, downstairs door and walked up the stairs. Unlocking his hallway door, he stepped inside the dark apartment and walked toward the kitchen. The street lights from the square provided just enough light to enable him to move from room to room. He pulled a milk bottle from the fridge and carried it to the living room window, where he swigged down a couple of mouthfuls. Below him the sidewalks were outlined in piles of snow.

It was too early to go to bed so, after putting the milk bottle back, he began peeling off his clothes with the intention of doing some reading. Brian retreated to his darkened bedroom, sitting on the edge of the bed as he removed the last of his clothing. On the nightstand beside the bed sat *The Dubliners,* a collection of James Joyce short stories he had begun reading in college and was now getting around to completing. Still sitting on the edge of the bed, he quickly realized something in the room was different. He sat motionless for a moment, trying to pick up on the nature of his sudden anxiety.

"I am glad you are finally back. It has been very hard on me waiting," came a soft voice. He jumped up from the bed, startled.

"It is me, Brian—Angel. I've been waiting for you."

"What are you doing here, Angel? God, you scared the crap out of me!" he exclaimed. He reached out and flicked on the light. Lying below him under the bed covers was Angelique, only her head and arms showing. "How'd you get down here—and *in* here?" rattled off Brian.

"You showed me, remember, where the keys were. I drove here after class this morning. I had to be with you—I just needed to be with you, that's all," she confided.

Before another word, he leaned down and kissed her on the mouth, his tongue sliding over her lips. She returned the kiss, pulling his head forward to her. He pulled himself closer to her, feeling the warmth of the bedcovers and sheets on his skin, the warmth created by Angelique's body. Reaching out, he let his arms encircle her, his hands sliding down her naked back and onto her buttocks. His hands touched nothing but soft, warm flesh. Beneath the covers she was naked.

"I want to stay with you. Will that be okay?" she asked. Brian could feel his heart pounding within his chest.

"Everything that's mine is yours, you know that. You can stay as long as you want."

The two were now intertwined, their arms and legs entangled. He continued peppering her lips with kisses, tasting the moisture from her lips while savoring every moment of the embrace. His hands and fingers continued running over her buttocks. He could not believe what he felt, her smooth, flawless skin was stimulating him beyond the power to resist. Her hands explored him in return, coming to rest on his briefs. He laid his head back on the pillow, defenseless. Following a few seconds of frustrated manipulation, she reached up and yanked his briefs down, then off his body. It was already clear that she had sex, in some capacity, on her mind.

"Wait, Angel, this is your first time. Lie back—let me give you pleasure." Brian sat up, and lifted the covers, allowing him to see her entire body. Her perfect face resting atop a perfect body. "Close your eyes and think about nothing but us—you and me—and our love. Then, totally relax, knowing you are perfectly safe here with me. Concentrate on how you feel as my mouth slowly moves up your leg from the knee. Slowly—so very slowly." Brian's mouth was already on her inner leg, drawing upon her soft flesh while moving almost imperceptibly upward. Meanwhile, his fingers tenderly circled her hardened nipples, causing her breathing to accelerate and her back to involuntarily arch.

"You don't have to only think of me," she blurted out.

"Angel, your body—the female body, is the most magnificent and beautiful thing in nature. When I do this, it's like playing an instrument, a perfect instrument. It gives me great pleasure, too—plus, I love you." He let one hand slide down her body, stopping at her vagina. She was wet, his stimulation resulting in her natural lubrication. "Remember, Angel, relax, it's me," he whispered. Her head was flung back on the pillow as Brian's mouth inched slowly up along her thigh.

His mind took him back to a stormy night years before and Linda Birch. It was she who had brought him his first, true sexual experience. On that blustery, autumn night, she had selflessly given herself to him. Brian knew it was his turn now to return the gift to another, and who better than to the woman he loved? He continued to touch her, arousing her, pleasuring her.

As her moment of climax drew near, she compulsively enveloped his head with her legs, locking her ankles behind him in midair. She cried out—not in pain—but in surprise and absolute pleasure. Her head lifted time and again off the pillow, then fell back, as Brian's tongue probed and explored her. He continued on, rubbing his hands over her and inwardly exploring her sexual landscape. He stopped abruptly at the sound of sobbing.

"Am I hurting you?" he asked.

"No, no—it just feels so good. I cry when I'm happy and this just feels so good." He looked up to see Angel's eyes closed, her head back on the pillow.

"Brian, please enter me," she begged.

"Angel, I've got no protection or anything. I didn't expect you here tonight—and it's not like there are girls coming through here all the time."

"It's okay, it's safe. My period just stopped yesterday, and if I know anything, I know that means I'm not fertile right now."

"It might hurt," he warned.

"It isn't pain if it is coming from you."

Brian cupped her face between his hands, began kissing her, methodically stroking her, until her breathing quickened again, and he brought himself down on her. They were both perspiring. With her arms wrapped around his head, he entered her, proceeding deeper and deeper in slow, deliberate thrusts. She cried out in what could best be described as ecstatic discomfort.

For him, the walls of her vagina provided the perfect domicile for his manhood. The two connected, they frantically kissed, their mouths drawing moisture from each other. Finally, with Angelique locked onto Brian and her teeth biting down lightly at the base of his neck, he reached fulfillment and the exchange of their mutual love was complete. It would be over a minute before he would draw himself from her. He pulled himself off of her, then collapsed breathlessly beside her.

"We sort of did that without much discussion," he stated.

"I'm eighteen—I think that makes it legal," she added.

"Do you have the slightest idea how incredibly magnificent you are?" asked Brian. She did not answer. She suddenly wore a pensive expression. "Oh shit! You're having second thoughts," he exclaimed. She turned squarely toward him.

"Will you marry me, Brian?" she asked.

"Okay—okay, what's going on? Why are you going off the deep end on me here? And why are you over here in the first place?"

Angelique looked directly at him. "I flunked out of college today. I've totally screwed up."

"Wait a minute, you just started the second semester two weeks ago—and you nailed your first semester. How could that be?"

"This morning—in one of my chemistry classes—we had an exam—and for the first thirty-five minutes, I went blank. Nothing! I just sat there looking down on the paper—my mind a blank. With half the time gone in the period, my memory came back and I started, but I started too late. I left two whole essay questions empty and some of the others I know I did poorly on. I've developed this bad habit of cracking under pressure."

"Why?" asked Brian in a concerned voice.

"It is very competitive at the school, and now I'm not the smartest in the class like I was at *l'Academie de Sacre Coeur.*"

"So, that's all it's going to take. One problem and pack it in?" admonished Brian. "For three years you've been telling me how much you want to be a doctor. I can't believe you'd just throw your hands in the air over one bad performance. None of us are perfect, Angel."

"There is a lot of pressure on me to succeed," she argued.

"You're creating a lot of it yourself," stated Brian, then brought her head down to rest on his chest. "In reality, you've got less pressure than most other people—not more. You've got me back here, behind you one hundred percent. You have me to fall back on. The others don't have someone like me behind them."

"Why did that woman send you that money?" asked Angelique, referring to the money order made out to Brian.

"Oh, you noticed that. That goes back a long way. I helped a lady once with her dentist bill. She promised to pay me back and finally did. That's about it."

"Is she pretty?"

"Angel, I was only a kid and she had three kids. You have no reason to be jealous."

"I have to go to the bathroom," she confessed. She lifted her head from his chest and scurried out the bedroom door into the bathroom. Brian clicked on the light, then rose and pulled down the shades. He was back in bed before she returned.

"Please, Angel, just stand there for a second," he called out as she came through the doorway. She stood in the light before him, her long, brown hair flowing down, partially covering her breasts. Brian looked at her, wishing he were a sculptor, so that this magnificent creation of God could be captured forever.

"You're perfect, you know," he said softly.

"My breasts are too small."

"No, you're perfect."

Brian spent the next three days restoring Angelique's confidence. By Sunday he had her convinced she would suffer no future blackouts under exam conditions. By the end of the weekend Angelique had fallen in love with the apartment and with Kennebunkport itself. Dining across the street at Alisson's on more than one occasion, the striking Angelique won over the hearts of a large number of regulars. On Friday and Saturday afternoons, Brian and Angelique bundled up and took walks out to Walker Point and Gooch's Beach. In the evening, they dined out and ultimately made love. Both saw this unscheduled weekend together as a preview to what their early years of marriage would be.

On the Sunday morning she was to depart, they enjoyed a leisurely breakfast together in the apartment. They were standing at her car preparing to say good-bye when she began to cry.

"Angel, don't do this to me," he implored.

"I can't help it. A great part of me does not want to go. It is a very long ride and it will be lonely," she sobbed.

"Wait here—don't drive away," he ordered, then raced across the square back to the apartment. Three minutes later, he emerged from the front of the building and jogged over to her car.

"I'm ready," he called out from the passenger side of her car.

"What are you doing?" she asked, astonished.

"I'm making the drive with you. I ran in to put some warmer clothes on and got some cash. Now, as long as you can put me up for the night we're all set. You've got me to ride with you all the way to Clarkson, and then I'll take a bus back."

Angelique smiled. Throwing her arms around his neck, she cried out, "Oh, Brian! I love you!"

Brian was ultimately smuggled into the dormitory where he slept on the floor that night. The following morning he caught the first in a series of disjointed bus rides that took him zigzagging across New York, Vermont, New Hampshire and, ultimately, home to Maine by the end of the day.

His memorable weekend with Angelique LaChapelle behind him, he spent the rest of a quiet winter putting together vacation packages and advertising programs for the coming summer season. He also began the search for an assistant manager. In April of 1980, he would interview no less than a dozen candidates for the job.

XXXIV

THE FINAL COUNT OF APPLICANTS who warranted personal interviews for the assistant manager's job at the complex came to an even dozen. Brian scheduled interviews with six candidates each on a Monday and Tuesday in early April. He scheduled interviews to run no more than an hour, beginning at nine in the morning. Of the individuals interviewed on Monday, only one merited further consideration. Tuesday morning proved no more encouraging, as each candidate seemed to have some glaring flaw, at least as Brian saw it. The first applicant on Tuesday afternoon was a no-show, leaving him time to kill before his next candidate. He looked down at the applications on the final two interviewees—a Catherine Plunkett and a Millie Pierce. Her résumé suggested to Brian that Catherine was young, reasonably well educated, but green. Millie, on the other hand, did not submit a résumé, was not well educated, and seemed to have no work experience.

Brian was stationed behind the front desk when Catherine Plunkett made her appearance. Young, impeccably dressed and brimming with confidence, the woman crossed the waiting area and presented herself to him.

She was pretty by any standards and appeared to know it. Brian directed her out into the kitchen, ushering her into a comfortable chair and taking his own place at the kitchen table, his note pad and her résumé laid out before him.

Every five minutes, as if on cue, she would unfold her long legs, then refold them in an elegant movement that drew his eyes downward. For Brian, the interview flew by as he peppered the young woman with questions while fielding her inquiries.

She had worked the previous two summers in Bar Harbor, so there followed an exchange of motel operation stories, and when he glanced up at the clock, Brian saw that the session had run over by twenty minutes. He quickly brought the interview to a close, checked his notes, and proceeded to escort Miss Plunkett out of the kitchen in the direction of the back door.

Waiting in the next office was his last interviewee, a plain, middle-aged woman with graying hair. He bid the youthful Miss Plunkett a good afternoon, then looked down at the stern woman seated quietly in the lobby.

"Mrs. Pierce I take it?" he asked courteously. The woman nodded her head. "Follow me, I've been doing all the interviewing in the kitchen." She rose and joined him in the next room, sitting by the wall. Brian returned to his chair at the kitchen table and proceeded. "You didn't send me a résumé, so I'm going to have to ask a few more questions than usual," he announced.

The woman sat erect in her chair, her handbag resting in her lap. "Maybe I can save us both a lot of time here. Having already seen little miss sugar britches on her way out—and knowing the way of the world a little—can I make the assumption that I don't have a snowball's chance in hell of landing this job?" questioned the woman in a matter-of-fact manner.

"Wow, you really don't have too high an opinion of me!" Brian, a little taken aback, laughed. "No, Mrs. Pierce, you cannot make that assumption," he answered. He flipped his yellow, legal pad to a clean page and proceeded. "Now, having no résumé to refer to, perhaps you can tell me about your work experience and any other pertinent information."

"I haven't had a paying job for thirty-one years, since I was twenty. I've raised three children, who've all moved out, and my husband's on disability—has been for six months now. His check isn't enough to keep the house afloat and that's sent me out looking," she answered.

"Is this the first place you've looked?" he asked.

"No, I've been looking since right after the holidays. Not much luck, so far. It's like I don't have the skills—not young or pretty enough for the good waitressing jobs—no experience or education for the others."

Brian glanced down at his notes. "Millie Pierce, that's your name according to my notes. Is that your proper name? Did your folks actually christen you Millie?" questioned Brian, a sly grin breaking across his face.

"No, my Christian name is Mildred," she responded begrudgingly.

"Mildred Pierce, is it? Just like in the movies," he teased.

"You look too young to remember that movie," she said.

"Now, Mrs. Pierce, or should I say Joan Crawford? Now, Mrs. Pierce, I'd like to find out a little bit more. You say you stayed home for thirty-one years—a housewife, no doubt. It seems to me you might have picked up some skills there. How about in the kitchen? Maybe baking skills?" he suggested.

"I can bake," she stated frankly.

"Well?"

"Very well," she said without hesitation.

"We have Congdon's across the street—and they also bake very well. What do you think? Can you and your baking stand up to that kind of competition? I don't want to look stupid down the road."

"My baked goods have always done real good at church functions—muffins, pies, turnovers, you name it. You can ask anyone in the congregation," she stated flatly.

"Just to explain this line of questioning: Our short-term plans here call for converting the upstairs of the main building into four bed and breakfast units. The baking goes hand in hand with the whole breakfast thing. Where are you from, Mrs. Pierce?"

"We live in York."

"Strike one! I can't stand York," called out Brian.

"Where do you get off saying that?" exclaimed the woman. Brian burst out laughing.

"Just trying to get your goat. Relax, Mrs. Pierce," he instructed, prompting the woman to raise her eyebrows and slump back into the chair.

"You are a very unusual young man, Mr. Kelly." Brian raised one eyebrow but did not respond.

"Does it feel awkward—addressing someone younger than yourself as mister?"

"Not really," she responded.

"Actually, I'd prefer that you not call me Mr. Kelly."

"And what would you prefer that I call you?" she asked.

"Oh, something simple like—grand potentate. That'll be fine," joked Brian. The woman rolled her eyes to the ceiling, but bit her tongue. "So, Mrs. Pierce, could you tell me in fifty words or less, what your employment would bring to the Atlantic Coast Motel and Cottages?"

"Well, that's a little hard without sounding like I'm blowing my own horn."

"You've already used up at least ten of your fifty words," kidded Brian.

"I'd work hard—real hard. I'd be here on time. I'm not afraid of a hard-day's work."

"Do you have an advanced degree in motel management?"

"No," she answered.

"Good—I don't want any smart aleck telling me everything I'm doing wrong." He paused for a moment, tapping his pencil on the kitchen table. "Do you think you would find it difficult working for someone younger than yourself—particularly someone as handsome as I am?"

"I have no problem answering to someone younger than myself; and as far as the handsome thing—I have no comment," she replied, smiling for the first time.

"Would you happen to speak any languages besides English?"

"Je parle français."

"Fluently?" he asked.

"Well enough," she answered.

Brian turned serious for a moment, appearing to be mulling over the applicant and her qualifications.

"You probably can't provide me with anything in the way of business references," he stated.

"No, I can't."

"Would you be available to work seven days a week, if necessary?"

"I will work any day of the week except Sunday morning. I would like Sunday mornings off for church," responded the woman.

"Strike two!" called out Brian. "That forces me to go to mass on Saturday afternoon."

"What's wrong with that?" she asked.

"Nothing, just trying to make you feel guilty," he added. "Do you have any questions about the job, or the pay, or how I got so darn good looking?"

"No, just how soon you'll be making a decision on the assistant manager's job."

"Does that mean you already have your own theory on how I got so good looking?"

The woman raised her fingers to the bridge of her nose, laughing under her breath. "Yes, I guess it does," she responded.

"Good," he answered. Brian clasped his hands behind his head and leaned back in the chair.

"And you'll be making your decision when?" she followed up, timidly.

"Oh, I've made my decision, Mildred Pierce." The woman looked up at him. "Welcome aboard, Millie," he called out, a wide grin spreading across his face. The woman suddenly broke out in tears. Brian jumped up from the chair and ran to her. "Are you okay?" he asked, concerned.

"Mr. Kelly, thank you. I can't tell you how much pressure we've been under—to find another paycheck and all," confessed the woman. Brian reached over and gave the woman a hug. "Was I honestly the best candidate?" she asked in astonishment.

"Millie, in all honesty, no."

"Then—why?"

"At least two candidates had better qualifications than you—including that redhead you passed on the way in. However, their skills were pretty much in line with mine, so what would I be gaining by having them around? You, on the other hand, have skills I don't have—baking and French—and the French is real important with all the Quebec traffic we get. You brought something in that I didn't already have. That, and the fact that you're drop-dead gorgeous."

"You're a lot smarter than you let on you are," she added, a measure of admiration in her voice and on her face.

"Next Monday morning—eight-thirty—here," Brian instructed. "Now back to York with you. Say hi to Nubble Light for me."

Millie picked up her belongings and marched to the door. "You won't be sorry, Mr. Kelly."

"It's *Brian*, now git!"

Brian was filled with an abundance of anticipation as the summer of 1980 approached, because Angelique was going to work the better part of the summer on the premises.

Millie was proving to be a find, as she had quickly caught on to the daily routine at the complex. Millie and Angel had already bonded over the phone and had expressed a strong desire to meet each other. Cottage #14 had already been prepared for the French-Canadian girl's arrival.

In mid-May, Millie had been left in charge for a couple of days while Brian disappeared, presumably to get his batteries charged for the coming hectic tourist season. Millie had just completed taking a phone reservation when she looked up to see Brian's pickup truck pull up at the back door. A moment later he was standing in the doorway, looking stressed.

"Mil, I'm about to do something that I am really not looking forward to, and I expect I'll be catching some garbage from you at the same time," he stated, avoiding eye contact. Millie turned serious, not knowing the nature of what was unfolding. "I've got to make a call to Quebec. God, if someone told me a month ago I'd be doing this, I'd have called them crazy."

"Okay, bucko, what's going on here?" questioned the woman.

"Two days ago, back in Lowell, I met what has to be the most beautiful girl in the world. In a minute I'll be bringing her in here. Now I know how you feel about Angelique, but, for my sake, I don't want any scenes or outbursts," ordered Brian before retreating back to the truck.

Millie felt herself grow rigid as Brian ushered in a young brunette. The girl's long hair flowed down her back, nearly reaching her waist. The beautiful but immature-looking girl had a lollipop stick protruding from her mouth. He guided her into one of the office chairs.

"Millie, this is Jennifer," he said proudly. Millie glared at the girl, then at Brian. The girl did not speak.

"I want to speak to you in private," ordered Millie, before withdrawing to the kitchen. Brian gave the young woman a smile, then joined his employee in the next room. Millie was already seated at the kitchen table, arms folded across her chest.

"You're not making this any easier, Mil. I've been dreading making this call to Angel all day."

"Have you totally lost your mind? How old is that little dimwit out there sucking on the lollipop?"

"Quiet, she'll hear you," he cautioned.

"Brian, come to your senses! How long have you known that little airhead?—and how long have you known Angelique?"

"Jennifer's gorgeous, Millie. I'm in love with her," confessed Brian.

"Stop being a typical man. For God's sake, think before you do something you'll be sorry for," she implored.

"I'm getting this thing over with," he exclaimed, then charged back into the office and picked up the phone. He punched out a long series of digits then paused as the call went through. Millie followed him back to the office, standing to his side and glaring at the young girl in the chair. "Hello, Mrs. LaChapelle, it's Brian. Is Angelique there?" He paused momentarily, his ear to the receiver. "You say she isn't there? She's where? You say she's down in Maine? You say she's in Maine and she's what? She's sitting in an office chair somewhere in Wells, you say?—sucking on a lollipop and watching a woman get totally taken in?"

Millie's face took on a confused look followed instantly by a look of embarrassment. "Angel?" she asked, gesturing to the girl in the chair.

"I'm sorry, Millie, it was all his idea," Angelique confessed in her discernible French-Canadian accent before rushing up to the woman. Meanwhile, Brian was already circling the television room, bent over in laughter. He glanced back to see the two women in a heartfelt embrace. "It's nice to know I have someone on my side if that crazy Irishman decides to dump me," confessed Angel in a voice loud enough for Brian to hear. With his laughter under control, he strolled up to the two women, stretching his arms around the pair.

"My two favorite women in the entire world, and I'm going to have them all to myself all summer," he proclaimed.

XXXV

THE SUMMER OF 1980 BROUGHT together all the heartfelt elements of Brian's life, collecting them at one time or another at the complex. The Clarkes spent the second week of July at the Atlantic Coast Motel and Cottages, allowing them to meet and socialize with the LaChapelles who stayed for two weeks just after the Fourth of July. Angelique worked the entire summer with Brian and Millie, leaving early enough to visit her parents for ten days in Quebec City before returning to Clarkson. Brian was delighted to observe the blossoming relationship between Angelique and Millie. His new assistant manager had begun to develop an almost maternal connection with her boss. She, on the other hand, saw Angel, a devout Catholic and Christian, as a positive influence on the young man who she now considered part of her extended family.

Over the course of the summer, Millie looked on as Angelique utilized cottage #14 as her principle domicile and Brian continued to sleep at his Dock Square apartment. Assuming, and correctly so, that these two young people were not practicing complete abstinence, she was still gratified to see a large measure of restraint exercised by them on the sexual front. On her last night in Wells, August 22nd, Angelique joined Brian in Kennebunkport for dinner at the Old Grist Mill and purchased a few gifts for her family downstairs at Julia's, before returning upstairs to the apartment. The setting sun was reflecting off a few second-story windows around Dock Square as she stood in the corner of the bedroom and took in a final sunset in Kennebunkport.

"Will you come and visit me at school?" she asked without turning.

"You know I will," he answered.

"I've hated the thought of this day—of parting. Being in love is painful in many ways," she lamented.

Brian moved across the room and stationed himself behind her, lopping his arms over her shoulders.

"When you finish your undergraduate work—before you start your graduate work and medical school—will you marry me?" he asked. "I'm not sure I can last until you're completely out of school. I'll be close to a one-third owner of the motel by then. I could sell my share and move on—or just finish up my five years and sell my full, one-third share. I'll work and support you while you're going through the whole grind. What do you think?"

She whirled around, her brown eyes locked onto his. "Are you serious?" she asked in a no-nonsense tone.

"I am absolutely serious."

"Yes—I will marry you under any conditions," she answered. Brian placed his lips softly onto hers, then lifted her, carrying her to the bed. Seconds later they retreated under the covers where, in total darkness, he used his four remaining senses to know the woman who had just agreed to be his partner in marriage. Conscious of the absence they were about to experience, they used the next two hours to share the most intimate and private of their physical properties with the other. No words were spoken as each used the subtlest of gestures to communicate, the sense of touch replacing the spoken word. It was Brian who broke the two-hour interlude of silence.

"You must know that I would do anything for you, including die for you."

"I think of death a lot, much too much," she confessed.

"I've heard there are two things you should never look directly at—death and the sun," injected Brian.

"Death presents me with a terrible dilemma. I will sometimes hope and pray that I will die before you because, loving you, I want you to survive. But then I imagine how this will make you sad and unhappy and I cannot wish this on you—so I pray that I be the one to suffer, and that you should pass away first. Do you see my dilemma? I ask God to make it me who is left to be unhappy. It is a terrible dilemma," she confided.

"Angel, you must outlive me. I can't even conceive of going through life without knowing you're with me. In all probability you will outlive me. Women outlive men, in general, by five years or so, plus you're five years younger than me. God, this conversation is really depressing. Wait a minute, I've got it! We die together, making love, our hearts exploding at the same moment. Agreed?"

"Yes, in fifty years—in this bed—in this apartment," she confirmed.

XXXVI

B RIAN WAS DISAPPOINTED when the call came from Angelique at Clarkson telling him that she would be returning home to Quebec City for a week before joining him in Wells.

It was the spring of 1982 and this upcoming summer showed signs of being the best yet. Reservations were ahead of 1981 and the staffing was in place earlier than usual. Although his time was at a premium now, Brian made a point of maintaining his friendship with Bobby Copeland. Through the winter and spring, the two friends enjoyed breakfast together on Monday and Friday mornings at The Embers, a cozy restaurant on Mile Road that catered to locals.

During the winter months, construction had transformed the top floor of the main building into four bedrooms, the rooms to be rented as part of the bed and breakfast concept set in motion by Brian. Each room had been furnished as a reflection of a specific decade ranging from the forties through the seventies. The complex's name was also shortened to the Atlantic Coast Lodge. Out front, a stockade fence had been put up paralleling Route 1 to cut down on road noise and increase privacy.

The following year, ten more cottages were to be built on the hillside sloping down the eastern end of the property toward the estuary and marshland. It was late afternoon as he walked the lower slope, trying to visualize the new cottages planned for the following year and any impact they would have on the view from existing units.

He was looking eastward across the wildlife sanctuary toward the line of beach houses along Wells Beach when a sense of depression descended upon him. After trying to dismiss the foreboding sensation he turned back toward the main house. His eyes caught Millie running toward him, clearly in a state of hysteria, and Brian immediately ran up the hill toward her.

"Brian, something terrible has happened! Mr. LaChapelle just got off the phone! Angel's been injured! You must leave immediately!" she blurted out through a combination of breathlessness and tears. Brian felt a spike of anguish drive through his body followed by a rush of nausea. "Hurry, it sounds serious!" urged Millie.

"Is she all right?" called out Brian, almost in denial.

"It sounds very serious," answered Millie before breaking out in tears.

He ran straight for his truck and left immediately for Quebec City. Joining the turnpike he sped northward, disregarding speed limits. With frenzied, delirious propositions spinning through his mind, he motored toward Quebec, stopping only to fuel the truck. During the brief periods his mind would clear, he prayed aloud, asking God to spare Angelique, at any cost to him. An abbreviated second stop saw him vomiting on the side of the road, his body attempting to shake the clutch of immense stress. It was late night before he reached Quebec City and sped to the LaChapelle residence. The entire house was lit when he pulled the truck to a stop and raced to the front door. The hallway was crowded with vaguely familiar people as he pushed his way in and searched for a family member. The spectators grew silent as Brian scanned the faces until Mrs. LaChapelle stood in the kitchen doorway before him.

"We've lost her, Brian, we have lost our precious baby," agonized the woman, sobbing. Reaching her, he slumped to his knees and wept unashamedly.

Minutes passed before Brian was led to the couch where he was told the specifics behind the tragedy. Angelique had been on an errand at the mall for her mother when an elderly motorist suffered a severe heart attack behind the wheel of his car. His body made rigid by coronary distress, his car sped out of control toward a crowd of people. After driving over a man in the roadway the vehicle bore down on the sidewalk where a four-year-old stood frozen in fear in its path. Witnesses reported that Angelique had rushed to the child's aid from a location of relative safety and the two were struck and thrown simultaneously.

Angelique succumbed to her widespread internal injuries two hours later in the hospital. The driver and the male pedestrian were pronounced dead at the scene. Jean Labrecque, the four-year-old, still continued to fight for his life.

With Henri stunned into a daze and Roland LaChapelle shattered by the events of the last twelve hours, Brian stood by the grieving mother as visitors vacated the house in small groups. It was after one o'clock when he announced that he needed fresh air and made his way out onto the streets of Quebec City. He walked the city for the next six hours, praying first to awaken from this grotesque nightmare in which he found himself. This was followed by an interlude in which he considered taking his own life. Curiously, he was aware of a certain shutting down of his own self. Perhaps he would not survive long without her anyway, he considered, drawing a sense of comfort from the prospect. He returned to the house just after seven. He was met by the ringing phone in the hallway as he entered. He picked up the phone.

"*Est-ce que c'est la residence LaChapelle?*" asked the male voice on the line.

"Yes, it is. Can I help you?" responded Brian. The caller switched the conversation to English.

"*Bonjour,* I am the uncle of Jean Labrecque, the little boy in the car accident yesterday. The family has asked me to inform the LaChapelles that Jean has shown the first signs of improvement. Would you be so kind as to tell Angelique's family of this?" asked the man. Brian agreed. "*Eh bien,*" said Jean's uncle, "*je vous remercie, je vous remercie beaucoup.*" Brian placed the phone down. He looked up to see the family sitting lifelessly at the kitchen table. Walking into the room, he announced word of the little boy's condition. The news brought only a meager reaction from the family. There was nothing left in them to discharge. Their grief had already depleted every ounce of humanity within them.

"I will stay on as long as you need or want me," Brian advised them. "If I may, I'd like to call my aunt and uncle in Massachusetts. I'm hoping one or both of them will come up to help," uttered Brian as he took a chair beside the family.

Brian was all too familiar with Roman Catholic wakes and funerals. It had been less than ten years since he had suffered through his mother's death. He found small consolation from

Roland and Collette LaChapelle's sharing of the grieving process. Most extended members of the LaChapelle family spent little time with Brian, owing at least partly to his minimal knowledge of the French language. Jimmy and Martha Clarke both made it up for the funeral, leaving Barbara in charge of the house for two days.

While Brian was relegated to a position of secondary importance by many at the wake, the LaChapelles nonetheless recognized his elevated position in the life of their daughter, and on the morning of the funeral it was Brian who would be the last to say good-bye to her earthly being before the lid would come down on her coffin. First her brother, Henri, then her parents, were ushered in for a final viewing before the room was emptied for Brian. Walking up to the coffin, he knelt down beside her as his eyes explored her beautiful face for the last time.

"Angel, I'm not going to be able to go on. I know you can hear what I'm saying—and you have to see that He calls me up to be with you. You can't let me stay here without you. We talked about this. You said you couldn't bear to leave first and have me the one who would suffer. I don't know how this could all happen? There was no chance to say good-bye. When my mother died there was no chance to say good-bye. You're with her, I know. Please ask Him to take me. I don't want to stay here without you. I love you, Angel—and I'll always love you," he whispered.

Brian knelt in silence, staring down on her until he became conscious of some activity in the next room. He rose from the kneeler and leaned over. Then, careful not to make any other contact, he set his lips down on hers, kissing her for the final time.

The Brian Kelly that Millie welcomed back to Wells from Quebec was a far cry from the young man she had grown to know over the prior two years. The loss of Angelique caused him to withdraw from those around him, the only exception being on matters dealing with the Atlantic Coast Lodge. If anything, his involvement in complex matters expanded to include even the most minute details. Pulling back from almost all his social contacts, Millie became one of the few people to maintain any role in his personal life. He took up jogging and was known to run from the complex on routes taking him to the end of Atlantic Avenue or even down to the footbridge in Ogunquit. In the colder months, it was not uncommon for people to report seeing Brian walking the frozen beach at Wells or Ogunquit in the late night or early morning hours. He did not seek the company of men or women his age and even his longtime friendship with Bobby Copeland ceased.

In the months immediately following Angelique's death, Brian kept a vigil in his apartment, knowing that if some form of mystical contact would take place, it would be in the only place that they had made love. He reasoned that if any two human beings could cross the boundary of death and be reunited, it would be them. For months he would climb the stairs to the apartment, harboring a shred of hope that Angel would be waiting for him, in some form, to communicate with him or perhaps to take him away with her forever.

As months passed and only the silence of an empty apartment was there to greet him, he became discouraged. There were nights when he would awaken and visualize her image, her perfect form, standing nude in the window, looking out to the river and the boats tied to their moorings. He prayed to die.

By the end of the year, Brian had discontinued the practice of his religion. Over the protest and sermonizing of Millie, he cut himself loose from all contact with the Catholic Church, a relationship only created after the aggressive prodding of Angelique LaChapelle. With his Catholic faith in ruin, Millie tried in vain to draw him down to York and the company of Congregationalists.

Finally, after nearly six months of loneliness and mourning, Brian packed his belongings and vacated the apartment, leaving behind forever the place where he and Angelique had consummated their love, decided to marry, and spent their last moments together on earth.

He took up residence back in the main building at the lodge, laying claim to the fifties room on the second floor.

XXXVII

BY 1985 THE YORK COUNTY SEACOAST was growing at a heart-pounding pace. Interest rates had dropped back from the nosebleed levels before the Reagan presidency. It had been nearly three years since Brian had moved back to the complex and he was beginning to feel the need to find something off the premises.

He had contacted a local real estate agent, asking her to let him know if anything came on the market that would fulfill his needs and that was within his price range. It was his hope to get something near the ocean where he could easily go for a stroll without throwing on his jogging outfit or hopping in the truck.

Just after the July Fourth weekend, he received word that a modest cottage in the Webhannet section of Wells Beach had just gone on the market and, based on initial reaction, it would not remain on the market long. Brian immediately arranged to meet his agent in front of the lodge and was taxied down to the cottage in question. Wendy Fitch explained the specific conditions that accompanied this particular piece of real estate. The property listed for $69,900 and would have to be financed through the sellers. The interest rate would be eleven percent, which was reasonable, and it came with a ten-year balloon payment. It was clear to all that tax considerations by the sellers figured strongly in the terms of sale.

With the conditions of the sale rattling through his head, Brian waited with anticipation as Wendy turned her car onto Deptula Drive and drove him to the end of the road. There, just before the tidewater estuary, sat a small, yellow cottage. The building was unassuming and dated, with a narrow screened porch and expansive deck.

"You'll be paying for the location and the land more than the building," cautioned the agent as they climbed from her car. It was true. The agent produced a key and ushered Brian onto the porch, then through the door into the small cottage.

The dwelling was poorly furnished, a condition Brian simply looked through. He was at once taken with the knotty pine walls and rustic doors and windows. The structure consisted of a small, narrow living room, a pantry-style, fully-equipped kitchen, a bedroom and half bath. He was able to survey the building in detail in just a few minutes.

Following his cursory inspection, the woman took him outside to review the land. The cottage rested on a one hundred by one hundred foot lot. In addition to the lot itself, the buyer would purchase ownership of the road in front of the land, Deptula Drive, being one of the few private roads at Wells Beach. He walked around the property quietly, observing estuary and swamp grass on three sides. At the end of the road in front of the lot, the water in the channel slurped up against the edge of the property.

"No one will ever build on three sides of you, Brian—the town, the state, and the environmentalists will see to that," advised the woman. He stepped up onto the L-shaped deck at the front of the cottage.

"What do I have to do to move toward purchasing this place?" he asked.

"First of all, you won't be alone. I know of five parties coming down to view it today. This is not some salespitch, it's the truth. Put a check in my hand for five hundred dollars and I promise you'll at least be in the running—but I'm making no promises," stated the woman.

"Take me back to the lodge and I'll write you a check. I'll have to run some numbers after to see if I can afford this place but so be it," answered Brian.

The two returned to Route 1, where Brian wrote the check and handed it over to Mrs. Fitch. She advised him that she would keep him posted on any developments or progress. Once back at the lodge, he buried himself in his room and ran the numbers. It would be tight, very tight, but the purchase was manageable.

The property at Wells Beach initiated the first sign of any excitement or fervor in Brian since the loss of Angelique three years earlier. This was abundantly evident to Millie and all of the summer help as the restrained Brian Kelly began to show signs of breaking out from the quiet demeanor that had enveloped his personality. Millie, in particular, observed a certain freshness in his disposition, long absent in recent years. Following a week of nervous excitement came a call from Wendy on a Friday afternoon.

"Brian, we've reached a point where you may have to sharpen your pencil if you want the property on Deptula Drive. The good news is—it seems to be down to two possible buyers, and you're one of them. The bad news is—your competition really seems to want the property badly, they've offered the sellers eighty grand. We're talking about a New York City doctor's wife—with deep, deep pockets. Is there any chance you can match the eighty thousand? I know it's a lot of money but it's the hand we've been dealt," related the woman, sounding frustrated by the turn of events.

"Oh, man, Wendy, give me a couple of hours to run the numbers again, but don't get your hopes up. It was tight at seventy thousand," he confessed. Brian called Wendy at home later that night, informing her that he was in no position to match the offer.

"Brian, I'll be speaking to the sellers over the weekend and I'll try playing a wild card. It's a long shot. I've gotten wind that the New Yorkers plan on leveling the cottage and putting up something elegant. There's a chance that the sellers may have some sentimental bond with the old cottage and opt to sell it to someone who'll leave it standing. It's a long shot but I'll play it."

Brian thanked the woman before hanging up the phone. The hectic pace of his Friday night duties and the following day's exodus of weekly renters acted as a distraction, taking his mind off the presumably ill-fated cottage purchase at Wells Beach.

Saturday afternoon found the complex reeling under the dizzying activity brought about by the incoming and exiting guests. With Millie handling all the activity at the front desk, Brian spent his time addressing problems, large and small, that cropped up in the temporarily vacated cottages, motel units, and rooms. With a total of thirty-five units rented, some as large as a small house, any number of complications were apt to occur. With only a few hours separating check out and check in times, it took a combination of quick thinking and repair savvy to carry out a smooth transition. It was in these areas that Brian's skills as a manager and supervisor were clearly present. While chambermaids worked their ways through the units in their assigned sectors, it was Brian who ferreted out and remedied problems with an assurance born of years of experience.

On this particular Saturday, he had already begun adding the required chemicals to the pool water when a chambermaid approached to advise him that Millie was in need of his help at the office. After removing traces of the chemicals from himself, he proceeded up the hill to lend his assistant manager a hand. Upon entering the office, he became immediately aware of a sense of tension in the air. Millie was standing behind the desk, an uncharacteristically unstrung demeanor present in her.

"How can I lend a hand here, Mil?" Brian offered, trying to bring a measure of calm to the room.

"Well, you can start by putting me in the unit I was promised over the phone last week," barked out a fashionably attired man behind tinted glasses. He stood in the middle of the office, arms folded defiantly. He stood about six feet on an athletic frame. His perfectly groomed salt-and-pepper hair framed a handsome face with chiseled features.

"Mr. Van Pelt claims that he was promised a two-bedroom, oceanfront cottage when he made his reservation," said Millie.

"One of your incompetent yokels must have thought it was a big joke—I know the routine—screw the tourist. What's he going to do about it? Well, in this case, you're fucking with the wrong tourist," railed the man, staring Brian defiantly in the eye. Meanwhile, no less than six guests looked on, clearly growing more uncomfortable by the second.

"I took this reservation myself. The idea that I claimed we were on the ocean is balderdash," stated a resolved Millie.

"Are you calling me a liar?" roared the man. Millie grew angry and upset, visibly shaking in reaction to the confrontation. "And I suppose you didn't tell me that my cottage had central air? Well, dummy, an air conditioner stuffed in the living room and master bedroom windows does not constitute central air! Even you morons in Maine have to know that!" admonished Van Pelt.

"Mr. Van Pelt, if I could have a moment to go over the situation with the lady here. After that, I'm sure we can work something out," suggested Brian in a soothing tone.

"I'm not going to be fucking patronized," asserted the man.

"Through that door into the kitchen—wait for me in there. There's some freshly brewed coffee—and soda in the fridge. Help yourself," suggested Brian, pointing the man toward the next room. The man muttered something about assholes under his breath and stepped through the door into the kitchen. He was joined by Brian following a short consultation with Millie. Van Pelt was standing in front of the window, looking out over the grassy lawn.

"This is what I get for waiting until the last minute. Why the hell I didn't just go back to the Cape is beyond me," he muttered, loud enough for Brian to make out.

"Millie has filled me in on some of the particulars here and I think the solution is clear," offered Brian calmly.

"Millie's filled you in. Oh, I can only fucking imagine. Listen, pal, and listen carefully, I don't give a rat's ass what Millie said. In fact, I'd like to see that incompetent bitch fired," spat out Van Pelt. Brian's head was down, filling out paperwork on the table.

"So you came here expecting a two-bedroom, oceanfront cottage—with central air, no less—for five hundred and fifty dollars?" questioned Brian sarcastically. "Ahhh, zip code 10110, New York, New York. Why doesn't that surprise me?" he added knowingly. "I think you'll find my remedy to our problem here quite satisfactory," he assured, still remaining calm under the circumstances. Upon completion, Brian tore off a form and passed it across the table to Van Pelt. The angry man's eyes widened in disbelief.

"What the fuck is this? This is nothing more than a credit for the rent you charged me. Apparently you didn't follow a goddamn thing of what I've been saying here," exclaimed the man. Brian folded his hands behind his head, leaning back in the kitchen chair.

"Van Pelt, I'll be brutally frank. I want your whining ass off the premises—now. That means I want you out the door in the next thirty seconds or—I'll escort you out—and by my count there are two door jambs between us and the back steps. I guarantee your head will make contact with both of those door jambs if I'm forced to haul your sorry ass off the premises."

"I'll have your ass in court so fast if you even lay a hand on me—you won't know what hit you," threatened the man.

"Oh, really!" answered Brian. "Let me get this straight. A Manhattan, gentrified yuppie will have me in court—we're probably talking Biddeford or Alfred—to file charges against me for escorting him out of my office after he throws a fit. I have witnesses to the fit. There, I'll be judged by a jury of *your*—no, correct that, *our*—no, correct that, *my* peers." Brian let out a laugh and took on a devious smile. "I can live with that," he concluded.

Across the room, Van Pelt visualized a jury of twelve men and woman seated in front of him, half with the surname of Kelly and the other half bearing a strange facial resemblance to the defendant, no doubt the direct result of generations of inbreeding. The New York City native rose to his feet, snatched the credit from the table, and stormed from the room and building. Brian emerged from the kitchen into the office a minute later, making an announcement to the assembled guests.

"To celebrate Mr. Van Pelt's departure, we will be providing free beverages, candy and munchies at the pool all day tomorrow." His words were greeted by a round of applause. The VACANCY sign was posted by the road and the vacated Van Pelt cottage was rented within ten minutes.

At mid-morning the following Monday, Brian was called downstairs by Millie. Reaching the bottom, he was surprised to see Wendy Fitch standing by the front desk.

"Don't tell me, Wendy, you're here to tell me the sellers became so incensed by the idea that their cottage was going to be torn down, they insisted on selling it to me at the lower price," commented Brian sarcastically.

"I'm afraid not. But I am here to let you know our competition threw a wrinkle into the deal. It seems they were going to be happy paying eighty grand for the property, but at four percent interest! Apparently, they thought the Wagners were idiots— Maine hicks. There was a message on my answering machine this morning from them. They were still angry over the doctor's wife's offer. They told me that I could write up the purchase and sales agreement." The woman produced a document and placed it on the countertop.

Brian glanced over at Millie, noticing her eyes already watering, her hand held up to her mouth. Over the last few days she had seen a partial rebirth in Brian's spirits, then seen them wane as the likelihood of the deal began to fade.

"It's all as we discussed, $69,900 at eleven percent, ten-year balloon." Brian picked up a pen and scribbled his signature everywhere he was directed. With the paperwork completed and a copy provided to her client, the agent excused herself and set off to meet with the sellers.

"Congratulations, bucko," Millie said, sounding greatly satisfied with this turn of events.

"We're going out for lunch, gorgeous. Name the place. Call Hal and tell him to get his lazy ass down here," called out Brian, unable to contain his enthusiasm. Hal Evans, a tall, sickly, young man with limited energy was employed seasonally to fill in at the complex.

"We won't go too far, bucko—maybe take a stroll over to the Windjammer." Brian nodded in agreement and the two spent a full two hours at lunch followed by another hour down at the new property at Wells Beach.

By mid-August of 1985 Brian had closed on his beach cottage and moved in. Somehow, in spite of his eighty-hour-per-week schedule that summer, he was able to devote a small amount of time to the Deptula Drive cottage, bringing in some new furnishings. Having now become a nostalgia buff, new furnishings meant an assortment of antiques. He surrounded himself with articles and items that reminded him of growing up back in Lowell. In the kitchen he brought in a glass orange squeezer, a hanging wooden match holder, a manual potato masher with a wooden handle, metal ice cube trays, and any number of outdated items he could lay his hands on. By autumn, he was strolling the aisles at Bo-Mar Antiques on a weekly basis, searching for items from the fifties to bring back to his cottage.

As Millie saw it, the cottage was therapeutic for him, partially taking his mind off the loss of Angelique. He had evolved into a loner by this time, content to paddle his canoe out into the estuary and meditate. She was not sure what went through his mind on his extended canoe trips or during his many off-hour walks along the shore. However, from her observations, she saw clearly that, even after nearly three and a half years, her friend had no inclination to pursue a member of the opposite sex.

For Brian, 1985 was, by any yardstick, a good year. At the Atlantic Coast Lodge, profits were up and his two partners were more than pleased with their return on investment.

In the final hour of the last day in the year 1985, Brian sat alone in his cottage. The house was quiet and, for the most part, Wells Beach was deserted. He had always found New Year's Eve a solemn time, and this year proved no exception. Pulling on his thermal winter coat, he stepped out onto the deck and looked up through the clear, frigid air to the stars.

He had just suffered through another Christmas, a holiday tainted years before by the death of his mother. When Angelique was alive he had experienced some measure of relief from these holiday doldrums, so great was her effect on him. But now, there was no person or thing to numb the pain brought about by the holiday season. This year, and since the death of Angelique, he had visited the Clarkes for Christmas, staying over two nights before returning to Maine. During trips back to Lowell, he would always drop in on Perez, the man whose company he still missed a great deal.

He walked to the end of the deck, taking in the sight of the night sky. The silence was interrupted by the eerie sound of cracking ice. The layer of ice settled on the estuary was being disturbed by the advance of the incoming tidewater, slowing lifting the ice from the floor of the muddy marshland. With his breath visible before him, Brian thought of the coming year and the possible calamities it might bring.

He need not have worried. The year 1986 would not be one to leave any lasting imprint in his life. It would be the events in 1987 that would change it forever.

XXXVIII

IT WAS LATE MONDAY MORNING, July 11, 1987, when Brian's curiosity was aroused at the sight of a taxi pulling up to the lodge. Taxis around York County were few and far between, but what made this cab particularly interesting was the unique markings it displayed, identical to the Yellow Cab Company back in Lowell. After about a minute of no visible activity, a lone figure emerged from the vehicle. The individual, a male, carried a single piece of luggage.

Brian stepped out from behind the front desk to get a clear look at the arriving guest. When the man stepped out from behind the apple tree, he was surprised to see Perez standing in the driveway looking up at the building. Brian immediately raced from the office to greet his friend.

The two embraced, each calling the other's name. Ushering Perez into the office, Brian proudly showed his friend the operation, then led him outside to view the entire complex.

"Well, my friend, I'm hoping ya can give me a room until Thursday," suggested Perez as they arrived back at the front desk.

"Man, we're booked solid, guy—it's July!" Brian said. "But wait a minute—wait a minute! Forget this crap about staying up here. I've got my cottage down at the beach. You can just stay down there with me. Did you say you're going to stay till Thursday? Stay with me, buddy. I'll squeeze a little time off and show you around. Whenever you decide to go home, I'll drive you. Forget taking a cab. What the hell did that cost you, anyway?" joked Brian. Perez fidgeted for a moment before speaking.

"You see, Bri, that's the deal. I ain't goin' back to Lowell, I'm goin' home."

"You're finally going home to visit your family in Puerto Rico?" Brian asked.

"No, man—I'm goin' home for good. I shipped everythin' worth shippin' back home already—I'm flyin' outta Logan Thursday mornin'."

Brian's face registered shock from the revelation.

"Ya know—I've been savin' my ass off for over twenty years now. With what I got, I won' be livin' like a king, but I'll be plenty comfortable."

Casting the unsettling news aside, Brian set Perez up in the television room, making him comfortable until Millie's scheduled arrival at one o'clock. He figured he could skip out for a couple of hours to take his friend to lunch, then get him settled down at the cottage. At precisely one o'clock, Millie arrived in a state of agitation.

"Well, they went an' done it! This morning it became official," she hollered as she burst through the doorway.

"What's got you so ticked off, Mil?" asked Brian.

"They went an' done it this morning! They went an' pulled the lighthouse keeper from Nubble Light! Became all nice and legal this morning—had a ceremony—course, no one could see it with the fog and all. Had to save money by automating it! Like they ain't pissing away millions and millions on a thousand other things. It just makes me mad! Tradition ain't worth a tinker's damn anymore!" she railed.

"Mil, I've got company. Any chance you can hold the fort until about three?" asked Brian, already knowing her reply. She glanced into the next room, spotting Perez for the first time.

"Bucko, you should've told me there was someone else downstairs. The poor man must think I'm a raving lunatic."

"Mil, you've heard me talk about my friend from Lowell—well, here's Mr. Perez in the flesh." Millie stepped forward to shake the man's hand as he jumped up from his chair.

"It's nice to put a face with the name," she said warmly.

"Likewise," he answered.

"Ya know, Millie, it's nice to hear someone speak their feelings as strongly as you. Too many people don' feel nothin' no more—about nothin'," Perez contended.

"Millie, I'll have you know that my buddy here and I were the ones out there protesting when they closed the lighthouse on the Merrimack River back home. It was right by where the Concord and Merrimack Rivers meet. We made sure there was hell to pay. It didn't help, of course, you can't fight city hall and all that," teased Brian.

"Now you're just making fun of an old lady—go to lunch, the two of you."

Before leaving for lunch, Brian offered his friend the fifty-cent tour, showing him around the grounds, providing a story and a date with most everything on the premises. Standing by the cottages that rimmed the southern edge of the property, he noticed Perez eyeing the immense, white building on the adjoining lot.

"Is that what I think it is?" asked a perplexed Perez.

"Don't tell me, let me guess—you think you're looking at the most magnificent chicken coop in the world!" said Brian.

"Ain't that what it is?"

"No, it is not. What it is is a luxury resort that, apparently, wants to *look* like a chicken coop. It went up last year, taking away a little of our view—not much—but a little. It took a lot of the view away from its neighbors up on Route 1," said Brian.

His friend continued to stare at the huge building, shaking his head. "I guess I'm not the first one—" Brian interrupted.

"No, my friend, you're not the first to think it was a chicken coop," laughed Brian before leading him toward the truck.

The old friends took a drive down Mile Road to Billy's Chowder House. From where they were seated, Brian was able to point out his yellow cottage across the marshlands. Following lunch, the beaming Brian brought his friend to the beach house. He escorted his guest inside, making a point to drop Perez's single piece of luggage in the bedroom.

"While you're here, the bedroom's yours. No arguments," ordered Brian, turning over his home to his friend. "I've got an accurate count on the silverware, glasses, even rolls of toilet paper. Don't try to pull something while I'm gone," he teased.

"I taught you well," retorted Perez, already beginning to unpack his things. Brian returned to the complex after asking his friend to wait at the cottage until seven, when they would dine together.

The three-day visit proved to be a relaxing one for Perez, with Brian spending as much time as possible playing host. The visitor from Lowell used his time alone to walk and lie on the beach. Late on Wednesday afternoon, the two men were sitting on the cottage porch, sipping beer, when the phone rang. Brian picked it up and learned it was Millie.

"Brian, slight problem. There's too much going on here this afternoon for me to do all by myself—and Hal wants to quit early and go home."

"What's his problem?"

"This is one for the books," she whispered in a voice clearly meant not to be heard in the next room. "Our little trooper was outside on his cigarette break—when an apple fell off the tree and hit him on the head. Now he claims he's got a headache and wants to go home."

"You've got to be shittin' me! Pardon my French," called out Brian.

"What's the problem, Bri?" questioned Perez. Brian covered the mouthpiece of the phone.

"You know that delicate little part-timer of mine—Hal? He says an apple fell off the tree and hit him on the head—and now he wants to go home and take care of it," repeated Brian in a sissified tone of voice, causing Perez to laugh aloud. "Put our little princess on the phone, Mil, will you?" Millie placed the phone down and called Hal in from the kitchen.

"Hello?" spoke a tentative voice into the phone. It was Hal.

"Hal, what's this shit about an apple dropping out of the tree onto your head?" barked Brian.

"Yeah, Brian, while I was outside on break. I've got a hell of a headache and I don't think I'm in condition to finish my shift."

"Listen to me, Hal. I don't care if an apple fell on you from the tree—I don't care if Isaac Newton fell on you from the tree. I want you there till nine—no if's, and's, or but's. Have you taken any aspirin yet?"

"No, I thought I'd take a couple when I got home," he answered timidly.

"Hal, kitchen cabinet, top shelf, with the rest of the medicine. Take two and settle in. I don't want you leaving Millie alone there, understood?" ordered Brian. He put down the phone and stood in the doorway. "Buddy, that's the kind of shit they can't prepare you for in college."

"Hey, man, screw beer—all of a sudden I'm up for some apple juice," laughed Perez.

The next morning, Brian roused Perez just after sunrise and the two men had a final breakfast together. The drive down Route 95 to Boston was spent reliving fond memories, including Brian's last Christmas with his mother. He confessed to his friend that that Christmas, spent in the company of his mother, his aunt, uncle and cousins, and his longtime friend, was among the fondest in memory. Reaching the terminal, he parked the car and escorted his friend inside.

"Brian, I've written down the name of my hometown—where I'll be livin'. It's called Arroyo and it's on the south coast. My mama lives near this real ole church and I won't be livin' too far from there. If ya ever need me or come down t'visit—or go on vacation—that's where I'll be." Perez reached out his arms and the two men embraced. "Twenty years over here an' you'll be the only thing I'm gonna miss—and that's the truth."

A sense of gloom had descended on Brian, leaving him speechless. His friend applied a final bear hug and turned away, both men knowing deep down that they would never meet again.

The drive back to Wells found Brian in pensive reflection. The pieces of his life, his boyhood life in Lowell, were breaking away from him. Now, with Perez's departure, only the Clarkes remained.

By late August the Atlantic Coast Lodge had already guaranteed the corporation its highest profits to date. A bonus incentive built into Brian's employment contract, which seemed unattainable two years earlier, was guaranteed in 1987. He had already spoken to his partners about issuing bonuses to Millie and Hal sometime in the company's fourth quarter, a proposal unanimously accepted by the other two stockholders.

It was after ten o'clock on a Wednesday evening when the office phone rang as Brian prepared his nightly deposit. He picked up the call following a single ring.

"Atlantic Coast Lodge, Brian speaking."

"Is it indeed?" said a female voice.

"In the flesh—so how can I help you, ma'am?"

"How are you, Brian? I hope you don't mind getting a call this late at night. It took a while to get up the courage," said the woman in a voice sounding vaguely familiar.

"The answering machine goes on at eleven—no problem at this time. May I ask who this is?"

"Someone you've probably long forgot about, but I haven't forgotten you," came the reply.

"Do I get a hint?" questioned Brian.

"Have you managed to get any peanut butter and jelly turnovers lately?" was the response.

"*Linda?*" asked Brian enthusiastically.

"How's my knight in shining armor these days?" she asked, laughing.

"All right—and you?"

"No complaints. Listen, Brian, I'm in town for a couple of days. The kids are visiting their grandparents. Of course, you know it's not Linda Birch anymore, it's Linda Turcotte. I was wondering if there was any way we might get together over a cup of coffee or something—do a little catching up. It would mean a lot to me. I know it's your busy time."

"I'll *find* time. How's tomorrow? If you can drop by anytime after one it'll work for me," he suggested.

"One's fine. God, it'll be good to see you again," she admitted.

Brian put down the phone as his mind began whirling at the prospect of seeing this woman. Piecing the seasons together, he calculated that it had been nearly twelve years since he had set eyes on her. He was still a teenager at the time while she was, in all likelihood, in her early thirties as best he could remember. Now, here she was, calling him.

He thought back to their night at the cottage and the sad, good-bye note that had followed. With the last of the lodgers upstairs and in for the night, he locked up the office, made his night deposit, and drove down to the beach. Inside the cottage he sipped on a cup of decaf and wondered about her visit.

For the first time since the death of Angelique five years earlier, Brian seriously thought about another woman. He was about to turn thirty-one, meaning that Linda would be in her mid-forties. It did not matter. There was something in her that he had found inherently beautiful years earlier, and he reasoned it would still be there.

The following day, a late-model sedan pulled into the driveway of the Atlantic Coast Lodge at twelve-forty-five and proceeded toward the main building. Brian did not catch sight of the vehicle until it coasted to a stop in the visitors' parking area. Millie had arrived early and was busy in the kitchen. A few seconds after the car's engine was turned off, he heard footsteps on the porch steps and Linda Turcotte appeared at the door.

Brian jumped to his feet and rushed to greet her. She was a changed woman from the harried housewife he had known living in a mobile home. Impeccably dressed and fashionably thin, she was a woman to whom the years had been kind. Her face beamed at the first sight of him. They embraced, holding each other tightly as Millie looked on from the doorway.

"I've been telling him to start greeting all our guests this way—but he won't listen," piped in Millie as the two pulled back from each other.

"Millie, this is a dear, dear friend of mine—Linda Turcotte. Linda, this is Mildred Pierce."

"Don't you start with that Mildred Pierce baloney," cautioned Millie before sending them off.

"There's been some changes since I was last here. Maybe you can show me around while we do a little catching up," Linda suggested. Brian pointed her toward the driveway leading down toward the lower cottages, catching her up on the complex and all the changes over the years, including his rise to partial owner.

"And how's Bobby?" she asked.

"He's fine. I don't see him all that often," he admitted.

"Oh, my God, and you two were so *close*."

"My fault. I've had a lot come down on me over the last few years. It hasn't been too pleasant."

When Linda asked, Brian went on to explain the painful circumstances brought about by the death of Angelique. As he spoke openly, he could see the sincere pain she felt hearing of his grief. Linda was still beautiful. It was a more mature beauty than had caught his attention years before but it stimulated him nonetheless. As a matter of fact, despite their very short time together, he was already reliving many of the sensuous feelings this woman had brought out in him more than a decade earlier. Walking beside her, it was as if the years had melted away.

"You must be wondering what on earth I'm doing contacting you after all these years," she admitted.

"It's just great seeing you again," he said.

"Well, as you know, Bub and I split just a few years after we left Wells. You must have figured that out when I sent you your money for the dentist work. I almost called you back then."

"You should have."

The woman shook her head and continued. "After about a year as a single mom, I met Jack, he's my husband. He's an older man, not much older—but older. It was Jack who brought me back—who showed me what it meant to be happy." Linda's face took on a look of true tenderness, as if just thinking of this man brought about rapture in her.

Brian noticed this and felt his spirits plummet.

"Jack and I have raised the kids pretty much alone. Bub's really just a father in name only."

"That was very good of him. He must be quite a guy."

"He is—and I would love for you two to meet."

Brian smiled but did not respond.

They stopped near the eastern end of the complex and Brian pointed out the changes at the Atlantic Coast Lodge. Linda tucked her arm around his as they made their way slowly back up the hill. They began crossing diagonally and upward in the general direction of cottage #15, the building that had housed their lone night together so many years earlier.

"I came here for a very real reason and now I hope I'm not getting cold feet," she confessed.

"Does this have anything to do with that whole thing with the dentist—and taking you home—and you passing out in front of me on the bed. Now, unless you have a taped recording of me confessing that I kissed you while you were out that night— your lawsuit isn't worth, as Millie would say, a tinker's damn," kidded Brian.

"I thought that was so sweet when you told me. Jesus, you were such a comfort to me back then." As she spoke there were tears welling up in her eyes.

"You know, Turcotte, if you're here because you suddenly need more dental work—forget it! That's a hell of a nice car you came by in and you look pretty well dressed. I think it's Jack Turcotte's turn to bring you to Biddeford," he joked, trying to bring Linda out of a deepening serious frame of mind. They walked past cottage #15, her body now leaning against his. Reaching the driveway behind the unit, they stopped and looked back at the simple, L-shaped structure.

"Have you changed it much since we were there?" she asked.

"Hardly a thing—too many great memories," he answered. She looked up toward the driveway and Route 1, then back to her friend. She reached down and took Brian's hand, slipping her fingers between his own.

"That young man walking down your driveway right now—that's my youngest."

"Is that Trevor?" asked Brian.

"No, Brian, that's Brendan—that's *our* son, Brendan," she confided.

Brian's eyes widened as the words registered with him. He felt the pressure from Linda's fingers as she held his hand firmly. The lanky boy, spotting his mother from across the yard, hustled toward them.

"Brendan, of course, has no idea—but in a few years I plan on telling him. Are you okay?" she asked. Brian's eyes were trained on the lad as he closed the distance between them. Upon reaching the grown-ups the boy let out a holler as he threw his arms around his mother.

"I'm out of money, Mom. I told you three bucks wasn't going to be enough," he shouted.

"Brendan, first I want to introduce you to someone—this is Mr. Kelly. He's the owner of this place."

"Wow, that's pretty good, Mr. Kelly. You must be real rich," uttered the boy.

"No, Brendan, not really. Your mom and dad could buy and sell me, and that's the truth," responded Brian while he stared down at the boy, taking in every detail of his face.

"Mr. Kelly and I are going to lunch in a few minutes. Would you like to join us?" Linda asked.

"Mom—you said we'd be doing things this afternoon and maybe going to the beach," complained the boy.

"Well, what would you like to do?" questioned Brian.

"I'd like to go swimming."

"There's a pool right here. How would you like that? You could stay and swim while your mom and I grab a sandwich."

"Yeah, that'd be great. I think my trunks are in the back of the car. Right, Mom?"

"Well, if they're not—I have a girl's bathing suit in the office that someone left behind. You could borrow that," teased Brian.

"No way!" cried Brendan.

"I wouldn't charge you much—only a couple of bucks," continued Brian.

"Your trunks *are* in the car," interrupted Linda. "We may have to borrow a towel, though, if that's okay."

"Not a problem—and I'll have Millie throw together a sandwich or something for Brendan for when he's through at the pool," added Brian. The boy had run to the car by now and was rummaging in the back seat for his bathing suit.

"Do you have any idea of the magnitude of the bombshell you have dropped on me?" Brian asked.

"I have wrestled back and forth with this whole thing for almost twelve years. I finally reached the point where I thought it was wrong to keep this from you any longer."

"We can talk it through over lunch. I'll make sure Millie keeps an eye on Brendan and you make sure he knows he can go to her if he needs anything. We should only be gone an hour or so."

As the two friends walked toward Linda's car, Brendan came barreling out from the office already dressed in his swimming trunks, a towel folded across his shoulder. Brian paused before stepping into the passenger seat and took in the sight of the youngster running at full speed toward the pool. Sliding into the car, he turned toward Linda Turcotte whom he saw studying him. His eyes were moist with sentiment, giving away his fragile emotional state.

"He's a terrific kid who's already beginning to resemble his dad in a whole bunch of ways—not to mention physically." .

"I don't know what to say—I don't," confessed Brian as they turned onto Route 1, catching a short break in the traffic.

They went to the Maine Diner for lunch. Following a brief wait, Linda and Brian were seated in a booth by the front window. After ordering, Linda began filling her friend in on the specifics surrounding the birth and raising of their son.

"Brian, if you recall, it was not long after our night together— a night I have never regretted—that Bub and I pulled up our roots and split. This move corresponded very closely with my realizing I was carrying your baby. I can't begin to tell you the turmoil that baby's coming caused between Bub and me. He was pretty clear about not wanting it. Take care of it—get rid of it, that's all he'd say. My in-laws even offered to pay for the abortion. I'd have none of it. It was the beginning of the end for Bub and me. I even considered naming it Brian, but I knew even Bub wasn't that dumb. He'd have smelled a rat. Brendan was sort of close to Brian—and it sounded good—Brendan Birch. The marriage went downhill real fast from then on—not that it was all that good before. Less than two years after Brendan was born, Bub and me were history. He sent along child support—sometimes. I took to waitressing and having my kids at daycare. I thought of you—God I did—but I wasn't going to tie you down with something like this or someone like me. Jesus, you were still only a kid—I couldn't do that to you. I got by. Then, Jack Turcotte showed up and entered my life. Suddenly, a very tired, practically middle-aged, mother of four was being pursued—then courted, by a man that reminded me of a boy back in Wells, Maine. Brian, Jack's got your heart. I know you'd like him."

The waitress approached the table, putting their salads down in front of them. For Brian's part, he sat silently, taking in every word spoken by this special woman.

"Brian, as I see it, I won't be telling Brendan who his real dad is for maybe five years. He's too young now—it would only confuse him. I just knew I couldn't keep this from you any longer. I know you'll honor my wishes," she stated confidently.

"Of course I will, Lin. But you have to promise me that you'll let me know where you are—you and Brendan—keep me in touch with your whereabouts."

"Before we leave today you'll have my address, phone number, and anything else you need," she promised.

"And if this Jack Turcotte fellow goes over the edge—starts in on his midlife crisis. Who do you come to when your hubby starts running around with *Sports Illustrated* swimsuit models?" kidded Brian.

"I call my boy lover in Wells, Maine, and we pick up where we left off—in cottage #15," she replied behind a warm smile that told him she had no misgivings about the events this day. He reached across the table and clutched the hand of the woman who, unbelievably, had borne his child eleven years earlier.

When Linda's meal arrived, a large bowl of the Maine Diner's famous seafood chowder, she scoffed at Brian who was content with a cheeseburger and fries.

"You're in Maine with the best and freshest seafood in the world, and you're wolfing down cheeseburgers?" she mocked.

"That's right, Mommy—but, don't forget, I live here! And even lobster gets old if that's what you see all the time," he answered.

They enjoyed each other's company through the rest of the meal as they kept the conversation light. Arriving back at the complex, they found Brendan seated at the kitchen table in the lodge, lunch and dessert set out before him.

Brian took a few moments to show Linda the rooms upstairs, those unoccupied at the moment, explaining the unique furnishings from the different decades. By the time they returned to the kitchen, Brendan was gulping down the last of his milk. Brian caught himself glancing repeatedly at his son.

"Millie, have you wrapped Brendan up that little girl's bathing suit for him to take with him?" he joked.

"Wrapped in pink paper—with a pretty bow," answered Millie.

"Hey, I don't want no girl's stuff," yelled the boy. Linda walked up to Brian, whispering in his ear.

"I'll get a picture or two out to you once we get home," she said. Brian extended her a smile.

"Say good-bye to Mr. Kelly and Millie—and thank them," instructed Linda. The boy walked over to Brian and extended his hand.

"Thank you, Mr. Kelly," he said politely.

"I want you to come back real soon—with your mom—for a visit. Do you hear me, Brendan?"

"Can I use the pool again?" asked the boy.

"Absolutely—no charge." Brian leaned down and hugged the youngster. Glancing across the room, he saw Linda's face beaming with approval.

"Now give Millie a hug and we'll be off," ordered Linda. Brian approached Linda, wrapping her in a long bear hug. Finally, mother and son waved good-bye and departed. Millie studied Brian's face as he watched his friend's vehicle turn out onto Route 1.

"Now that is one classy lady," she uttered, almost involuntarily. Brian smiled sadly, then turned away without replying.

XXXIX

FOR THE PEOPLE LIVING AT WELLS BEACH in 1988 it was a common sight for them to observe one of their neighbors running and walking the beaches and roadways throughout the year. Over the years, Brian Kelly had evolved into a dedicated, if not exceptional, runner. In addition, he still had a reputation for walking the beaches in any and all kinds of weather. Always seemingly lost in thought, he would pass by neighbors or strangers with a friendly wave or gesture, but hardly anything beyond that.

However, that changed when he made the acquaintance of an older man whom he had passed on numerous occasions over the years. William Regan was a widower who lived a short distance from Brian off of Fisherman's Cove. He owned a well-maintained, turn-of-the-century cottage directly across the street from the ocean. Following a mild heart attack, Regan had been encouraged by his doctor to take up walking and it was after passing by Brian on countless occasions that he introduced himself. On Regan's suggestion, the two men scheduled two walks a week together. They used their time to discuss serious issues including politics, religion, and philosophy, finding intellectual stimulation in the other's arguments and viewpoints. Personal matters were rarely brought up.

In November, Brian saw the need to have some heavy vegetation on the north and south sides of the complex trimmed or removed. He knew that his old friend Bobby Copeland was still in the landscaping and lawn care business and contacted him first to see if he was interested in the project. Bobby jumped at the opportunity and performed the work during the week prior to Thanksgiving Day. On the third and final day of the project,

Bobby dropped by the office, collapsing in a television room chair.

"Done!" he cried out. "You know, Bri, this work couldn't have come at a better time. Is it me, or are things slowing down around here?" he asked.

"No, you're not imagining things. I've noticed it, too," Brian answered. Bobby was clearly tired as he sat slumped in the chair, his cap pulled down over his closed eyes. "Bobby, you quoted six hundred and fifty. If that holds, I could write you out a check right now and you could just send me the invoice next week," suggested Brian.

"You wouldn't mind?" questioned Bobby.

"No big deal."

"Bri, that'd be great—if you don't mind. Things are as tight as my mother-in-law's asshole at home. This'd really help," he said, peeking out from beneath his cap. Brian pulled out the three-ring binder checkbook and began preparing the payment. "It's been too long buddy, you know? Any chance you joining Annie and me out somewhere? Or just coming over to the house sometime?" Brian's glance conveyed the idea that the suggestion was not out of the question.

"Wait a minute!" Bobby continued excitedly. "Annie and me's goin' to a Christmas party over at Goose Rocks—on Saturday night, the 10th. Big fuckin' house! I do the lawns there. They invite the Copelands to show they mix with the common people. They're fuckin' loaded. Last year we went and felt like a penny waitin' for change. Great food—terrific lookin' broads. Mostly Kennebunkport people. Annie's talkin' about not goin', but if you come, I know she'll change her mind."

"I wasn't invited," said Brian.

"No, it'll be okay. The party's always swarmin' with people. No one knows who's invited. If you were a bum or something— someone might say something, but you'll fit right in. Come on, say you'll come," encouraged Bobby. Brian tore off the check and brought it over to his friend, setting it down in his lap. "Damn this looks good," he confessed, looking down at the check. "Will it be okay if I run this to the bank before they close?" Bobby asked as he jumped to his feet.

"It's covered," answered his friend.

"Say you're comin' with us to the party," ordered Bobby. Brian mockingly raised his eyes to the ceiling.

"I'll be there," he relented. Bobby shot him a thumbs-up sign as he hurried out the door.

The Copelands picked Brian up at the complex the night of the party and the three proceeded on to Goose Rocks. Annie spent the better part of the drive turned to the back seat, catching Brian up on the couple's children and family woes. Money was tight in their household, as Brian had suspected from his talk with Bobby.

"Hell, the last time the three of us spent any time near Goose Rocks was during the Storm of '78—remember that night, Bobby?" teased Brian from the back seat.

"Oh yeah, Kelly, the night I saved your ass when you ran your car off the road, then let you stay in my apartment in Dock Square. Oh, I remember it well."

"Yeah, Bobby, I would have been screwed without you that night. Whatever happened to that gorgeous chick you were with that night? Did you ever see her again after that?" continued Brian.

"Thank you, Brian—it's true—I was a gorgeous chick back then," added Annie, digging her elbow into her husband's ribs.

Bobby turned the car down the roadway toward Goose Rocks Beach and soon they were driving by the impressive, oceanfront home where the evening's festivities were being held. The driveway and road in both directions were lined with the vehicles of attendees. Driving his car about one hundred yards beyond the house, Bobby finally pulled the vehicle up in front of a neighbor's darkened two-and-a-half story and the three got out. The threesome locked arms with Annie in the middle and strolled toward the party.

"Remember, the rich are just like you and me, they just have more money. Hemingway or Fitzgerald said that, no one's quite sure which," injected Brian.

"I say we look down our noses on everyone—beat them to the punch," suggested Annie.

Bobby, Annie, and Brian entered the front door without knocking and were unceremoniously greeted by no one. Brian lightheartedly removed his own, then Annie's, finally Bobby's coat, to a chorus of laughs. Finally, he heaped the three on Bobby and asked that he find the cloakroom. They made their way through a maze of rooms before coming upon what appeared to be the main room. Annie spotted three unoccupied chairs and raced over to claim them, followed by Brian. Bobby stood awkwardly in the middle of the room, the three coats obscuring most of him.

"I'll find the bar," called out Brian. "Annie, guard the chairs—Bobby—if you want, continue to act as a coat rack until it's time to go."

By now the trio were being observed by a number of snobbish onlookers. Brian winked his eye at Annie and set off in search of the bar. Five minutes later he returned with a mixed drink for Annie and himself and a beer for Bobby. The two settled into conversation as the rest of the room resumed their chatter, mostly gathered in groups of three and four. A few minutes passed, then Bobby arrived back in the room, joining his wife and friend.

"If you're smart you'll stay downstairs. I made the mistake of wandering upstairs. You wouldn't believe the crowd of crones up in the library—real man-haters. Man, I just had to stick my head in the door and they were on me like flies on shit. There's one in particular—a bitch and a half! With any luck they'll stay up there all night."

The gathering was proving to be pleasant enough—open bar, a buffet table in three rooms, pleasant background music. Brian and the Copelands used the evening to further catch up on happenings in their lives. Bobby was already on his third beer when he stopped in mid-sentence and stared in the direction of the doorway.

"Oh shit, someone's let her out of her cage!" he exclaimed. Brian and Annie turned to see a young, blonde woman standing in the doorway, surveying the room. The woman, or girl, it was too close to call, had short hair that framed her face perfectly, setting off her elegant features. She was tall, even in flat heels, and wore her clinging red skirt four inches above the knee. A fashionable, long-sleeved white blouse completed her wardrobe. After a few seconds spent scanning the room, she was joined by two other females of approximately the same age. En masse, they moved across the room and claimed a group of chairs in the far corner.

"That's the one with the mouth on her that I was telling you about," advised Bobby.

"She's only a kid," observed Brian.

"That's a beautiful outfit," Annie commented, clearly impressed by the young woman's wardrobe. The three friends resumed talking with Brian catching himself involuntarily glancing over at the blonde. Periodically, the women in her group would erupt into bursts of loud, irreverent laughter. On one occasion, the girl looked over, catching Brian staring at her. She boldly established eye contact, unsmiling, until he felt pressured to look away. There came an announcement from the next room that a fresh table of dessert items had just been placed down. Brian volunteered to fight his way to the next room and return with goodies for the group.

He returned to the main room a full fifteen minutes later, the backed-up line at the dessert table having snaked its way through two rooms. On returning, he was quick to observe that the brash blonde had switched chairs. She was seated closer to the Copelands, but now was in the company of a young male. Returning to the company of his friends, Brian laid a small platter of goodies down in Annie's lap and fell back into the chair to her right. Flanked by her two male companions, Annie portioned out sweets between the three. Brian's chair was positioned at a severe angle, allowing him to casually glance over at the blonde girl while still carrying on a dialogue with his friends. When Bobby excused himself and set off in search of his sixth and seventh beer, Annie directed the conversation to the object of Brian's undivided attention.

"You missed quite a little show while you were out in the other room. That little bitch, and she is a cunning little bitch, is moving in for the kill. It's so obvious," she whispered, fearing to be overheard.

In the near corner, the blonde stranger had angled a young man away from the rest of her group, now engaging him exclusively in conversation, her chair moved in such a way to largely block any interference. Brian and Annie looked on as the girl monopolized the conversation with the handsome young chap. Brian watched as she spoke with an almost hypnotic intensity, all the while her willing companion's eyes remained locked on her.

"God, to be a fly on the wall," commented Brian, eliciting a positive response from Annie. Both, now, were caught up in the unfolding melodrama. In an effortless motion, the young woman lifted her legs and placed her feet on the side of the fellow's chair, totally cutting him off from the rest of the room.

"God, it's like watching a lion cut off an antelope from the rest of the herd," muttered Annie, transfixed by the developing episode. Brian, too, was hard-pressed to look away. The two were able to view the proceeding without fear of detection, so intense was the girl's concentrated effort. Brian and Annie were no longer even putting up the pretense of conversing, so absorbed were they in what was unfolding before them.

"Oh my God, I don't believe it!" cried out Annie before turning and burying her face in Brian's chest, trying unsuccessfully to muffle laughter.

"What? What is it?" asked Brian in a whisper.

"Look—look carefully—she's not wearing underwear!" exclaimed the shocked woman. His eyes descended and he could see it appeared that this was quite true. Annie, her face remaining buried in Brian's chest, fought unsuccessfully to contain her nervous laughter.

"I just can't believe this—I really can't," she confessed. Brian, meanwhile, could not look away.

"What a shameless bitch," she muttered. "And what about *him,* Brian, what's *he* doing?" she asked, not daring to look back.

"He's *gone.* In fact, if this were a boxing match, the referee would be stepping in and stopping it," he joked. This was true. The boy appeared almost in a trancelike state, clearly having fallen prey to a combination of liquor and this young female's seductive skills. Moments later the room was joined by a swarm of women, all approximately the blonde girl's age. Commandeering the entertainment center providing music and the lighting, the young women brashly brought down the lights and replaced the passive dinner melodies with a driving beat. The rhythm, which seemed a cross between Latin and African, drew a handful of these females to the center of the room, where they broke out in free-form dance.

Impacted by the invasion of her peers, the blonde slipped off her shoes, handed them to the young man, and joined her sisters in the middle of the room. For the next few minutes Brian watched the girl dance, finding himself taken in by her natural, graceful movements. Occasionally, he would glance at Annie, who also appeared totally absorbed. With the realization now fully upon him that this young creature posed a threat to his mental stability, Brian leaned down and spoke to Annie.

"Maybe we should go look for your husband—and find somewhere else in the house to park ourselves. This room is getting to be a bit much, don't you think?" he suggested.

"Yeah, let's find my old man," she answered.

They found Bobby two rooms away, arguing sports within a circle of middle-aged men hiding from their wives. Annie was anxious to get home to the kids while Bobby was enjoying the open bar. A compromise was reached when it was decided to limit their stay to one more round. It was clear from Bobby's speech that his intake had accelerated during his absence. The three found an empty couch some distance from the darkened main room. Annie tried to fill Bobby in on what he missed in the last forty-five minutes.

A half hour later, the friends made their way out into the cold December air and hiked up the road to the car. With Annie behind the wheel and Bobby propped against the passenger door, the three prepared to leave.

"Wait a minute—I had my hat when we got here. It's not in the car," Bobby complained. After scanning the floor and the back seat, Brian volunteered to go back inside and retrieve it. Reaching the front door, he pushed himself through a small crowd only to come face-to-face with the brash, young female and her male prey. Brian's mouth dropped open at the sight of the boy being led to the door by this aggressive girl, her belt looped around his neck like a leash. He stood before them, speechless.

"What the fuck are you looking at, grandpa?" she snarled. Brian stood mute for a moment. He took in her face at close range for the first time. Her face, flawless but for a few traces of acne covered well by makeup, was remarkable. He recovered, looking down at the hapless chap before him.

"Don't forget, you're going to have to look in the mirror in the morning," he counseled the boy.

"Fuck off. You only wish," she spat out, pushing by him.

"Molly," cried a voice from within the house. "Your Christmas present," called out the man, who, by all appearances, could have been the host of the party. The girl turned and, pulling her willing captive, walked back into the noisy crowd. Brian stared from behind at the curious couple, then quickly located the cloak room and Bobby's hat.

He emerged from the house and made his way to the Copelands' car out front. On the drive back to Wells, he filled Annie in on the last chapter of the evening, the brief confrontation in the doorway with the acid-tongued Molly.

XL

A FEW DAYS AFTER THE PARTY at Goose Rocks, Brian called
Bobby at his apartment in Ogunquit and informed him of
another project, this time for a motel operation in Kennebunk.
Bobby was overjoyed, the work coming so late in the year, and
offered to treat Brian to dinner. Brian accepted and the two scheduled dinner for just after the holidays at Alisson's Restaurant in
Kennebunkport.

Brian cleared the front door of Alisson's on a frigid Thursday night in January. He was to meet Bobby at six o'clock for
dinner but found himself twenty-five minutes early. The restaurant and bar were barely half full as he entered the main dining
area. He was about to sit down at a small table by the window
when his eye caught sight of a familiar face across the room.
Bill Regan, his walking partner, was seated by himself near the
bar. Catching sight of Brian, the man gestured him over. Brian
crossed the room and took a chair across from his friend.

"What are you doing all the way up here? No, let me guess—
a hot date," said the man. Brian shook his head.

"Meeting an old friend of mine for dinner. I'm early, though,
so if you can stand me, I'll just hang around till he gets here."
With the onset of the bitterly cold weather, the seventyish Regan
had decided to take a break from the walks, promising to resume
by mid-March. Brian learned that Bill, too, would be meeting an
old friend for dinner. During the course of their many walks, he
had learned that Bill was a widower, but had never pushed the
man for details. On this night, Bill Regan seemed inclined to
speak of matters aside from the usual politics, religion, and the
like.

"I asked a friend of mine, Abe Rosen, to join me tonight. Today's the anniversary of my darling's passing away. I need company on this night, above all others."

"I hope you'll always feel free to call on me, if you ever get in a pinch for company and your friend Abe's not available," offered Brian.

"You know, I sort of know your story. We older folks have a way of passing on information and—we do live in a small town. Can I tell you a little story—and maybe share a little more of my philosophy with you?" Brian smiled and prompted him to continue. "I lost my sweet Emily nearly twenty years ago. As I told you—it was on this very day. When you lose someone that means everything, well, it's real easy to just throw your hands in the air and stop trying. Now, I'm going to share something with you that I've never shared with anyone before, not even Abe. I've always made a point of getting out of the house on this night, for my sanity's sake. On this night—it would have been eleven years ago now—I was sitting alone in a lounge, it was after nine o'clock, when the door opens and this beautiful lady, and I mean lady, strolls in and takes a seat at the end of the bar. Dressed to the nines and truly beautiful, she looks absolutely miserable, like she's lost her best friend. Now, this woman can't be more than forty—and here I am past sixty at the time. Somehow, I gather enough courage to walk up to her and ask if she'd like a little company, just to chat. Now, I'm looking at her close up and, if it's possible, she looks even better close up than from across the room. You're a young guy, and forty may seem old to you—but, you'll find out, women have a beauty at forty that no girl in their twenties can even dream of having. Anyway, incredibly, she invites me to sit and talk. Two hours fly by like they didn't happen and now the bartender's picking up our glasses for the evening and the lights are being put out all around us. In the course of the two hours all I've learned about this woman is that she's leaving Maine the next day and, in all likelihood, never coming back. Now the next couple of minutes are real fuzzy but I asked her if there was any way she'd consider spending her last night here with me. Imagine how dumbstruck I became when she up and says yes! We go back to my house at the cove and settle in, all the while I can't believe what's happening to me! This woman and I, Jesus, I never learned her name—made love and never let go of each other until the sun rose the next morning. I won't go into any more detail than that. She left the next morning in her rented car as I fought back the urge to plead with her to stay, knowing damn well she wouldn't."

Brian sat transfixed by what his friend had shared with him.

"Brian, when I count them up, I realize that I spent less than twelve hours with this woman. What plagues me is that when my time comes and I'm about to go—I'll be thinking of her right along with my Emily," he said soberly. Brian remained quiet, searching the man's eyes in front of him for even the hint of insincerity. There was none.

"My young friend, here's what I'd like to share with you— and why I shared that story with you in the first place. Don't bury your head in the sand. Life is always worth pursuing. The reason is, every time you turn a corner, every time you open a door or someone opens a door in on you, every time you walk through a crowd, you never know if you're going to—in the next instant—come face-to-face with the most fantastic woman in the world, the woman who'll give you a glimpse of paradise right here on earth. Life's an adventure my young friend. Don't bury your head in the sand. Life's a great adventure! Do you follow me?" asked Bill.

Before Brian could answer, a pair of hands came down on his shoulders.

"What, you found someone better to have dinner with?" asked the stranger.

"No, Abe, sit down. Brian Kelly—Abe Rosen."

The two men shook hands and Brian relinquished his chair to the older man, then looked up to see Bobby entering the room and settling himself in at a table by the bar. He took this opportunity to excuse himself and wish the two men a good evening.

"Bill, about what you told me earlier—and you can take this observation with a grain of salt. I'm not entirely sure that that lady in the lounge and your Emily aren't one and the same. Just an observation from a sentimentalist—and I'll give what you told me some serious thought."

Bill Regan looked up from his beer and smiled at his young friend.

Brian carried his drink across the room, joining Bobby at a corner table by the door and adjacent to the bar and they began catching up on developments from over the holidays.

"You know, my friend, you've more than earned your dinner tonight. That work you sent me in Kennebunk saved my ass. Things are getting real tight at home and that money helped keep us afloat," exclaimed a grateful Bobby. When Bobby's beer arrived at the table, Brian lifted his glass for a toast.

"To old friends—they're the best," said Brian. Bobby echoed his agreement and the two men struck glasses.

"Now, I want you to feel free to order anything you want, Bri, don't hold back. The people you sent me to in Kennebunk, asked me to give them a bid on their lawn work next year and, lo and behold, I got it. That's another two grand of income I can count on next summer. You've friggin' *earned* yourself a good dinner!"

"I'm glad you feel that way, Copeland, cause I purposely starved myself all day for this. There'll be no mercy tonight," responded Brian. An instant later the front door opened in the next room.

Out of the corner of his eye, Brian caught sight of a blonde female and her date speaking with the hostess. Even from the back, the young woman seemed vaguely familiar. When the couple turned and moved toward the main dining area, the young woman and Brian established immediate eye contact.

"Don't look now, but the creature from Goose Rocks is on her way in here," whispered Brian across the table.

"Jesus Christ, I don't believe it! *Grandpa,* they've let you out of the home for the evening! No, don't tell me: your social security check came in today and you're out celebrating. Is that it?" scoffed the smartly dressed blonde.

"Let me see, now—the last time I saw you, you were leading some poor, emasculated, young man to your car in a noose. How'd that evening turn out for the princess and her prey?" asked Brian behind a forced smile.

"They'll never find the body, so I think I'm home free," she retorted. "By the way, this is Phil Hackett, my escort for the evening. Phil, this is grandpa. I'm sorry, do you have a first name, grandpa?" needled the girl.

Brian extended his hand to Hackett.

"No, it's just grandpa—and this is Bobby," he said, introducing his friend. Hackett, clearly feeling uncomfortable, reached out and shook the hands of both men. Shortly thereafter, Molly and Phil pulled up stools at the bar a short distance away.

"Be careful, Phil! Somewhere between the main course and dessert is when our little princess here usually tries to clamp on the leg irons," called out Brian.

"I can hardly wait," replied Phil, albeit nervously.

"Oh, grandpa—I fully expect you'll be falling asleep at the table before too long, dining out being so tiring for people your age. I'll be sure to call a cab for you and make sure you get home okay. Now, what retirement home is it again you live in?" she taunted.

"Now, don't you worry your pretty little head about me, sweet Molly. I'm going to have to stay awake and on guard. When I see the townspeople gathering outside in the square, lighting their torches, and cursing the mad scientist on the hill for his hideous, blonde creation, I'll let you know, kid—'cause you'll want to be getting a good head start," answered Brian.

The wisecrack brought a laugh from Bobby and Phil. However, Molly just turned and stared at her tormentor. She noticed that Brian had remembered her name.

With the flurry of verbal jousting seemingly over, Brian and Bobby returned to their dinner conversation while Molly and Phil carried on their own banter. The main course had just arrived at the fellows' table when a husky, fashionably attired man took the stool to Molly's left. After a few minutes, Brian noticed that the dark-haired man with a prominent, hooked nose was boldly trying to inject himself into Phil and Molly's conversation. Following a series of crystal clear hints that his company was not appreciated, the man's demeanor turned noticeably ugly, a fact not lost on a few of the nearby customers. As luck would have it, George Martel, the regular bartender, had the night off. On any other night, George would have already prepared the aggressive stranger's bill and began the process of removing him from the premises. However, in his absence, the situation between Molly, Phil, and the stranger was rapidly growing worse. Phil Hackett appeared paralyzed with fear, reduced to ineffectual attempts at reasoning with the man. Finally, Bobby turned to his friend.

"If I stick my nose in this, will you stand behind me?" he asked. Brian nodded yes. Bobby let his silverware drop down onto the table.

"Why is it," he began in a loud, complaining voice, "that when I finally get out of the house—and away from my wife's cooking—and have a chance for a really, good meal—that's when some idiot will park his fat can on a bar stool nearby and screw up my meal? Why is that, Brian?" roared Bobby, his voice escalating with each phrase.

Incredibly, the boorish stranger did not pick up on Bobby's tirade. Molly was now in the act of forcibly removing his arm from her shoulder. Bobby jumped to his feet, determined to try again. He walked up behind the stranger and lifted the collar on his suit.

"God, is this a cheap suit, or is this a cheap suit?" he asked his friend.

"That is one crappy, cheap suit," agreed Brian.

"What the *fuck* did you say?" asked the man, turning on his stool to face Bobby.

"We all couldn't help but notice the suit you had on—and what a piece of crap it is!" explained Bobby.

"Maybe you'd like to step outside and say that?" came back the man.

"You know, Bobby, we may be being too hard on this guy. I've heard tell that when the boys in Ogunquit get done with a guy—you know used him up bigtime—over—and over—and over and when they've just exhausted every orifice, well, it's a tradition—they always buy him a cheap suit before they run him out of town. Now, take a look at this guy. Do I have to paint you a picture?" tormented Brian.

"No, Bri, you're right—this is a man that's been *used*." The words were barely out of Bobby's mouth when a Kennebunkport police officer walked through the door and was ushered up to the stranger. It took less than thirty seconds for the sergeant to hand the man his coat and escort him out the door. Led by Bobby, the patrons broke out in song: ". . . Nah nah nah nah / Nah nah nah nah / hey hey hey, goo-ood-bye. . . ."

Brian and Bobby returned to their table to the sound of light applause. Moments later the men were taken aback as Molly pulled up a chair from an adjoining table.

"Excuse me," muttered Brian to the girl. From his bar stool, Phil Hackett called out to his date.

"Molly, I'm a lover, not a fighter."

"I'd say you're not much of either," she called back. Now mortified, the man removed a few bills from his wallet, placed them on the bar, and exited the building.

"So, where were we?" asked Molly.

"I believe I was just about to ask you to remove your scrawny ass from the table," answered Brian in a low voice. An angry look broke across the blonde's face.

"Fine!" she exploded, picking up her coat and whipping it across Brian's face as she stormed from the room.

"Is she a sweetheart or is she a sweetheart?" asked Brian sarcastically.

"She seems to have drawn blood," observed Bobby.

Brian brought his hand to his face, rubbing his fingers across the bridge of his nose. On inspection, the tips of his fingers were wet. He dabbed the minor wound with his handkerchief while Bobby resumed his dinner.

Two hours later the friends settled their tab and stepped out into Dock Square, promising to breathe life back into their friendship.

XLI

IT WAS TWO DAYS AFTER HAVING DINNER with Bobby in Kennebunkport that Brian sat in front of his computer terminal and worked on the corporation's finances, attempting to reconcile the company's checkbook with the general ledger. The complex was in complete darkness, save for the light at the front desk. Outside the temperature was unseasonably warm, about forty degrees. This was the part of his job that he had the least interest in. He glanced up and saw it was nearly nine o'clock.

He was playing with the idea of calling it a night when a set of headlights flashed through the windows and a car stopped at the rear of the building. Thinking a misguided traveler must have wandered to his door, Brian switched on the outside light above the porch. A few moments later the office door was pushed open. Brian did a double take at the sight of Molly marching boldly into his office. In her hands she carried two containers of coffee.

"Who's the asshole with the Bush/Quayle bumper sticker on his truck?" she asked.

"That'd be me," he said.

"Why doesn't that surprise me?" she mocked, walking across the office and placing one cup down on the front desk. She followed this by removing her coat and flinging it onto a chair in the corner. Making herself at home, she nestled into the most comfortable of the office chairs, removed her shoes, and assumed the full lotus position. Brian looked on as she removed the cap from her coffee cup and sipped her beverage.

"You weren't the easiest person in the world to track down, *grandpa*. I thought it was only fair to look you up and give you a chance to apologize for the other night."

315

"You must be a real glutton for punishment. I thought I was pretty clear about where you and I stood at Alisson's," answered Brian, reaching down for his coffee.

"Grandpa, I may be young, but I can tell in a heartbeat when someone's interested—and you're an open book," she gloated.

"You forget, Molly Malone—I've seen you in action. I know how you treat people."

"*Men* aren't *people*," she snapped back.

"Some of us are," he countered.

"I think you're afraid of me—afraid of what I can do to you. That's what *I* think." Brian smiled and shrugged his shoulders.

"Did you think I didn't see the way you watched me at the party? You wanted to be right where Kenny what's-his-name was—wondering what I had in store for him once we left the party. If you say you didn't—well then, you're a fucking liar," she scoffed. Brian forced himself to look away. Her brashness, her directness, the unbroken eye contact—she was wise beyond her years in the art of seduction.

"I want you to think of this coffee cup as an hourglass, and the coffee in it as sand. When my coffee is gone, the sand has run out, and I'll be asking you to leave," he advised.

"You can *ask* me all you want. I'll leave when I'm ready to leave," she countered. For the next thirty seconds Brian could only stare across the office at this young, confident, aggressive female. For all his bravado, he felt himself slowly falling under her influence—and she sensed it.

"How old are you, grandpa? Sixty? Seventy?" asked Molly, now beginning to toy with him. He did not respond. Instead he began drinking down his coffee in generous mouthfuls, finally emptying the cardboard cup in a flourish.

"Ahhhh—gone. Time for someone to leave. The sand has been emptied from the hourglass."

"And who's going to make me?" she asked, folding her arms. He stared across the room at the bold, young woman, conscious that she had accomplished what she had set out to do. He felt the passion inside him heating his blood and clouding his judgment.

"I'll put it this way: I'll give you sixty seconds to finish your coffee, grab your coat, and leave. If you're not out of this building by that time, I'm carrying you upstairs—and you won't be coming down until morning. That is a goddamn promise!" threatened Brian. Molly answered with a derisive snicker.

"And I'll have your ass behind bars so fucking fast your head will spin," she threatened.

Brian glanced up at the clock. Fifty three—fifty two—fifty one— "When the jury hears I gave you an entire minute to leave they'll laugh you out of court."

"I'll tell them I said no—and when a woman says *no*, it means *no*,"

Forty six—forty five—forty four. Brian folded his arms defiantly across his chest and stared directly into Molly's eyes. "There'll be a scandal the likes of which you won't believe. They won't believe you when you say you gave me sixty seconds to leave—it's moronic!" Forty one—forty—thirty nine.

"You'll spend the next twenty years in jail!" she railed.

"I don't give a shit—can't you tell? Leave!" he ordered. Thirty three—thirty two—thirty one. Molly responded by spreading her arms and yawning.

"You're bluffing, grandpa," she said, with a little cat smile. Twenty two—twenty one—twenty.

It was decision time for Brian. It was becoming quite clear that his visitor was not about to back down. In his mind he drew a line in the sand. He would carry through with his threat. However, he would stop if, at any time, she broke out in tears. Molly looked up at the clock and broke into a gale of laughter.

"You haven't got the balls, grandpa," she scoffed. Twelve—eleven—ten. They stared across the room at each other, not speaking a word while the clock ticked down—until—three—-two—one. He crossed the room and threw the lock on the door. He was now standing right above her.

"*Fuck off*," she spat out.

He bent forward and grabbed hold of Molly's wrist, then, in one motion, hoisted her over his shoulder in a fireman's carry. Balanced atop his shoulder, she pounded on his back, hollering at him to put her down. With his right arm wrapped over her lower buttocks he kept her weight distributed upon his right shoulder. With his free hand, he flipped off the porch and office lights and proceeded to make his way to the stairs. Molly continued to scream and rain blows on his back. He was amazed at how light she felt as he climbed the stairs, walked to the end of the hallway, and pushed open the door to the fifties room.

Light from the hallway flooded the bedroom and the queen-sized bed that dominated it. The bed was fitted with an oak headboard lined with books. Brian half placed, half threw, Molly down, careful not to strike her head on the oak headboard, and deposited himself on top of her. With her hands temporarily free, she ran her nails across his neck, leaving a line of abraded skin. He responded by bringing his mouth down on hers, then secured both her wrists with his hands. She attempted to bring her knee up into his midsection but he now had her completely under his power. His mouth left hers, then found its way to her soft, exposed neck. He tasted the floral essence of her perfume as his tongue, then his teeth, brought pressure upon her flesh.

Brian felt the resistance from her arms and wrists subside, prompting him to relax his grip. Pulling her hands free, she grabbed him by his hair and guided his mouth back to her own. Their bodies were now aligned. Brian's head swam from the rush of erotic passion that soared through him. Their lips remained engaged as their tongues explored each other's mouths. Ten minutes passed before he pulled back and began peeling the clothes from her, his passion rising with each additional garment he stripped from the magnificent creature beneath him. She reciprocated by ripping the shirt from his back, removing two buttons in the process. There would be no further foreplay. Following the hasty removal of Brian's jeans, the two warring lovers became one as Molly pulled him down upon her, guiding his erect penis inside her. They began moving in instant, perfect rhythm. Aroused beyond the point of recovery, they shared the exhilarating pleasure of each other's bodies, testing each other's limits. Amid the ecstasy, Brian felt Molly's sharp fingernails dig and tear into his back. Finally, their bodies drained and wet with perspiration, Brian's passions were released as the girl writhed with passionate bliss and completion beneath him.

Looking down, he saw Molly's yellow hair wet and clinging to her forehead. He kissed her face tenderly, showering kisses across her forehead, down the bridge of her nose, and eventually back to her lips. He could literally feel her heart racing within her chest. He stood up, lifted her from the bed, pulled back the covers, and placed her down upon the sheets. Joining her under the covers, he pulled her slender body against his own. They would wake twice in the middle of the night and, without speaking, repeat the lovemaking ritual from earlier.

Brian awoke the following morning to an empty bed. He paused before rising, realizing the bedding retained the scent of young Molly. He was still for a short period, breathing in the air that still preserved this small bit of evidence of the night before. Finally rising, he searched the bedroom, then the downstairs for a note from the girl. It soon became apparent that she had not left one.

In the small bathroom of the fifties room, he examined the marks on his neck and back left by her. Returning to the bedroom, he fell back upon the bed, looking up at the walls. Portraits of Marilyn Monroe and Dwight D. Eisenhower stared back at him. He could not help wondering what was running through Molly's mind at this very moment.

Millie dropped by the complex during mid-afternoon. She was receiving unemployment compensation over the winter, there not being enough work to require anyone besides Brian in January through March. Millie, who was not one to miss much, noticed Brian wincing while reaching down to pick up an object from the floor.

"You got a sore back or something?" she asked.

"No, not really—it's nothing," replied Brian.

"And what's with the turtleneck shirt?"

"Just wearing it for a change of pace," he answered, covering up. The woman squinted her eyes and stared at her employer, waiting on a straight answer.

"Okay, if you must know, I had a little company last night. Okay?"

"What kind of company?"

"Female company."

"So what does that have to do with you grimacing every time you have to move?" Brian raised his eyes to heaven, but did not respond. "Let me take a look," ordered the woman.

"Millie!" exclaimed Brian.

"All right—have it your way. But, you know, I'm wondering when you're going to let me introduce you to one of the ladies from the church?"

"One of your Congregationalist friends?" he laughed.

"That's right—it's been way too long since you had a good, Christian woman in your life. Not since Angel," lectured Millie.

"I'm not interested right now."

"Brian, I have a couple of young woman in mind—good women—and handsome women, on top of that!"

Brian laughed. "*Handsome* women! Oh, I don't like the sound of that! There's something about those two words when put in that order,—handsome—women—that strikes fear into most men's hearts. *Men* are handsome, not women. Women are pretty, or gorgeous—but they're *not* handsome. When's the last time you heard someone say—boy, that Kathy Ireland sure is *handsome*? I picture myself waiting for one of your handsome women on a blind date—I open the door and there she is—with Paul Newman's eyes, Robert Redford's smile, Clark Gable's ears, and Arnold Schwarzenegger's muscles!"

Millie raised her eyes to the ceiling but did not muster a response. Meanwhile, Brian was growing a little concerned about the lack of any word from Molly. He saw her as a loose cannon and began wondering if she might follow through on her threat from the night before.

"Mil, there's just an outside chance that something could come up, publicly, about what happened here last night. I may have done something stupid—largely because of whom I did it with."

"What is this all about? Does it have something to do with you hurting all over?" Brian nodded yes.

"All right, now let me take a look at you," she ordered. He peeled down the collar of his turtleneck, exposing the line of broken skin across his neck. "What in the world?" exclaimed Millie.

Then he untucked his shirt and slipped it up to his shoulders. "What in heaven's name happened to you?" she gasped. "What sort of business did you have going on here, anyway?" she asked in astonishment.

"I may have done something very, very stupid," he admitted. In the next instant, the phone rang within reach of the woman.

"Atlantic Coast Lodge," she parroted. Millie's eyes darted to Brian as she listened to the voice at the other end of the line. "It's a Molly Windsor for you," holding out the phone.

"Hello, Miss Windsor—I was hoping you'd call. I was disappointed when you weren't here this morning," he stated in a pensive voice.

"With or without cream and sugar?" questioned Molly.

"Excuse me?"

"Your coffee—with or without cream and sugar?" she repeated. Brian felt his nervous stomach unwind.

"If it's all right with you, I'd like to take you to dinner—maybe even a movie in Sanford. You know, so we can talk and stuff," he suggested.

"I'm not riding in that beat-up rattletrap of yours with the Bush/Quail sticker on it."

"And I'm not taking it off. I guess we'll take your car."

"What time?" she asked.

"Six would be nice."

"Fine—I'll be by at six," she answered before hanging up the phone without a good-bye.

XLII

THROUGH THE WINTER AND SPRING OF 1989 Brian continued to keep the company of Molly Windsor. He learned that she came from a good family of comfortable means in Kennebunkport. Stubborn and extremely independent, Molly did not join her graduating high school class in setting off to college, a fact of major concern to her parents. To a great extent, it was at the urging of Brian that she applied to and was accepted at the University of Vermont. Their relationship remained largely intact through her freshman year. She returned home during all semester and holiday breaks and worked back in York County in the summer of 1990. By the time she returned to Vermont to begin her sophomore year, the couple's association was little more than a familiar, sexual one. During the Christmas break of 1990 there was an unspoken agreement between the two that they would eventually pull away from each other; however, it went unsaid, pending the outcome of the upcoming summer.

In January, Bill Regan passed away. Brian learned of his death from the *York County Coast Star* shortly before the funeral, allowing him to attend. Being the winter, he had not seen Bill for two months. Brian had sat alone in the back of St. Mary's Church. He did not mourn for his friend although he knew that he would miss him. He comforted himself with the knowledge that Bill was with Emily. Aside from Abe Rosen, he had recognized no one at the service.

It was on the morning of April 15th that Brian sat at the kitchen table, cursing the Internal Revenue Service as he wrote out a check to attach to his federal tax return.

"I'd love to know where those bastards get off taking this much money from me," he hollered to Millie in the next room. "When we're kneeling over a toilet with a brush in our hands in mid-July, I don't see these IRS slugs showing up to lend a hand."

"When I saw how much they took out of my bonus check last Christmas, I mean, I wanted to cry," shouted back Millie.

"By the way, Mil, I still haven't heard you comment on the new furniture in the TV room."

She walked into the room. "It's beautiful, Brian—it really is. But, I do have one question. What is it with you and that dumpy, old, gray thing in the corner? Good Lord, I swear that's been here since I came to work for you." He did not answer. There was a sadly thoughtful look on his face.

"What is it?" asked Millie.

"I just can't seem to get rid of it," he acknowledged quietly. Millie just looked on, knowing she had touched upon something of importance to him, and that he would tell her if he wanted to.

"The day I first set eyes on Angel—I was sitting in that chair—and she came over and stood up on it—bold as brass. From that moment, I have never been the same. It's one of my few remaining links to her, Millie, that chair—and the pickup. The truth is—I've never recovered—and I'm sure I never will."

Millie walked up and wrapped her arms around him.

"It wasn't fair—I know that. The good—they really do die young. I know I'll never forget that day—never!"

"Enough of this! Damn the IRS! This all started thinking about those thieves. The thought that my taxes are paying for those lying cockroaches' lunches and stuff—while we plug away up here."

"I haven't heard you talking about Molly lately. Isn't she due home in a few weeks?"

"Still not sure—all's quiet on that front."

"My offer still stands—good Christian women," said Millie.

"Don't tell me—and they're very handsome women, at that," needled Brian.

The two friends returned to work eventually, Brian opening the last of the cottages after their long, winter's sleep, and Millie manning the phones and assembling promotional material.

It was nearly nine when Brian closed the office and headed back to his beach cottage for the night. He was scheduled to attend a tourism seminar in Augusta the next morning. Before retiring, he took a short walk down to Crescent Beach. On this night he thought of Bill Regan. It brought on a melancholy frame of mind, which was hard to overcome. It was not even ten o'clock when he reached up and threw the switch on the light over the bed.

Brian slowly became aware of the feel of cold sand beneath his feet. Around him the fog seemed to envelop everything. There was water nearby although he could not see it. He knew this from the repetitive, lapping noise of the water washing up on sand close by. He walked toward the sound and eventually made out, through the fog, the hull of a lobster boat anchored just off shore. The air was cold and he was dressed only in his sleeping attire, a T-shirt and briefs. He wandered away from the water and shortly made out the rocks of the jetty. He scrambled through the cold sand to the rocky walkway, climbing up onto its flat surface. There was no sound except that of the nearby Atlantic Ocean. He was on the jetty on the Drake's Island side of the entrance to Wells Harbor. He headed eastward, having decided to walk to the end of the walkway. The rocks beneath his bare feet were even colder than the sand he had just left.

He walked swiftly, careful to step squarely on the flat stones that made up the pathway. In the distance a light shone through the fog. He deduced it was close to the end of the jetty. He walked toward it, accelerating his pace. The sound of water rushing against the rocks and his own breathing were the only things audible to him. He was nearing the end of the jetty when the light began to take form, the form of a woman, her back turned and looking out to sea. Brian drew to within twenty feet of her.

"I don't want to startle you—so you should know you're not alone out here," he called out. The figure turned to him. Brian's spirit soared as his eyes beheld the image of Angelique.

"Angel!" he cried out before scrambling over the rocks to her. Falling to his knees, he wrapped his arms around her, feeling the contours of her body within his grasp. Her body brought warmth to his own.

"Hello, my love." She spoke in a quiet, soft manner. "As you see, I have brought you out to a very meaningful place."

"The jetty—the jetty where I swam to you," he exclaimed. Her hand reached down, lifting his head up to look at her.

"Brian, I'm here to say good-bye—and to bring you some peace." He looked up at her, once again looking into the brown eyes that had silently spoken to him so many times before.

"Take me with you, Angel. I'll have no peace without you. I've been here long enough without you. Just bring me with you—that's all I ask," he implored.

"It is not your time, my love—and you are not ready," she answered.

"I don't care about any of this here anymore. I want to be with you. Please, Angel."

"Your work is not done here. There are things you must finish. Your son, Brendan, will need you—and he will not be your only child."

"Why did you have to go?" he asked. Brian remained on his knees, acting from a sense of subordination.

"When you have completed everything set out for you— and if you have righted yourself, we will be together again," she promised. "You've turned your back on Him. The lessons given to you by your mother and me—and the guidance from Millie—you ignore. Open your eyes, my love—open your eyes."

"You can't come to me like this and then leave me, Angel—I won't survive this."

"You have a busy and long day ahead of you," stated Angelique, ignoring his words.

"I'm supposed to go to Augusta tomorrow."

"Yes, you will travel to Augusta—and before the day is through you will meet with her."

"Meet with who?"

"You will meet with the one who will pull you through all of this," she answered.

"I don't understand what you're talking about—and how would I even know her?" he followed up.

"When you see her, you will know her," she answered.

"How?"

"When you see her, you will know her," she repeated.

"I can't let go of you, Angel. I can't let you slip away from me again," voiced Brian, ignoring her words and tightening his embrace.

"Get to your feet," she ordered. Brian rose to his feet but would not surrender his embrace.

"Look to the horizon, my love," she said. He lifted his eyes. The fog dissipated before him, revealing a strip of blue sky above the horizon. He saw in that line of color, a shade of blue brighter, more luminous, than any other within his experience.

"If you begin to doubt what has happened here, think of the color before you," she instructed. Brian looked on, bewildered by the brilliance of the horizon. Gradually, the fog returned and the strip of blue was gone. He turned his eyes back to Angelique. She beckoned him to kiss her. He obliged, convinced that he once again could taste the magnificent moisture from inside her mouth.

"Good-bye, Brian, my love," she whispered, pulling back from him.

"Angel, don't leave me!" he called out frantically.

"Heed my words and I will be waiting on you—there to bring you over," she promised, before fading from view.

Brian was jolted up into a sitting position in his bed. The room was dark but the shades in the window and the sporadic sound of birds indicated that dawn was upon Wells Beach. He was wet with sweat, but his body felt cold in spite of the triple layer of blankets he'd had covering him. He jumped from the bed and staggered into the kitchen, flicking on the light. He was filled with a sense of wonderment, fear, and depression, the three emotions battling with each other within him. His feet were so cold, they felt warmth from the linoleum beneath them. He was convinced he could still taste the kiss from Angelique in his mouth. He walked into the living room and collapsed onto the couch, his logical and spiritual selves fighting inside his head. The dream had attributes he could not dismiss. It was not only the vivid feel of the cold from the elements and the warmth from the body of Angelique, it was more than that. He thought of the strip of blue on the horizon, the one pointed out by Angelique. Brian knew that he always dreamed in black and white, without exception. He had heard discussions about how women were more apt to dream in color than men. He had always believed this because of his own experience—he had never dreamed in color. His logic was finding this particular element of his dream difficult to rationalize.

Brian did not return to bed. With no appetite, he brewed himself a pot of tea as he ran the details of the dream over in his mind. The logical and cynical part of him scoffed at his preoccupation with the specifics of this dream. He went so far as to jot down the words spoken and respoken by Angelique: '*When you see her, you will know her.'* To him, this could only mean that this woman would stand out in the crowd, be quite attractive or maybe distinctive looking. It could not be a coincidence, he reasoned, that he would be among mostly strangers in Augusta on this day. Brian theorized that, in all likelihood, this woman would appear at the seminar in Augusta, and if this dream was a genuine spiritual encounter, she would stand out from all others, at least to him. How circumstances might bring her to him was another question which he would address when confronted with it. Before setting off for Augusta that morning, he took the drive down to Drake's Island where he walked to the end of the jetty, all the while internalizing the painful specifics of the dream and this encounter with his beloved Angelique. The maddening aspect of this whole matter was he dared not discuss this with anyone, not even Millie, for fear of appearing melodramatic, or worse, insane.

With his thoughts monopolized by the dream, Brian finished the trip to Augusta via the turnpike with no recollection of the journey. Arriving a full half hour before the scheduled opening remarks, he took a chair near the back of the spacious hall that allowed him an unobstructed view of the room and attendees. As the conference hall filled, his eyes followed each of the females as they strode through the door and searched out a place to sit.

Less than five minutes before opening remarks, a tall, sophisticated-looking woman paused in the doorway. Brian's eyes locked onto her. She was slender and blonde and wore a fashionable pair of eyeglasses. After sweeping the hall with a glance, she made her way to Brian's side of the room, dropping her material at a table two rows in front of him.

Throughout the early morning, Brian's attention was divided between the material being presented from the podium and the sophisticated stranger seated two rows in front of him. During mid-morning break he noticed her standing alone out in the hall, balancing a cup of coffee. He approached her in a matter-of-fact manner and managed to strike up a conversation that lasted over the fifteen-minute break. However, it was during the luncheon break that he was able to essentially break the ice. The catered luncheon for the attendees was staged in an adjoining hall in the facility. The floor of the hall was dotted with circular tables, each seating six persons. Brian had learned during the break that the woman's name was Ramona Tardiff, and he followed her and sat down beside her at a table in the corner of the hall. Fortune shone down on him when no one joined them at the table, allowing him to monopolize all of Ramona's attention. During the meal he learned that she managed an upscale inn and guest house on the hillside overlooking Camden. The meal flew by as the two shared war stories from prior years. When the seminar was called back into afternoon session, Brian moved to Ramona's table where he continued to get to know the meticulously dressed and accessorized woman. It was less than a half hour before the session concluded that he broached the subject of dinner.

"Ramona, I hope you won't think I'm being way too forward but—well, I intended on having dinner here in Augusta before heading home. I would love to have your company—if that fits into your schedule," he asked politely.

"That will be fine—as long as we can stay here in the facility," she responded, following her acceptance with a polite smile.

The hotel and convention center had an in-house restaurant and lounge, allowing the two to walk directly from the seminar to dinner. The words from his dream the night before continued to play in his head during the meal as Brian looked deeper and deeper into Ramona Tardiff, and behind the facade of chic sophistication. Her rounded glasses did little to disguise her natural beauty. As the two near-strangers conversed over their meals he was impressed with this woman's use of language, as well as her knowledge of current events and politics.

The restaurant served gourmet food in measured portions. Brian and Ramona both opted for dessert. The time together passed effortlessly. The sound of live music from the lounge wafted in just as the desserts arrived at the table. Brian thought how different Ramona was from Molly, and how much more difficult to read. When the check arrived he reached for it.

"It's all mine—under one condition," he bargained.

"And that is—?" came her response.

"I may have one dance before you leave."

"It's getting late, Brian," she countered.

"One dance—nothing more," he reiterated. Her eyes retreated to the table as she accepted his offer.

After settling their tab, they walked into the lounge where they joined about a dozen other patrons. Brian ordered a beer as they settled in at a table by the dance floor. The music was coming from a trio of piano, drums and guitar. Following a few seconds of fumbling, the group started in. After only a few notes Brian recognized "Something Stupid."

"I don't think we'll be having Frank and Nancy singing any time soon, so—" he said, reaching out his hand. Ramona took it and they stepped onto the floor, joined by two other couples. In seconds he knew that his partner was no stranger to the dance floor.

"Is there anything you don't do well?" he asked, prompting her to laugh. They swayed back and forth in perfect rhythm, as if from years of common experience.

"Ramona, I'm wondering if perhaps we can exchange cards before you go. I'd like to think we might stay in contact somehow," said Brian softly. She hesitated before answering.

"I'm sorry, Brian, but—I don't think that's such a good idea. You seem like a wonderful guy—and you're certainly not a bad looking guy. The truth is—I don't feel anything, and—it's either there or it's not. I'm sorry," she concluded, politely but with resolve.

They finished out the dance before returning to the table. Reaching down for her coat, Ramona Tardiff applied a light squeeze to Brian's shoulder before heading out into the hallway and out of his life. With her departure, Brian felt an immediate sense of depression come over him.

He moved his beer to the bar where he sat, waiting on the arrival of anyone who might fulfill the promise of his dream the night before. There was nothing in Angelique's visitation that could have been misinterpreted. It was to happen today and Ramona Tardiff had been the only woman to come close to fulfilling his expectation from the dream. *"When you see her, you will know her,"* was the message from Angelique and Ramona Tardiff had been the only woman to touch Brian that way. On this Tuesday evening the lounge saw few patrons. Brian slowly nursed his beer for another hour, hoping to see someone appear in the doorway to drive off his deepening depression. It was just before nine-thirty when he picked up his change from the bar and made his way out to the truck.

The drive back to Wells provided Brian with little in roadside distractions. He found his spirits plummeting as the visit from Angelique replayed in his head along with the details of his aborted evening with Ramona Tardiff. It was not long before he was reprimanding himself for the stupidity of his actions.

Had he actually *believed* that Angel's departed soul had returned to direct him? But the dream had seemed so *real*! The human mind—and its power to deceive! But the color, the vivid color in the dream—and his cold body temperature on awakening! The human brain—mind over matter!

As Brian's rational side slowly took possession of his thought processes he felt his mental state continue on its downward spiral. He began pondering the utterly purposeless nature of his existence since the death of Angelique. He asked himself if he was going mad. Might not clinical depression lie ahead? He felt himself psychologically collapsing beneath the weight of the events of the past twenty-four hours.

Angelique was gone—and had been for nearly ten years! Remarkably, at the urging of a vision manifested through a dream, he had foolishly followed through on a directive from his long departed Angelique, with embarrassing results. He cursed himself for being simpleminded and gullible. As he drove back to Wells, Brian tried to blot out the memory of this day.

Guiding the truck off Route 1 and up the complex driveway, Brian saw a reasonable number of cars parked in front of units, four vehicles in front of the motel and a couple more behind the lodge, including a BMW. It was nearly eleven o'clock. He pushed in the door and was greeted with a smile from Millie.

"I'll bet you're glad to finally see me," he commented emotionlessly.

"Not as much as someone else is going to be," she responded under her breath. He walked up to the front desk and examined the key board.

"Nine units—damn good for a Tuesday in April," he observed. Millie stared into his face at close range, grinning ear to ear. "Mil, this has not been a good day. No, correct that, this has been a friggin' rotten day—and any clowning's going to be lost on me," he warned. She put her finger up to her mouth, signaling him to keep his voice down. "What's the matter with you?" he asked, becoming slightly irritated. She picked up a registration form and handed it to him. Brian looked down and scanned the card.

It read: Margaret Keogh-Olson, Bedford, New Hampshire.

"She's been here since early this afternoon."

"What is she doing here?" he asked.

"Well, I'll put it this way—she's not here for the lobster or the clean, ocean air. She's here for you! Make no mistake about it. Oh—she tried to ask about you in this matter-of-fact way, but—please, she was quite obvious," whispered Millie. He walked over to the doorway leading into the television room. In the darkened, far corner a female sat snuggled in the old, gray chair.

"And did you notice where she parked herself? She's in your old chair! She had all the chairs to choose from and she flopped herself in that one." Brian's eyes were growing moist as he stood contemplating everything unfolding before him.

"You okay?" questioned Millie. He could only look down at his friend in bewilderment, lost for words.

"In case you haven't figured it out yet—she's waiting up for you. She's been there since eight-thirty or so." Having said that, Millie scurried out to the kitchen, returning with her pocket book. "I've got to get home to the old bear. Now you—you be a good boy now with your little friend—play nice," she heckled. She planted a peck on his cheek and made for the door while he stood immobilized in the middle of the room. He felt ashamed.

"When you see her, you will know her" were the words directed to him in the dream by Angelique. He looked back on his reflections over the last hour. He pondered on his misinterpretation of the dream, on his willingness to disbelieve the words spoken to him at the jetty. How incredibly disappointed his Angel must have been in him as he drove back from Augusta, discounting everything she had said. As thoughts surrounding his experiences over the past twenty-four hours swirled through his head, he walked toward the near stranger resting in the television room. He picked up a hassock and placed it down in front of the gray chair. Seating himself, he stared at the face of the young woman that, years earlier, had lifted his spirit to the clouds and then plunged it into a state of extended despair. He studied her face closely, taking in the most minute detail. It was still a beautiful face, albeit somewhat harder. There was some darkness under her eyes, perhaps from extended working hours. She appeared prosperous.

"So it's Margaret Keogh-Olson now," he thought. On her left hand, a wedding band and an engagement ring sporting a substantial stone, no doubt a diamond. So, what was a married woman doing looking for a man from her past, he wondered. Brian's eyes dropped down to the pair of folded legs balanced on the edge of the chair. She appeared fit, his Maggie May posing as Margaret Keogh-Olson.

He thought of his conversation with Bill Regan more than two years earlier. The message had stayed with him. Yes, perhaps life was a great adventure that we must embrace! Now it seemed that he was being propelled into a new adventure, an adventure with a woman who had already broken his heart years before. If she had retained any of her former resolve, Maggie May Keogh posed a threat to Brian's future mental well being. However, her arrival fulfilled Angelique's promise, and now this new adventure was about to begin. For Brian, an inner peace had replaced the feeling of guilt brought about by this woman's arrival. He gazed down on the sleeping woman for an extended length of time.

It was indeed the girl whose bedroom he had sat in a dozen and a half years before; the girl he had sat on a hill with in York, waiting out a passing shower; the girl who had wagered with him in English class at Southside High School so long ago. He watched her breathe, her chest rising and falling almost imperceptibly. She was everything he remembered, and perhaps more. It was time. It was time for another of life's adventures. Brian gently placed his hand on her forearm and spoke softly.

"Madam, you're sleeping in my chair."

About the author

Thomas Coughlin is the author of *Maggie May's Diary*, the sequel to this book. He is a practicing certified public accountant and former disc jockey. Lowell, Massachusetts; Wells, Maine, plus Berlin and Chester, New Hampshire, are claimed as his hometowns.

The author standing outside Maggie May's pub in Loughrea, County Galway, Republic of Ireland.